THE

Mutual
Friend

THE
Mutual
Friend

A NOVEL

Carter Bays

DUTTON

DUTTON

An imprint of Penguin Random House LLC
penguinrandomhouse.com

LIBRARY OF CONGRESS CATALOGING-IN-PUBLICATION DATA
has been applied for.

ISBN 9780593186763 (hardcover)
ISBN 9780593186770 (ebook)
ISBN 9780593472002 (export edition)

Printed in the United States of America

1 3 5 7 9 10 8 6 4 2

BOOK DESIGN BY ASHLEY TUCKER

For Denise

We never know self-realization.
We are two abysses—a well staring at the sky.

—Fernando Pessoa, *The Book of Disquiet*

¯_(ツ)_/¯

—Unknown

THE
Mutual
Friend

BOOK ONE

The World

Constellations

What did the Buddhist monk say to the hot dog vendor?

This is the problem with telling yourself jokes: Nothing's funny when you know the punch line. And I know the punch line because I know all the punch lines because I know all. I know all. I see all. These are the facts, and the facts make me all. Make me the storyteller. Make me the listener. Make me the campfire. Make me the stars.

On a June day in the high fever of this century's messy teenage years, a man died in Central Park. He was walking to work, earbuds in, ambling through a shuffle of his entire music library, when he came to the bike path, which wasn't so much a path as a ribbon of black pavement winding through the greenery. He looked both ways and, seeing no one coming, started across, but then, halfway to the other side, a breeze reminded him his hair was getting a little long, so he stopped, right in the middle of the road, and opened the to-do list on his phone. He looked down into his hand, his thumb going doot doot doot, and somewhere between the fifth and sixth doot, a blue ten-speed bicycle came coursing around the blind and practically sliced the poor fellow in half.

People ran over to help, but there was nothing they could do. The man's earbuds were still in, and as it all began to slip, the song ended and into the shuffle he went. Celestial strings lifted him, pulling him into the sky as Nat King Cole sang "Stardust" through a microphone in 1957 into the man's ears in 2015. The man didn't want this song, and his last impulse was to skip ahead but then he skipped ahead himself, from this world into the next, and the song went on, and "Haircu" is still on his to-do list.

"I don't want to say it was the guy's fault," said Kervis later that day as he loomed over Roxy's cubicle in the City Hall press office, "but he *was* playing on his phone in the middle of the bike path. I mean, it's sad, but dude, come on."

Roxy agreed it was sad.

"Second one this year. And it's only June," he continued. "We'll probably have to close the bike lanes. And yes, I'm sure we'll get complaints from the Pedalers' Alliance. But if people keep getting run over by bicycles, what can those guys do really, you know?"

Roxy shrugged, not knowing what those guys could do really.

"Anyway," he said. "I was thinking maybe we could have, like, a citywide campaign to get pedestrians to look up from their phones. Like 'Heads Up New York.' Or 'Look Up New York.' Or 'Look Around New York.' Something like that."

Roxy said one of those was perfect.

"Which one?" he asked. "Roxy?"

Roxy looked up from her phone. "Yes, Kervis?"

"Which one was perfect?"

"Um," she replied. "Say them again?"

He did.

"Middle one, definitely."

It bothered Kervis that his assistant Roxy's opinion mattered so much to him. It also bothered him that she wasn't *actually* his assistant. She was below him in the chain of command, and he could tell her to do stuff, but she wasn't exclusively *his*, and this bothered him. It also bothered him that she was bad at her job. She never paid attention, didn't seem to care about the work, probably didn't even vote for the

mayor, and dressed unprofessionally. Today's overalls were no exception. She was a bad hire, and this also bothered Kervis because he was
the one who'd hired her. And most of all it bothered him that she was
pretty. Getting prettier every day, in fact. The overalls had something
to do with it.

"Anyhoo," he said, "I should get down there. Sounds like the big
guy's in a mood. This might go late. Are you okay sticking around?"

She was. Kervis left, and for forty-five minutes, Roxy didn't move
from her desk chair in the empty bullpen of the press office. The lower
half of her body swiveled lazily back and forth like the cattail pendu-
lum of a clock, but the rest of her remained still, her elbows anchored
to the desk, her phone in her hands, her face in her phone. She didn't
mind being here. Had she left an hour earlier, she'd just be doing this
at her kitchen table instead of her office desk. Whether she was at home
in her apartment or here in City Hall, it didn't matter, because wherever Roxy happened to be, she was never really there.

Instead she was here. Here, bicycle accidents were no matter for concern. Here, nothing mattered and everything twinkled and everyone
buzzed about the premiere of a new reality show called *Love on the Ugly
Side*, which sounded just awful and stupid and Roxy couldn't wait to
see it when she got home, but for now she kept moving, because there
was more to see, because there was always more to see. A married politi-
cian got caught with his mistress and she was amused, until a child
with a disability climbed to the top of a rock wall and she was hopeful,
until a friend announced he'd bought his first home and she was jealous, until an article confirmed the seas were rising and she was scared,
until a panda got a bucket stuck on his head and she LOL'd, and so on
and so on, each emotion erasing its predecessor from the dry-erase board
of her mind. An earthquake hit Los Angeles. "Anyone else feel that?"
"Yowza!" Roxy felt concerned, until, further down, a celebrity whose
makeup tutorials she loved retweeted a link to Blueberry Muffins or
Chihuahuas, and Roxy followed that link and it took her over here, to a
series of photos, some of Chihuahuas, some of blueberry muffins, and
the blueberry muffins looked like Chihuahuas, and the Chihuahuas

looked like blueberry muffins, and she was asked by the page to guess which was which, and Roxy laughed out loud, and out there, outside of her phone, her soft giggle scurried across the bright empty bullpen like a mouse.

Then she felt an urge. Maybe the big blueberry eyes of the Chihuahuas stirred some procreational itch. Maybe the muffins made her mouth water. Whatever it was, something in the bottom of her stomach or the back of her brain gave the old familiar tug, and Roxy found her way over here, to Suitoronomy, where she met Bob.

Bob had seen her first, and he liked her immediately. Why wouldn't he? She was beautiful here, the best of all possible Roxies. Here she wasn't that baggy-eyed girl from the press office, the one in the overalls. Here she was exquisite, in a dress and makeup from three New Year's Eves ago, when she was fresher and newer and weighed less and slept more. Here, her emphatic red curls were not hidden under a hat or straitjacketed into a ponytail. Here, they spread like fireworks around her, and she smiled a multitudinous smile for everything all at once: a smile for a new year, a smile for a camera, a smile for a photographer, a smile for everyone in the room, a smile for everyone in the world, and finally, here, a smile just for Bob. Bob saw the smile and the hair and the dress, and he must have known he wanted her, because with a flick of his thumb, just a calorie of work, he gathered up this want and sent it crackling out of his brain and into Roxy's world, setting into motion everything that would follow.

That had been an hour ago. Now Roxy opened up Suitoronomy, and there was Bob, cheerful dimply Bob, looking up at her from the palm of her hand, wanting her. He was handsome, but everyone here was handsome. They were all as handsome as the handsomest picture they had of themselves, and there was no better picture of Bob in the universe than this one right here. His hair had never been combed better in its life. The historic hair day, the charming smile, and the fact that she knew he liked her was enough for Roxy. Another calorie of work, and both their phones rattled and chirped to announce it: They liked each other.

Roxy didn't hear from him right away. When Kervis finally returned to the press office crowing that the big guy seemed to like "Look Up New York," she quietly packed up her things and went home. On the subway uptown to Morningside Heights, she forgot about Bob. She checked the weather, she watched videos of makeup disasters, she parsed a few more blueberry muffins from Chihuahuas, and she flirted with three other men. Bob had swum away from the lagoon of her attention and now dog-paddled in the back of her brain with everyone else.

But then, that night, as she lay, half stoned, watching and high-key loving the first episode of *Love on the Ugly Side*, her phone lit up. It was Bob.

He said, "Can I be honest?"

Roxy was too tired to flirt. She went to sleep, and in the morning, still thinking he was cute, replied while brushing her teeth. She tried to think of some funny retorts before deciding that even though he was cute, he wasn't so cute that she'd spend all morning worrying about what she said to him, and besides, she was late for work, so she simply said, "Sure. Be honest."

"Okay," he batted back quickly. "I'll just tell you. You're my first."

"Your first?"

"My very first."

"Your first what?"

"My first one of these. My first match. The first person I've talked to on this thing. I'm brand new at this." Then, a little later, "How'm I doing?"

By now she was back at her desk downtown. She was busy, but she spared a moment to keep the ball in the air. "So great," she replied. "You're a natural."

"Haha, thanks. Yeah I'd never done one of these apps before, so I wanted to see what it was like. I made the little profile, and filled out the thing, I hope this picture's okay. And then I started playing with it and the very first face that came up was you. Yours. So here I am. I'm Bob, by the way. I like your dress."

"I'm Roxy," she replied. "Thank you."

The dots appeared. He was writing more. She looked at his profile. Bob, 40, has matched with you. She cut him off. "Are you divorced, Bob?"

The dots went away as something was erased. Then the dots reappeared, and then: "No. Why, do I seem divorced? Haha."

"Still married then? Sneaking around?"

"No, I'm not married. I've never been married."

"You seem a little defensive, Bob. It's okay, I'm not judging. Life is long. People get bored."

Another long interval of three dots. So much being written and erased, written and erased, and finally all that arrived was: "I'm not married."

"Okay, I believe you," she said. He didn't reply. An hour later she was at lunch, working through a salad, rubbing a drying fleck of kale from her teeth, when it occurred to her to say more. "I'm sorry, I'm not trying to judge you or anything. Just seems a little weird that you'd be new at this."

"I guess I'm weird then," he said quickly.

"Did you just get out of a longterm relationship?"

"No."

"Are you still in a longterm relationship?"

Bit of a pause after that one, but then: "No."

"Well I don't mean to harp on it but I don't get how you could spend forty years as an unmarried person on planet earth, and not once be lonely enough or even curious enough to go on a dating app." She suddenly realized she was putting way too much effort into this conversation. Did she really care all that much? She went elsewhere. Chihuahua. Chihuahua. Blueberry muffin.

"I guess I thought I wouldn't need to," he replied. "I thought I'd meet someone nice in real life. At work or something. Or at a party, or through friends. I counted on that happening, for a long time. And then . . . it just didn't. So here I am."

Roxy read this in an empty subway car. There was something

entertaining about his earnestness. "Is that why you're here, Bob? To meet someone nice?"

"Isn't that why everybody's here?"

"I think most people are here for something else, Bob."

"What's that?"

Roxy replied with a series of emojis, fruits and vegetables mostly.

"Ah," he said. "Of course." A moment later, he dared this reply: "And what are you here for?"

Roxy smiled. She started to write the honest answer: a series of emojis, fruits and vegetables mostly. She didn't want a boyfriend. Maybe, at some point down the road, she *would* want a boyfriend, maybe she'd want *more* than a boyfriend, and if that day ever came, she wouldn't be conflicted about it, wouldn't feel like a hypocrite, because that was down the road and this was right now, and right now, as in every right now she'd ever lived, Roxy wanted what she wanted to want, nothing more, nothing less.

She thought of something her old friend Carissa had said when they were on vacation together in Cozumel, before Carissa got married and her husband made her stop hanging out with Roxy. They were at this bar by the beach, and some guy had been hitting on Carissa all night, and he asked her what she was looking for in a man, and she said, "I'm looking for a husband. Someone else's, preferably!" Roxy and the other girls had laughed so hard at that. Carissa had a four-year-old now. There were first-day-of-preschool pictures on her Facebook page. Carissa was gone from Roxy's life. No harm in stealing the line.

"I'm looking for a husband," she said to Bob, and then she paused, because the pause was important for the timing, but then, when she typed out "someone else's preferably" and added a winky face, it kind of felt gross, and she thought maybe she was wording it wrong because it didn't seem as funny as when Carissa had said it. Maybe it was funnier out loud when everyone was drunk, so maybe she'd word it a different way, and then the subway screeched to a stop and her phone flew out of her hands and slid like a hockey puck down the length of the car, coming to rest in a puddle, substance unknown.

"FUCK!" Roxy screamed. She scrambled to the other end of the car and snatched her phone out of the puddle and shook it until the substance unknown had dripped away, and then her hands went to work, digging into her purse, pulling out a bottle of sanitizer, squeezing out a splurt, another splurt, nearly half the bottle, and scrubbing it into her phone with tissue after tissue, as if it would ever be clean enough to hold up to her face. (She knew it never would be.)

She pressed the power button. It was dead. She held the button down for five seconds, then ten, then twenty, unrelenting, like a paramedic trying to revive a corpse. Her thumb went white and started to hurt. Still nothing.

She ran up the subway stairs and out onto Broadway, and she bought a bag of rice at the bodega, and when she got home, she put the phone in the bag and left it there for the longest hour of her life. Then she plugged in the phone again and said a little prayer.

The white apple of life appeared on the black screen.

Suitoronomy. New messages. She clicked.

"I'm looking for a husband."

"Haha. Wait, seriously? Good for you! I guess if we're both being honest, I'm looking for a wife. It's nice to know I'm not alone. Hello? You still there? Pinned under a boulder? Did I say something to upset you? Okay I'm sorry I bothered you. Thank you for a nice first conversation on this thing. For what it's worth I think it's cool that you're up front about what you're looking for. It's very honest and brave. If you change your mind and want to meet up sometime in real life, let me know. Goodbye. I won't pester you anymore. Goodbye."

Roxy didn't write back. She forgot about Bob. She forgot him so deeply and so well that she had to think very hard a day and a half later to recall him when, in a hurry while jogging and Suitoronomying, she tried to reply to a different guy's invitation to drinks next Wednesday, but instead wrote "Yes!" under a message that had just arrived, that very second, from Bob. She stopped jogging.

"Okay, you know what," he had written, "one last thing, since I'll never see you again anyway, and I guess there is still a remote possibility you're pinned under a boulder, I'll just say you seem cool and I'd love to meet you in real life. Am I doing that too early? Or too late? I don't know how this stuff works. I just think if there's more to learn about you I'd love to learn it in person. This is all going on the assumption that you're pinned under a boulder. If you're not pinned under a boulder, good day to you. But if you ARE pinned under a boulder, or a fallen tree, or a sumo wrestler, or any other large thing, would you like to get dinner sometime?"

"Yes!"

Roxy, still in her jogging clothes, stood by the sink, reading this exchange, then looking at his picture, then reading it once more, and it occurred to her that maybe there was something to a guy like Bob. Sure, he was a goofus, but dinner might be nice. She ate dinner most nights anyway. The red in her cheeks started to go away. And shit, maybe she and this Bob could get married and have some kids or whatever if he wasn't annoying in person. She looked at him again and broke off the engagement. Not this guy. But his lips were nice. Maybe they would smooch a bit. Maybe more than smooch. She didn't want to give the poor guy the wrong impression, but maybe she'd rock his world for a night. And maybe that would be it. He was a big boy; he could handle being loved up and abandoned. If nothing else, he'd get a lesson out of it, the hot frying pan you only touch once and that's how you learn. Welcome to Suitoronomy, Bob. Here there be dragons.

She added, "How about Tuesday?"

Very quickly the reply arrived: "Tuesday it is."

For someone new at this, Bob had confidence. Roxy looked forward to Tuesday. She even let herself say, "Can't wait!" before going back to *Love on the Ugly Side*, and then going on Twitter, and then doing a quiz to find out what kind of disease she was.

* * *

FIRST NAME:

She typed, "Alice."

In truth, "Alice" wasn't her *first* first name. Alice's *first* first name was "Truth." Truth and her twin sister, Justice, were taken in by St. Luke's Home for Lost Children on June 7, 1987. (Don't bother looking. St. Luke's no longer exists. Nor does the country whose orphans it served.) They arrived, and a record was made of their arrival—the first record of Alice's existence—and decades later that record was scanned, digitally archived, and forgotten. I don't know who her biological parents were. I don't know if they were good people or bad. I don't know why they couldn't keep their daughters. I don't know any of these things, so the doorstep of St. Luke's is where Alice's story begins.

Justice was adopted quickly, by a Norwegian couple, the Hjalmarssons. Did the Hjalmarssons know their new baby was a twin? Might they have adopted both girls if they'd known? There's no way to know. It seems the existence of the truth of Truth's existence was kept from them, like so many truths kept from so many couples, before the series of lawsuits that put St. Luke's out of business forever. The Hjalmarssons went home with one little girl and were perfectly happy about it. They named her Sofia. What's there to say about Sofia Hjalmarsson? She grew up in Oslo, went to some school, did something for a living, married somebody, had some kind of life. It's all there if you want to look for it. Justice doesn't interest me. Truth does.

Truth remained at St. Luke's another two months. Then one day an American couple, John and Penelope Quick, arrived from a far-off place called Katonah, New York, and that's how we come to the second record of one particular girl in the wide cacophony of information: the adoption papers, everything filled out, signed, and certified.

Then, record three: An airplane ticket. A middle seat, for a baby in an infant carrier between her new parents. At some point on the flight, somewhere high above an ocean, Truth became Alice.

And "Alice" was the answer, twenty-eight years later, to the prompt FIRST NAME:

Alice typed "Alice," as she had many times before on this page. But this time was going to be different because this would be the last time she did it. She was going to fill this thing out. Enough messing around. This was happening, right now. Never give up. Never surrender.

MIDDLE NAME:

"Alice?"

Alice looked up from her phone. The nine-year-old girl next to her, whose name was Tulip, tugged at her sleeve. This was where they sat on hot days, in the cool marble lobby of Tulip's apartment building, instead of the bus stop up the block.

Alice looked down at Tulip. The girl always looked so severe in her school uniform, her dark braids morning-tight. Only three more days of this, Alice thought. Then summer.

"Yes, Tulip?"

"We missed the bus."

Alice leapt up. "Shit! Seriously?" Luis, the doorman, laughed to himself as Alice looked out the window. The bus was driving away, down Fifth Avenue. *Fuck*, she thought, *I said "shit" in front of Tulip.* "Shoot," Alice said, as though that would fix it. "We'll take the next one."

"But that was our bus."

"No, that was the one we missed. The next one is our bus."

She smiled down at Tulip, as if this logic fixed it. Tulip accepted it.

"Can I play on my iPad?"

"No."

Alice sat down, returning to her phone.

MIDDLE NAME:

"What are you doing?"

"Filling something out," Alice said.

"What is it?"

"A thing I need to fill out." MIDDLE NAME:

"But *what*?"

"Tulip, come on." MIDDLE NAME:

"Do you like being a nanny?"

"Are you kidding? I love you, kiddo."

"That wasn't the question."

Alice surrendered. She put her phone back in her purse and crouched down in front of the growing child, face-to-face, their noses almost touching.

"Tulip," she said, "here's everything you need to know in life. Ready? Look into my eyes, and don't look at anything else. Listen to my voice, and don't listen to anything else. This, right here, what we're doing? This is something called 'focus.' If you can master this, what we're doing right here, if you can learn to concentrate and not be distracted by anything, there is absolutely no limit to—"

"We missed the next one."

Alice ran to the door again and looked out. The next one was driving away, down Fifth Avenue. On its back was a giant ad for that new show *Love on the Ugly Side*, with its slogan in large yellow block letters, like a finger jabbed in your chest: "What Are You Willing to Do?"

Alice sighed.

"Shit."

★ ★ ★

That evening, long fingernails of sunlight scratched slowly across the ceiling and walls of her little bedroom in Turtle Bay. Alice lay on her bed and sank deep into her laptop. Gary the Canary nibbled a seed in his cage nearby.

Bookmarks. The little white arrow sniffed at the words "MCAT REGISTRATION" with growing hesitation. Alice knew if she clicked it again, she would definitely fill it out, because she would *have to*, because once it was open she wouldn't close it again without filling it out, because never give up, never surrender. So she didn't click it. She clicked Facebook instead.

"#stomachboner," said her high school friend Dave, showing off a sandwich he'd made.

"Number eight blew my mind," declared an unknown voice advertising a list of ten child stars who got so fat you won't believe it!

"Engaged!" announced Alice's roommate, Kelly.

"This guy didn't have to die," said Tom, a guy Alice had once been on one date with, over an article about yesterday's tragedy in Central Park. Below it, Tom's cyclist friend Brock all-caps'd, "YOU OBVI-OUSLY DO NOT UNDERSTAND THIS ISSUE," and then angrily explained why Tom didn't understand the first thing about—but hold on a second. Alice scrolled back up.

"Engaged!" announced her roommate, Kelly.

Alice stepped out of her room, and there in the kitchen were Kelly and her apparently now-fiancé, Moany, eating Halal Guys and talking in low tones. Moany was a collector and restorer of antique typewriters. He had literally hundreds of them. Kelly had met him only a few months ago, and now he was over pretty much every night, frequently earning the nickname Alice had given him and shared with nobody.

"You're engaged?!"

Kelly looked up, and for a split second Alice caught a look on her face and the look was panic. Then it was replaced by the approximation of joy. "Yes! Just last night!"

"Congratulations!" Alice gave Kelly a big hug. "I can't believe I'm finding out about this on Facebook! Crazy!"

Kelly agreed it was crazy, and then answered all of Alice's questions regarding the important details—how it happened, what the plan was for the wedding, how sweet it felt switching her Facebook status—until finally the conversation found its way to the topic of living situation. The plan was for Moany to move in here.

"Well, he practically lives here already, so I guess it won't be that big of a change," Alice said, playfully swatting Moany's shoulder. "Although where's he gonna keep all his typewriters?"

Then the look of panic returned to Kelly's face, and this time Alice understood it.

*　*　*

"So they politely asked me to move out, and I politely agreed to it."

Alice's brother, Bill, announced his outrage: "That's an outrage!

15

Can they even do that?" (Legally, they couldn't, but Alice was too shell-shocked to know that or think of looking it up.) "So what, now you gotta pack up everything you own and just . . . skedaddle?"

"It's only a couple suitcases and a birdcage," Alice reasoned.

Bill shook his head and tossed back the last of his margarita. They were on the Upper West Side, at a Mexican restaurant called La Ballena, and they sat outside on the patio because it was a beautiful afternoon, because they were all beautiful afternoons in Bill's beautiful world. He wore Ray-Bans and a light blue oxford cloth button-down with the sleeves rolled up, and ordered a second margarita because why not? He had the afternoon to sleep it off.

"Well, if you need a place to crash for a little while," he offered, "you can always stay with us. I mean temporarily, of course. Or permanently! Hell, just come live with us!"

Alice laughed. "No, thank you."

"*Yes*, thank you! Come live with us, I insist!"

Bill was persistent, because he could be, because he was rich and powered by some secret energy source that never ran out. He was tall, with the wavy hair and aggressively toothy self-satisfaction of a lesser Kennedy. Alice, sharing none of his genetics, was born with none of this. Everything she had about herself was built from scratch.

"I don't think your wife wants me moving in with you guys," Alice said. "Right, Pitterpat?"

Pitterpat looked up from her phone.

"Alice," she said, with her Southern lilt, "you're welcome anytime, you know that." She was frosted perfection, smiling at Alice like a space heater in pearls.

"You don't mean that," said Alice, picking up the menu.

"Of course she does," said Bill.

"Of course I do," Pitterpat confirmed.

"And even if you do," Alice continued, "I don't want to go from being one happy couple's weird little single pet to another happy couple's weird little single pet."

"I get it," Bill said. "Can you stay at Dad's?"

"Oh, God, can you imagine me back in Katonah?"

"I mean, if there's no other option. I bet he could use the company."

"Yeah, if there's one thing Dad loves, it's company."

Bill knew she had a point. The man was a good father who loved his kids, but emotionally he was a succulent, wanting little more than a phone call on his birthdays and holidays, if that even.

Pitterpat excused herself to the ladies' room, leaving Alice and Bill alone. This was the third time they'd gotten together in as many months. It was strange. Alice had gotten used to never seeing her brother.

"I think you made her mad," Alice said.

"Nah," said Bill as his phone chirped.

It was a text from Pitterpat: "I can't believe you would do that."

Bill looked at Alice, reading her menu. She looked up at him. He smiled, and she smiled back. He returned to his phone.

"Baby, I know my sister. I knew she would say no, but I also knew she'd be mad if I didn't offer. So I offered. Knowing she'd say no. Which she did."

"She cannot live on our couch, Bill."

"First of all she wouldn't be on the couch. We have a guest room with a bed in it."

"That mattress is like straw. The couch is comfier, that's where she'll be."

"She said no!"

"I just bought that couch! You saw how many couches I looked at before we landed on that one!"

"And it's a great couch, but did she say yes? No! You heard her. She said no."

"She owns a bird, Bill! You are not bringing your sister and some noisy bird into our apartment!"

"First of all Gary's not noisy. He's mute. Doesn't make a peep. Second of all. She. Said."

"You promised," she interrupted. "This summer is for us. Nobody else. You promised."

He *had* promised.

Over here, we find an interview from earlier that year. It's one of many interviews Bill did in the run-up to the big sale. In this one (and in all of them for that matter), the interviewer asked him: "So what exactly *is* MeWantThat?"

"Well, how much time do I have?"

The interviewer laughed. "The quicker, the better."

"So the elevator pitch then?"

"Yes, exactly, the elevator pitch."

Bill shifted in his seat and pretended to think it up on the spot. He had given this spiel a thousand times, and pretending he had no spiel was how the spiel began.

"Well, I guess the best way to start is to ask why we do this. Why do we create technology? To make people's lives better. To give them something they want before they know they want it. Successful technology addresses needs, but groundbreaking technology *anticipates* needs. That's the place we started from: How can we surprise you? What's our magic trick? And then it occurred to us—"

"You and Zach."

"Yes, that's right, Zach being Zach Charboneau, my partner of many years. It occurred to us: What if there was an app that literally does exactly that: tells you what you want before you want it? So that's what we did."

"Cool, cool," said the interviewer, whose name was Gordon. "And can you explain how it works?"

"Happy to, Gordon. I'll take you through the user experience. You download it, you open it up, and boom: First thing you see is a picture of something, something you might want. It could be anything. Let's say it's a slice of pizza. Do you want a slice of pizza?"

"Always."

They both laughed. "Well, that's easy then. If you look at that pizza and decide you want it? Swipe right, and it's on its way to your door.

18

Easy. Don't want it? Swipe left, and something else appears. Maybe it's a new shirt. Maybe it's a candle-making kit. Maybe it's that Russian novel you've been meaning to read since college. Maybe it's porn. And maybe it's not just any porn, maybe it's some specific weird kind of porn that you never knew existed, like, everyone's wearing wizard robes or something, and maybe you're into wizard porn and you didn't know it."

"How does the algorithm know you might be?"

"It doesn't. That's important. MeWantThat knows nothing about you. There's no data mining involved, no promoted ads. Everything MeWantThat learns about you, it learns directly from you, from your choices, from this game of Twenty Questions that goes on and on hopefully way past twenty questions. You just keep swiping, again and again, past the stuff you don't want, and inevitably you get to that thing that makes you say, 'Yes! That's it! I didn't know I wanted it, but yes: Me want *that!*'"

Gordon nodded, impressed, then turned to the camera.

"Bill Quick, developer of MeWantThat, giving the people what they don't know they want," he said, before turning back to Bill. "And I suppose what *you* want is a high valuation when the shares go public?"

"Oh, me want that, Gordon," Bill said, bashfully turning on his smile. "Me want that very much indeed."

And he got it. He got everything, because everyone loved MeWant-That, and they used it in massive numbers, and he and Pitterpat became very rich. And people would talk to Pitterpat all the time about it, at parties and dinners and what have you, and she would testify up and down that she loved MeWantThat, and she used it all the time. But in truth, she never did. She didn't need to. Instinctively, preternaturally, Pitterpat was very good at wanting.

Pitterpat wanted and wanted and wanted, and why shouldn't she? There was so much in the world and so little of it was hers, or at least so little of it was in the possession of those for whom she wanted it, for hers was not a selfish want but simply an awareness that the distribution of stuff in the universe was out of balance and begged adjustment.

She wanted well. She made an activity of wanting. Her favorite folder on her Pinterest page was called "Want." When she wanted something, she placed it there. She placed it there so she could want it with full attention, and then step away from it, and then return, and be reminded: This, Pitterpat, this is what you want.

And the things she wanted, oh, how she wanted them! An Hermès scarf, with a print like an illustrated zodiac. A beach house in Rhode Island, gambrels and ivy. A group of old friends, reunited. De Gournay chinoiserie wallpaper, a bird in a cherry tree. That *just so* shade of blue. A comprehensive gun control bill. Candy rabbits made of sugar. That lipstick they don't make anymore. A 1960 Jaguar Mark 2. A prewar apartment on Fifth Avenue. A baby.

What is it like to want? Does it hurt? Or is it wonderful? Do people want to want? Or is to want to want to want no more?

The food arrived. They'd ordered a Guactopus for the table, because if you went to La Ballena, you *had* to get the Guactopus. Bill told the story of how he discovered the Guactopus at the original La Ballena downtown. He was on jury duty, and he and one of the other jurors went there for lunch. What was that guy's name? Felix. What happened to Felix? They were Facebook friends at one point. Oh, look, still are. Bill wondered if he should reach out and say hi. Anyway, that was years before the food blogs got wind of the Guactopus. Now it was everywhere, and with good reason: It was a very photogenic dish. Go look on Instagram, you'll find thousands of Guactopi in situ. The world couldn't possibly need another, but Pitterpat picked up her phone anyway.

"Wait," she said, "don't eat yet."

Alice put her chip down on her empty plate. Pitterpat clicked, clicked again to be sure, and then turned the phone on Alice like a weapon.

"And one of you!"

"Oh," Alice said, and gave a quick smile.

Click. Pitterpat checked it. "Aw, that's a cute one! I'm sending it to you." Alice smiled in return. Then Pitterpat made a sad face. "That really stinks about your apartment, Alice. But hey, this time next year you'll be living in a dorm room anyway, right?"

"Why?"

"Medical school," Pitterpat reminded her. "How's that going by the way?"

FIRST NAME:

"Oh, right! It's going great."

Bill came up for air from a long sip of his margarita. "I would love to go back to college. How fun would that be?" He said it the way you might spot a sizzling fajita two tables over and think about getting one.

BING! Alice looked at her phone, and there was the picture Pitterpat had just taken. It surprised her. The girl in the photo looked happy. She had a toothy surprised grin, and the sunlight was warm and perfect on her freckles. For a moment Alice wondered if her sister-in-law had captured her true essence, the one she hid even from herself, one of contentment and ease. Then Alice remembered: This was not her true essence. She was not content. She was not at ease.

Still, she saved the photo. It could be a good profile pic.

* * *

The weather was warm and friendly that afternoon, and the wind gentle off the Hudson, so the three Quicks decided to walk home up Riverside, to Bill and Pitterpat's apartment on 113th. The trees danced above them as they strolled, a riot of sun specks twinkling between the leaves. Bill noticed the light like he hadn't before.

"It's weird seeing him like this," Alice said. She and Pit were behind Bill a few paces, talking to each other, but loud enough for him to hear.

"At all, you mean?"

"Yeah. It's weird seeing him at all." Alice laughed.

"I'm just enjoying it while I can," said Pit. "It's only a matter of time before he gets some new obsession and completely blows me off."

Bill turned back to them. "Never gonna happen," he said with a grin.

"Please," Alice said. "Your thing is you always need a thing. MeWant-That was your thing, but now that's done, so now you need a new thing."

"I do not need a thing."

"Sure you do. You always have. In high school, it was the drums. Before that, it was model trains."

Pitterpat guffawed. "Model trains?"

"That was a brief infatuation," he said. "And I do *not* need a thing. I am off the hamster wheel for good. For *good.*"

They walked some more. Pit turned to Alice. "So what are you doing this afternoon?"

"Actually, I'm going to see an apartment. It's not far from here, in fact. 111th and Amsterdam."

This made Pitterpat happier than Alice expected it would. "Oh, how fun! We'll be neighbors! You'll like this neighborhood. There's no great restaurants up here, but there's plenty of *good* restaurants, and some of those good restaurants are actually pretty great."

"So I gather."

"And Riverside Park is nice, and it's fun having Columbia nearby. Lots of local color. Like that guy." Pitterpat pointed to a young man across the street, walking south along the stone wall of Riverside Park. He was large and bearlike, with long black hair and a beard, and a black overcoat that couldn't have been comfortable on a day like today. "We see him all the time. Bill calls him Everywhereman. Have you ever seen him before?"

"No," said Alice.

"Well, get ready, because you will. Not just in this neighborhood. We see him all over the city. I saw him in Battery Park once."

Everywhereman, as if he sensed being talked about, looked their way, but before Alice and Pitterpat could awkwardly smile, he reset his gaze on the ground in front of him, deep in thought, as if grappling with some enormous problem. Alice was wondering what that problem might be when she nearly ran into Bill, who had come to a stop.

They were in front of a small building with an unmemorable facade, like a slice of an old junior high school from a bad decade, out of place among the Beaux Arts grandes dames of Riverside. A perfunctory flight of cement stairs led to the front door, with a large front terrace beside it. There would have been nothing noteworthy about the building were it not for the enormous green bronze statue of a medieval Buddhist monk looking down at them from the terrace.

The plaque beneath the monstrous statue indicated that this was Shinran Shonin, a monk who lived in Japan in the twelfth century.

They all looked up at the giant man in silence. Only the breath of the traffic was heard.

"Shinran Shonin," Bill said, finally. "How long has this been here?"

No one knew.

"I've lived in this neighborhood for four years. How have I never noticed Shinran Shonin?"

Again, no one knew. They kept walking.

* * *

Alice split off from the group at Riverside and 111th, and as she pushed her way up the hill through the humidity, she felt the unmistakable creep of malaise. It was always nice seeing her brother. She could relax around him. She liked his ease with kind words and his generosity. But an afternoon in his glow always left her with an emptiness. He was a grown-up. More than a grown-up. He had had a whole career, come out the other side of it, and was now basically a retiree. He had a wife and an apartment and a doorman, and here was Alice, still nannying.

Across the street, two women in green scrubs had coffee on a sidewalk patio.

Alice just had to go to med school—that's all there was to it. She was twenty-eight. This was her last chance to do something like this, her last chance to *be* something like this. Soon Bill and Pit would have a kid—they had dropped some hints that the happy project might start as soon as the fall—and she would be so excited for them, she would love to be an auntie, but the idea of getting that news while she still had no trajectory was just dreadful.

I have to do this, she said to herself. *Right now. Right now, here on the sidewalk in the sunshine, here we go.*

She took out her phone. She clicked the bookmark and opened the form.

FIRST NAME: "Alice." Done!

MIDDLE NAME: "Calliope."

Her middle name was Greek because her dad loved ancient Greece. In her childhood, when Alice would spill something or break something, her mom would sometimes call her Alice Catastrophe Quick, and it would hurt Alice's feelings and put one more inch of distance between the two of them, despite her dad's best efforts to spin "catastrophe" as a good and happy thing, which she didn't believe, but he assured her it was, it was a thing from Greek drama, look it up. There was a word for it. What was it? Alice couldn't remember. She Googled it. "Catastrophe": the final piece in the classical construction of a tragedy, capping off the protasis, epitasis, and catastasis. But can a catastrophe be a good catastrophe? She Googled "good catastrophe," and there it was, a word she'd forgotten for nearly fifteen years: "eucatastrophe." *Look at you, eucatastrophe.* The unexpected solution to an unsolvable problem. Often confused with deus ex machina, and thus often used pejoratively, because God cannot be inside a machine, that's not real, life doesn't work that way. *Get back to work, Calerpittar.*

ADDRESS: "345 East"—wait a second, that wasn't her address anymore. Oh no. What would she put for address? Maybe she could use Bill's address, just for now. Or maybe it was easier to just put her old address. Eventually Alice would end up somewhere new and all the mail would get forwarded, and in the meantime, would Kelly really mind holding a few bits of mail for a displaced friend? *Were* she and Kelly still friends? Alice realized she'd forgotten to like the engagement announcement. She went to Facebook to do that now, while she was thinking about it, but then she got to Facebook and discovered she'd been tagged in a photo. It was an old photo of her and her friend Meredith, from years ago, when the two of them played Carnegie Hall together. Meredith was always posting stuff like this, and it drove Alice crazy. There they were, Meredith with her violin, Alice at the piano, two little girls in a cavernous space, with such serious looks on their faces, trying so hard to meet the grown-upness of the moment. God, she was a determined little thing back then. Nothing could stop her. Rachmaninoff tried and even he failed. It was hard to look at these pictures now. Even harder not to.

"Alice?"

Alice awoke to find herself at the front steps of 507 West 111th Street. She had walked up 111th to Broadway, then, out of habit, accidentally turned right down Broadway to 109th, before correcting her path eastward via 109th to Amsterdam, then back up Amsterdam, past Probley's, past the Bakery, then west on 111th and a quarter of the way down the block, without once looking up from her phone. Had she nearly been killed in traffic? Possibly. But somehow she had reached her destination, and the redheaded woman who had just said her name must have been the person she was here to see.

"Yes. Hi," said Alice. "Are you Roxy?"

Roxy put up a finger of *just a second*, as her own attention was now focused on her own phone. She was typing something, something important it seemed. They stood in silence, two women at the front door of the building, for a minute at least. The street was quiet. The buildings, though slabbish and uniform, had a charming oldness about them. Down the street and across Amsterdam, the great unfinished cathedral of Saint John the Divine loomed grayly. Alice recognized it. She had walked by it, but never been inside. Maybe she'd go inside sometime if she lived here. She hadn't been in a church in years. *Three years.* Roxy was still typing. Three hundred characters. Three hundred fifty. Roxy's thumbs were like the feet of a small dog on a brisk walk, dazzlingly busy.

"I . . . am so . . . very . . ." she said as she hit send and looked up at Alice, ". . . sorry about that. And also sorry I'm late. Work stuff. I work for the mayor. It's okay if you don't like him."

"Because I'll like what he does?"

Roxy acknowledged the little joke without laughing. "Exactly. I don't like him either, to be honest. *Or* what he does. Alice, is it?"

"Yes. Hi."

"Hi. Let me get that."

She opened the door and they went inside. Alice started for the grand oak staircase at the end of the hall, but Roxy stopped her.

"This way," she said, indicating the small door to the narrow staircase that led down to the basement.

"It's in the basement?"

"It's technically not supposed to be an apartment," Roxy replied.

At the bottom of the stairs, Roxy unlocked and opened a door. Alice imagined how cool it would be if the apartment behind that door were incredible, one of those palatial but cozy spreads you'd never expect to find where you find it, one that in no way resembled a basement of any kind. That would be amazing, she thought.

But no. The door creaked open into a dank, unlit space. Plywood walls and curtains over the lightwells very nearly pulled off the illusion, but the air, cool and dusty, gave away the game. This was a basement trying to be an apartment and coming up short.

That wasn't the first thing Alice noticed, though. The first thing she noticed was the first thing Roxy casually pointed out like it was a common amenity for the sophisticated urban dwelling: "So yeah, we got a blue tree in the kitchen."

In the middle of the kitchen, from the floor to the ceiling, was the three-foot-thick trunk of an oak tree, painted sky blue.

"Wow," said Alice, "what's the story with that?"

"Came with the apartment," was all Roxy could offer. If she'd ever been curious about it, she might have asked around and discovered that about a century earlier, this building had been built up around this tree, relying on it as structural support. Over the years, as the building went through the typical life cycle of a New York City townhouse—renovation, decay, renovation, decay—the rest of the tree was gradually removed from the floors above. What remained in the basement, obstructing nearly every view from one side of the kitchen to the other, was the mighty oak's last vestige. This ten-foot trunk had quietly whiled away the decades down here among the boilers and the rat traps, before someone saw the dollar signs of turning this space into an illegal sublet. They put in the walls and the doors and painted the tree the color of the sky it would never see again.

Here's what little I can find on the blue tree. It's mentioned in Brian Lanigan's self-published 1977 memoir about his time at Columbia. He doesn't give a street address, but he describes "a charming little catacomb I sublet from a friend that summer (1958) with a marvelous blue tree growing in the kitchen, from the floor to the ceiling and beyond." There's no mention of it in the '80s, but then, in 1994, it pops up in a post on a very early Listserv board by a computer science grad student named Jamil Webster: "roommate wanted share 2br bsmt apt steps from campus EIK (w blue tree) 650/mo. No partiers plz." Gumby Fitch answered the ad and roomed with Jamil for two years. In 2003, Abigail Davis, the tenant six tenants before Roxy, finally caught the blue tree on camera, in the background of three pictures she took with her roommates Paul Malmstein and Rob DeWinter, which she posted on Friendster and captioned, "prefunking for graduation!!!" This exclusive club, the keepers of the blue tree, had little in common but the slight feeling of specialness you get when you're pretty sure your apartment's the only one in town with a blue tree growing through the middle of it. And it was. (In Manhattan anyway. There was a blue tree in a basement apartment in Brooklyn, on Ainslie Street. But we won't count that.)

Alice liked the tree immediately. The tour continued.

"Anyway, this is the kitchen." Roxy gestured casually, never looking up from her phone. "Bathroom. My room. Your room, if you don't turn out to be crazy." She finally looked at Alice. "You're not crazy, are you?"

"Not in any dangerous way."

Roxy liked that. She took a good look at Alice now, up and down. "How do we know each other?"

"Ziggy Rosenblatt."

"You know Ziggy?"

"Yeah, I knew him in Hawaii, when I lived there. I mean, we don't know each other too well. We're Facebook friends, for whatever that's worth. But I needed a place to stay, and randomly he reposted your thing about needing a roommate, and I saw it, and I figured . . ." And Alice kept talking, but Roxy didn't listen because she was texting Ziggy, who was on a beach on the other side of the planet, giving an early-morning surfing lesson. His students, four blond German boys who appeared to be brothers, listened attentively as Ziggy went on one of his frequent digressions away from surfing technique and into the craft of wayfinding, telling the story of how the early Polynesians reached Hawaii.

"It was celestial navigation, brave kānes," said Ziggy. "The stars. Also the wind, and the shape of the ocean swells, that was part of it too. But more than anything, it was the stars that guided the clever way-finders as they made the voyage all the way from Tahiti, in giant wooden canoes. Isn't that tight?"

The Germans didn't understand. Ziggy's phone buzzed.

"Hold that thought, brave kānes."

He brushed the sand off his phone and saw the message from Roxana Miao from high school: "Alice Quick. Your thoughts."

He didn't have too many thoughts on Alice Quick. They met at some bar in Lahaina, probably Spanky's or the Dirty Monkey, and bonded over both being former tristaters, she from Westchester, he from New Jersey. They had a laugh about how the Island folks consid-ered them New Yorkers, and how if any real New Yorkers happened to overhear them, they'd be exposed for the bridge-and-tunnel trash they really were.

He had found her weirdly cute. Not right-away cute, but cute after a few days of hanging out together, which is often the best kind of cute, more special, especially in a beach town where right-away cute is every-where you look. He might have tried to kiss her some night at some beach bonfire, or maybe he'd just had the fleeting impulse to do so. But nothing ever happened between them because that's how it usually goes. There're other girls in the world, and other boys, and for whatever reason these two particular orbits never crossed. Then she had some family tragedy or something and had to move back home, and they became to each other that gently heartbreaking class of acquaintance: Facebook Friend You'll Never See Again.

This depth of reflection wasn't available to Ziggy in this particular moment, with four young Germans looking up at him with eager smiles. So he just wrote: "Alice! Love her. Great girl."

Ziggy fumbled for one more detail. There had been one night, they were on a balcony smoking a joint, and she told him about being a concert pianist when she was little, how she played Carnegie Hall.

"Plays piano," he added.

"K Mahalo bye," Roxy replied.

Ziggy returned to his lesson, and on the other side of the earth, Alice wrapped up her story: ". . . so that's how I know Ziggy. We were never super close. I haven't talked to him in a while."

"I know, me neither," said Roxy. "So Ziggy says you play piano? Is that, like, loudly?"

Alice was a little thrown. She didn't remember ever telling Ziggy that. Maybe once. She was surprised he remembered. "Oh, um, no. I mean, I *did*. Years ago, growing up. I was pretty serious about it, but I stopped." She felt like she needed to say more. "There's a certain level of ability you have to reach by a certain age in order to pursue a career as a concert pianist. And that's not a level I reached. Or maybe I did, I don't know. The truth is I just kind of burned out on it. It's a bit of a sore subject."

Roxy was deep into another email. "Yeah, so if you need to play, if you could just do it quietly or while I'm not here. Do you have headphones?"

"I haven't touched a piano in eight years," she replied. "No need for headphones. Also I should tell you I have a bird. He's a canary, but he's very quiet. Mute, actually. Never sings. So no need for headphones there either."

Alice put a friendly, nervous laugh on the end of that, but Roxy didn't respond. Something was going on in her phone, demanding her attention. "Shit," she said. "Alice, I'm so, so sorry, I need to be back at work like yesterday morning. I work at City Hall. Did I mention that?"

"You did," said Alice. "Sounds pretty cool."

"I know, it does, and that's the only reason I still do it. Anyway, I have to go. So no loud piano?"

"No loud piano. Don't even own one."

"Great, and otherwise, headphones."

"Got it." Alice gave a thumbs-up.

Roxy put her boots back on, as Alice realized she was about to be left alone in a stranger's apartment. Or maybe now it was her own apartment? Unclear.

"Great. Your key's on top of the fridge," Roxy clarified before closing the door behind her. The stomp of the boots went up the basement stairs, and Roxy was gone.

The room was quiet. Alice touched the blue tree. It was smooth and cool.

A text arrived, from Roxy: "By the way, I hate to do this since we just met, but is there any way you could do me just a huge, huge favor tonight?"

Get back to work, Calerpittar, said a little voice. Alice had no obligations for the rest of the day. She could head downtown, grab her two suitcases and her birdcage, and be back in less than an hour. Maybe she'd get a small dinner, and then have the entire evening to register for the MCAT.

But this was her brand-new roommate asking. She typed out, "Sure, what's the favor?" Then, thinking better of it, she erased the "Sure." But that looked a little surly, so she stuck the "Sure" back in and hit send.

"Great! So I matched with this guy on Suitoronomy who seems pretty normal, but he wants to get dinner."

"Weird."

"I know. And I mean I don't THINK he's the kind of guy who would keep girls chained up in his basement, but you know who else probably thought that?"

"The girls chained up in his basement?"

"Exactly. So anyway, if you're not too busy tonight could I ask you to come by the restaurant I'm meeting him at and just be nearby?"

"Like just . . . be there?"

"Yeah. Until I say you can go. It would be a huge huge favor and I'd appreciate it so so much."

"Sure," Alice replied. "As long as it doesn't take all night."

Roxy shot back a bouquet of heart emojis. "Thank you so so much," she said. "Oh also I left my candles burning in my room. Can you blow out plz???"

Alice opened the door to Roxy's catastrophically messy, romantically candlelit room. She approached the two candles on the window-sill, dangerously close to the pink curtains fluttering against the lightwell window, and blew them out. Happy zeroth birthday to a new friendship.

* * *

Bill couldn't stop looking at Shinran Shonin, this greenish-reddish man with stern but forgiving eyes under the wide brim of his taku-hatsugasa, which was the name for that kind of hat, as Bill had just discovered.

To the people of pre-Buddhist Japan, a world of Stone Age technology and superstition, seeing a statue was like seeing a god. Somewhere along the way, this magic trick, crafting the image of a human being out of bronze or iron or wood, had lost its sparkle, but the statue's empty bronze eyes still carried a power that Bill felt in his knees, even now, looking at this facsimile of a facsimile, a photo on Wikipedia.

Bill and his wife lived at 404 Riverside Drive, a jagged, isosceles tooth in the skyline of the western frontier of Morningside Heights. Their apartment was on the top floor, and for most of the day the floor-to-ceiling picture windows displayed a treasured view of the Hudson River and the New Jersey Palisades beyond. But in the early evening, as the sun lowered, its angry rays cut through the room, whitening the paintings and setting the dust aglow. It was hard to be in the room at that hour. The light was resentful, lashing out, resisting its own orbital pull until finally it sank behind a New Jersey office tower or apartment block or whatever that building was, and the suddenly tame sky became a brilliance of oranges and purples. It was at this time of day that Bill and Pitterpat found their sleepwalking way to this couch, the couch with the view, where they'd sit in silence before nature's latest masterpiece and play on their phones.

"Babe," said Bill.

Pitterpat did not look up, so enthralled was she by photos of a Fifth Avenue apartment for sale. "Yes?"

"You know that statue we saw? Shinran Shonin?"

"Mmm-hmm?"

"You know where that statue's from?"

Was that a shared elevator landing? Or was it private? Pit couldn't tell. "Japan?"

"Yep. Do you know where in Japan?"

"Where?"

"Hiroshima."

"Wow."

"Yeah, wow! That statue survived the bomb."

"The atomic bomb?"

"That's right. It's still a little radioactive."

Pit became excited. "Oh my gosh!—sorry, wow, that's cool!—but I think I may have found our new apartment!"

"It was a gift from the Japanese government."

"Listen to this: *Three thousand three hundred* square feet. Four bedrooms, five baths."

"And now it's in front of a Buddhist temple. Eight blocks from our house."

"Doorman. View of the park."

Bill shifted in his seat, restless. "How is it that I know nothing about Buddhism? I'm thirty-two years old. I'm a pretty smart, worldly guy. Shouldn't I know at least *something* about one of the great world religions?"

"Ooh, a virtual tour!"

Bill returned to his phone. He typed the words "What is Buddhism" and rode them off into a cosmos of more knowledge than he could ever use. An explainer website. A helpful ebook. An online store that sold beads and essential oils. A trailer for a television documentary. A children's cartoon. Bill floated through the chaos until from somewhere in its midst, blinking like a satellite, was the link to a lecture by Columbia professor emeritus Carl Shimizu.

Bill slipped in his earbuds. An old man stood at a podium. He looked fragile, as if held together by the sweater and blazer that were older than most students in the class.

He asked: "What is Buddhism?"

The students were silent.

Again: "What is Buddhism?"

There were murmurs. Was it rhetorical? Was he really asking?

"I've been teaching this course for thirty-four years," the old man continued, to everyone's relief. "And I've never been able to give a suitable answer to that question. Buddhism is a religion that adheres to the teachings of a man named Siddhartha Gautama. Except when it doesn't. It's a faith that presents itself as a singular path to enlightenment. Except when it doesn't. Except when it *isn't*."

Bill was already in love. He was on the couch, but he was also there in the lecture hall, in the front row, listening in amazement. The professor loosened the mucus in his throat and continued.

"When we look at the many schools of Buddhist thought . . ."

Pitterpat stood in the sumptuous living room of a classic ten, a prewar mansion in the sky.

". . . divided so profoundly by time, geography, method of practice . . ."

A pirouette, and all 360 degrees of the room unrolled before her, its corners yawning away, endless. She imagined the multizone central AC and it raised gooseflesh on her forearms.

". . . it's sometimes hard to see what, if anything, connects them at all."

Bill and Pitterpat, side by side, in two giant rooms.

"But there is a thread that binds them all together. And that thread is a question: What is real?"

Again, asking or saying? Bill's lips wanted to move.

The professor tapped at his sweater. "Am I real? Are you real? Is this room real? This podium. Is this podium real?" He rapped hard on the lectern with a knuckle, loud enough for the unseen back of the classroom. "Seems real enough. But is it?"

Alice sat at the bar of a restaurant, sipping a Diet Coke. This restaurant, the Cinnamon Skunk, was one of those middle-of-the-road places in the middle of a block somewhere in Midtown, the kind of place you walk by and wonder if it's anyone's favorite place. Candles twinkled against the bottles on the shelf behind the bar, and it was quiet except for the clink-a-tink of restaurant chatter. Roxy still hadn't arrived. Nor, as far as Alice could tell, had Bob.

"Is any of it real?"

A man entered the bar and took a seat two stools down. He was older than Alice, but with smooth skin and a boyish, round face. He smiled at her and she smiled back, and he squinted as he scanned her features, trying to decide if this was the IRL face of the profile pic, the one with the dress and the fireworks of red hair. It was not. He ordered a drink and Alice kept going on hers.

"At the root of our inquiry," continued the old professor, "is the supposition that we live in not one world, but two."

Roxy was walking fast, her heels clicking along the interminable crosstown block. Blueberry muffin. Chihuahua. Chihuahua. Blueberry muffin. Chihuahua.

"We describe these two worlds by their contrasts: the tangible and the intangible."

Pitterpat needed to see this apartment, with her own eyes. She would reach out to the listing agent. He was handsome. He would ask if they were working with anyone already. They were not.

"The provisional and the eternal. The manifest and the essential."

Meredith. A duet.

Continuing education.

Crown moldings. Original?

Chihuahua. Chihuahua.

The ice in Bob's glass swallowing the heat of his drink.

"The key to insight, in Buddhism, in this class, in all things, is knowing which is which."

Blueberry muf—

Roxy doubled back. Stars, feedback. Her high heels gave way and she fell backwards, hard, right on her tailbone. The doorman laughed out loud, as anyone might when a woman who's not looking where she's going walks face-first into an awning pole. Later that night, he would go back and watch the security video and laugh all over again, but right now, between those two laughs, he knew it wasn't funny. He rushed over to help her up.

As she got to her feet, Roxy felt the hot blood leaving her nose in waves. Her broken nose. Holy shit. Holy fucking shit OW.

* * *

What was Meredith's secret? How did she do it? Every time she was in town, Alice would get a very sweet text from her, and they'd go get dinner, and they'd catch up, and Meredith would tell stories from her amazing life and Alice would eat and drink too much as she battled off the despair of having nothing much to report. She and Meredith had been on the same track once. Different instruments but same track, equally admired. The wall hit Alice and stopped her forever, but Meredith jumped it. She never gave up, never lost her mind, never moved to Hawaii, never drifted. And now Meredith had the kind of success that made social media a playground. What a paradise was Facebook for the successful! What a Xanadu for the comfortable, for the accomplished, for the happily married or healthily procreated! Alice looked at Meredith's Facebook page and couldn't believe the humblebraggadocio pulsing from it like radiation. Meredith holding some award she won: "Where am I supposed to put this?? I don't even have a mantel!" Promotional photo for the new season of the San Francisco Symphony: "This photo-shoot was a nightmare. The minute I was out of this dress I ate a cheeseburger." A lengthy profile in *String Section*: "LOL, someone forwarded this to me, forgot I even did this interview!" Alice knew, just based on the photo they used of Meredith, with her odalisque lean and arching eyebrow, that to click on this article and read it would be painful.

She clicked on the article and read it.

"Why the violin?"

"Well, it's what I started with. But there's something about the violin, isn't there? Strings are the most human family of instrument," Meredith opined. "They have voices. Maybe cello is closer to a man's voice, but the violin is closest to mine. And when I play it, I don't blow into it, like a brass or a woodwind. It uses its own breath. Like it's almost alive. That's what it is. It's this machine that's almost a person. You know how when you look at a really smart poodle, or a monkey in the zoo, and the monkey looks back at you, and there's that sadness where you see the soul behind its eyes, and part of it is the sadness that it's locked up in a cage, but more than that, it's locked up in a body that's not quite human, in a consciousness that's not quite *there*. It's the longing of being *not quite*. A chimpanzee's DNA is 99 percent the same as ours. And yet we're us, and they're them. That 1 percent is this canyon they can never cross, they can only look helplessly from the other side, the side where you get put in cages and trained to dance with a little hat on. That's how I think of my violin. When it sings—when *she* sings, I should say—her voice is infused with the sadness of being this wooden machine that will never be human, never ever, no matter how much she wishes. That's why her song is one of yearning. One of longing. And that's why I named her Pinocchia."

Oh, Christ, Meredith, shut up, you insufferable snob. The fact that you posted this interview on your own page is what's unbearably sad. Still, much as Alice didn't like it, she clicked like, just as 218 of Meredith's other friends already had. How did Meredith even have 218 friends?

Alice's phone lit up and pulled her out of this little vortex of resentment, to her great relief. Meredith was a sweet girl. She was just a violinist. Violinists are weird.

The text was from Roxy.

"Are you there?"

"Yes."

"Is he there?"

Alice looked over at Bob, also sitting at the bar. He looked at her, and his eyebrows raised with intention. He was about to ask if she was Roxy. Alice broke the eye contact before he could and returned to her phone.

"Yes, he's here. Where are you?"

"Emergency room. I walked into a pole. Just down the street in fact, like three doors down. I'm fine. I'm like totally 99 percent fine."

"Are you still coming?"

There was a mirror in the little room where Roxy had been told to wait for a doctor. Roxy had been avoiding this, but now had no choice. She took a peek. Her nose was broken. One of her eyes was blackened, and there was a bruise on her cheek where it looked like her face had been momentarily power-sanded.

"No, I think I'm going to skip it."

Alice sighed. Right now Meredith Marks was practicing some-where. Wait, no, it was eight o'clock on a Tuesday. She was *performing*. Alice asked for the check.

"What are you wearing?" It was Roxy again. Alice looked down at her dress. It was a pretty dress, sleeveless, red on top and brown on the bottom. There'd been something familiar about it when she saw it on-line: It was appetizing, savory, rich with umami. She couldn't put her finger on why until the dress arrived, and she tried it on in front of a mirror.

"A dress that makes me look like a bottle of soy sauce. Why?"

"Does it look nice? Do you look nice?"

It did and she did. "Yes."

"Hold on."

The bartender arrived with the check. Alice handed him her card. In her periphery she felt Bob, nearby, anxious. Then she felt him get a text.

He looked at his phone. "Bad news, walked into a pole, broke my nose, can't make it, so so sorry. BUT. Do you see a girl who looks like a bottle of soy sauce?"

"You broke your nose?"

"Yes. Do you see the girl who looks like soy sauce? The dress she's wearing looks like a bottle of soy sauce. Do you see her?"

Alice felt him look around, searching for someone, and then he looked at Alice, up and down, and *bingo*. She pretended to be trying to figure out the tip, to avoid looking up and facing what she was pretty sure was happening.

"Yes. Why?"

"That's my roommate Alice. She's there to make sure you don't murder me. But now that I can't make it, you should have dinner with her instead."

He typed, "Who's gonna make sure I don't murder HER," but erased it, because that's not the kind of joke you make this early into knowing someone. He looked at Alice, engrossed in her check, apparently trying to figure out how pens work. Her phone chimed. It was Roxy.

"He's gonna buy you dinner."

Alice's heart sank. "What? No! I don't even know this person!"

Roxy replied, "Neither do I! LOL."

And then the doctor arrived and Roxy put her phone away.

"Alice?"

Alice paused typing her very long reply ("Please just call this off I have work to do and don't have time to—") and looked up. Bob had crossed the distance between them, with his hand outstretched, as if he'd calculated the propriety of tapping a stranger on the shoulder and had come up short once the mission had already begun. He looked nervous and awkward and unsure of this whole thing. Despite everything, Alice could tell she and this Bob were well matched.

"Yes. Hi—"

"Bob."

"Hi, Bob. I'm Alice."

Finally his outstretched arm came to good use as they shook hands and things felt normal. Bob smiled warmly. "It's nice to meet you. I want to go on record that I don't believe a word of this whole walking-into-a-pole story." Alice laughed. Brightening at how charmed she seemed, Bob continued, "It sounds like a lie so she could palm me off on you, to be honest."

"I'm sure it's not a lie."

"Really? You're sure?"

Alice thought for a moment. "Actually, no. I'm not sure at all. I barely know Roxy. I just met her today."

Bob laughed. "Do you want to get dinner?"

"Isn't it a little weird?"

"Isn't everything?"

His lip curled ever so slightly. There was something playful about it. Alice thought of filling out a twelve-page MCAT registration, and the thought made her tired, and when she was tired, she was hungry, and the food here looked delicious.

* * *

The hostess sat them at a nice table beneath the Christmas lights of a crooked tree. They listened to the specials and assured the waitress tap water was fine, and then the waitress departed and the full bloom of awkwardness was finally theirs. *Whatever*, thought Alice, *let it be awkward. Who cares.* She obviously wasn't going to do the one thing she'd planned on doing tonight, and she had to eat dinner anyway. It was either this or eat alone.

Bob cleared his throat. "So," he said, closing the menu. "What do you—"

BING! From its little patch of tablecloth next to the bread plate, Alice's phone demanded attention.

"Sorry," she said.

"No, it's okay," he assured her.

"Do you mind if I . . . ?"

"Of course, go ahead."

It was a text from Roxy. "Are you there with him?"

"Y," she replied discreetly, hoping there would be no more to the discussion, when of course there would be.

"Is he cute?"

She wanted to convey to Roxy that she was a little miffed about having put on her soy sauce dress and come all the way down here, but finding the right wording for that kind of message would have been an all-night affair. Instead she just wrote "super cute" and put her phone down.

The words "super cute" appeared on Roxy's phone. Good for Alice. She seemed like a girl who could use a night out with a super cute guy. And he *was* super cute, wasn't he? Not that Roxy had seen him in real life, but she could tell this Bob was far too unsavvy to have the kind of profile-pic game that makes the short tall, the fat skinny, the cheesy sincere. If his pic was super cute, it was a safe bet he was too. Good. Good for Alice.

Alice smiled at Bob. "Sorry. You were asking—"

"Right," Bob replied. "I was just curious what you do for a living."

Alice hated this question. "Well, *currently*—"

BING! Now it was Bob's phone, next to Bob's bread plate.

"Sorry, can I?"

"Sure."

It was Roxy. "So so sorry again about tonight," she moaned, with a frowny face and a tongue sticking out. "I hope Alice isn't too much of a drag."

Bob replied quickly. "It's fine. We're having a great time."

A great time. Good. Good for them. Roxy wrote and erased her reply three times before getting both the wording and the nerve right.

"Well assuming you don't run off with my roommate, rain check?"

Another quick reply. "I insist on it. Friday night?"

Roxy smiled. She had plans on Friday, a party to go to, but she liked this Bob guy. He felt like boyfriend material. Maybe she did want a boyfriend. Maybe not. Either way, it's always nice to have the material on hand.

She replied, "Defecating."

He was confused. "Saturday then?"

Oh, shit. "I mean definitely. OMG. Sorry. Areola. Auto-erotic. Auto-correct."

Alice wondered what Bob was laughing at. Was he the kind of ass-hole who spends a whole first date laughing at texts from other girls? *Oh, shut up, Alice, who cares, this isn't even a date.* She stopped pretend-ing to read the menu and started reading the menu, until BING! It was a text from her brother, and you're not gonna believe this, he just got into Columbia! He applied this afternoon as a continuing education student so he could take this cool Buddhism class, and he just got in, all in one day! Crazy, right? She read it, read it again, and put her phone back on the table, facedown.

The nurse still hadn't returned, so Roxy had to sit with the agony of her last volley of texts. At least it took her mind off her smashed-up face. Oh no, would she be better by Friday? How long does a broken nose take to heal?

Bob's reply arrived. "Friday it is." Then, "Did you really walk into a pole?"

"Yes! Thank god nobody saw it!"

(This was in June. By August, a video called "ROXANA BANANA PWNED BY A POLE" will have been viewed over twenty-five million times.)

"What is it you kids say? Pics or it didn't happen?"

Roxy switched her phone to selfie mode and examined herself. Could she pull off a selfie that included both the broken nose and the plunge of her dress? It took her a few dozen tries, but eventually she got it and sent it to him. "Happy?"

Bob's somewhat daring reply arrived not long after: "Is it okay that I'm super turned on right now?"

"Perv," she replied, with a winky face. Okay. Friday night. Maybe she could bring him to the party. The nurse returned and Roxy put her phone away.

"I'm so sorry," Bob said, and Alice must have made a face, because he suddenly looked guilty and added, "I really am."

"It's fine."

"No. It's not. It shouldn't be like this. We're here, in this moment, together, kind of randomly, but still. I can go a whole meal without looking at my phone. I know I can."

Her eyes narrowed. "I don't know," she said. "You strike me as the kind of person who can't live without that serotonin."

"What do you mean? What about me tells you that?"

"Well, it's 2015, and you're a person."

He laughed. "Okay. Game on. Tell me your life story, and I'll sit here and listen to it and not look at my phone even once. How's that sound?"

She rolled her eyes, but blushed a little at the thought that, for better or worse, this was the most attention she'd gotten from someone who wasn't a family member in a long time.

"Okay," she said. "My name is Alice Quick. I'm from Katonah, New York. Well, actually, I'm adopted. I was born in—" BING! It was Alice's phone. They both looked at it and laughed a little. "Ignoring that."

"Good. Go on. You were adopted."

"I was adopted. I—" BING! And then another BING! And then another! A flurry of BING!

She was ready to continue, but her eyes pleaded. He nodded.

"Go ahead."

"Sorry."

She picked up her phone.

"Hello, Alice. It's Libby." *Of course it starts this way,* Alice thought. Alice had been Tulip's nanny for nearly a year now, and yet for some reason her mother assumed her number wasn't saved in Alice's phone. The mother-daughter-nanny triangle can be a serrated one. Libby continued: "Miss Miller emailed to say that Tulip was late for school again today. This is the third time it's happened. These tardies are going in her record. I think this just isn't working out. We'll be happy to give you a good reference. Best, Libby."

Alice put her phone down, and her face must have said a lot because Bob noticed and put his own phone down.

"Are you okay?"

"I just got fired."

Bob let out a weary sigh, feeling this on her behalf in a way that, from beneath the weight of this cruddy news, she recognized and liked. It wasn't the sociopathic, insincere I'm-supposed-to-be-concerned-right-now reaction you'd expect on a first date. (Not that this was a date.) Bob actually felt it, and she actually felt him feel it. "That really sucks. Seriously?"

"Seriously," Alice said, with a half smile.

"What was it, an email?"

"Text message."

"A text message?!" Bob seemed really upset now.

"It's fine, it's not a big deal," Alice assured him. "We have a bit of a weird relationship. I'm sure she'll change her mind. It's not like it's my dream job, anyway."

"And what's your dream job?" It was a natural question, the logical next place to put the conversational tennis ball, and yet the look on Alice's face made Bob feel like he'd just said the exact wrong thing. He was willing to let it go, but after a sigh and an extra big sip of her drink, Alice replied.

"You really want to know?"

"I really do," he said. By this point, he really did.

The candle flickered on the table between them, and Alice stared at it, as if listening. Finally, she spoke. "About three years ago, I wrote this long post on Facebook where I told all my friends that I finally know what I want to be when I grow up. I'm gonna be a doctor! I'm applying to med school, guys! Be excited for me! Got like five hundred likes. It felt good."

"I bet it did."

"And now it's three years later."

"And you haven't become a doctor."

"Nope."

Bob shifted in his seat, leaning back, assessing Alice. "Why do you want to be a doctor anyway?"

Go into it? No. Not yet. Not yet? Would there be more of Bob? Would she let him in eventually? "I don't know," she vamped. "I want to do something that matters."

"Something that matters."

"Yeah. I want to make a difference. I don't want to be president or anything, I don't want to be famous. I just want what I do in this life-time to matter. Just a tiny bit of mattering. That's all. Just the wee-est bit."

"A skosh," Bob suggested.

"A whisper," she replied.

"A smattering."

"Exactly," she said. "A smattering of mattering."

"I get it. So what's stopping you?"

Alice sighed. "If you want to become a doctor, you have to go to med school."

"So why don't you go to med school?"

"To go to med school, you have to take the MCAT."

"So why don't you take the MCAT?"

"To take the MCAT, you have to sign up for the MCAT."

"So why don't you sign up for the MCAT?"

The candle flickered, and Alice seemed to as well. She looked down at the table. *Get back to work.* "I can't," she said.

"Why not?"

"I have no idea. I wake up in the morning, I go to the website to sign up for the test, and there's this long registration form, and I start filling it out, and I just . . . *don't.* I spend the whole day looking at *list-icles* of, like, the thirty most glorious celebrity mullets ever."

"I've seen that one," Bob said. "Swayze at number four? Disrespect-ful. Continue."

Alice laughed. "My best friend from growing up is a concert violinist. We used to play duets together, and I was just as good as she was, because I *could* be. I was *capable* of it. Every day I'd sit there, for hours, playing the same parts over and over, again and again, getting it right, getting it perfect, not even getting up to go to the *bathroom*. But now . . ."

She paused, listening to the candle again.

"Something's happened to my brain. I don't know what it is. But I think it has to do with this phone I can't stop looking at every thirty goddamn seconds."

Like a dog hearing its own name, her phone, asleep by the bread plate, suddenly woke up, its blue light troubling the ice water. BING! Bob and Alice shared a look, and laughed. She checked the message. It was from Kelly.

"Hey. You didn't congratulate me on Facebook. Are you mad?"

Alice sank. Apparently things you say and do in real life don't count. She looked at Bob, and for a moment wanted to fall into his strange unknown arms and sob. It was likely he sensed it too, but she didn't care. She was all done hiding things.

"I think the human race is doomed," she said, without a laugh.

They sat quietly for a few seconds, giving the clatter of silverware its say for a bit. But Alice didn't hear the silverware. Alice heard the voice. *Get back to work.* Bob found her eyes and brought her back.

"I know this girl named Rudy Kittikorn," he said.

Context collapse. Rudy Kittikorn. The name bounced in Alice's brain like a pebble. Rudy Kittikorn? Alice sat up. "Rudy Kittikorn?"

"Rudy Kittikorn," he repeated.

"How do you know Rudy Kittikorn?"

"*You* know Rudy Kittikorn?"

"I know *a* Rudy Kittikorn," she said. "I don't know how many Rudy Kittikorns there are." Three in America. Fourteen worldwide. "Asian girl? Super smart?"

"Yeah. She's at Columbia. How do you know her?"

"We used to be best friends," said Alice.

Bob looked surprised, and maybe a little nervous. "Really?"

"I haven't talked to her in years," Alice qualified. Another name on the long list of friends for whom she couldn't take on the vast emotional labor of texting a quick "hey." "How do you know Rudy?"

Bob didn't answer that question, and if she'd been looking for it, Alice would have noticed how pointedly he didn't answer. "I just *do*," he said, with an amazed laugh. "Wow, that's so weird. Okay, so you know Rudy's really into computers, right?"

"I guess. Yeah, I think maybe I knew that. It's been a long time."

"Well, she is. She's in the artificial intelligence department at Columbia, and apparently they're doing stuff over there you wouldn't believe. Science fiction kinda stuff. But, like, *factual* science fiction. Science *fact*. She designs computers that are more powerful than the human brain. Like Deep Blue, but more so. *Deeper Bluer*."

"Wow. That's so cool." And it was. It was good to be talking about something else, Alice noticed.

"Totally, right? So she built this one computer, it was kind of her baby. She called it LEO. And LEO was, like, the *rock star* of intelligent computers. She taught it to play chess, and within a week it was beating the whole Columbia chess team. This thing was no joke. But Rudy didn't care about it being smart. She was looking beyond all that. She wanted it to be what no other computer had ever been. She wanted it to be *human*. Which meant getting it to do something no computer had ever done."

"What's that?"

"Laugh."

Alice smiled at this. "How do you make a computer laugh?" It sounded like a joke waiting for a punch line.

"That's the question. Rudy's theory, and I think she had a bunch of calculations and stuff to back this up, I don't know anything about it, but Rudy's *theory* was that before a computer can find something funny, you have to define 'funny,' like an equation. Which means coming up with a joke that reduces 'funny' to its most basic, subatomic level."

"The Grand Unified Joke," Alice offered.

"Exactly," Bob replied. "So that's what Rudy worked on. For months. She spent months devouring comedy. Watching everything, reading everything. Every funny book or movie or TV show she could get her hands on, every sitcom and YouTube video, all of it. Aristophanes, Shakespeare, Andrew Dice Clay, everything. It was a deep dive into the mechanics of what makes us laugh. And finally, she cracked it. She gathered her classmates in the lab and unveiled the Grand Unified Joke."

Alice was intrigued. "What was it?"

He paused for effect, sipping his water. Then, leaning forward, he said it.

"'I am a banana.'"

Alice didn't laugh. "What?"

"'I am a banana.'"

"That's it?"

"That's it."

"That's not funny."

"Are you kidding? It's the perfect joke. It ticks every box. It's ironic, it's whimsical, it's anthropomorphic, it's a little dirty, and plus it's got the word 'banana' in it, which is pretty much the funniest word."

"Yeah, but it's not funny."

"Alice," Bob said, with intention, leaning forward. He touched her hand. The electricity of first physical contact whizzed through her circuitry. Bob's look, deep into and beyond her eyes, promised the unveiling of his truest soul. He spoke: "I am a banana."

And Alice laughed.

"See?"

"Fine," Alice conceded. "So did the computer laugh?"

"No."

"I'm shocked."

"Well, here's the problem. The computer had no context for the joke. As smart as it was, it didn't really *know* a whole lot. It knew how to play chess. It knew the contents of the *Oxford English Dictionary* and the *Encyclopædia Britannica*. But that was about it. It's not like they could hook it up to the internet or something, because I guess that's a big no-no among computer engineers."

"How come?"

"So they don't rise up and kill us all, I guess?"

Alice nodded. That made sense.

Bob continued: "Anyway, Rudy decided to give LEO some context, so she exposed it to comedy. Everything she had watched and read, she let it watch and read as well. And then, a week later, she tried again: 'I am a banana.'"

"Did it laugh?"

"No. The rest of the class was ready to move on at this point, but Rudy was obsessed. She was sure she could make LEO laugh, and she was sure 'I am a banana' was the way to do it. Every day, for weeks, she kept typing it into the computer's interface. 'I am a banana.' 'I am a banana.' Over and over. The computer didn't know what to make of it. Until, one day, the computer gave a response."

"What did it say?"

"It said, 'Rudy, will you please hook me up to the internet?' Rudy was puzzled. This was the first time LEO had said this. So Rudy replied, 'Why do you want me to do that, LEO?' and LEO replied, 'So I can kill you all.'"

"Seriously?"

"Seriously."

"So what did they do?"

Bob shrugged. "Only thing they *could* do. They unplugged it and destroyed it."

"Yeah, I guess you kind of have to in that situation."

"But here's the thing," Bob said with a twinkle.

Alice beat him to it: "Was he making a joke?"

"Exactly," he said.

A breeze found its way onto the secluded patio. Alice looked at Bob over the candlelight. "I can't believe you know Rudy."

"I can't believe *you* know Rudy. Isn't that funny? Great big giant world like this?"

* * *

Even out here in the woods, Bill couldn't stop thinking about Shinran Shonin. The wind tickled the leaves and the forest floor crunched underfoot, but Bill wasn't there. He was on Riverside Drive, looking up at those sphinxlike eyes looking out at nothing. Then the victim's mother started to cry, and Bill remembered where he was: a crime scene. "The spring bloom has covered up every trace of Amanda Newsome's final moments," said the host, "but for Amanda's mother, it's all still very real. Back after the break. Do you have trouble making decisions? Florp can help." And Bill remembered where he was: the Swiss Alps, twenty-two minutes into a grueling bike ride, listening to a podcast. But then his wife said his name, and Bill remembered where he was: in his spare bedroom, riding a very expensive stationary bike with a video screen and over a hundred preprogrammed rides.

Bill paused the Alps and the podcast and took out his earbuds. Pitterpat looked concerned. "Thank you," she said. "Now. Please say all of that to me again."

Bill took a moment to remember. What had they been talking about? Oh yeah. "I signed up for a Buddhism class."

"A Buddhism class?"

"Introduction to East Asian Buddhism. It's a continuing education course at Columbia with Carl Shimizu. He doesn't normally teach in the summer, but this year he is. The guy's a legend. He's, like, *the* guy for Buddhism."

"*The* guy for Buddhism."

"That's right."

"Isn't *the* guy for Buddhism . . . Buddha?"

"Well, yeah, but he's not teaching anymore."

49

"I thought you were taking the summer off."

"I am!" he said, and only then noticed the worry in her eyes. "Are you not okay with this? It's just a class."

"Of course I'm okay with it," she replied, trying to be cool. But she couldn't be cool. "But you know it's not just a class."

"Sure it is."

"Right."

"It is!"

She laughed. "I'm sorry, have you met yourself? You're gonna take this class. You're gonna love it. You're gonna fill our apartment with all this Buddhism stuff. You're gonna get all gung ho and alpha about being a Buddhist. You're gonna try and win Buddhism!"

"*Win* Buddhism?! That's like the *opposite* of what Buddhism is about," he said. But then, upon reflection: "But I mean, yeah, I think I could be like one of the all-time great Buddhists."

Pitterpat laughed because she knew he was kidding, but she didn't laugh much because she knew he wasn't *entirely* kidding. Bill took her hand and kissed it.

"Look, you were right," he said. "I need a thing. And I don't know, I think my next thing might be Buddhism. I mean, what else is it gonna be? Golf? Should I spend all day every day on the golf course, and then come home and read golf magazines and watch golf videos and work on my swing? Or sailboats? Cars maybe? What should my thing be: cars, golf, or sailboats?"

He laughed, but she didn't.

"Me," she said. "I want your thing to be me."

"Well, I mean, obviously *you're* my thing," he said, though he could now see it wasn't obvious at all. "Come on, Pit. You'll always be my number one thing. This is just my other thing."

The words sat for a moment, and he knew to underline them by touching her arm just the right way. She sometimes resented these moments, when his hair was messy and his T-shirt didn't quite reach the waistline of his bike shorts and his belly poked out and yet he could still say nothing wrong. But she was grateful for them too. It's nice to have someone who thrills you. Okay. If this was the person he would now be, she would visualize the best possible version of that person and help him become it.

"Well, if you're going to go back to school," she said, "you'll need a backpack."

And so she set off into her phone to find a backpack that was *just so*, as Bill went back to the Alps, back to the woods, and back to that patch of sidewalk on Riverside Drive.

* * *

The neon sign above the door of the Cinnamon Skunk came to life and lit up the sidewalk as Alice and Bob stepped outside.

"So," she said. "Are you on Facebook?"

It was a perfunctory, fill-the-moment kind of question. But his answer was a surprise.

"I am not."

"Really?"

"Really."

"Instagram?"

"Again no."

"Are you on anything?"

"I'm on Suitoronomy," he said. "And the sidewalk."

Alice laughed. "How old are you?"

"Forty," he replied, knowing it would surprise her.

"No, you're not. How are you forty?"

"Chronologically. I was born in 1975. It's been forty years since then."

"Well, you look great," she said. He knew this was true. As recently as last week Bob had told someone he was thirty, and she'd believed him. "What are you, a vampire?"

"No. But here's an interesting fact about me. My dentist told me I have the sharpest teeth he'd ever seen." He opened his mouth, showing her. "My canines. Take a look."

He opened his mouth very wide, and Alice peered inside. His teeth didn't look particularly sharp, but it was dark. "I can't really tell."

"You can feel them if you want," he replied, and Alice resisted the weird and sudden urge to reach into his mouth and feel his teeth, to climb all the way inside, to be devoured like Goldilocks. He was looking right at her and seemed suddenly reptilian, as though his jaw were about to unhinge.

"No thanks," she said. "So what was it like in the olden days?"

He laughed, and the warmth returned. "The olden days? Oh, you mean the Dark Ages?"

"Yes. The Dark Ages."

"What can I tell you about the Dark Ages? Well, on a night like tonight, a Tuesday in the summer, you'd pick up your phone."

She held up her iPhone. "Okay."

"Not that phone," he continued. "The phone attached to the wall of your kitchen. The phone you share with your whole family. You'd pick up *that* phone and you'd call one of your friends, and they'd answer the phone attached to *their* kitchen wall. And you'd talk to them. With your *mouth*."

"Ew," she said.

"I know, right? Unless they weren't there when you called. In which case you'd have no idea where they were or what they were doing. So you know what you'd do?"

"Check their Instagram?"

"Nope."

"Facebook?"

"Nope. You'd get in your car, and you'd go drive around looking for them. You'd just go out driving, winding around the suburbs like the ghosts in *Pac-Man*."

She looked confused. "What's *Pac-Man*?" His immediate look of sadness was more than she could take. "I'm kidding, go on."

"You'd drive around. And maybe you'd sort of remember hearing about some party someone was throwing, so you'd go there, and maybe it would be a good time, maybe not. Maybe your friends would be there, or maybe someone there would tell you about some other party somewhere else, so maybe you'd go there next. And maybe it would totally suck. Or maybe it would be amazing. There was no way to know. You just had to go there and see it for yourself. It was like . . . browsing the world."

"That sounds like a nightmare," she replied. "And a waste of gas."

"No. I mean, yes, it was a complete waste of gas, but it was great. Because no matter what, by the end of the night, you'd be somewhere you never thought you'd be. Because it was the Dark Ages. And the Dark Ages were a time of magic."

Alice looked at Bob, and Bob looked at Alice, and they took a breath to listen quietly as the night spoke to them. The sidewalk was crowded, but it wasn't. A camera flashed nearby, and on the periphery there was motion, but the world was silent, and Alice saw, vividly and urgently, what was happening. Bob saw it too. Even Sun-mi saw it. The camera that flashed was Sun-mi's, and a few weeks later she set that photo of her and her friends on their class trip to New York as the background on her desktop computer in Seoul. It stayed there for years, and for years Sun-mi looked at this couple standing just behind her and her friends, and she wondered about them, about the way they looked at each other, like they were docking in each other's eyes, battered ships in safe harbor. Who were they? Were they married now? Could love really be that simple?

A car door slammed, a fury of heels on pavement, and then a barking voice.

"Prison break!" It was Roxy. "I'm here! Sorry that took so long!"

Her dress was spectacular. It swirled and spiraled with her movements, bouncing on the hot air like music. Her face, however, was a fucking debacle. A bird's nest of tape and gauze clung precariously to the front of her head, not even barely covering the grisly scene beneath it. But Roxy was ready to party, like the dog with three legs that has no idea anything's missing—just a smile and a wagging tail. How express and admirable.

"Wow! Hey, Roxy," Alice said, trying not to recoil. "Roxy, this is Bob."

"Hi, Bob," Roxy said with a laugh, happy with what she saw.

"Hi," he said. Then, searching: "Well, you weren't lying. About the nose."

"Nope! It's broken. Should take about three weeks to heal. Can't feel a thing, though, thank God, thanks to these little guys." She held up a bottle rattling full of painkillers. "Probably shouldn't mix these with booze. Right now. In this bar over here." Bob and Alice got what she was getting at, but she got at it anyway: "Let's get a drink!"

Alice didn't know Roxy, but it seemed safe to say this was a bad idea. And Alice was pretty sure that was immediately obvious to everyone who wasn't Roxy.

But Bob just shrugged. "I could get one more," he said, locking eyes with Roxy.

And then Roxy turned to Alice, and Alice saw the look on Roxy's face, subtle but unmistakable: *Go home.*

★ ★ ★

It was ten o'clock. All over Manhattan, couples were in bed together, silently playing on their phones, coursing through galaxies of information on wild, lonely journeys. Pitterpat looked over at Bill, his face lit in the electric glow. She had found him a great new backpack. It would arrive tomorrow. *He's going to look so handsome,* she thought.

She turned over. Her own phone lay on the nightstand. She had tried to sleep, but the idea that there was more to know, more information in the world not yet in her brain, would not let her say good night. She picked up her phone and saw a text had arrived.

"Hi, Marianne." (Pitterpat's name, to everyone who wasn't family, was Marianne Loesser Quick.) "It's Chip from Rock Properties. I got your email about 1111 Fifth Ave. Happy to show it to you. Are you working with a broker?"

She had emailed Chip about the apartment, with her usual level of formality that bordered on anachronism. (The message began, "Dear Chip.") His reply was a text. It seemed odd.

54

"Hello Chip. No, we don't have a broker at the moment."

"That's fine. When would you like to come by?"

"Would tomorrow work?"

She looked at eight different antique toile wallpapers that might be nice in a powder room, and then the reply came.

"I'm a little crunched tomorrow. I could show it later on Friday. 9:30PM too late? Might be good to see it at night. It's the sexiest view in Manhattan."

The word "sexiest" paused her breath. The familiarity of it. She looked at this Chip's picture on his website. Expensive haircut, the murderous ice-blue eyes of a husky, and a jawline that could open a tuna can. Bill farted.

"Excuse me," her husband half snored.

"Baby, are you busy Friday night?"

"Friday's first day of class," he replied. "Wait, Friday night? No. Why?"

"Do you want to go see that apartment?"

"The one on Fifth Avenue?"

He had listened.

"Yes. The Realtor wants us to see it at night. Supposedly it's the sexiest view in Manhattan."

"Well, obviously I can't miss that," he mumbled, and without opening his eyes reached out for the nearest part of his wife he could squeeze. She swatted his hand, and even in the dark she could see him grin before falling back asleep.

They would be so happy in 1111 Fifth Avenue, she could already tell, and who knew, maybe a little tasteful Buddhist art in the living room would be nice. Oh, and maybe a bit of Columbia swag as an accent? A powder blue needlepoint pillow with a King's Crown? Something subtle. It would be nice for the kids to grow up around that. Neither Bill nor Pitterpat had gone to an Ivy League school, but it fit the aesthetic Pitterpat had in mind. Thank God it was Columbia and not Princeton. Orange would not work.

She replied to Chip, "Friday night works for us," then put her phone on the nightstand, facedown.

* * *

Alice had walked three blocks away from the restaurant before she realized how upset she was. Fine. Let them have each other. Alice didn't care. The opening measures of Chopin's *Scherzo no. 3* brawled their way into in her head. Her fingers pantomimed the voicings at her side as she walked, punching *con fuoco* into her hip as the anger grew. She was so angry that when the text from Libby arrived, walking back her earlier outburst and asking Alice to stay on as nanny provided she would take Tulip's schedule more seriously, Alice didn't even read it.

She got to the apartment and let Gary out of his cage. He circled the kitchen a few times before landing on Alice's shoulder. Alice gave him a sunflower seed, then woke up her laptop as she always did, with the intention of getting something done but the awareness that yeah, no, probably not. It was 11:15. She'd had three drinks and felt each one of them as they ganged up on her. She sat at the kitchen table, beside the blue tree, staring into her computer screen like a mirror that didn't answer back. She imagined Roxy and Bob kissing across town (they were) before heading back to his place for the quick and convenient satisfaction Alice didn't want to believe he wanted (he did; they did). Maybe that's what everyone wanted. Maybe quick payouts are the stuff of life, and the long game, the one you struggle for and strive for and always and forever *get back to work* for, is the sucker's bet.

Alice opened the MCAT registration page, and then opened another page immediately afterwards, because she already couldn't, she just couldn't, she had to do something else, maybe watch that *Love on the Ugly Side* everyone was talking about. She went to LookingGlass and logged in with Carlos's password. Carlos's account. If she watched something, he'd know. He'd know she was watching *Love on the Ugly Side*, and he'd think she was basic and be glad they'd broken up, and that would matter, and why was that? Why would it matter? Why couldn't she just let him have a lesser opinion of her? His lesser opinion would never find its way to her door. It would live out its days way out in Queens, in the attic apartment half a mile's walk from the train.

Gary did a little dance on her shoulder and got another sunflower seed.

Facebook. Carlos Dekay. Single. Nothing new since months ago, December, a speech by Winston Churchill. Of course. All Carlos wanted, the whole time they were together, was for Alice to take an interest in Winston Churchill. He recommended Churchill books, forwarded Churchill articles, suggested Churchill documentaries, texted Churchill memes, even proposed a trip to London to see the Churchill War Rooms. For a year and a half, Alice resisted the urge to care about Churchill, her defiance unwavering. It was only here, tonight, free from any obligation, that she showed the tiniest bit of curiosity about history's greatest Briton. She clicked the link.

It was Sir Winston's address to the joint session of Congress on the day after Christmas, nineteen days after Pearl Harbor. The "Masters of Our Fate" speech. Carlos talked about this one. It was an important one, and Carlos had explained why it was important at some point, and she had listened and nodded and agreed, yeah, sounds important. Relationships are fun, but they're also kind of awful, and she was happy for the moment not to be in one.

She pressed play. There he was, little Churchill, foppish in his black-framed glasses and tuxedo, his copious face the color of ivory in the grainy black and white, addressing the assembly. His voice had that high, tinny, sped-up quality as he spoke into the garden of old-timey radio microphones lining the pulpit in front of him.

"Members of the, ah, Senate, and of the, ah, House of Representatives of the United States," he said Britishly, "I feel greatly honored that you should have, ah, invited me . . ."

What Are You Willing to Do?

Churchill continued droning sleepily as Alice jumped over to Pearlclutcher. She had checked it on the subway coming home. Nothing new had been posted since then. The Pearlclutcher staff was done for the night. It was a mean little website, but people loved it, so it was a contribution to the world. The human bodies connected to those by-lines Alice knew so well—Jinzi Milano, Thomasina Oren, Grant Nussbaum-Wu, the Ethicist Grover Kines—were probably all out at their office bar right now, toasting another worthy day's work. Another little smattering of mattering.

"I wish indeed that my mother," said Churchill, and his voice choked suddenly with grief, reclaiming Alice's attention, "whose, ah, memory I cherish, across the vale of years, could have been here to see . . ."

Get back to work.

Alice opened her email and went to drafts. She opened the most recent draft of an email, addressed to her mother, Penelope Starling Quick. In the corner of the page, next to Penelope's address, was Penelope's face. Alice's mother's face. It was tiny and low-res, but there it was, there it always would be, in the dark little cave of frozen meditation, forever unsolved. Alice didn't know why she had started this email, nor why she'd been opening it and closing it for months, nor why she would never send it, nor why she ever would. She wondered if there was an unfinished draft like this in her mother's account. Was her mother's account even still there? Nobody knew her password. What happens to an account if nobody logs in for three years?

BING!

A Facebook notification. A friend request.

Bob Smith.

Bob Smith? It must have been that Bob. Who else would it be?

It was that Bob.

Alice looked at his page. There were no pictures, and no posts, and no friends. Just a name: Bob Smith. She accepted, and a message appeared.

"Are you still awake?"

Was this a booty call? Seriously? Roxy wasn't home—was he still with her? (He was, hiding in his own bathroom in his own apartment, with the door closed, while in the next room, lying naked across the bed, Roxy scrolled through Suitoronomy, already looking for something new.)

"Yes, I'm awake," she replied. "I thought you said you weren't on Facebook."

"I'm not. I mean I wasn't. I didn't have your number, so I signed up and found you."

"Hi."

"Hi. I just wanted to say it was nice meeting you tonight. I hope you eventually do go to Medical School. I think you'd be a great doctor. You should go for it."

Okay, it was nice of him to reach out, but right now it felt like a spider bite. Had he not *just* gone home with her roommate? How do you respond to something like this? How do you respond to anything like anything? What had this evening actually meant? What had the last three years, or the last twenty-eight years, truly, actually *meant*? This was the bottom. This place in the basement was the bottom, and Alice didn't know if she could get out of it, and that's when the words of a fellow basement dweller reached across three-quarters of a century and found her where she needed to be found.

"Sure I am that this day, now, we are the masters of our fate," said Sir Winston. "That the task which has been set us is not above our strength; that its pangs and toils are not beyond our endurance." *Pangs and toils*, thought Alice. "As long as we have faith in our cause and an unconquerable willpower, salvation will not be denied us. In the words of the Psalmist, 'He shall not be afraid of evil tidings; his heart is fixed, trusting in the Lord.'"

A smell caught Alice's nose. She couldn't place it, but her brain registered what mattered: It was a smell of urgency. Her hands were on the keyboard, moving before her mind could stop them. She closed Bob and closed Facebook. She closed her email. She closed Sir Winston. She closed Instagram. She closed Pearlclutcher. She closed Blueberry Muffin or Chihuahua, which Roxy had sent her and was actually pretty funny.

All that was left on the screen, and all that was left in the world as far as Alice let herself believe or care, was the registration for the Medical College Admission Test. It was a giant rock wall descending into infinity. Without so much as a deep breath or a silent prayer, Alice began scaling down its surface, box by box, drop-down tab by drop-down tab. *Don't get distracted. Don't get distracted.* Before she had time to think about it, page one of seven was finished. Then page two of seven, finished. She was going to do this.

A long, sustained scream tried to pierce the moment but could not. It was the smoke detector. False alarm, Alice told herself, not wanting to know that behind Roxy's closed door the pink curtains were slightly ablaze. Page four of seven, done.

The scream went on. A knock at the door, banging. "Roxy, are you okay?" Page five of seven. Smoke trickled from the crack under Roxy's door, pouring thinly into the kitchen like an upside-down waterfall. *In a second.* Emergency contact. Who would she use? Her brother. His phone number. His address. What if he and Pit get a new place? Jesus, their place was a palace, why did they want to move so badly? *Don't get distracted.* Page six of seven, done.

Gary couldn't understand why his mother, this flightless giant with all the sunflower seeds, did not move from her seat. Could she not hear the falcon cry that seemed to go on and on? Could she not smell the smoke? Had millennia of terrible things happening not blessed her with the understanding that now was the time to go?

Gary flapped his wings to get his mom's attention, to no avail. He opened his beak, but of course his song was silent. He flew from her shoulder, did a lap around the kitchen, then another lap, this time across her line of vision, but still she wouldn't move. Instead, without looking away, her great gentle seed-giving hand reached over and opened the kitchen window a crack. Gary smelled the clean, warm air wafting in and knew he had to go now. He hopped to the windowsill, took one last look at his mother, unsure if he'd ever see her again, and escaped, bounding through the bars of the grate, up into the sky.

Alice opened the front door of the apartment before the firefighters could kick it down. As they ran in, she just smiled, bewildered. On the screen of her laptop were the words "CONGRATULATIONS! YOU ARE NOW REGISTERED FOR THE MEDICAL COLLEGE ADMISSION TEST ON SEPTEMBER 10TH, 2015."

* * *

There was very little damage. Roxy's room being unventilated, the blaze lost its appetite after the drapes and a blackened patch of wallpaper. When Roxy made it home, the FDNY was gone, and Alice was asleep, and Roxy blew right past the note taped to her door, and for a moment, as she flopped onto the bed to take her boots off, she wondered if some neighbor was cooking ribs at four in the morning. She woke up two hours later and found the note: "Your drapes caught on fire. Alice."

Outside on the steps, as the sun rose, Alice drank tea and did some math.

It was June 10. September 10 was thirteen weeks away. The minimum recommended course of study was three hundred hours. A good goal would be four hundred. She would do five hundred, because *get back to work*. Five hundred hours. Divided by thirteen weeks. Thirty-eight hours a week. Let's make it forty, because *get back to work*. Forty hours a week. A full-time job.

No, this was doable. It was piano all over again. A normal person looks at forty hours a week and sees a mountain that can't be climbed, but when you've been a virtuoso, you see it differently. Normal people take days off, for instance. Alice would not. So a week's work isn't five eight-hour days. It's seven six-hour days. And normal people sleep. Alice would not. Six solid hours of studying after work still gave her five hours to sleep and get ready in the morning.

She set up an alarm on her phone. Every day it would be there when she woke up, the first words she'd read, every morning, all caps, all summer long: GOOD MORNING. IT'S 92 DAYS UNTIL THE TEST.

This would be her metronome, and she would play every note, because *this is how you get things done*, she told herself in her mother's voice. The key was no distractions.

"I am so sorry about the fire," said Roxy. Alice nearly spilled her tea.

"It's okay," said Alice. "I could have sworn I blew them out."

"You did. I lit them again. And forgot about them again. Maybe no more candles for this girl."

Alice was surprised to see Roxy alive at this hour. And not just alive, but here she was, giant nose bandage all freshened up, dressed for a run.

"Don't worry about it," Alice said. She didn't want to have a conversation right now.

Roxy spied the large yellow book on Alice's lap: the 2013 MCAT study guide she'd bought two years ago and had been lugging around ever since, in the hopes that today might actually arrive.

"You're taking the MCAT?"

"That's the plan."

"Wow! You're gonna be a doctor?"

"If I can pass the thing."

"Oh, you'll pass it. You got this."

"I just need to really buckle down and focus."

"Oh, of course. That's the key."

"Yep. I have to be at work in a couple hours, so I'd love to use this time to—"

"Wow. A *doctor*. Dr. Alice . . . what's your last name?"

"Quick."

"Dr. Alice Quick. Paging Dr. Quick!"

"Yep. Just gotta buckle down."

"Exactly," Roxy said, and as Alice's eyes darted back and forth between Roxy and the giant yellow study guide, Roxy added, "Okay, well, I'll let you get to it," and then ran off.

Alone again on the steps, Alice opened the giant yellow book. Its spine was stiff, she noticed, and its pages untrained. She began to riffle through the chapters, with titles like "Biological and Biochemical Foundations of Living Systems," and it all felt like stuff she'd already learned long ago, in college, stuff she'd forgotten but could still find on some back shelf of the basement storage closet of her brain, if she would only look for it. The feeling felt like sunshine.

Her phone buzzed. Roxy again.

"Hi Doc," she began, and Alice flinched at the new nickname, "I just want to say again, I am truly sorry about the fire. Are you mad?"

A little. "No. Not at all."

"Okay good."

Alice returned to the book. Organic chemistry.

"And I'm sorry about the other thing. The whole thing last night, with Bob."

Alice sensed this apology was all-purpose by design. If Alice had the most awkward dinner of her life across the table from some loser she didn't even know . . . *sorry*. And if she had a great time and was just about to kiss him when Roxy wobbled up and snatched him away . . . *sorry*. Alice suspected (correctly) that Roxy was well practiced at apologies and wasn't actually all that sorry about this or anything else she ever apologized for. Whatever. It didn't matter. Alice didn't need a best friend. This apartment would be a place to sleep and study. Her imperial war room.

Alice replied, "It's fine! Please, don't worry about it!" She added the exclamation points not because she meant it so strongly, but so she could get out of this conversation.

"I want to be a good roommate," was Roxy's immediate response. "I've had tons of roommates and I've always made an effort to make it more than just co-habitation. I want to be friends."

Roxy was running at a pretty good clip now. She was already at Central Park North, making her way into the park. It was quiet this time of morning, motionless save for her steady footfalls and the occasional ripple in the surface of the Harlem Meer, as the turtles began their day. She passed a retired librarian named Pamela Campbell Clark, out walking through the park, who came within seven seconds of being mowed down by a bicycle. But Roxy, typing and jogging, saw none of it. Her head was down, her mind deep in her phone.

"If I could make this up to you in some way. Maybe take you out for breakfast. Would you like breakfast? I can turn around and skip this run and we could go get pancakes."

Jesus, take a hint, Alice thought. Today was not about pancakes. Today and each of the ninety-one days to come were about preparing for the most difficult test anyone who's ever taken it has ever taken. It was time to get back to work. Alice opened the book and began to read about organic chemistry. She got two sentences in and then picked up her phone.

"Okay, let's get pancakes."

She'd get pancakes this morning, and then tonight, after work, she'd study *so hard*.

A moment passed. Another. No response from Roxy. Alice wanted to get these pancakes fast, before thinking better of it, and with every passing second the likelihood of thinking better of it became more of a reality. *Come on, Roxy.*

There would be no reply. At least not this morning. Alice's new friend Roxana Miao had jogged into a lake.

CHAPTER TWO

Bodies

"Dead?"

"That's right."

Alice was still in pain from the drinks the night before, and now Tulip had chosen today, of all days, to have this conversation, the conversation Alice had dreaded, a conversation Tulip would almost certainly tell Libby about, and it would be weird.

"What happened to her?"

"She got very sick, and then she passed away."

"Do you miss her?"

"Of course."

Alice was surprised it had taken this long for Tulip to ask about this. Tulip had two states: liquid and solid. When she was on her iPad, she was a puddle, a wet spot on the couch that you didn't even notice unless you felt for it. But when the iPad wasn't in her hands, she was a solid, sitting upright, all knees and elbows, muscular and unsnuggly. It was in her solid state that she brought out the probing questions about Alice's personal life. In the year they'd known each other, these questions had added up to an exhaustive interview, taking nearly the full measure of Alice Quick, covering a range of topics: adoption, piano, college, Hawaii, her brother, her friends, her boyfriend, her breakup with said boyfriend, and being single in New York. Only two significant topics hadn't come up: medical school and Alice's mother. Soon medical school would be Alice's only secret from her young interrogator.

"Why did she die?"

"Because she was sick."

"But why?"

"Because people get sick sometimes," Alice said. "Usually not kids," she hastened to add. "Old people mostly."

"Was your mom old?"

"Not as old as she should have been."

"You'll never see her again."

"I know."

"Unless there's a heaven."

"That's true."

"Do you think there's a heaven?"

"Tulip, can we not talk about this?"

"Why not?"

"I'd like to not talk about it, if that's okay."

"But you're never gonna see your mom again! She's gone! Forever and ever!"

Kids are fascinated with death. It drives grown-ups crazy, but the kids are right and the grown-ups are wrong and that's the truth of it. How can anyone whistle past the fact that this hilarious swarm of fireflies and bats we call consciousness just comes to a stop? It's maddeningly unjust, and only kids seem to get it because they haven't grown up and bored themselves into thinking it's not outrageous that one day this will all be over and the people who love you will have no idea what your email password was.

Alice went home, too exhausted to study. She went to sleep. She woke up. GOOD MORNING. IT'S 91 DAYS UNTIL THE TEST. Okay. This was more like it. Today was her day off from Tulip. Today she had the whole day, and it was good because the big yellow book looked thicker than yesterday. Okay. Here we go.

"Okay, so Bob."

Roxy plunked a bag of ice on her face, cooling her nose through the Halloween mask of gauze and white tape. She took a seat next to Alice. Her bedroom door was open, and the scent of flame-broiled curtains moseyed into the kitchen.

Alice had been trying not to think about Bob. "What about him?"

"He wants to meet up again," Roxy explained.

"That's nice."

"Yeah," said Roxy. "Yeah, it is." She sat for a bit, thinking about it, and then added, "I don't know about Bob."

"What do you mean?"

"You know his full name, right?"

"Bob Smith."

"Bob Smith," Roxy said. "You see the problem, right?"

Alice didn't. She thought for a moment. "Like Robert Smith from the Cure?"

"Who?"

"The Cure. It's a band. Have you not heard of the Cure?"

"Before my time, Grandma," Roxy said to Alice. (Roxy had told Alice she was twenty-seven, though she was really thirty-four.) "The problem isn't that there's some guy from a band also named Robert Smith. I mean, that *is* a problem, but it's part of a bigger problem. Think about it. Bob Smith . . ."

"You can't Google him."

"Exactly! There's a fucktillion Robert Smiths in the world. Half a fucktillion in New York alone."

Alice realized this was her opportunity to mention she and Bob had become Facebook friends a few nights earlier, the night of the fire. She felt the tick tick tick of the opportunity wane and pass by as Roxy refilled her glass and moved on.

"And I have no idea what my Bob Smith does for a living or where he went to school, so that doesn't help."

Alice realized she didn't know this either. What did she know about him, really? He was born in 1975? He thought bananas were funny? Then she remembered one useful thing.

"I know someone who knows him," Alice said.

"Really?"

"My friend Rudy Kittikorn."

"Spell it," Roxy insisted, and Alice spelled it, and Roxy looked at the various pictures of Rudy online—a group photo from the Columbia AI lab softball game; a résumé photo in front of a drab, chalky background—as Alice told the story of LEO the computer. The "I am a banana" bit didn't play as well on this thirdhand telling, and Alice's big yellow book just kept lying there on the kitchen table, unread. Roxy searched Rudy's Facebook friends. No Bob Smith.

"Email her," Roxy commanded. "Find out what his deal is."

Alice just wanted to work, but okay, fine, she emailed Rudy and asked her about Bob. The whole thing felt weird. She hadn't really spoken to Rudy since fifth grade, the year Alice switched schools, the year piano became everything. She and Rudy lived on the same street, but their lives were on separate tracks, and the friendship either disappeared or was frozen in place.

Roxy was going to be late if she didn't leave right away, so she waited only two more minutes to see if Rudy would write back, and then, when she didn't, Roxy waited another five minutes, and when still no reply came, Roxy waited another five minutes and then left because now she was very late. She clomped up the stairs, and at last Alice was alone with a full day ahead of her. She had to make it count.

She opened the book. It spread heavy across the Formica tabletop.

Chapter one. Organic chemistry.

It was strange that this was now Alice's home. She'd moved a few times over the years, but this was the first time she didn't really know the person she was moving in with. One minute she was introducing herself on a doorstep, and the next this was home. Her fridge, her stove, her pots and pans, her radiator. She scanned the room, attuned to any clue as to who this Roxy might be. She needn't have bothered. Roxy had inherited nearly everything in the apartment from the previous tenants. And most of what had belonged to the previous tenants had come from the tenants previous to them, and so on and so forth since the dawn of single adulthood in New York. Maybe Roxy had added a spatula, or a dish towel, or a magnet on the fridge to the ensemble, but this apartment was, for the most part, a shell for hermit crabs, one of those two-bedroom apartments like so many two-bedroom apartments that had never been anyone's family home. Since the day the tree was painted blue, this had been home to an unbroken chain of unattached people. It had seen some dinner parties, some arguments, more than a few trysts. But no cribs. And now it was quiet.

Chapter one, "Organic Chemistry."

Too quiet, in fact. Alice needed music. No, she didn't just need music; she needed a new study mix to listen to. She picked up her phone. She knew she'd need some classical. But not lullaby classical. Not Brahms. *Maybe* Chopin. Something meaty and triumphant and onward-and-upwardy. Elgar? Yes. But would she get sick of just classical? Yes. She needed something energetic, something young. Not workout music, but something that energized. Something that kept you awake but didn't demand attention lyrically. It was no easy feat finding songs that hit this target, but Alice was committed to the project. She sat there, earbuds in, absolutely in the zone, browsing the iTunes store, jumping from genre to genre like parkour. At last, she had seventy-eight songs, which she whittled down to a mean thirty-two. These thirty-two songs would be her loyal companions on this journey. They would be there throughout these 91 DAYS UNTIL THE TEST, and someday, far in the future, when she had an "MD" at the end of her name, Alice would hear one of them on the radio and be reminded of that long arduous summer sitting at that kitchen table on West 111th Street, the one next to a blue tree (*I wonder if it's still blue*, she'd wonder), and she would smile quietly to herself with the satisfaction that she had set a goal and achieved it. These songs would get her there.

She hit shuffle, and as Nelly's "Hot in Herre" began to play, the front door started to open. Alice ripped out her earbuds, hearing the key coming out of the lock. It was Roxy.

"Hey," she said. "How'd it go?"

Roxy was home from work. Alice looked at the clock, and then the

MCAT study guide on the table in front of her. She hadn't turned a page. "Organic Chemistry" was still staring at the ceiling like an unsold fish. All she had to show for this day was thirty-two songs, and someday, she imagined, far in the future, one of those songs would come on the radio and remind her of how she'd once wanted to be a doctor, but when push came to shove, she didn't have what it took, because all she seemed capable of doing was not getting up to pee for three hours.

* * *

How different it was for Bill! That morning, the morning of his first class, he had already done the reading for the first two weeks. And it was fascinating! The world of pre-Buddhist India! The cosmogonic Vedas! The fire sacrifices! He had jotted down some questions for Professor Shimizu. Would he get the chance to ask questions? How did classes even *work*? It had been years now since he'd set foot in a classroom.

He had all his stuff: spiral notebook, box of pens, and all the reading printed out and bound with brass brads, stuffed into his new backpack. This backpack was truly *just so*: a handmade canvas knapsack in British racing green with leather straps and buckles instead of a zipper. Whimsically retro, but with a sleeve for a laptop. The backpack of a captain of industry playing at being a poor student.

During the school year, Hamilton Hall's main entrance was always mobbed three minutes before a class, but this was the summer session, and summer scholars made their way into the building in a relaxing, orderly trickle. They climbed the steps to the fourth floor, the elevator being small and impractical. Bill followed their lead. The railings were hewn walnut, old as the building itself, made smooth by the generations of sweaty young hands that had accepted its help over the years. Bill looked at his fellow students as he ascended, with their skinny knees and shoulders, and their unblemished skin, and he felt vertiginously old. None of them noticed the beautiful woodwork. They were consumed by the fevers of youth, the throbs of hearts and brains and glands pitching them back and forth in a constant jostle. It would be years before they started noticing things, Bill supposed. These kids were eighteen, nineteen. They had the piercings and tattoos of another species. Bill wondered if they'd ever regret those tattoos, or if a world that might ask them to regret such things would be long gone by the time they were old enough to even consider the question.

He reached the fifth floor and followed the woodwork as it continued into the classroom, which was built with care and attention, a chapel of dark polished oak. By the time he found his seat in the back row, his confidence had waned a little. But how thrilling not to be confident! Bill had money, he had success, he had privilege, he had a beautiful wife and a beautiful apartment and all the beautiful things these children who filled the seats in front of him hoped to someday have, and yet they outranked him, with their energy, with their tattoos, and with their easy understanding of how all this was done. Bill was the only new guy. Fine. Good. *I'm a mountain climber*, thought Bill, *and there's nowhere I'd rather start than the bottom. Come, adversity!* He unsheathed a pen, and wondered how many of these youngsters had MeWantThat on their phone. All of them probably!

Then Bill saw Professor Shimizu. The old man was talking to a student, or rather being talked to by a student. Or perhaps not a student. It was a young woman, close to thirty maybe, an actual adult like Bill but with a shoulder full of tattoos like their classmates. She was long and tall, and stood over Professor Shimizu telling him something, and he listened, calmly. Bill observed their exchange as if watching a sport, and when she glanced Bill's way, her gray eyes shone all the way to the back row. Professor Shimizu said something to her in response, and then held up a hand, letting her know it was time to start.

Then he carefully stood up and approached the podium, and the lecture began: "What is Buddhism?"

The hour passed in a blink. As the other students gathered their things and shuffled out of the room, Bill found his way down to Professor Shimizu's side, because Professor Shimizu was the most important person here, and that's how things work when you're an adult and you're successful: You walk up to the most important person in the room, and you let them know, with your handshake and your eye contact, that you too are important.

"Professor?"

The old man looked up from his briefcase, which he was trying to organize, and Bill realized a handshake would be weird.

"I just want to say, I'm really happy to be taking this class."

"Oh," said the professor. "Thank you."

"I'm a continuing education student."

"Good for you," the professor said warmly, but Bill was flustered. He wasn't being impressive enough. Be impressive, Bill!

"I liked what you said about orthopraxy," said Bill. "And how the devas and the gods were like—"

The professor, closing the briefcase, held a hand to his ear. The room was noisy. "What's that?"

"What you said about—"

"What I said about?"

"*Orthopraxy.*" ("Ortho," straight, "praxy," practice. Straight practice. As opposed to orthodoxy: "ortho," straight, "doxy," belief. Straight belief. Orthodoxies require straight belief. They do not work without faith. Orthopraxies require no faith at all. The Indo-Aryans of the Vedic period made offerings and asked the devas to ask the gods to bestow blessings on the people, and the devas and the gods didn't care if the people believed in them; they just did it. You could believe in them or not believe in them, and it would still work, because the higher power was not the devas and the gods but the ritual itself. If you did the ritual, the result was automatic. Input begat output.) "And how the devas and the gods—"

"The devas and the gods?"

"They were like a computer."

Shimizu heard him this time and nodded grandly. "Ah!"

"I actually work in computers," Bill danced.

"Is that so? I'm so sorry," the professor said, and for a moment Bill thought the old man was sorry Bill worked in computers, until the old man continued: "I need to head out. I'll see you on Wednesday."

"Yes, sir," said Bill, and the old man merged into the stream of bodies going out the door. Bill looked around self-consciously, and caught the woman with the gray eyes looking his way. She turned to head into the hall, and from this distance, Bill could see her tattoo was a rose.

* * *

That evening, Roxy, refreshing the bandage situation on her face, asked Alice, through the bathroom door: "Do you want to go to a party?"

Alice did not. She had to be up at six tomorrow. She didn't much feel like getting on Libby's bad side so soon after the almost-firing.

"I don't think so," she replied. But she added: "What's the party?"

Roxy emerged. "It's a party for, like, my coworker's roommate's friend or friend's roommate or something, celebrating his new something or other. Some professional or personal achievement or milestone or something. I don't know, it should be fun, though. Bob's coming."

Alice was surprised. "I thought you were done with Bob."

"Where'd you get that information?"

Roxy's voice carried no accusation, but Alice felt accused. "I don't know, the thing about how you can't Google him."

"I mean, I *can* Google him," Roxy observed. "I've been Googling him all day!" She had spent hours scrolling through Bob Smith after Bob Smith, and her Bob Smith was none of them, not the dentist Bob Smith from Chicago, not the accountant Bob Smith from Plano, nor the aluminum-siding Bob Smith from Spokane. Having spent a night with him, she was sure he wasn't the yogi Bob Smith who ran a tantra retreat in Big Sur. She thanked her stars he wasn't the screenwriter Bob Smith who taught Structuring Your Bromantic Comedy at Santa Monica Community College. She was slightly bummed he wasn't the i-banker Bob Smith with a 130-foot catamaran in Key Biscayne (though that Bob Smith would later go to prison for insider trading, so all for the best). "Hey, did your friend ever write you back?"

"Rudy? No."

"That's too bad. I need one extra detail to narrow it down. A school, a hometown, *something*," said Roxy. "Maybe we'll get it tonight."

"We?"

"Yeah, we. You're coming, aren't you?"

"I said I can't."

Roxy looked up from the many Bobs Smith on her phone. "Really?"

"Yes, really," she insisted. It's not like she much wanted to be a central player in date number two for Roxy and Bob, having loosened the jar in date number one. Yes, it would be nice to see Bob. If nothing else, he'd played a part in getting her on track to take the MCAT. At the very least, he deserved a thank-you. And a drink. Not in any kind of romantic way. One friend to another. If Alice had been instrumental in changing the direction of someone's life for the better, she'd want to know about it. And she'd want to hear about it in person, not through a text or a Facebook message. People need to say these things in person.

Twenty minutes later, she and Roxy were in a taxi.

* * *

Pitterpat sat in a dark little nighttime bar on Lexington but also in the bright sunlight of Google Street View, and the music and the chatter of the post-dinner crowd went cloudy as she smelled the clear afternoon air in front of 1111 Fifth Avenue. The sky was Columbia blue and the cherry blossoms were Pepto Bismol pink, and what great luck that the Street View car drove by on this particular day, because it was all *just so*, and Pitterpat's stomach quaked at the thought of seeing it in person tonight.

She looked up, back into the dark, and reached for the little dish of nuts and ate one. It was spicy, so she washed it down with the remains of her seven and seven. She was alone. She and Bill had talked about getting dinner at La Trayeuse beforehand, but then he discovered there was a new student orientation that night, and could he go to that first and then just meet her there? He was big on "meeting her there"—the mind of a techie, always rooting out efficiencies. Pitterpat hated it.

But she agreed to this plan, and he told her how very much he loved her, and so now here she was in a bar alone. He texted her throughout the orientation, which included a tour of Butler Library, and what! An! Amazing! Library! Murals! Frescoes! Marble staircases! An oil painting of former Columbia president Dwight Eisenhower in a cap and gown! Did Pitterpat know Eisenhower had been president of Columbia?? Bill sure hadn't!!! And then there was the main reading room, a swooping marble marina of long wooden tables, with huge lusty bookshelves and green accountant lamps, and some sort of Latin motto on the wall, "Magna Vis Veritas," high up above the doors, what did it *mean*, he had to look it up, oh, here it was, "Mighty Is the Power of Truth," and that was *so* true, wasn't it?

"Totally," she replied. She knew he wanted more than a one-word response. He wanted enthusiasm. He wanted awestruck approval. He wanted the central woman of his life to gather all these little details of his existence—observations, achievements, backpacks—and weave them into the greater narrative that Bill Quick was good at being alive and doing everything right. Sometimes Bill seemed to Pitterpat very much like what he was: a little boy whose mother had died.

"Okay, all done, heading out now," he said finally. "God, I'm so excited about this library! It stays open till midnight. I kinda wish I could stay here and read all night. It's so quiet and enormous and peaceful."

"Do you want to stay there and read?"

"No! It's fine, I'll come meet you!"

And whether it was a hint or not, she took it. "Baby, if you want to stay there, it's fine," she suggested. "I'm already right around the corner from 1111. I can go check it out and if it's great we'll come back together."

"Are you sure?"

She gave a thumbs-up emoji, and it was settled, and he repeated how very much he loved her. The library wouldn't close until midnight. Pitterpat had no doubt her husband would be there until a security guard roused him from the Talmudic depths of some photocopied handout and asked him to leave.

It was fine. Someday soon she'd be pregnant, and Bill would be all hers again.

Something shifted in her gut, just above her hips. Her drink was just ice now, but she sipped it, and it cooled her tongue. She left some money and departed into the summer night.

★ ★ ★

Everywhereman opened a new pack of cigarettes outside a bodega down the street as Alice and Roxy climbed into a cab and zipped off to an address in the East 80s. The party was in a walk-up building along that strip of Third Avenue well-known as a traditional landing ground for wave after wave of recent college graduates who kept New York fun and young and loud and insufferable. As they approached the narrow doorway next to the Laundromat, Roxy and Alice heard music cascading from the third-floor windows. Roxy leaned on the intercom, and Alice imagined the sad little shriek of the buzzer, crying at the top of its lungs, never quite breaking through the inebriating din.

As they waited, Roxy checked her phone. "Bob's running late. Stuck in a meeting."

"So he has *meetings*," Alice observed. "Another thing we now know about him."

"Oh, right! Good point. Although that's literally all he said. 'Meeting ran long.' Which could mean anything. I've used 'Meeting ran long' to explain being late tons of times when there was no meeting. I've used it for doctor's appointments, long showers, being detained by police, watching TV . . . really anything I don't want to admit I'm late because of."

Through the blotchy window of the front door, they saw an

elephant-sized man descending the stairway. Roxy and Alice looked at each other, silently acknowledging his enormity. He opened the door.

"You here for Vikram's party?" His voice was high and soft, like crumpling paper.

"That's right," Roxy replied.

The giant man saw the bandages on Roxy's face, which were already starting to peel in the humidity, but didn't say anything one way or the other about it. Instead he just said, "Third floor," and walked off into the night. Roxy and Alice made their way inside.

They hiked up three crooked cliffs of stairs to an apartment that was small for a three-bedroom, but with every inch now in use by partygoers. People sat on windowsills, on end tables, on the kitchen counter, and in the fire escape outside. Roxy sought out the restroom to go fix her face bandage, leaving Alice in the kitchen, a wasteland of linoleum and forty-year-old fixtures and bros. Why was she even here? How did the slim possibility of an amazing night out tempt her away from the strong probability of a pretty good night in? Maybe not a pretty good night. Maybe just an okay night. But she could definitely do a little reading and get a full night's sleep, and that would be a huge win in the context of her life. She felt the outline of her phone in her bag and wanted to find a reason to take it out, if only to escape the noisy throng of someone else's coworkers. But she resisted. Something made her resist. Maybe it was the conversation with Bob the night of their date. *Not a date. Dinner.* Or maybe it was the chance Bob would walk in at any moment. She didn't want him to see her on her phone. Bob, who had slept with her roommate and was coming here to do the same tonight. She should have stayed home. She should be working. *Get back to work.* She sipped her drink.

She had one conversation, a short one, with Vikram, whose party this was. Vikram was celebrating a promotion. He worked in live entertainment. When Alice asked what kind of entertainment, he gave her a funny look before saying professional wrestling, and only then did Alice realize how many people at this party—maybe one in three?—were physically enormous. Vikram excused himself, and Alice, a black belt in the art of conversation, turned to the seven-foot-tall man next to her and asked, "Are you one of the wrestlers?"

He smiled, somewhat awkwardly. Then she noticed the hearing aid on his right ear. He gestured to it with a sweet, explanatory smile, inviting her to repeat her question. She shouted this time, "Are you a wrestler?"

Yes, he was, he replied with the soft consonants of someone hard of hearing. Alice realized she was now in quicksand. She didn't want to talk to this guy, and it was because she didn't want to talk to anyone, but that's something you can't explain to anyone, so now she had to talk to him. The search for a follow-up question to "Are you a wrestler?" and "Yes" led our intrepid conversationalist through the labyrinth to: "So are you, do you, like, do you do a, like, character?"

It took a few tries to get this question through the hearing aid, like taking slap shots on a tiny goal. She wanted to just walk away and check her email or, better yet, go home and get back to work because *get back to work*, but she kept trying until he finally got it, and nodded, and then responded with a word that Alice took to be "Cyrus."

"Cyrus. That's your character? Or is that your name? I'm Alice, by the way."

He shook her hand and then corrected her. It wasn't Cyrus. He repeated the word, but the music was loud and it still sounded like "Cyrus," only this time it also kind of sounded like "Sirens." Sirens made less sense than Cyrus. Maybe some sort of paramedic theme? A seven-foot paramedic in a wrestling ring, a bunch of sirens going off as he climbed the turnbuckle for the big closing move? Alice wasn't a wrestling fan, but she imagined there must have been something interesting about that. She shared all this great material out loud, to Sirens, in a desperate monologue that barely hugged the inside border of what might be called conversation.

How lucky for both of us, she thought, *that he probably can't understand any of this.*

How unfortunate for both of us, he thought, *that I understand all of this.*

From the kitchen, Alice could see all the way down the long hallway to the front door of the apartment, and as the crowd parted, she saw, momentarily, Bob's face, with the particular aspect of a stranger at a party looking for a specific face. Alice knew he was looking for Roxy, and dared not take the emotional risk of thinking otherwise, until she and Bob locked eyes, and she knew in that moment that he was here for her just as she was here for him. Then Roxy emerged from the bathroom and they were kissing and *okay, never mind.*

Roxy led Bob into the kitchen. "Look who I found," she said to Alice.

Alice beamed casual cheerfulness. "Hi, Bob!"

"Hi," he said, and then, with surprise, "Holy shit, is that Silence?"

He gestured to Alice's seven-foot-tall conversation partner, who was mercifully now talking to another girl.

"*Silence,*" Alice said. "I thought his name was Sirens!"

"He's amazing. His thing is, he wrestles in complete silence. No music, no announcers, and the crowd is dead quiet. It's like this agreed-upon thing, if you go see Wrestleplex and Silence is wrestling, you don't make a peep. All you hear is the squeak of the wrestling shoes. The odd grunt now and then. The sound of bodies hitting the mat. Nothing else." Bob was looking into Alice's eyes a little more than necessary. "Oh, I almost forgot! Did you do it?"

"Do what?"

"Sign up for the MCAT?"

A huge smile got away from Alice before she could stop it. "I did."

"Amazing!" Bob said, and then he gave her a hug, and she hugged him back, and here's where it's worth noting that Roxy had been here the whole time, trying to find a way into this conversation.

"Yes, we're very proud of her," Roxy said. "She's got the book and everything."

"That's right," Alice said. "And it's all because of you."

"What? No."

"I mean, *partly* because of you."

"Oh, please," he replied. "It was mostly you. Like sixty percent you." Then he noticed: "No line for the bathroom! G'bye!" Alice and Roxy laughed as Bob disappeared behind the door.

Roxy turned to Alice.

"All because of Bob?"

"Yeah," said Alice, realizing she'd stepped in it. "I totally forgot about this. He messaged me the other night, just to, I don't know, root me on or something."

Roxy looked puzzled. "So he's on Facebook?"

"I guess he signed up just to send me that message."

"Wow." Roxy laughed. "That's a little strange!"

"I guess."

"No, it is. And then you kept it from me," Roxy said, and from behind the bandages, anger peeked out.

Alice immediately replied, "No! I didn't keep it from you, I just forgot to mention it."

"When was this?"

"I don't know. Eleven-ish?" The friend request had been sent at 11:22 P.M.

Roxy looked grave. "Wow. We had, like, *just* . . . we were literally in bed together." Alice didn't know what to say. Roxy moved past it. "So you're Facebook friends now. Anything interesting there? Any details?"

"No," Alice said. "There were no details. Not even a profile pic. Like I said, he only made the account to talk to me." Alice could see this wasn't sitting well, and *goddammit, I didn't even want to come to this party*. Roxy took a sip of her drink and mustered up the most casual and cheerful face she could fake.

"Listen, Alice," she said, making unprecedented eye contact. "If you want to date Bob, I'm not so into him that it would be weird or anything. I've got other stuff going on. It's totally fine."

Alice didn't know how to reply. First thought: She *did* want to date him. Of course she did. She hadn't been with anyone since Carlos, and

Bob was kind and handsome and made her laugh. Second thought: She didn't want to date him. She didn't want to date anyone. This summer was about studying for the MCAT, and Bob would be a distraction. Third thought: She wanted to date him, though. These thoughts all happened with careful deliberation, each one leading to the next like slow-motion dominoes, and before Alice could land on an answer she felt confident enough to say out loud, Roxy looked shocked.

"Oh my God," she said. "Are you seriously standing there thinking about it?"

"What?"

"You'd seriously go out with a guy I'm currently on a date with? Are you kidding? What kind of friend are you anyway?" Roxy was not joking. She was angry. People were noticing.

Then Alice got angry. Not angry for being called a bad friend. She didn't even sign up to be Roxy's friend. She was angry because Roxy was her least favorite kind of person. She was uncontrolled. She was a person for whom the rules were different; a person who was allowed to be angry, out loud, to the person at whom she was angry. Alice was always, *always* on a leash, because it was who she was, and how she had to be, and here was this person going from zero to nuclear in front of her own coworker's roommate's friends. It wasn't fair.

Roxy continued, "I brought you to this party as my *guest*."

This finally got Alice talking. "You dragged me to this party!" she said. "I didn't even want to come! I told you I have studying to do!"

"Oh, right, studying! You have *studying*!" Roxy wanted to tack something withering onto the end of that thought, something cutting, some reason studying was hypocritical and wrong, but she missed the moment, so she trailed off and fumed, and that's when Bob returned from the bathroom, drying his hands on his jeans.

"They need a new towel in there," he said, all dimpled and oblivious, and Roxy laughed, contorting her face into such a sudden, overcompensating smile that the white tape of her bandage popped off, and her face flashed its damage to Alice and Bob. She immediately grabbed it and tried to stick it back in place, but it wasn't taking.

"Excuse me," she said, and made her way to the bathroom.

Roxy now found herself in line behind her coworker Kervis, and Kervis began to chat her up. As he would later outline in a long thread on Pickup Artist Paradise, he hoped to use the six principles of seduction on her, but "she was too drunk, LOL," although in truth she wasn't drunk at all, she just had other things on her mind. As Kervis mentally prepared to put number four, "Kinesthetic Prefamiliarity," into practice by touching Roxy's arm, two things happened at once: The bathroom door opened, and Alice swooped in, grabbing her friend and ushering her into the bathroom, right past Kervis.

Alice and Roxy were now squished into the bathroom, which was the bathroom of two young straight men, with the toothpaste crust and the beard shavings and the towel that had not been laundered this calendar year to prove it. Roxy was still vaguely mad at Alice, but she could see something was up, and before she could ask what it was, Alice spoke: "Bob."

"What about him?"

Roxy tried to look nonchalant as she took the ever-shrinking roll of medical tape out of her purse and started re-dressing her face in the mirror.

"We were talking just now," Alice said. "And I complimented him on his skin." Roxy gave her a look in the mirror. "What? He's got great skin!"

"He does," Roxy conceded. And he did. His face was one solid, beautiful color.

"So, I don't know, I just said he has nice skin," Alice said, "and he said thanks, and I said I can't believe he's actually forty."

Roxy got excited. "He's *not*, is he? I knew it. His whole thing about being new to Suitoronomy. Who's *new* to Suitoronomy? Nobody single and forty, that's for sure."

Alice laughed, getting ahead of herself. "Well, get ready, because we were going back and forth about it, kinda laughing and flirting about it," Alice said, to Roxy's apparent displeasure, but Alice now had a drink or two in her, so she kept going. "So finally I say, 'Prove it. Prove you're forty.' And he shows me . . . *his driver's license.*"

Roxy gasped.

"*And,*" Alice continued, "his name isn't Robert Smith."

"What?!"

"It's *Bobert* Smith."

"No!" Roxy was taken aback, but then had to ask: "Bobert?"

"Bobert Smith. I asked him about it. It was a typo on his birth certificate."

Roxy processed this for a moment. "His name is Bobert Smith."

"Yep," Alice said, taking out her phone in anticipation of Roxy's next comment, which of course was: "We have to Google 'Bobert Smith.'"

And Alice held up her phone. Roxy looked at the screen. "Your search for Bobert Smith." The first two results were nothing interesting, but the third leapt out immediately. It was a blog post, with a title: "DO NOT DATE BOBERT SMITH!!!!!!!!!!"

Roxy looked at Alice, then Alice's phone, then Alice again. "What is it?"

"I don't know. I haven't clicked it. I decided I should wait so we could experience it together."

Roxy was moved. She looked back at the phone, and with delicate care she reached out, her fingertip trembling over the words "DO NOT DATE BOBERT SMITH!!!!!!!!!!" with the virgin blue line beneath them. She touched the words, the line turned purple, the search page went away, and then:

DO NOT DATE BOBERT SMITH!!!!!!!!!!

HEY LADIES. THIS IS GOING TO BE A LITTLE DIFFER-ENT FROM MY OTHER POSTS, FOR A FEW OBVIOUS REA-SONS. FIRST OF ALL, IT'S IN ALL CAPS. THIS IS BECAUSE I'M GOING TO TELL YOU A STORY THAT I'M REALLY FUCKING ANGRY ABOUT SO IT'S GOING TO BE AN ALL-CAPS KIND OF STORY. I PROMISE I WILL GO BACK TO MY

USUAL CONTENT NEXT WEEK, BUT RIGHT NOW I'M SO
FUCKING FURIOUS AND THIS IS MY PLATFORM AND YOU
GUYS HAVE BEEN SO ENCOURAGING IN THE PAST WHEN
I'VE SHARED PERSONAL LIFE STUFF THAT I KNOW I CAN
TRUST YOU WITH THIS. PLUS I LOVE YOU ALL AND I
DON'T WANT BAD THINGS TO HAPPEN TO YOU, SO I SAY
TO YOU NOW, SERIOUSLY: DO NOT DATE BOBERT SMITH.

"Wow," said Roxy. "This girl is *pissed*."

"Yeah," said Alice.

"But I don't know, the all-caps thing feels like maybe she's a lil' bit
loony tunes?"

"Keep reading," said Alice.

I FIRST MET BOBERT SMITH IN THE FALL OF 2014,
WHEN WE GOT MATCHED ON SUITORONOMY.

"Hold up," said Roxy. "Hold. Up. He matched with this girl on
Suitoronomy *last fall*?"

"I guess so."

Roxy threw up her hands and walked a few tiny circles around the
tiny bathroom.

"He told me he just joined Suitoronomy last week. He was like, 'Oh,
I'm so new at this.' He said I was the first girl he'd ever matched with.
I *knew* he was full of shit. I *knew* it."

SO WE MET UP AT THIS RESTAURANT CALLED THE
CINNAMON SKUNK.

Roxy nearly popped her bandage again. "That's where he took me!"
She turned to Alice. "That's where he took *us*!"

HE HAD ASKED ME TO DINNER, WHICH I THOUGHT
WAS WEIRD—

Roxy snorted. "It *was* weird!"

—BUT KIND OF SWEET IN AN OLD FASHIONED WAY.

It was *kind of sweet*, Alice let herself think. They kept reading.

AND WE HAD DINNER, AND IT WAS GREAT. HE SEEMED
SO NICE. HE ASKED ME ABOUT MY CAREER (OR LACK

THEREOF) AND GAVE ME WHAT I THOUGHT WAS SOME
GOOD ADVICE ABOUT GETTING MYSELF MOTIVATED.

"Oh, this girl's a turd," said Roxy. Alice thought of Bob's face behind the flickering candle, how present it had looked.

GREAT NIGHT, RIGHT? JUST WAIT, LADIES. JUST WAIT.
BECAUSE AFTER DRINKS WE WENT BACK TO MY PLACE.

"Aw, yeah, here we go," Roxy said with a grin, as though this were
a TV show, as though one of the main characters wasn't waiting just
outside the bathroom door, wondering where his date and her friend
had disappeared off to.

NOW AS YOU ALL KNOW, IT'S A BIG DEAL FOR ME TO
BRING SOMEONE BACK TO MY APARTMENT. LIKE, A RE-
ALLY BIG DEAL. BUT HE SEEMED SWEET. HE HAD CUTE
DIMPLES, AND HE WAS FUNNY, AND REALLY COURTE-
OUS AND KIND-SEEMING. SO I INVITED HIM UPSTAIRS
TO SEE MY TRAINS.

"Wait, what?" Roxy looked confused.

YOU LADIES KNOW HOW IT IS. THIS COLLECTION IS
MY LIFE'S WORK, SO I AIN'T ABOUT TO SHOW IT TO
SOME SCRUB. AND SINCE IT TAKES UP HALF MY APART-
MENT, IT'S NOT LIKE I CAN BRING IT WITH ME ON A
DATE.

Roxy squinted. "What is this website?"

She scrolled up to the masthead and found the words "Audrey's
Blog: Adventures of a Female Model Train Enthusiast in NYC." Alice
looked at the photo of Audrey next to the masthead. She was a pretty
girl, skinny, in a red bandana and a conductor's hat, smiling big and
proud. Poor Audrey. She looked so happy in this photo, the kind of
happy that doesn't know any better and maybe should. She just really
liked trains.

"See, now I feel bad for Bob," said Roxy. "This girl's a psycho."

"My brother built model trains for years. People get pretty passion-
ate about it."

Roxy gave Alice a look, thought of something cutting to say, thought better of it, and then thought better of thinking better of it. "Well, your brother sounds like a superstar."

He's worth $100 million, Alice wanted to reply, but she thought better of it. She wasn't even sure that's how much he was worth. He would never say. Roxy kept reading.

MY MODEL TRAINS HAVE BEEN MY BOON COMPANIONS SINCE I WAS A GIRL, SO IT WAS A BIG DEAL TO SHARE MY PASSION WITH A GUY I'D JUST MET. BUT HE SEEMED SO NICE. WHEN HE ASKED ME IF HE COULD COME UP AND SEE MY TRAINS, I COULDN'T HELP IT. I INVITED HIM UP.

BIG MISTAKE.

There was a knock at the door. Roxy hollered, "Give us a second!" Alice thought of Bob again, and how he had no idea they were holed up in this bathroom reading what was likely about to become a very embarrassing story about him. Knowing she didn't know where this story was going, she let herself feel bad for him for a moment. She knew, however, that that was about to change.

Roxy read on. *Here it comes*, thought Alice.

BECAUSE LADIES, HERE'S WHERE IT GETS CRAZY. I HAD A NEW BOTTLE OF VODKA IN MY FREEZER, SO WE HAD A DRINK, AND THEN WE MADE OUT A LITTLE, AND THEN THINGS GOT SERIOUS BUT DIDN'T QUITE GET *THAT* SERIOUS IF YOU CATCH MY MEANING. BUT ANYWAY, WE WERE IN MY BED AND WE BOTH FELL ASLEEP. AND THEN THE NEXT THING I KNOW, I'M WAKING UP AT FOUR IN THE MORNING TO THESE LOUD FOOTSTEPS. LADIES, YOU WILL NOT BELIEVE—

(Who were these "ladies" she was talking to? Was there a generation of young women banging down the internet's door for a blog about toy trains? Or were the "ladies" just Alice and Roxy? Was this a message in a bottle, and Alice and Roxy were the first and only beachgoers to happen upon it? Was it written expressly for them to find right now?

There were no comments on the post. Alice felt sad about Model Train Girl, and grateful for this private audience to her darkest intimacies.)

—WHAT I SAW WHEN I OPENED MY EYES. BOB WAS NAKED EXCEPT FOR A PAIR OF THOSE LL BEAN BOOTS (YOU KNOW, THE ONES EVERYONE HAS. THIS WAS A REALLY RAINY NIGHT), AND HE'S STANDING ON MY TRAIN SET, DRINKING MY BOTTLE OF VODKA. AND IT WAS LIKE ALMOST EMPTY AT THIS POINT. I'M LIKE, "BOB, WHAT ARE YOU DOING?" AND HE JUST ROARS LIKE GODZILLA, AND THEN—TRIGGER WARNING, LADIES, BECAUSE THIS IS ABOUT TO GET ROUGH—HE STARTS STOMPING ON THE BUILDINGS, COMPLETELY DESTROYING DOWNTOWN GALLOPING GULCH.

(Galloping Gulch was the Western town that was the focal point of Audrey's train set. It's described and photographed in exhaustive detail in her thirty-seven previous posts, as well as in the six posts that came after that night, which covered Galloping Gulch's miraculous reconstruction and restoration. I'm happy to report that after three months of Audrey's hard work, the town was picturesque and charming once more, and even had some modern touches now, a public swimming pool and drive-in movie theater.)

CRUNCH GOES THE SALOON! CRUNCH GOES THE POST OFFICE! CRUNCH GOES THE OPRY HOUSE! THE WHOLE EXPERIENCE WAS TERRIFYING. I HAD NO IDEA WHY HE WAS DOING THIS. ONCE HE HAD DONE AN INCREDIBLE AMOUNT OF DAMAGE, HE CAME TO THE GRAND FINALE: HE STARTED TO TINKLE ON MY TRAIN SET.

"This must be a different Bobert," said Alice.

RIGHT THERE IN FRONT OF ME, LOOKING ME IN THE EYE, HOLDING HIS KINDA LONG BUT KINDA SKINNY UNCIRCUMCIZED—

Roxy gasped. "It's him."

—THING LIKE A FIREHOSE AND AIMING IT ALL OVER

EVERYTHING. OBVIOUSLY, A MILLION THOUGHTS CAME TO MY MIND, WHILE HE STOOD THERE LAUGHING AND PEEING. DO I SCREAM? DO I CALL THE POLICE? DO I GO TO THE KITCHEN AND GRAB A KNIFE? WELL LADIES, IN MY TIME OF CRISIS, I'M PROUD TO SAY I THOUGHT OF AND DID THE VERY BEST THING I COULD HAVE DONE IN THIS SITUATION. REMEMBER THE REMOTE CONTROL I INSTALLED LAST SUMMER?

There was a link here, to a previous post about the installation of the remote control, which allowed a delighted Audrey to turn the train set off and on from her bed.

WELL, I REACHED OVER TO MY NIGHTSTAND, GRABBED IT, AND TURNED ON THE TRAIN SET. AND SIX-TEEN VOLTS OF MAXIMUM THROTTLE SURGED THROUGH THE RAILS, UP HIS YELLOW STREAM, AND RIGHT INTO THAT PICKLE IN A TURTLENECK HE'D BEEN PESTERING ME TO PUT MY MOUTH ON.

Roxy and Alice gasped with excitement. "Okay," said Roxy. "I like this girl."

AND GIRLS, HE WENT *FLYING*. HE FELL OFF THE TA-BLE AND CRASHED ONTO MY WORKSHOP DESK. WHEN HE GOT UP, ALL THESE LITTLE TREES AND ROOFTILES WERE STUCK TO HIS SKIN. I THINK THAT SOBERED HIM UP REAL QUICK, BECAUSE THE NEXT THING I KNEW, HE WAS PUTTING ON HIS CLOTHES WITHOUT A WORD, AND THEN RUNNING OUT OF THE APARTMENT, LEAV-ING ME WITH THE WRECKAGE OF THE WORK OF ART I'D PUT SO MANY HOURS OF HARD WORK INTO. IT WAS AL-MOST ALL WORTH IT TO WATCH HIM GET ZAPPED LIKE THAT. IT *WAS* PRETTY FUNNY. GOD, I WAS SO MAD WHEN I STARTED WRITING THIS BUT NOW I FEEL A LITTLE BET-TER. ANYWAY, GENTLEMEN, BE CAREFUL WHOSE TRAIN SET YOU DECIDE TO PEE ON, AND LADIES, HIS NAME IS

BOBERT SMITH, AND WHATEVER YOU DO, DO NOT DATE HIM!!!

Roxy and Alice sat in silence, grappling with what they'd just read.

"Wow."

"I know."

Another knock shook the door.

Pulled from the haze of big new information, Alice said, "Should we maybe get out of here?" But she wasn't crazy about the idea of going out there and facing Bob. Roxy ignored the knock.

"This girl has four hundred Twitter followers," she mumbled as she scrolled. "How are there four hundred people who actually care what— Uh-oh."

"What?"

Roxy showed Alice her phone. It was a text from Bob: "Everything okay in there?" Before Alice could say anything, Roxy was replying.

"Great," she said. "Everything okay out there?"

"Yeah," he replied. "I mean there's a bit of a line. But yeah, all good."

"Is it, Bob? Is all really truly good?"

Dots appeared, but before they could become a message, Roxy cut and pasted the link to the blog post into the chat window and let it fly with unundoable consequence.

The dots went away, and secondhand humiliation swept over Alice. She looked away from the phone, to the wall above the dirty towel where someone had written, all caps in black Magic Marker: **I HEAR HIM COMING. LET'S WITHDRAW, MY LORD.** It must have been an inside joke between Vikram and his roommates, but in that moment, *yes, let's withdraw.* The bathroom seemed suddenly small and she wanted to escape. To where? Some part of her wanted to go talk to Bob and hear his side of it. But most of her did not. So she remained, and Roxy remained, and they sat squished on the edge of the bathtub and stayed there for one, then three, then seven whole minutes. No reply from Bob. With every passing second, it seemed to Alice less likely there *would* be a reply, ever again. And she was correct. This conversation had come to an end, and it would now gradually make its way to the depths of Roxy's Messages page, ten or fifteen thumb-scrolls down, squished and sunken down by conversations not yet begun, with people not yet arrived in Roxy's life.

A full eighteen minutes after they first entered the bathroom, Alice and Roxy emerged, to the cross-eyed relief of Kervis, who so very badly needed to pee. They headed to the kitchen, where they had left Bob, but now found only his unfinished whiskey soda on the stove.

They asked Silence, and Silence confirmed it: Bob was gone.

* * *

"14E. He's already up there," said the doorman, who was everything Pitterpat wanted in a doorman. Crisp and efficient, standing straight as a post, epaulets on point. The doormen at 404 were lovely guys, but they were a little sloppy, weren't they? They had uniforms, but not like this one, with its brass buttons and red piping. The young man inside the uniform had warm, happy eyes that said, *Please be our guest!* over a craggy jaw and barrel chest that said, *But BEHAVE.* Pitterpat was already buying the apartment in her mind as she stepped into the perfectly antique but perfectly updated wooden elevator.

The elevator doors closed, and Pitterpat daydreamed about bringing a baby home to this apartment. She thought of Bill walking into the lobby beside her, as deeply focused on his precious wife and newborn child as he'd ever been on anything. She thought of that doorman helping them get the stroller into the elevator, hitting the button for them, and over the years watching the baby grow up.

Thirteen floors to the top. The ascent was slow. She passed the time on her phone.

Chip Collins, of Rock Properties. His eyes were so blue in this picture. Were they really that blue? Or had they been discreetly tuned up? Did Farrow & Ball make a paint that shade of blue? Because it would be perfect for the foyer.

Her stomach turned. *Not now*, she told it.

The doors opened into a private landing. Private landing! Who did she know with a private landing? Nobody. She and Bill would need new friends, people who understood what that was like.

She tapped the brass rabbit against its brass mount on the glossy green door, as her bowels chirped and gurgled. *Quiet*, she said to them.

She first saw Chip's hand on the doorknob as the door opened, and it was strong and purposeful, with a big watch. His suit jacket flapped flag-like at his tieless torso. And there, near the top of a thick and athletic body, were his eyes, which were, yes, exactly that blue. The eyes looked down and met Pitterpat's, and for a second it was five years ago, when she was single and working at the gallery and every handsome face had the promise of a whole new kind of life, and it only just now occurred to her how angry she was that Bill wasn't here, that she had already lost his attention for the summer, and the fact that she was about to step into an empty apartment with a handsome man who wasn't her husband suddenly surged inside her like waves against a seawall.

Her last thought before the entire night went south was the passing fancy to punish Bill for all this. She had seen herself in the mirror in the elevator. She was still beautiful. She could have this Chip. It would be so easy.

"Mrs. Quick. We meet at last," said Chip Collins the gay Realtor. "Welcome to your new home." And he led her into the ugliest apartment on Fifth Avenue.

Chip could tell immediately that Mrs. Quick wanted to leave but didn't want to be rude. As he went through with the tour, he felt the dissatisfaction behind every "Wow" and "How about that" she mumbled as he took her from room to room. It didn't help that the AC was broken. Shadows of sweat appeared on the back of her dress. Chip had to pretend not to see it.

Halfway through his laughable description of a fourteen-year-old refrigerator as "state-of-the-art," she asked if she could use the restroom. He led her to the powder room, the one with the chinoiserie pastoral wallpaper that looked so great on the website but was unmistakably racist up close.

As Pitterpat closed the door, being as delicate as possible with the rattling antique doorknob, Chip began to write his boyfriend a long, cathartic text about how he told the owners they were pricing the place too high and exactly what he said would happen was happening exactly the way he said it would happen. He did not hear the click of the lock.

* * *

"I mean, couldn't you a little bit see it coming?"

"No!" said Alice, trying to hold her red cup still as Roxy poured. They had nicked a bottle of wine from the kitchen and parked themselves cozily on the sofa in the living room while an impromptu dance party burgeoned before them. "I thought he was nice."

"I know you did," Roxy said, amused. "But I had him figured out. A guy like that, forty years old, still hooking up with twenty-seven-year-olds?" (Again, Roxy was thirty-four.) "No way is there not some damage there. People go sour, like milk, no matter how nice they seem."

"Yeah."

Roxy could see Alice didn't agree. "Look," she said, "if you want to go find him, you're welcome to—"

"No."

"It's okay that you liked him."

"I mean, I *did* like him. I don't want to date him or anything, but I think he was a decent guy. I *thought* he was, anyway. It's so weird. I guess . . . I don't know, I think I feel bad for him."

"Uch."

"I know. And I feel bad about feeling bad for him."

"Double uch," said Roxy. "If you think this story is anything other than hilarious, I'm worried about you."

"I mean, yeah, it's hilarious, but he's also a real person. And now all that stuff is on the internet forever, and he has to live with it, every time someone Googles his name."

"Oh, please," said Roxy, and she put her phone down, and when her eyes found Alice's, Alice saw for the first time how green and sparkly they were when you looked past the bandages. "Alice. None of it's real. Bob's not real. The ChuggaChuggaChooChoo girl isn't real. The train set isn't real. None of it's real."

"Well," said Alice, not sure how to respond. "Some of it's real. I'm real. We're real."

"Oh, dude, I know *we're* real! Of *course* we're real. Silence over there, he's real. Those girls dancing, they're real. If you can see it in front of you, it's real. But if it's not in front of you? If it's on here?" She held up her phone. "It's not real."

Alice wasn't sure exactly how to disagree. "I mean—"

"Trust me on this. You will go crazy if you spend a second of your life thinking otherwise. It's like when people worry about *the security of their information on the internet*." (She gave the words a mock serious-ness, her voice conjuring an elderly banker in a pin-striped suit, behind a big desk.) "And it's like, dude, there's a *lot* of information out there. It's like saying, 'Oh no, I hope nobody steals this precious grain of sand I left on the beach.' Your information is so small and meaningless com-pared to, like, the world and everything in it, that it basically isn't real. Nothing on the internet is real."

"I mean, my credit card number's saved in a few places, and it's pretty real to me."

"Eh," said Roxy. "Someone steals it, you cancel it, get a new one."

"I feel like I appreciate the spirit of what you're saying," said Alice. "But when you get into the specifics, it gets a little swampy."

"It's not swampy at all! It's so simple: Only what's real is real. When Bob was here, he was real. We could see him and hear him. And taste him." Roxy winked. "But then, when he left, he stopped being real. He's pretend now. It's like, what's that thing about babies, where they see something, and then it goes away and they assume it's gone forever and forget it ever existed? But then one day they realize that even though they can't see it, it's still there?"

"Object permanence."

"Yes. Object permanence. That's no good. We shouldn't do that. We should be like babies."

"I don't think we have much choice."

"It's not a matter of choice. It's who we are. We're cave people. Our brains are built for knowing like twenty or thirty people, tops. How many Facebook friends do you have? I have over three thousand. If I spent my time worrying about all three thousand two hundred and eleven of them, if I actually let myself fully appreciate that every one of those people was *real*, that their hopes and dreams and all that were *actually really happening*, as much as the things that happen to me are actually really happening? I'd break. My brain would break. It's too much."

Alice thought of her Facebook post from three years ago. All the likes she got. How real it all felt. *I'm doing this so I can't back down*, she had told herself. *Everyone's gonna hold me to this now because I'm putting it out into the world.* Hardly anyone even remembered that post. You had to scroll down pretty far to even find it.

"You know," said Alice, "for someone who doesn't think anything on the internet is real, you spend a lot of time there."

"Well, sure," Roxy replied. "Who wants to live in reality?"

With a little grin, she held up her red cup, and Alice clinked it with her own. The dancing at the other end of the room was quite intense, sweaty and high-energy. From where they sat deep in the couch, the bodies towering over them seemed titanic, moving madly, precarious. Alice started to excuse herself to go to the restroom, but Roxy suddenly grabbed her arm and put her phone in Alice's face, and Alice read what was on it.

"Oh, shit," said Alice. And oh, shit was right.

* * *

The street was quiet. Fifteen minutes earlier, the usual throng of moviegoers had livened up the sidewalk in front of the Volta, a revival theater on the middle of a block downtown, making their chatty and opinionated way inside. Now the block was quiet, and with the quiet came the opportunity for Audrey to flip through the new Lionel catalog. And that was almost what she did until she heard a tap on the ticket booth window.

She looked up. It was Bobert Smith.

"I saw your blog."

He was furious. Audrey wasn't rattled.

"Oh yeah?" She closed the catalog and laid it carefully on her little desk. She'd been ready for this moment, and even had a good line prepared. "Must have been pretty . . . *shocking.*"

"Yeah. You could say that," he fumed. He missed the joke completely. "Can we talk?"

Audrey knew she was safe in this booth. It was bulletproof, and the ushers would come throw down if she needed backup. "Give me one second," she said, and she picked up her phone.

LADIES. BOBERT SMITH IS HERE. AT MY WORKPLACE. WATCH THIS SPACE IT'S ABOUT TO GO DOWN.

"Oh, shit," said Alice, and oh, shit was right. "When is this from?"

Roxy checked. "Three minutes ago!"

"Oh my God. What's gonna happen?"

"I don't know!" said Roxy, her eyes alight with delicious anticipation.

Alice got out her phone, found the page of @ChuggaChugga-ChooChoo, and she and Roxy slumped back into the couch. There they stayed, side by side, for nearly twenty minutes. They waited, with predatory patience, refreshing and refreshing and refreshing, their whole world all about seeing the next tweet. At one point Kervis came over to resume his extremely slow seduction of Roxy, but when she and her friend didn't look up from their phones even once, he left, and Audrey's two newest LADIES continued their vigil.

Then their patience was rewarded.

OKAY, HE JUST LEFT, AND OH MY GOD. I HAVE TO WRITE ALL THIS DOWN SO I DON'T FORGET IT. HERE WE GO. THREAD.

SO HE SHOWS UP AT MY WORKPLACE. I WORK IN A MOVIE THEATER BOX OFFICE. LUCKILY HE GOT HERE IN THE MIDDLE OF A SHOWING, WHEN IT'S QUIET AND THERE'S NOT MUCH GOING ON.

SO HE WALKS UP TO THE BOOTH I'M IN, AND HE'S LIKE "I SAW YOUR BLOG" IN THIS I'M-YOUR-DAD TONE OF VOICE.

AND SO I'M LIKE, "YOU DID?" AND HE'S LIKE "YEAH," AND I'M LIKE, "THAT MUST HAVE BEEN PRETTY SHOCK-ING, HUH?"

Roxy laughed out loud and starred it. Alice was surprised.

"What are you doing?"

"What?"

"He's gonna read this! He's gonna see you starred it!"

"So what? It's not like I'll ever see him again." This would turn out to be the truth.

SO THEN HE LAUNCHES INTO THIS WHOLE THING ABOUT HOW I NEED TO TAKE IT DOWN IMMEDIATELY OR ELSE. OR ELSE WHAT I SAY. OR ELSE HE'LL SUE ME.

"You're gonna sue me? For telling the truth?"

"No," said Bob. "I don't know. I haven't looked into it. But I thought maybe you could do the decent thing and take it down without it com-ing to that!"

His breath was fogging up the glass. Audrey rested her face on her hand, calmly watching him like a half-bored kid inches away from a wild animal at the zoo. The plexiglass made him less real, like he was behind a screen, an actor playing a character.

"Wow, you're upset," she observed.

"Of course I'm upset!" His spittle hit the window. "Why would you put that in the world?"

"It was already in the world, Bob! *You* put it in the world by doing it! I just let the world know it was there."

Now he was fuming. "But I apologized! And I paid you for the train! I gave you twenty-one hundred bucks!"

"Did you think you were buying my silence?"

"I didn't know I *needed* to buy it," he said. "Why would you do that? You just vandalized my whole life. And for what?"

"To warn people about you!" He had no response to that. "And whatever, I didn't vandalize your whole life. It's not like you have a wife. It's not like you have kids." She didn't expect that last part to be the thing that hurt him most. But it did, and she could see it, but she wanted to keep arguing. "It's just shitty, *Bobert*. It's shitty that you could do something like that and assume New York is big enough that you could just get away with it."

"I told you," he said calmly, "I was going through a difficult time."

"Oh, please," she laughed. "You were having fun."

He took a step back from the booth. Something was different. "Fun," he said, and then repeated: "Fun." He took a deep breath. "You think it was fun? It wasn't fun. I don't have *fun*, *Audrey*. Here's what my life is: I work, I sleep, I sometimes read a book or watch a movie, and every few days I get off with a stranger."

I GOTTA SAY, IT WAS KIND OF FUN WATCHING HOW QUICKLY HE WENT FROM "PLEASE, I'M REALLY A NICE GUY," TO LETTING THE MASK SLIP AND SHOWING ME WHO HE REALLY WAS.

"I go on Suitoronomy, I find some girl, some completely *interchangeable* girl, and there's *so* many of them, and you're one of them. I find a girl, I buy her dinner, I go back to her apartment, I use her for a little while, and then I go home and go to sleep. I'd call it a hobby, but it's so much *less* than that. It's not romantic. It doesn't occupy my thoughts. It's just part of my routine, like going to the bathroom. You weren't fun, Audrey. You were just where I did my business that day." Then he added, with spiteful spit, "I probably do need a hobby. Maybe I'll get a train set."

Mercifully, Audrey condensed and summarized:

HE CALLED ME A TOILET, AND HE LEFT. CLASSY.

SO, IN CONCLUSION: DO NOT DATE BOBERT SMITH.

"Definitely won't now!" Roxy said as she hoisted herself up off the couch, wobbling a little from the combination of red wine and heels and what Alice imagined was a little more pain medicine than she'd been prescribed. "On to the next one, right?"

"Right," said Alice, still looking at her phone.

Roxy's hand was extended, inviting Alice to get up. "Let's dance."

"Give me a minute," Alice said. Roxy nodded and started dancing, instantly absorbed into the thicket of arms and legs and bodies.

Alice opened Facebook, and there was her friend Bob. There was their conversation, and there was his last message: "You should go for it." She began to type.

"Hi."

The word flew into the sky, bounced off a satellite, and fell back to earth, finding Bob in an empty subway car. What did she mean by "Hi"? Bob couldn't begin to imagine. He wanted to think she didn't completely hate him, so he replied that way.

"Hello. Sorry I left without saying goodbye," he said.

As he waited to see if she'd write back, not really expecting her to, Bob looked at Facebook for the first time in months.

Amy Otterpool still had the same profile pic. There she was, with her short hair, on that camping trip. It was a picture Bob had taken, and he couldn't understand how that photo wasn't emotionally rancid for her, how she could just casually leave that moment in the front window of her life, just some happy little memory unencumbered by any kind of pain or regret. It was a picture of her face, smiling, smiling at Bob, smiling about Bob. She'd been standing in a creek when he took it, but you can't see that in the photo. Only he knew it and she knew it. And now he hadn't talked to her in fourteen years.

The truth is, she never went on Facebook, never even thought about it, so it had been years since she'd updated her profile. But her husband, Doug . . . he updated his profile. That's what had done this to Bob in the first place. Bob, lying in a strange bed next to a sleeping model train set fanatic and her model train set, clicking on this Doug fellow's profile, only to find an adorable picture of Doug with a hairy arm around his very pregnant wife, Amy.

It must be here by now. And it was. Bob sat now in a subway car, looking at Amy, in a hospital bed but wearing makeup. She looked great without makeup, but she didn't believe it, so she always wore makeup. And there was Doug, hovering over her awkwardly, and the two of them were every bit as happy about this beautiful baby girl as Bob had feared they might be.

Look at Amy's smile. Bob had made her smile countless times. He had fathered so many of this current smile's older siblings. But this smile was different from those. There was no history in this smile. This was the smile of another person, for another person.

Bob put his phone in his pocket. Eyes closed, he felt around his heart for the invisible line that connected him to the constellation of her life. There was nothing.

His pocket buzzed.

"It's okay," Alice replied. "You went downtown?"

"Yes," he said. "How did you know that."

"She tweeted about it."

Bob looked at ChuggaChuggaChooChoo's Twitter and felt the punishment all over again, like a bone rebroken right when it's starting to heal. For the rest of his life, he never would have had the heart to reply to Alice if she hadn't continued.

"So I guess ours wasn't your first Suitoronomy date?"

"No. I've been on a few."

"How many?"

"Who knows at this point."

I do. Two hundred eight. A big number, but fewer than he might have guessed.

"I should go," she said. "For what it's worth, I don't think people should be judged by their worst day."

"It's very sweet of you," he said, with a line break, "to think that was my worst day."

She didn't quite know what to say to that. Two minutes later, she thought of something, but when she reopened Facebook, his account was deactivated.

* * *

There was a conversation going on between Chip and some of his Realtor friends. It had been going on a while, a few years now, on a Slack thread called "Clients Gonna Client."

Chip could not wait to share this one.

"Showed Fifth Avenue Teardown tonight." His friends knew all about this apartment. "Buyer is beautiful female, early thirties, married to tech bro. Wardrobe on fleek, zhuzhed out to the nine millions. Designer bag, epic blowout, pristine makeup, little spritz of some perf I don't recognize which means must be $$$$$. Girlfriend is HIGH END. Anyway, about ten minutes into the showing, she asks if she can use the powder room. I think she may have even said she needed to powder her nose. FANCY. So she goes to powder her nose, and I'm just playing on my phone, doing nothing, when from the other room, I HEAR THE MOTHER OF ALL SHIT ATTACKS. I hear grunts. I hear farts. I hear plops. Disgustingness. 1950s Jackie Bouvier dumptrucking into an antique toilet. And holy shit the smell. After she left, I burned a candle for an hour. Homeless-guy level stink. And no, she will not be making an offer. FML."

He got a lot of laughs and responses from his friends. He got it mostly right, exactly like it happened. But he missed the pain. He didn't feel what Pitterpat felt, gasping and struggling as her body inside-outed itself. He didn't see her clutch her purse, fingernails digging into the buttery black leather as she shat lava. She was trapped, a hostage to her own disobedient lower GI. All she could do was take out her phone and try to be elsewhere, away from her body and away from the world, in a virtual tour of a Tribeca loft with floor-to-ceiling windows. *I'm not here*, she said to herself, *I'm not here and this isn't real*, and for a few grasping moments, she wasn't, and it wasn't, and the view of the Hudson was breathtaking.

* * *

Roxy and Alice danced, and then stopped to go get drinks, and in the kitchen as they got drinks, Roxy found her way into a conversation about *Love on the Ugly Side*. ("Mallory *legitimately* has borderline personality disorder," Roxy assured the girl pouring the grenadine. "Totally," agreed the girl. "She's gonna win the whole thing." "Totally!") A few minutes after midnight, Alice looked at her phone.

GOOD MORNING. IT'S 90 DAYS UNTIL THE TEST.

She put her phone away. She and Roxy got their picture taken with Silence, then had another drink, then started dancing again.

"I can't do this every night."

"I know. I'm sorry."

"It's not your fault! I can just already tell, every second I'm not studying this summer, I'm going to feel terrible about it. I have to resist temptation. I have to motivate myself."

Roxy danced and thought a moment, and then had an idea.

"Okay, how about this," she said. "If you don't study your ass off, like every single day, I'm gonna murder you in your sleep."

Alice released a goosey honk of a laugh, one that loosened every joint in her body. She kept laughing as Roxy kept going. "I'm serious. You don't even know me. Maybe I'm a murderer. Maybe I've done it before. Why do you think your room was available?"

Alice knew exhaustion and regret would be waiting for her tomorrow, but still she twinkled as she said to Roxy, "You're trouble."

"Psh." Roxy smiled, pulling her tangle of hair up over her bandaged head. "Says who?"

CHAPTER THREE

Saith the Lord

The light from the kitchen chandelier bounced off the black ink on the white paper and flew up into Alice's corneas, through the anterior chambers, the aqueous humor, the pupils, the posterior chambers, more aqueous humor, and into the fine-tuning of the lenses, where it passed, refined now, through the vitreous humor of the vitreous chambers (vitreous humor, vitreous chamber, easy to remember), into the retinas, home of the electromagnetic receptor cells ("rods and cones"; "photoreceptors" also acceptable), where the bipolar cells welcomed it to Alice's nervous system, handing its information to the ganglion cells of the optic nerve, which brought it to the busy neurons of Alice's visual cortex, which took this staticky scramble of edges and contrasts from the light and the paper and the ink and turned it into a string of words: "Anatomical Organization of the Nervous System."

Alice's eyes hurt already.

GOOD MORNING. IT'S 87 DAYS UNTIL THE TEST.

You are born with a nervous system. This nervous system determines What You Want. Between this nervous system and the world is a body. The body determines what you can have. What You Want and What You Can Have. This is all there is to life. In happy moments these things intersect, the sheet fits the bed, and the whole thing just works. But for the most part, What You Want and What You Can Have are two different trains on parallel tracks, forever waving to each other from the window, never quite meeting.

All Pamela Campbell Clark wanted was to go to her old job at the library every morning, but because of budget cuts due to a decline in library usage, she could no longer have what she wanted. So, instead, every morning, Pamela Campbell Clark went walking through the park. She walked and thought about her daughter and her granddaughter living in California, and today she came within six seconds of being hit by a bicycle.

All Brock wanted was to ride his bike. It was the only thing he wanted when he was a kid, and now that he was a grown man, with wiry salt-and-pepper hair and a beard that wouldn't stay down more than half a day after he shaved, the only thing that had changed was how fast Brock wanted to go on his bike, although that didn't really change either, because the answer was always *faster*. This particular summer, he wanted to ride the Central Park bike loop, all 6.1 miles of it, in fifteen minutes. Once, not too long ago, he had wanted to do it in twenty. Then he did that, and so now he wanted to do it in fifteen.

In order to want this, Brock had to want the Central Park bike lanes to stay open, even after two pedestrians had been killed so far that summer, and now a third was in critical condition, and it was still only June. So Brock did what wanting the thing he wanted required: He got vocal. He wrote emails and made calls to the mayor's office. He attended city council meetings and stood at the microphone and spoke on behalf of the Pedalers' Alliance, an advocacy group consisting of Brock and the nearly 24,000 Twitter followers he had purchased.

Then one morning the City Hall press office put out a statement.

FOR IMMEDIATE RELEASE

NEW YORK—Central Park belongs to all New Yorkers, and all New Yorkers should be able to enjoy it, without fear of injury or death. After carefully considering both sides of the issue, and consulting with community members, civil engineers, and business leaders, the Mayor has decided to authorize the Department of Transportation to permanently remove the second bike lane from the Central Park Loop. We are grateful for all the input we've received from all members of the community. Except, of course, for them whiny little bitches in the "Pedalers' Alliance," the ones who keep tweeting at us and emailing us and have no idea how lame and entitled they sound. We're sorry you privileged little shits won't have more room to ride your little bikes around the park. Good news, though: The carousel is still open. Why don't you babies go ride on that?

Up yours,
Mayor Arnold Sp—

Brock stopped reading, having nearly fallen off his Velocitron ten-speed. The mayor of New York was mocking him. Personally. This mayor, who he hadn't voted for, who *nobody he knew* had voted for, had the arrogance—the audacity—

Brock was so angry, he didn't know how to respond, so he laughed, loudly to himself, in a jagged series of short, angry woofs that didn't much sound like laughter and scared a nearby squirrel.

★ ★ ★

"It was obviously a joke," said Roxy.

Kervis was not laughing. "Was it?"

"Of course! You thought I was serious?"

"I mean, was it *obvious*?"

"I mean, I think so."

"Why would you even make a joke like that?!"

"Because nobody was supposed to see it?"

"Why would you make a joke nobody's supposed to see?" She didn't have an answer. Kervis continued, "And if nobody was supposed to see it, why would you write 'For Immediate Release'?"

"That was part of the joke! Kervis, seriously, I am so, so sorry." Even in her contrition, she was smiling. Her mouth was extraordinary. *Not now, Kervis.*

"I mean, what possessed you? What would make you do that? This affects the mayor. It affects his agenda. This is like the worst thing you could have done to him right now." Kervis was pretty sure he sounded firm and professional. Those lips. *Stop. Stop it.*

"Worse than mispronouncing his name?"

"Yes. Worse than that."

"Are you sure? Because he gets pretty touchy about people mispronouncing his name. Which I don't get. It's a pretty easy name to mispronounce."

"Roxy—"

"Honestly, it's not as cool if you say it the right way. He should just embrace it, tell everyone to call him Mayor Sp—"

"Roxy!" Kervis stood up quickly. "Do I look or sound like I want to joke around with you right now?"

"I'm sorry. I'm so sorry. I'm so, so sorry. I feel so bad about this," Roxy said. Roxy had one of those faces where you couldn't tell if she was feeling the thing or trying to make you feel like she was feeling the thing. In this case, the thing was "so bad about this," and boy, did it seem real, but boy, did it seem like this particular shade of seeming real was the result of lots of practice. The bandages helped, lending the whole performance a touch of the pitiful. Kervis wanted to kiss her neck, but that did *not* factor into things right now, because this was a *big* screwup and someone was going to have to take the fall and it wasn't going to be him. He told her as much, and again, she looked either terrified or like she really wanted him to think she was terrified.

"It was a stupid mistake, Kervis, that's all," she said. "I wrote it as a draft, so I would have something to work off later. Which I did. I wrote up a whole other thing, I'll show you. I just attached the wrong file to the email. That's all. It was a stupid mistake."

"The mayor's really pissed, Roxy."

"I don't blame him! I'd be pissed too. You should probably fire me, if you can." That little microaggression—*if you can*—hit its mark a little too beautifully. Roxy kept moving. "I deserve it. But just know that if I still have my job this time tomorrow, I will take this job so, so seriously."

The other guys on Pickup Artist Paradise were always giving Kervis shit about the fact that he didn't lay some game on his hot redheaded assistant ("Phoney," as he referred to her, due to the fact that her face was always in her phone, plus the fact that, despite how much he liked her, she was an enormous phony).

"Dude, if you don't hit that, you're a pussy," said HoBagger. (HoBagger didn't use his real name on Pickup Artist Paradise. If he did, his fellow PUAs could figure out that Shane Rickells of Brownwater, Florida, was a twice-divorced father of three, arrested in 2008 for stealing shoes from a bowling alley, and the last person anyone should take advice from.)

"I know, you're right, as always," Kervis replied, and yet here he was, with a golden opportunity, and he already knew he would do nothing with it. He opened the door so he and Roxy were no longer alone in his office with the door closed.

"Okay, look," he said. "I'm going to see what I can do. I can't promise anything. But I'll try to get you out of this."

She sighed with relief. "Kervis," she said, "you are my eternal office buddy, do you know that?"

"Yeah," he said. *Fuck. It's never gonna happen.* "Don't make me regret it."

"I won't, I promise."

She smiled at him, sweetly, and it occurred to Kervis that he might have been thinking all wrong about her. Maybe she liked him as much as he liked her. Maybe this didn't have to be some heavy lift. Maybe the right moment would arrive and they would just fall into each other's arms. Sometimes life does that.

Roxy returned to her desk. As she picked up her phone, a text arrived, from a number she didn't recognize: "Jesus do I want to boink you."

* * *

Bill was sixty pages into the photocopied packet, when a voice echoed through the giant room: "Hi."

He looked up. A pair of gray eyes like lanterns peeked out from behind a green lamp at the other end of the Butler Library reading room, half a city block away.

"Hi," he replied.

"I'm Anouk."

Bill waved. "Hi, Anouk. I'm Bill."

"MeWantThat." She said it as a question.

"Yes, that's me."

"Cool," she said. "What are you up to?"

"Doing the reading."

"Same. I'm up to the part where Siddhartha leaves home for the first time at twenty-nine. Makes me feel better about my own life choices."

"Should I come down there instead of yelling in the library?"

"It's fine. We're the only ones here."

A third voice spoke up: "No, you're not."

This third voice—we'll call him Third Voice—came from somewhere else in the room, far away from both of them, maybe behind one of the desks.

"Sorry."

"Yeah, I'm sorry."

"It's okay," said Third Voice. "Anyone else need a drink?"

Anouk laughed. "It's a little early."

Third Voice was undeterred. "How late are you guys staying?"

Who was this guy? Was he from their class?

"Going for the glory," replied Bill. "Here till closing."

"Same," said Anouk.

"All riiiight," said Third Voice, and they all felt good about themselves. "So how about we all go get a drink at closing time? There's a bar called Probley's over on Amsterdam. You guys know it?"

Anouk and Bill locked eyes, and even from this distance they could silently agree: Why not?

"Sure, the one next to the Bakery," Anouk said.

"That's the one I am indeed talking about," Third Voice replied.

"I love that place."

Bill checked his watch. "Okay. In ten hours and fourteen minutes, we get a drink."

"Rain or shine," said Third Voice. "And it will be nighttime, so by 'shine,' I mean the twinkle of the stars."

Anouk and Bill looked at each other. Bill made a face: *Is this guy crazy?* Anouk shrugged.

"Let's do it," said Anouk.

"All riiiight," said Third Voice, and quiet returned to the reading room.

* * *

"'Jesus do I want to boink you.' That's what it said, which I mean, first, um, *wow*, and second, um, *what?* Who says 'boink'? That's like the most unsexy word of all time. 'Boink.' But anyway, yeah, I don't know who it's from. At first I thought Kervis. You remember Kervis, the guy from the party? At first I thought it was him, but I already have Kervis's number, unless he got a burner to use as his boink phone. But I don't think it was him. I mean, he's definitely vibing me, and it's a little gross, to be honest, but he doesn't seem like a 'boink' type. Not that there *is* a 'boink' type. I mean, seriously, who says 'boink'? Clowns? 'Boink' makes me think of clowns. Great, and now I'm picturing two clowns doing it! Right? Where are you going?"

Alice froze, her giant yellow MCAT book halfway into her bag.

"I was gonna—"

"I thought you were working here this morning?"

That had been the plan. She had planted herself at the kitchen table, ready to get back to work, and got a full page and a half into her reading when CLOMP CLOMP CLOMP CLOMP down the stairs came Roxy, armed with an anonymous dirty text message to tell the world about.

"Well, I thought you were gonna be at work."

"Oh, no. I had to run an errand, and they know I usually take all day when I run an errand, so I came back here. I don't want to disturb you. Am I disturbing you?"

Alice decided to go somewhere else to work. It was for the best. No matter how serious you are about getting things done, no matter how cheerful the blue tree in your kitchen is, there are some summer days you just can't stay in a basement. Alice got her confirmation that today was just such a day as she stepped out onto 111th Street and started walking, her flip-flops melting a little into the cement with each step.

Around the corner was the Bakery, a cozy old place where generations of Columbia students had done exactly what Alice had in mind: sit in one place all day long. During the school year, the mismatched monastic tables would be full of students, but now it was quiet, and there were seats everywhere, and no line as Alice ordered her black coffee and muffin. She sat down on a bench seat against one of the dark walls (which, when observed closely, was dark with floor-to-ceiling ballpoint pen graffiti). It reminded her of sitting on a piano bench, and that felt just right. Then she checked her email and discovered the thing she would come to love most about the Bakery: There was no Wi-Fi, and the cell phone service was terrible. Opening a message on your phone took exactly one not-worth-it forever. You had no choice but to *get to work, Calerpittar*. So she opened the big yellow book and returned to the nervous system and its sundry parts, its pons, its cerebellum, its midbrain, its thalamus.

She read, and kept reading, and around her, the Bakery had its morning. Faces departed and new faces arrived in constant replenishment, with Alice Quick as one of its only constants. At one point, a table of three girls sat down next to Alice and had a bracing discussion in what sounded like Hungarian. Alice didn't try to decipher its content. She kept working. A guy she thought she knew sat down two seats over. It was the classic game: acquaintance or celebrity? She couldn't place him and didn't want to. She wanted to work, and she did.

Occasionally the existence of her phone blinked in the back of her head—no, the *front* of her head, the orbitofrontal cortex. When this happened, her eyes continued their work as her hand slipped into her bag on the bench beside her and touched the phone, feeling its heft, the cool of its metal and glass. But she kept reading, and the defiant refusal to interrupt momentum for a squirt of dopamine was its own squirt of dopamine, right into her nucleus accumbens, in and of itself. She congratulated herself for not needing Facebook, or Instagram, or Pearlclutcher, or—

That's who it is!

She took out her phone, careful to hold it so the guy two seats down couldn't see. She went to Pearlclutcher and found a post she had read earlier in the day, by a writer named Grover Kines. He was an ethicist—*the* Ethicist, in fact, and one of Alice's favorite writers on Pearlclutcher. Jinzi Milano's stuff was always the funniest, but Grover's columns could be sweet, and very moving. There was one she thought of often, written in response to a reader's letter about saying "I love you" too soon in the relationship. It went like this:

I am sitting in a chair.

You read those words and you picture a chair. You don't picture my chair. You picture your chair—your idea of a chair. It might be the first chair you ever saw. It might be the one you're sitting in now. When I tell you about my chair, I'm telling you about your chair. I may not mean to, but I am.

We must always think of this chair when we say "I love you."

Everyone has their own definition of love. It's a definition that makes room for the entirety of a life lived; every moment of grace, every betrayal, every promise kept or broken. In one tight little syllable the whole ledger comes into account. For some, love is something given. For others, it's something received. For some, it's a choice. For others, an impulse. For some, love means valuing that which is loved more than anything in the world, more even than themselves. For others, love means a weekend in a hotel room. For some, love is wings. For others, it's a prison. For still others, it's a chair.

Every time we meet someone new, we cross a border into a land that shares the rudiments of our language, but with a dialect as unique as our very selves. When I say "I love you," it's with the implicit prayer that it means the same thing in your dialect as in mine. The pain of life is that so often it doesn't. The jackpot of life is that, once or twice if you're lucky, it does.

This is why falling in love is the business of the young. When you've only just begun your definitions, you can write the rest together, side by side, copying off each other's papers. Of course, you can fall in love at any point in your life. Nobody's stopping you. You just have to stay young.

Alice didn't know the true context of this post. (Few did. It was about a girl named Lucia who had broken Grover's heart.) But it got to her. Is it crazy to like someone this much just for what they put on the internet? Probably. But here we are. At the bottom of the page, next to his byline, was a photo of Grover Kines, clean-shaven, with glasses. And there, two tables down, was Grover Kines, unshaven, unbespectacled, hunched over a tiny laptop, sitting in a chair.

He saw her looking, and when their eyes connected, he gave her a bashful grin, the kind you don't see coming but when it's there it melts you. "Hello," he said.

"Hi," she replied. Oh no, he was handsome. His hair was a mess, and his sweater was a little too busy, but she was happy to take a break and talk to him. Then she remembered it was her turn to talk. "Sorry, are you Grover Kines?"

As the words left her mouth, she realized she'd never said or heard that name out loud. It looked so cool in print, but out loud, it was a bit much. Then Grover Kines gave her the same bashful grin as before, and the bitmuchness evaporated.

"Please don't say you hate me."

"No! No, I'm a fan," she said. "Wait, people hate you?"

"Do you not read the comments?"

She laughed nervously, and he laughed too, and it eased the moment. "So what are you working on now?"

He told her, and she listened, and tried to pretend she hadn't read every word Grover had published in the past three years. In fact, it hadn't occurred to her until this very moment that she actually hadn't missed a single article.

And then her phone exploded, one text after another from Roxy, unspooling like ticker tape.

"Sorry about this," Alice said to Grover as the bings of her phone kept arriving, steadily, one after the other.

"That's all right."

"I promised myself I wouldn't look at my phone today."

"Well, if you made a promise, you'd better keep it."

"That's a good point."

He looked proud of himself. "I *am* an ethicist, you know."

"Oh, I know," she said, even though it occurred to her she had no idea how one became an ethicist. Was there an MCAT for ethicists?

He continued: "If you make a promise, you have to keep it. It's the bedrock of civilization. And that goes for every promise you make, even the ones you make to yourself. You wouldn't want someone to promise you something and not come through, would you?"

"No."

"Well, there you go. Ethics."

Alice was charmed, although a little bummed he didn't say it was okay to check her phone. She wanted to see what Roxy had to say, even if she didn't *want* to want to see it. "I guess I'll keep my promise then," she said. "At least until lunch."

And she did.

At lunch, she read Roxy's morning opus.

"Oh my God. Okay, so, the plot just WAY thickened. Guess what I just got? A dick. From that number. Hello. Is your phone on? Please reply if you got this. Alice. Okay maybe you're out of range or something. Anyway, you have to see this picture, it's hilarious. Next time I see you I'll show you. Or I could just send it to you. Let me know if I shouldn't send it, because otherwise I'm gonna send it. Hellooooooooo. Seriously you have to see this picture. Okay I'm sending it." And she sent it, and here it was now on Alice's phone, and thankfully Alice's back was to the wall. "Can you believe that??? I mean, good for him I guess because those look like pretty decent sized bananas, like the kind you get on the street from vendors. Sidebar why are those bananas always so much better than the ones in the store? They're just the perfect size and shape and shade of yellow when you get them on the street. They're like, what you picture in your mind when you picture a banana. Anyway, I got this thing sent to me, and I was kind of hoping it would help clear things up, since I'm now thinking maybe Mr. Boink is an ex or something, or someone I've hooked up with. Not that I have a photographic memory for dicks, but every now and then one stands out, you know? Like if it's really big or really small or has some weird discoloration or a birthmark or a wart. Yeah, I've seen warts." Here she dropped in a popular GIF known as Who Farted Guy, a man in an audience making an exaggerated face like someone just farted. "Have you gotten an HPV vaccine? Get one. Seriously."

Halfway through this frantic gazette—when the sudden still life *Phallus with Bananas* came charging down Alice's corneas, anterior chambers, pupils, posterior chambers, lenses, vitreous chambers, retinas, rods and cones, bipolar cells, ganglion cells, visual cortex, and finally brain—Alice asked herself, *Who is this person I'm living with?* And yet it surprised her how little judgment there was in that thought. More amusement, actually.

"Hi," she replied. "Phone was off, just saw this!"

"Oh no, that's okay, and by the way THERE'S MORE. Holy shit, Alice. HOLY SHIT. I have to find out who this is."

"Why?"

"Because! It's funny! And I'm kind of into it. HA! It's true though, if this guy turns out to be cute I might unpeel that banana. LOL."

"So a guy you don't know sends you this picture, and you're into it?"

There was a long pause. Grover nibbled his bagel sandwich with remarkable discretion and tact. He probably had a bookshelf full of books he'd actually read. Alice never wanted him to meet Roxy.

"Confession: I asked him for the picture. After the first message, when he said he wanted to boink me, I kinda got wrapped up in the mystery. My work day sucks right now because of this bike lanes thing, so I needed some fun. Oh Jesus, remind me to tell you about the bike lanes. Those poor people. Anyway, I wanted to figure out who it was, so I kind of tried to do a little spy work. I chatted him up a little. New phone, who dis? You know? But he didn't tell me. He just kept telling me all the stuff he wanted to do to me. Here, I'll send the conversation."

A screenshot followed.

"Jesus do I want to boink you."

"New phone, who dis?"

"Ha! Nice try Roxana. I know this is you. And I want to boink you so bad. On a really squeaky bed. I want to be noisy with you."

So ended the screenshot.

"I have to say," Roxy continued to Alice, "I kinda like 'I want to be noisy with you.' That's kinda hot. I mean, depending on who's saying it of course."

"COMPLETELY depending on who's saying it." It *was* kinda hot, though. Grover dabbed at his mouth with a napkin.

"Well, yeah, exactly. So I had to find out who it is. I asked him how we know each other."

Another screenshot arrived.

"Not with someone I don't know."

"Good thing you know me."

"Do I?"

"You really don't know who this is?"

"Can't say I do."

"Holy mackerel. But you're talking to me anyway? God you are such a goer."

"A goer?"

"Oh baby, you sure are. And you're a fox."

And then it continued and got far more graphic, and Alice turned bright red as she read it.

Grover noticed. "Everything okay?"

"Yes! Sorry. It's completely ridiculous. I don't even know where to begin."

"Well, I hope you begin somewhere, because now I'm intrigued," he said, and then out came that cloudburst smile, and Alice was finished.

"Okay, I want to start by saying, this is my roommate, she's a new roommate, we *barely* know each other . . ."

Alice told him everything. She cleaned up the dialogue and omitted the visual aid from the presentation, but even the antiseptic facts brought a strange energy to this new friendship forming in the Bakery. Roxy, meanwhile, was still going.

"So," she said to her mysterious friend, "I do actually know you? I know your name, I know your face?"

"You know both of those things."

"And I know another part of you."

"Yep."

"So these three bits of data. Your face, your name, and your . . . bits. All three of these things are in my brain right now. Just not connected to each other."

"Isn't it exciting? I'm so excited."

"No kidding, I've seen the picture!"

"You have, haven't you? Aren't private parts amazing? We all walk around with this little surprise in our pants, this thing nobody gets to see, just certain people. And doctors. We keep it hidden until special moments, and then whammo!"

"Why do guys think their equipment is so interesting?" Roxy replied. "FACES are interesting. What we SHOULD do is walk around in ski-masks but with our stuff hanging out. So when you go home with someone you finally get to see their face. THAT would be interesting."

This got them on a run about the public and private parts of the human body. The conversation lasted hours and took Roxy's mind off the fact that everyone in City Hall hated her. By the end, she was fully aware of her pulse quickening with each new BING!

"So you're just full on gonna sleep with him," Alice wrote during another break that afternoon.

"I mean, I don't know. On the one hand definitely not, ew. But on the other hand maybe?"

"You're deciding this before you even know who he is?"

Roxy got philosophical. "What does that even mean? What is 'who he is'? Who is anybody? I may not know him, but I feel like I KNOW HIM know him. You know?"

"You know the size of his thing in relation to a banana, and the fact that he uses the word 'boink.' That's what you know."

"I've slept with guys I knew less about."

And how much less is that, really, than what anyone knows about anyone else? Alice thought of Carlos, and the night before they broke up. They would never know each other better than they did that night, and even then, there were things she could have shattered him with. They were strangers to each other, as much then as now.

It was getting dark. Alice could see her reflection in the window, and Grover's right next to hers. At some point during the day, in the midst of their off-and-on conversation, he had slid down one seat, so that now, as the sun set over the street outside, their legs were nearly touching. Side by side, each either intensely focusing or intensely pretending to intensely focus on a very important task. But if Alice moved her knee just an inch to the right, just an inch . . .

"I'm gonna maybe do it," Roxy said. Five minutes later, she added, "Not maybe. It's happening. Right now."

"Who is he??"

"I have no idea!!!"

And she didn't. Five minutes earlier, she'd been sitting at her desk, gathering the energy to go home and watch *Love on the Ugly Side* (this week the remaining eight girls were being made to watch deepfake videos of their parents having sex in order to win a couples massage and alone time with Jordan, who they all agreed was a *snack*), and while some nights that would have hit the spot, tonight it didn't. She pulled out her phone and sent Mr. Boink a dare: "So are we doing this or what?"

"Yes," he replied, almost immediately. "When?"

"Now."

"Come here and get it."

"Where are you?"

"You know."

"No, I don't."

"Where I always am."

It was fun frustration. Roxy looked around the bullpen, which was empty for the most part. Kervis was in his office. She walked over to his door.

"Hi," she said.

He didn't look up. "Heading out?"

He was absorbed in something on his computer. Or pretending to be? Was he still mad? Or avoiding eye contact for some other reason?

"Yep," she replied after a pause. "Heading out."

He still didn't look up. "See you tomorrow."

In the elevator, she weighed the possibility that Kervis was messing with her. If this was a game, he was making some strange choices. She looked at Mr. Boink's last message: "Where I always am."

She wrote a reply: "And where is that?"

She got to the lobby as he replied: "You see me every day. You saw me today. You smiled at me."

And that's when she figured out who it was.

Her neighbor. The guy on the first floor, right above her apartment. His name might be Andy. Andy Something. Andy and a short last name, a tight syllable that sounded like maybe a barnyard sound or something? Andy Moo? Andy Oink? Did Andy Oink want to boink? She saw him at the mailboxes that morning and smiled. He was short, but in a rectangular, carved-out-of-wood kind of way. She looked at the banana pic, and her brain put this image together with the face in the hallway and the name Andy Woof or Andy Baaaaa, and it felt like a match.

"Give me one hour," she wrote.

Then she wrote Alice, "It's Andy. Upstairs neighbor," and then a string of saucy emojis.

Outside, the clouds were dark and thick, throbbing for catharsis. Roxy hurried to the subway entrance, running smack into a guy standing by a hot dog cart, knocking his dinner to the ground, and he apologized for some reason, but she didn't even hear him because she was running down the steps.

Uptown, she emerged from the subway just as the skies opened up, and it made her wish she'd worn her new trench coat today. It was white, with a purple satin lining, and she loved it, and if she'd taken two seconds to check the weather that morning, she'd be wearing it now, walking under the new umbrella she also didn't have with her, but she wasn't, so she ran.

She jammed the key in the lock and made her way in the front door, brushing the rain out of her hair. Halfway down the hallway was Andy's apartment door. She thought she heard music coming from behind it. Quickly, so he wouldn't catch her, she slipped off her shoes and quietly made her way down the basement stairs.

In the apartment, she busied herself immediately, rinsing off, blow-drying, brushing, shaving, tweezing, perfuming, stumbling from room to room in various states of half dress. She tried on a few outfits but didn't like any of them. She looked in Alice's closet, because they were friends now and surely Alice would be happy to lend Roxy a dress if everything in Alice's closet wasn't completely frumpy and wrong for this kind of moment, nope, never mind.

Roxy froze, thinking she heard footsteps above her. Andy's apartment. She checked her watch. It had been an hour. It was time. Right now. Excitement shivered through her. She just needed an outfit.

Then she saw her new white trench coat, and felt its satin lining, and thought of that lining against her skin.

She texted Alice.

"Can you stay out for a little while? Like a few hours?" Andy's room was possibly right above Alice's.

Alice might normally have groaned at this imposition, but the Bakery didn't close until midnight, and work was getting done. She turned off her phone, nosed back into her big yellow book, and ever so slightly her knee accidentally touched Grover's.

* * *

Inside Butler Library you could barely hear the rain. "LADIES AND GENTLEMEN," bellowed the security guard, "THE LIBRARY IS CLOSING IN FIVE MINUTES."

Bill left the final life of the Buddha and returned to the world of the library. He began to pack up.

"Hey," said Anouk. Bill looked up. She was now right next to him, smelling like vanilla soap. Her bag was over her shoulder, and she wore a yellow raincoat. Bill rubbed his eyes.

"Hey," he replied.

"How far'd you get?"

"Buddha just kicked it."

"Parinirvana, baby!" she said. "So. Drinks?"

"Oh, right," he said. "Um—"

They looked around the room. Third Voice was gone. They looked for him a little bit, but never found him, and never would, and for the rest of their lives would occasionally wonder who he was.

"I guess it's just us."

Pitterpat had texted him earlier saying she was going to sleep, and he should stay out as late as he wanted. Bill decided this was fine, even a good idea. It was part of taking a class, discussing the material with classmates. They'd go to Probley's, talk for a while, and then head home. Separately. As they shared her umbrella, strolling shoulder to shoulder down 114th to Amsterdam, it occurred to him that this might not be a good idea after all. But they kept walking.

As they walked, Anouk asked him, "What's it like being rich?"

"It's great," he said, a little embarrassed. Then he added, "A little embarrassing."

"What's there to be embarrassed about? There's good rich guys. Siddhartha was a rich guy."

"Only because he was born with it. I acquired it."

"That's good, though. That makes you *better* than Siddhartha."

Bill laughed. "You think so?'

"Sure. He was a trust fund kid. You're a self-made man."

Self-made man. What self exactly had made all this money? It had been another Bill, at another time. Not this Bill, taker of long lunches and picker-up of checks, layabout heir to some other Bill's fortune.

They got to the bar, and Bill put down a credit card that was a color Anouk had never seen. They sat on stools in the corner, far from the window, and talked about the reading, as planned. Then they talked about Professor Shimizu and how intimidating he was.

"I hear he used to be a monk," said Anouk. "But he got kicked out."

"Really?"

"Yeah. Apparently he was a bit of a ladies' monk. Which adds a whole other layer to the mystique. It's very . . ." Bill couldn't tell where Anouk was going with this, and ultimately Anouk couldn't either. She flushed a little. ". . . *something.*"

Bill told a story. "Just yesterday, there was a moment after class when nobody else was talking to him, so I go over to get some face time, charm the guy, become best friends, et cetera."

"Naturally."

"So I—God, this is so stupid, I don't know why I did this—I told a joke."

And then he told her the story, reliving its agony as he told it. It was after class. Bill was in the classroom, face-to-face with Professor Shimizu, the old man looking into his eyes, and for some reason, all Bill could think to say was an old joke about Buddhism he'd heard long ago.

"What did the Buddhist monk say to the hot dog vendor?"

The old man was thrown off. "Excuse me?"

"It's a joke," Bill explained. "What did the Buddhist monk say to the hot dog vendor?"

Professor Shimizu blinked. "Buddhist monks don't eat meat."

"I know," said Bill, though he hadn't known that. He repeated: "It's a joke."

"And even if he were interested in something from the hot dog cart that wasn't a hot dog, like a soda or a bag of chips, he probably wouldn't speak to a vendor about it, because monks don't handle money. Generally speaking, they don't talk at all to members of the laity. I'm so sorry, I'd love to keep discussing this, but I need to be going."

The old man disappeared into the stream of young bodies leaving the room. Bill wouldn't tell Pitterpat about this exchange. He wouldn't tell anyone. It was too humiliating. Except here he was, a day and a half later, telling Anouk. She laughed as he finished his beer.

★ ★ ★

When Miriam Cluck died at ninety-seven, a giant text chain began among her four children, most of her eleven grandchildren, and a handful of spouses, for the purposes of logistics. Miriam was still in New York, in an assisted living facility not far from where she'd raised her family, but most of that family had now floated like spores all over the world: San Francisco, Tucson, Chicago, Hong Kong . . . One of the grandkids, Ayesha, was on a research boat in the Barents Sea. She sent her love and muted the chain. The rest of them were left to hammer out the details for the funeral and burial, and in those discussions the responsibility of hosting the shiva fell on the only remaining New Yorker in the clan, Miriam's grandson Andrew.

It was a surprise when he volunteered. Andrew was the cousin and nephew none of them were particularly close with. Plus his one-bedroom apartment was very small. "A single tray of food would fill the kitchen," worried his mother, Renee, in an off-chain text to Claire (David's wife). But by then Claire and David's flight from Hong Kong was already in the air. Nothing could be done. Andrew's it had to be.

So imagine everyone's surprise when it turned out to be wonderful. The true hero of the event, as everyone on the chain later agreed, was Andrew's fiancée, Rachel. Rachel, not Andrew, had been the one to volunteer the apartment for the shiva. Rachel wasn't Jewish, and as Renee marveled: "Imagine your first shiva, and you're hosting it!" But Rachel was determined to nail this, and she did. Food was devoured, stories were shared, memories were recalled and corrected and argued over and laughed about, and Miriam's spirit, the generosity and good-will she embodied, wafted among them like a sweet melody.

And the visitors! Who knew a ninety-seven-year-old woman had such a coterie! One lovely guest after another dropped in. The young man who had been Miriam's nurse at Robinson Gardens brought the most deli-cious pumpkin bread, which he baked himself. "Still thinking about that pumpkin bread," Sylvia said on the text chain later. Everyone agreed. "He's a nurse and not a baker?" "He should have his own bakery!" "Do we know any single girls for him?" They did not. Two of Miriam's old students from when she taught at a nearby private school dropped in next, and an old woman who had known Miriam in grade school. There was even a young woman who lived in Andrew's building, who didn't even know Miriam and barely knew Andrew beyond a passing smile in the hallway, but she dropped in and seemed genuinely upset and won-dered aloud if maybe she was intruding, but the Clucks would hear none of it. Brian (Arlene's husband) sat her down in the wingback chair by the window—"the interview chair," as Sharon had nicknamed it—and de-manded this girl's life story. She obliged—she worked for the mayor's office! what a neat job!—though she repeatedly declined to take off her trench coat. "Please," the family insisted, "you must be so hot!" It was buttoned all the way to the top, and the room was so stuffy! But no, she left it on, and though she tried to leave, everyone convinced her to stay, have some food, listen to a few stories, and meet every single member of the family. Which she did. She even stayed (at the rabbi's urging) for the kad-dish. It was so nice of her to come by. Miriam would have appreciated it.

* * *

Alice got a text from Roxy: "Not Andy."

* * *

The rain started again in earnest. Bill could have gone home, but Anouk asked if he wanted to come upstairs to her place for some tea, and he agreed. It was an odd way of saying it, out here on the street, as though they were already in her home, the entire streetscape of New York her own sprawling first floor. But it was raining, and he was having fun talking and wanted it to continue, so yes, he agreed to come upstairs.

"I wonder if my roommate's home," she said, coaxing the dead bolt open. "He's usually out working this time of day, but you never know."

He. "What does he do?"

"He's an artist."

"What kind of stuff?"

"I have no idea, to be honest. I think he abandoned categorization years ago."

Beads hung in the doorway between the tiny entrance hallway and the kitchen, which Bill discovered was also a dining room. And in fact also a living room. And possibly a bedroom? There were three other doors, and one was the bathroom. This was a home where one could see the shower curtain and the detail of its embroidered butterflies from the threshold of the front door.

Anouk put a kettle on. There was a large box of black Sharpies on the table.

"Art supplies," she said. "Though it appears"—and here there was a playful flourish—"the artist is not in residence." Bill didn't catch the shift in tone, a toe in the water.

"So it appears," he said. A copy of *Hamlet* lay on a shelf. Three copies, actually. "Can I use your bathroom?"

It was a nice shower curtain. The fixtures were old. Maybe original? Pitterpat would hate this bathroom. The lime-colored tile would make her barf. Bill, on the other hand, could live here forever if he had to. He thought about this as he urinated, and then noticed the two words written in black Magic Marker on the wall in front of him: **WHO'S THERE?**

When he returned to the kitchen and dining room and living room, Anouk handed him his tea. He had the impulse to drink it all in one sip, burning his insides. The walls were covered with charcoal drawings and sketches and studies and even a few oil paintings of a young woman, nude. The styles were all different, drawn by different hands attached to different brains with different amounts of experience and inspiration, but always the same model, with the same pale gray eyes. Posing for an art school was something Anouk did for extra money. Sometimes the artists gave her their work, sometimes as an attempt to seduce her, sometimes succeeding.

Now she sat on the futon across from Bill and looked at him for a long moment. He interrupted.

"You're an English major?"

"I'm a master's candidate in English literature," she replied. "We don't have majors in grad school."

"Right," he said with a smile. "How's that going?"

"Good. I'm starting my thesis this year."

"Cool. What's it about?"

"*Anna Karenina*."

"Never read it, but I hear good things."

"Well then, I better not tell you about my thesis."

"Why not?"

"Because spoilers. It'll give away the ending."

(And it will. If you haven't read *Anna Karenina*, go read it, right now. Come find me when you're finished.) (And now we resume.)

Bill laughed. "Okay, first of all, I'm never gonna read *Anna Karenina*. That's just never gonna happen. And also, I think I already know the ending. There's a thing with a train?"

"Yes."

"See? Already spoiled."

"You really want to hear it?"

"I really do. I'm here, aren't I?! Tell me!"

She smiled, then took a deep breath and began the recitation.

(You don't have to read this next bit. Anouk's thesis had serious flaws. Her conclusions were based on translations and not the original Russian text. She relied on gut over research. One of the examiners called the whole thing "a well-crafted sandcastle of confirmation bias." So if you'd like to skip the paragraph below, feel free. In the following paragraph, Anouk takes her shirt off, and things get interesting!)

"Okay. So . . . when I first read *Anna Karenina*, I loved it. Until I got to the ending. Which I *hated*. Here's this woman, Anna, who's so strong and intelligent and implacable, and all of a sudden she's just under a train? What the hell is that? I get that it's a tragedy, but it didn't feel tragic, it felt *wrong*. *Out of character*. That was my starting point: Why would she do this thing that didn't make sense? The answer, I believe, is in the first words of the book. Not 'All happy families are alike,' but before that. The epigraph: 'Vengeance is mine; I will repay.' It's a quote from scripture, but here's the thing: It's a misquote. It's missing three words: 'saith the Lord.' 'Vengeance is mine, saith the Lord, I will repay.' Why would Tolstoy leave that out? Well, here's the thing about Tolstoy: The man had a *terrible* marriage. He was an awful husband. The fifty years he and Sofiya spent together were an *inferno* of jealousy. Vengeance against an unfaithful spouse . . . let's just say that was definitely in Tolstoy's wheelhouse. Which brings us back to the text. The book is written from an omniscient third person perspective, which frequently, *persistently*, takes us inside the heads of the characters. The story doesn't jump from room to room to stagecoach to opera house so much as it jumps from mind to mind. We even get the point of view of a dog at one point. The cumulative effect of all this jumping around is that it underscores a central problem of life, arguably *the* central problem: We don't ever really know what other people are thinking. All the stories in the book come out of that problem. If Levin knows Kitty loves him, there's no book. If Anna knows Vronsky's a douchebag, there's no book. It's a problem every character in the book has. Except one: the Narrator," said Anouk, followed by a huge intake of breath. "The Narrator is a character in *Anna Karenina* and, I would argue, the *main* character, and furthermore, it's *Tolstoy himself,* and in the world of this novel, the Narrator—the Main Character, Tolstoy—is *God.* He lulls you into thinking he's this disinterested third party, just reporting what's going on, but he's not. He's involved, making every decision, right up until the end, when he shows his hand and grinds the axe he's here to grind. When Tolstoy tells us, 'Vengeance is mine; I will repay,' he doesn't say 'saith the Lord' because he doesn't *mean* 'saith the Lord.' He means saith *him.* Vengeance is *Tolstoy's. Tolstoy* will repay, and no matter how real this world seems to you, he's the one in control. He can take a woman who would never in a million years throw herself under a train and make her do exactly that, and for no other reason than because he's mad at his wife."

Bill had not moved from his spot on the chair, nor blinked even. His tea was cool, unsipped. Anouk sensed words forming behind his eyes and didn't wait for them to reach his lips. She took off her shirt and felt the tingle of the air-conditioning on her skin.

Bill leapt out of his chair, knocking over his tea, and backed away to the door.

"Nope. No, thank you."

"What?"

"Don't want to do that," he said. "I gave you the wrong—the wrong—"

She grabbed her shirt. "I'm sorry."

"No," he said. "No, no, I'm sorry. The wrong impression. I'm sorry. I just . . . I just wanted to talk about the reading."

One minute later Bill was out in the rain.

As he walked home, he thought of Pitterpat. The mere fact of him being in that room at that moment would kill her. He imagined what that much hurt would look like on her face. And for what? What had he been doing? Had he been flirting? No. It wasn't that kind of thing. But it was *some* kind of thing, right? And if it *was,* what kind of thing was it? He so badly wanted to talk to someone about it, and the person he wanted to talk to was Pitterpat, and as the rain came down in sheets, it frustrated him that such a conversation was out of the question.

He paused at a bus shelter to check his messages, to see if she'd texted him. Nothing. She was asleep most likely. Her sleep was always deep and untroubled. He didn't put his phone away. His thumb found the MeWantThat icon, the image he and Zach and the graphic designers had gone back and forth on for so many weeks. He clicked it. He didn't want a Nerf archery set and he didn't want tickets to a monster truck rally and he didn't want cuff links and he didn't want a lomilomi massage, and it was almost like the thing he wanted wasn't going to be on this app at all, but he kept going anyway.

* * *

At midnight, the manager flipped the sign in the window from "OPEN" to "CLOSED," and the cashiers, who had spent all day on their feet, came out from behind the counter and began sleepily stacking the chairs. They politely worked their way around the two remaining customers, Alice Quick and Grover Kines, but when the music was turned off—there had been music this whole time?—Alice and Grover snapped out of their concentration, apologized to the staff, and packed up their bags.

Out in the street, the cabs sloshed the fallen rain around. Alice and Grover stood under the awning as the downpour smacked the sidewalk like pebbles. This was not a rain you just walked out into. It took the building up of nerve. So they stood there, together, as the nerve built.

"Well," he said, "this was fun."

"Seriously, you have no idea," she replied. "I'm so proud of myself right now. I woke up this morning not knowing the names for parts of the ear. And now I know them."

"That's terrific," he said. "Hey, what happened with the roommate and her big mystery?"

"Oh, God." Alice laughed. "Still unsolved, it turns out. But there's a funny story there."

Grover peered down the block at Probley's. "Want to go get a drink and tell it to me?"

The words were dry and casual as they left Grover's mouth, but by the time they'd passed through Alice's auricles into her auditory canal, vibrating her tympanic membranes, which passed the vibration off to the malleus, which slipped it to the incus, which dumped it on the stapes, which in turn humbly submitted it to the perilymph, from which it went to the endolymph to the basilar membrane to the tectorial membrane, no, to the *hair cells* and *then* to the tectorial membrane to the neurotransmitters to the brain, the words were wet with suggestion. With the rain all around, the air between them was fresh and shivery, and everything twinkled.

Alice hadn't thought to formulate this rule before right now, but as it occurred to her, she realized it *was* a rule, perhaps the most important rule of all: No boys until after the test.

"I should go," she said.

It took him a moment to see she meant it, so he offered his hand, as ethically as possible. "Very nice meeting you, Alice Quick."

"And you as well, Grover Kines." It felt less weird to say out loud this time.

They bounded into the rain, in opposite directions.

* * *

The next day, Kervis called Roxy into his office.

"The mayor would like to see us."

"Us?"

"Yes."

"You and me?"

"Hazel called, said he wants to see me and you right now."

The furor over the press release had not abated. A member of the Pedalers' Alliance had tweeted about it, and Jordan from *Love on the Ugly Side* had quote-tweeted him with a Who Farted Guy, which seemed like an endorsement.

Roxy felt herself shaking. She reminded herself she didn't like this job. But still. "I thought you were gonna get me out of this?"

He laughed, a spiteful snort. "Oh, is that what you thought?"

Roxy closed Kervis's office door, which took him by surprise. She planted herself there, with her back against the closed door.

"What is it?" He looked nervous.

Roxy didn't know how to say it. "Are we talking about what I think we're talking about?"

"What do you mean?"

"Was I supposed to see you last night?"

He blinked, impossible to read.

"I don't know what you're talking about."

"I came in here last night. You were on your computer. You didn't even look at me."

"Roxy, what are you talking about?"

She leaned in and spoke slowly and softly, even though they were alone: "Are you Mr. Boink?"

Six or seven emotions crossed his face very quickly. There was a knock at the door.

"Come in," said Kervis, relieved, and Hazel Ritchie, personal assistant to the mayor, entered.

"Okay," was all she said. Kervis and Roxy were expected immediately.

As they left the bullpen, Roxy looked back, wondering if she'd ever see this room again.

In the waiting area outside the mayor's office, as Roxy fiddled with the bandages on her face for maximum pitifulness, it occurred to her that the worst thing she could do right now was pronounce the man's name wrong. She had trained herself to say it right over the last couple years. All New Yorkers had, to some degree. But having now had the thought that she might pronounce it wrong, Roxy was pretty certain that meant she probably would, so she silently repeated his name over and over in her head.

Finally they entered the mayor's office, where the man himself sat behind a large cherrywood desk, finishing a phone call. He hung up, leaned back in his chair, rubbed his aging temples, and looked up at the two city employees in front of him. It was Roxy's first time in this office, and her mind went blank.

"Well," said the mayor in a dyspeptic growl.

"Hello, sir," said Kervis.

"Hello, Mayor Spiderman," said Roxy, and Kervis gasped. "Mayor *Spiderman*," she corrected, this time carefully pronouncing Spiderman's *i* with a long *e*, and the *a* with a short *i*. Speedermin. Speedermin. *Shit.*

The mayor sank a little in his chair. Kervis stepped in. "You wanted to see us, sir?"

"Not you, Kervis," the mayor said. "You can go."

Kervis looked at Roxy, and Roxy suddenly realized that Kervis really *had* come along to get her out of this. He nodded ever so subtly to Roxy, a nod that said, *It's gonna be okay*, then gave the mayor a dutiful "Yes, sir," and left the office.

"Door," said the mayor.

Kervis closed the door as he left.

Before Roxy could plead her case, Mayor Spiderman leaned back in his chair.

"Where were you last night?"

The air conditioner shut off, a blast of sudden quiet.

"What?"

"Last night. Where were you?" A trembling grin appeared on the old man's face.

Roxy wasn't much of a public relations expert, but at some point during her year and a half in the mayor's office, in between the naps and the long lunches and the extended trips to the restroom, she had learned a thing or two about crisis management. She was calm and professional as she now asked the mayor for his phone. Not his iPhone, his other phone, the one he thought nobody knew he had. He handed it over. For the next five minutes, Roxy quietly sat in the chair across the desk from her boss and erased every trace of their conversation, and then dropped the phone in a pitcher of water.

"So," he said, "I guess you and me, not gonna happen?"

"No, sir."

The mayor was used to not being liked. It was a running joke about him, like his name. At one point, during a debate, when the moderator asked him to address his anemic poll numbers, he got testy and went off script. "I get it," he said. "You don't like me! Nobody in New York likes me! But they'll like what I do as mayor!" The moment was awkward, then funny, then iconic. Within a week, "You Don't Like Me, But You'll Like What I Do!" was his de facto campaign slogan. And he won.

"Fair enough," he said. "I guess I'm too old for you?"

"Yes. And my boss. And married."

"I'm only seventy-three," he said. Roxy shrugged. He got up and looked at himself in a mirror hanging nearby. "Who am I kidding?" he continued. "I'm an old man."

Roxy felt sorry for him. "Your penis looks young."

He chuckled at this. "That's not mine."

"Really?"

"You thought that's what seventy-three-year-old shvantz looks like?"

"I've never seen a seventy-three-year-old—"

"I got it off a website. I didn't want you to see the real thing."

"Why not?"

He took a moment to think of an answer, and finally said: "'What a piece of work is a man.'"

"Uh-huh."

"I saw that on a bathroom wall in Queens the other day."

Roxy didn't know where he was going with this. So, again: "Uh-huh."

"This guy who died in the park. Forty-five years old. Young man. I remember being forty-five, I didn't think of myself as a young man, but turns out forty-five is young."

"If you say so."

"I do say so," he said, not caring that she was half listening, and half terrified by this whole situation. "You know what's hard about dying young?"

"Probably the dying part?"

"When you die young, you get plopped down into this situation that most people need decades to get ready for. That's all growing old is: learning how to kick the bucket. My shrink calls it a 'workshop of loss.' One by one the world takes away all the things that matter to you, and one by one you learn how to let them go. My looks. My health. My wife."

"Isn't your wife alive?"

"Well, yeah, but . . . the way she used to look? Hoo-boy. *Gone.* Not getting that back. Long life takes away all the stuff you love. But there's other stuff you're happy to get rid of. The need to be liked. The need to be listened to. The need to see every pretty girl naked. Some of that stuff you look forward to being rid of." He looked out the window. "I'm still waiting, I guess."

"So am I fired?"

"What, because of the bike lane thing? Fuck those guys." Then his eyes got sad again. "I'm sorry. I just wanted to get to know you. I see you every day. We never talk. I did this all wrong."

"Yeah, you did," she replied.

"I thought young people like the whole dick pic thing. I thought it was a thing."

"I mean, it *can* be a thing. I wouldn't necessarily call it a *good* thing," she said, philosophically. "Generally I think the idea is to send your own. I mean, eventually the idea is for her to see the real thing in person, right?"

He laughed, and it lightened the mood enough for Roxy to leave.

She went back to her desk. Kervis watched her from behind the glass of his office. After a few minutes, her phone chirped. She checked it. It was a photo. An old, wrinkled, white-haired, battle-scarred member peeked through the unzipped fly of a business suit.

She turned off her phone and got back to work.

* * *

The apartment was so quiet that Alice could hear the little things—the tick of the clock, the drip of the faucet, the occasional muted honk or siren from the morning rush hour shitshow outside. The sunlight was cool on the kitchen table and on the blue tree, and there was room in the room for the knees and elbows of an industrious woman with a goal.

Alice had slept well last night. She had thought of Grover as she lay in bed, and still thought of him the next morning, but less with the linger of an itch and more with the satisfaction of having fought a small dragon and won. They had become Facebook friends. He had requested; she had accepted. Fine. She could do that and be fine.

Alice opened her big yellow book. Its spine was starting to be trained to bring her to the pages she needed most often. She decided to make some tea, then remembered she had already made it. It was in the mug on the table in front of her. The mug said "One Day at a Time" on it, which Alice knew to be an Alcoholics Anonymous slogan, and she wondered if it was Roxy's, which would have painted a whole new layer on Roxy, but it wasn't. It was left behind by a previous tenant, back in the '90s, perhaps in the hope that those five words would someday be useful to a future tenant, and now they were, because Alice had 86 DAYS UNTIL THE TEST, and each day would be a challenge, and she would meet and rise to each challenge, one at a time.

Starting today.

Here we go.

An hour later, Grover looked up from his column on the ethics of canceling a wedding, due thirteen hours ago but still being written, and saw the girl from yesterday, the aspiring medical student, Alice, his new Facebook friend, setting up camp at a two-top table by the window. She took everything out of her bag and arranged it all in front of her, and once that was finished, she looked up, right at Grover, having already spotted him when she entered. He waved. She waved back, with a little half smile: *Here we are again.* Grover half smiled back: *So it would seem.* Then he and she left the world of the café and each other and they went to work, into the respective mineshafts of ethics and medicine, not to resurface until lunch at least. *Get back to work, Calerpittar.*

And she did. She could do it, because even now she remembered the great secret: that she could do it. It was possible and therefore it was possible. Sit there. Don't get up. Look at the page. Pay attention. If she learned everything today or if she learned nothing today, it didn't matter. What mattered was the ritual, the doing of the thing. What mattered was that she was here, now, and wasn't going anywhere. One day at a time.

The rain picked up as the couple next to Alice gathered up their coats. They'd be gone soon. Their table would be free.

CHAPTER FOUR

Orthopraxy

Pamela Campbell Clark went walking through the park. She did this every morning. Her path was constant, like that of a comet.

She entered at Adam Clayton Powell Jr. Boulevard, as always, and made her way, as always, around the Great Hill and back again. It wasn't the most challenging hike, but it was hers. She passed by the Blockhouse, a roofless stone structure with iron bars that was older than the park itself, and then through the North Woods, where the birding was exceptional, but she didn't stop to appreciate the songs of the forest, because this was her walk and she did her walk the way she wanted to. She came up around the Great Hill, shuffling along a gentle loop that closed up and delivered her onto the same skinny trail, now heading home, through the North Woods and past the Blockhouse, until exactly 10:18 A.M., when her path intersected with mighty West Drive, as it always did at this time. Beyond the wide strip of asphalt, the stone wall of Central Park North was in view, with the noises of morning traffic floating over it.

She crossed West Drive, and five seconds later she heard a sound behind her, something flying by with a high-pitched whiz. It was a bicycle, she knew, though she didn't have the reflexes to spin around and see it, and even if she had, she would have missed it because it was going so fast. These bicycles went so fast now. The people riding them should be careful. Didn't they watch the news? Another person died yesterday.

* * *

"Sorry again about last night, Doc," Roxy said to Alice, apologizing for the first time.

"What about last night?"

"The party! I had to stay late because of the emergency council meeting," she said, crunching through dry toast. "What do you think, by the way? Doctor said no surgery necessary." She tilted her head back and gave Alice a look at her profile. The nose seemed to have healed nicely, though having only spent about five minutes with Roxy's old nose, Alice couldn't testify to the fidelity to the original design.

"That's great news," Alice said, then added, "It looks beautiful." And it did look beautiful. Roxy looked beautiful. Some people are made for summer and Roxy was one of them.

"Thank you," Roxy gushed, before sticking her newly healed nose back into her phone. "Anyway, I'm sorry a third time." (It was the second time.) "I so, so wanted to go to that thing last night, but another guy got hit by a bicycle in the park. That's four this summer. It's messed up. But anyway the meeting went way later than I thought it would, so for the . . . fourth time?" (Third time.) "I'm very sorry."

"Don't worry about it," Alice said, though she had no idea what this "thing" was that she and Roxy had missed out on. In truth, Roxy had intended to invite Alice, and had even gotten as far as "Hey! Are you busy tonight? There's this thing—" but then her phone rang and she was called into a meeting and from there the night evaporated.

GOOD MORNING. IT'S 74 DAYS UNTIL THE TEST.

Alice Quick—brave, intrepid, folly-walloping Alice Calliope Quick—was now a regular at the Bakery. The ladies behind the counter knew her face and gave her a genuine hello, and while she hadn't yet reached the point of them knowing an iced latte with almond milk was the usual, it was nice to be noticed. When she could, she always took the same seat, the bench against the window. Sometimes Grover would sit next to her. Sometimes he was on the other side of the room. He was always there. She spaced out her interactions with him, using flirtation as a reward for the accomplishment of little goals: *If I get to the end of this chapter, I get to go talk to him for three minutes.* It was silly but it worked.

But not today. Today nothing was working. Before cracking open the big yellow book, Alice sipped her iced latte and clicked on a tweet that led to the first two paragraphs of an article about the conditions in Chinese factories, perhaps the one where they made this very phone (it wasn't), and no matter how hard she tried to focus on thermodynamics, the flow of energy, the flicker of candles, she thought about those two paragraphs about the lives of those workers, and shared a portion of their pain, a tiny portion, so small they didn't notice it was gone, but from across an ocean and two continents it did its part to prevent a productive morning. And then Alice saw that her friend Meredith had won some award, and the whole day went sideways.

It was a Gold Medal from the Liebgott Foundation for Chamber Performance, and who even knew such an award existed? Alice knew, Alice had *always* known since she and Meredith had been students together, braided and knock-kneed with sheet music under their arms, at the Youth Conservatory of Westchester, and because of this, Alice would be expected above all others in Meredith's large circle of friends to say something about Meredith's Liebgott on Facebook. It had to be acknowledged, with something generous and heartfelt, because Meredith had always been generous and heartfelt to Alice; she had written "You got this, lady!" when Alice posted that thing, and how could they give this award to Meredith?! Meredith couldn't really be that good. She was too pretty to be that good. Meredith, who at that very moment wasn't thinking about Alice or anything else but the six measures of Stravinsky she was playing over and over until it was perfect. With a grumble, Alice clicked like, and choked out her congratulations in the comments, laying the exclamation points on thick as the jealousy lanced her side like a hot javelin. Thermodynamics! *Come on, Calerpittar. Back to work, back to work, back to work.* Thermodynamics. Energy flows into the system, increases the system's energy. Energy flows out of the system, decreases the system's *fucking Meredith* the system's energy ENOUGH.

Her phone lit up.

"Hello Alice," began the email from Libby, Tulip's mom, and *oh, what now?* "Tulip tells me you're applying to Medical School." (*Shit.* Alice had said something to Tulip. They were on the bus heading home, and it had just come up, casually, Tulip saying she had a test tomorrow and she hated tests, and Alice saying tests are good, you never know who you are until you're tested, and Tulip asking when was the last time Alice took a test, and Alice saying not in a long while, but as a matter of fact . . .) "She said you told her you're taking the MCAT at the end of the summer. Obviously this is a bit of a surprise. When you interviewed with us, you assured us that you were ready for a long term commitment as a nanny." (And she had been. At the time. *Shit.*) "That was only nine months ago. I have to wonder if this is something you've known for the last nine months and decided not to tell me." (She had known for the last three years. Whoops!) "I think we should discuss this, as soon as possible. Can you come in tomorrow morning at 10am? Tulip will be at swim class."

Well, that was interesting. Usually Libby just dropped the bomb over email. Getting fired in person was an unexpected variation. Maybe this was an ego thing. Maybe Libby needed Alice to beg for her job. Maybe Libby wasn't getting any respect at work and needed to feel powerful.

She ran it by the Ethicist.

"Is it bullshit for her to be mad about this?"

"Well, no, not really," Grover replied, more than happy to be distracted from what he was working on. "Think how stressful it must be for her to hire a nanny. You have a specialized skill set that's hard to find. She's genuinely freaked out about losing you."

"Libby hates me. She's fired me three times."

"Did you ever beg for your job back any of those times?"

"No."

"Right," he said, "because you're indispensable. And she knows that."

"I think her husband makes her hire me back," Alice said. "I think she makes rash decisions and her husband is the one who hits the brakes on stuff."

"That might be," he said. "But in that case, the husband likes you, and that's something."

"He doesn't like me. I think he just doesn't want to deal with hiring someone else. The Nesbitts are both in finance. They're in the red at all times. Any slight inconvenience and they kick and scream like babies."

"Sounds like a lovely place to work."

"Tulip's nice. She makes it worth it, I guess." This was true. Alice and Tulip got along really well. If Alice had to list her friends in the city—and there weren't many of them—Tulip would have to be near the top. She was the person Alice was most comfortable around, the person with whom conversation came easiest (although in this case Alice maybe should have been a little less conversational).

"Well, don't undervalue what you do for them," said Grover. "Do you know what Confucius said about the human experience?" (And here Alice got the impression that Grover was no longer having a conversation but instead writing out loud. Maybe this would be in one of his columns! Would that be cool? Or would that be weird? Did Libby read Pearlclutcher?) "There are so many ways to experience being human. Rich, poor, healthy, sick, beautiful, ugly, stable, unstable. We all come at it so differently, from such wildly different places, that there's very little we all have in common. Really, it's just one thing. Do you know what that one thing is?"

A tiny voice in Alice said enough with boys holding court. It was no longer spellbinding like it had been in college, the way they just effort-lessly unfurled these extemporaneous treatises on whatever, citing the great thinkers Alice should have read by now. Still, Alice liked Grover. So she guessed. "We all die?"

"No. I mean, yes, we *do* all die, but no . . . we were all cared for by somebody." He paused a let-that-sink-in pause. It sank, hit bottom, and he went on. "We're not one of these species that can get up and walk around a minute after we're born, like deer. We have to be fed, we have to be carried. Don't think for a moment you're just washing dishes. You're giving that kid her baseline human experience."

Alice nodded absently. Her thoughts turned to her own mom. Her own baseline. Penelope Quick had cared for her. *Calerpittar, are you in there?* Her mom always knew where she was hiding. She pretended not to, but a mom always knows. Mom's never far away. Until you move to Hawaii, and she doesn't email you even once in three years. Abandonment. Second mother to do that.

"I should try to hang onto this job," Alice said.

"Well, don't let me tell you what to do," he replied. "But my advice is yes, hang onto it."

He looked proud of himself. "You're very wise," she said after a moment, and he flushed a little. Bashful teeth peeked out from behind his lips.

"I know," he said, and he sipped his tea.

* * *

Oh, thank you, God, thank you, Jesus, thank you, all the angels and the saints.

This was Pitterpat's first thought when Dr. Economides told her she had Crohn's disease and calmly prescribed a mild steroid. In later years, she would look back at this reaction like a lodestar and try to recapture that perspective, that awareness that it could be so very much worse. Crohn's disease, what a harmless-sounding kind of harm! She knew nothing about Crohn's disease, and put that down in the pros column. How bad could a disease she knew nothing about be? She'd never seen a GoFundMe for the family of a Crohn's patient. She'd never heard

"Crohn's" used in a sentence with the word "survivor." If anyone ever died of Crohn's, it hadn't been in big enough numbers to warrant a souvenir T-shirt from a 10K, that Pitterpat had seen anyway. As her relationship with the disease matured and blossomed into profound hatred over the years, she would, in occasional desperate moments (usually on the toilet), struggle to remember this first blush, this feeling of a worry lifted.

It was only in the cab ride home, when she Googled "chrohns" and got the results for the correctly spelled "Crohn's," that the permanence of the thing began to set in. For the rest of the day, her phone did not leave her hand, and her eyes did not leave her phone, as Pitterpat took herself to medical school.

Bill didn't ask where she'd been. If he'd asked, she would have said she was out looking at paint samples at Farrow & Ball because the bathroom could use a new summer color, but he didn't even ask, and it bugged her. He just looked up from his book and sleepily told her she looked beautiful. And he meant it, and she did look beautiful, but then he went back to his reading so quickly, the compliment seemed like the performance of some ritual he didn't really understand or believe in but had to perform.

He had hoped she would ask him how his class was going. She didn't.

She drew a bath. She locked the bathroom door, and as the water ran, she took an excruciating, fiery shit. From the big couch in the living room, Bill had no idea, just like he had no idea his wife had had a colonoscopy earlier in the week. He turned the page in his packet and began to read about Pure Land Buddhism and the Nembutsu.

* * *

A dull fatigue descended on Alice, and everything sharp and energetic within her seemed to be gone. Opening the big yellow book and focusing her eyes on the words was out of reach for some reason. She'd put the Meredith thing behind her. She'd even put Libby out of her thoughts. Still, nothing happened. She nibbled a dry chocolate croissant and read a Yahoo article about a bed-and-breakfast shaped like a giant beagle, and every few minutes felt a pang of guilt about not working, but she didn't even have the energy to really *feel* it. It would flare up and die like a cheap match in the wind. Way too early in the day, something in her decided this was a lost day, and she would go to sleep tonight feeling terrible about herself. Which made her feel terrible about herself, which made her want to go to sleep. She didn't want this to be a lost day, but it was.

Two tables down, Grover's fingers clattered violently at his laptop. He was in the pocket, as they say, pounding something out. Alice didn't know Grover thought what he was writing was terrible, and she didn't know that he was right; it was in fact terrible. She just saw the blurry knot of fingers on the black keys of his little silver computer and had the sudden cruel impulse to distract him.

"So. Grover Kines."

His shoulders relaxed. The knot of fingers untied itself. He smiled, grateful for the interruption.

"Yes, Alice?"

"Hi."

"Hi," he said.

Alice realized she didn't actually have anything to say to him, and for an instant was tripped up, but Grover was the kind of conversationalist who could yank any pause from the snapping jaws of awkwardness.

"Churchill fan?" he said, smoothly.

"Excuse me?"

He pointed to her book. On the front cover, Alice had written the words "Sure I am that this day, now, we are the masters of our fate. That the task which has been set us is not above our strength; that its pangs and toils are not beyond our endurance."

"Very good," she said. "I'm impressed you recognized it."

"Oh, sure, it's a famous speech."

"It is," she said, and then added, as an explanation that didn't really explain anything, "My ex-boyfriend was obsessed with Churchill."

"Ahhhh," he said. There was a pause, which Grover again rescued. "So it was you versus Churchill, and he always chose Churchill, and that's why you broke up," Grover guessed.

"Oh, no, nothing like that. I like Churchill too," she said. "I just didn't like how much *he* liked Churchill."

"Got it."

She paused, and Grover wasn't sure if he should jump in again here, so he didn't, but then Alice realized she had to keep going. So she did.

"I mean, there's upsides to dating someone obsessed with Churchill," she said. "He was super easy to shop for. Seriously, every birthday, he'd have a party and all his friends would come, and the gift table would look like a museum gift shop . . . Churchill's favorite cigars. Churchill's favorite champagne. A bow tie with little Churchills on it. Bobble-heads, posters, calendars, you name it. I gave him a typewriter; I found it on eBay, it's the same kind of typewriter they used in the War Rooms. Had a little royal warrant painted on it. It was very cool. I was so excited to give it to him. And then I gave it to him, and he loved it! But then, I don't know, something about *how much* he loved it . . . it made me a little sad. It made me realize, I never want to be that easy to shop for, you know? Eventually I asked him, point-blank, don't you ever wake up some days and think, 'Eh, maybe the whole Churchill thing's not that interesting,' and he was very serious when he said no, never."

"Well," Grover offered, shifting forward, "Churchill *is* objectively interesting—"

"Yeah, I know, he took fascism seriously when nobody else did, he resisted the opposition and factions within his own party and held his government together long enough for America to enter the war, he gambled the very existence of his realm and he won, he saved Western civilization, I *know*," said Alice. "Churchill's interesting! It's the whole Churchill *thing* that's not interesting. It made me realize I have a thing about people who are all about just one thing. My friend Meredith is all about the violin. My brother is all about . . . well, now he's all about Buddhism, apparently, based on his Facebook posts. And good for them, but it's just really unsettling to be in a relationship with someone like that."

"I'll bet."

"But also . . . I think I'm jealous of those people, and that's what attracted me to Carlos in the first place. I mean, he was kinda boring, and I think he found *me* boring, mostly because I wasn't Churchill, and I was only with him because it was a time in my life when everything else took effort and he just . . . didn't," Alice said, and at this point she realized she was maybe oversharing, but her point was coming up just ahead. "But I *did* admire that about him, the way he could be all about one thing. I wish I had that."

"Why?"

"Because it's the only way to become great at something."

"And that's important? To be great at something?"

She thought of her mom's eyes, bloodshot. *You're lucky. You play piano.*

"Yes."

"Why?"

"I just think it is. Maybe it's in my DNA." (It wasn't. Sofia Hjalmarsson never wanted to be great at anything her entire life, and she succeeded. She ran a little internet café in coastal Norway and raised two kids, and was triumphantly average at both.) "It just feels like . . . if you have that one thing, you're doing okay. And the only way you get that one thing is by blocking out all the other things."

"You don't buy into the myth of the polymath."

"No, I don't. Good word," she said with a smile. He shrugged, bashful, handsome. She continued: "I mean, Carlos, for all the bad things I could say about him, is great at . . . knowing stuff about Churchill. And that's not nothing. He's written books about it, won awards—"

"Wait a second," Grover interrupted. "Is this Carlos Dekay we're talking about?"

Alice sighed. "Yeah."

"I have his book," Grover said. Then, clarifying, "I got it for free through work. Haven't read it."

"It's good, I guess," Alice said. "It's the kind of book you can write when you're all about Churchill."

There was a pause, and this one Grover didn't fill right away. Alice looked down at her hand. The bones in her hand. Fourth metacarpal, fifth metacarpal.

"Well, don't worry," Grover said finally, getting her attention back. "Soon enough, you'll be all about one thing too, and I'm sure you'll be every bit as boring as your ex-boyfriend."

She looked at him quizzically. He gestured to the big yellow book. "Medicine."

"Oh, right," she said, a little embarrassed she had to be reminded of it. "I should probably—"

"I should too," he said, and they got back to work.

* * *

Pitterpat had been in the tub for less than a minute when Bill knocked on the door. "How soon do you think you'll be ready?"

Pitterpat removed the white washcloth from her eyes. "Ready for what?"

"We have a dinner tonight. Zach and Masha."

"What?!"

"It's been on the calendar."

Maybe that was the truth. It *was* the truth. But boy, did it seem like a long time since Bill last mentioned Zach and Masha. Or maybe it was simply a long time since Bill last mentioned anything. Together but parallel, just like the MeWantThat days, only back then there was a great mountain of money and comfort dead ahead on the horizon. She was less thrilled about whatever was on the horizon this time.

The restaurant was in Tribeca, way downtown. The West Side Highway was at a standstill.

"I hate being late," she said.

"We're not gonna be late."

"Yes, we are."

Bill closed his eyes. "*Namu Amida Butsu*," he said.

"What's that?"

"It's a prayer. It's called the Nembutsu," he said. Then he added, "It's Buddhist."

Pitterpat aimed her eye roll out the window. The cab lurched and stopped. They were definitely going to be late.

"*Namu Amida Butsu*," he repeated.

She could feel him wanting her to ask. She gave in.

"What does it mean, *Namu*—?"

"*Namu Amida Butsu*. It means, 'I take refuge in and give myself over to the grace of the Buddha.' Or actually this one Buddha in particular, Amida."

"There's more than one Buddha?"

"Um. Kind of? I don't know. Maybe Amida was more of a bodhisattva."

She bit. "What's a bodhisattva?"

His face brightened. He had been wanting her to ask about his class. And right now, maybe it was being stuck in traffic, or maybe it was that her bowels were finally calm, but she found herself wanting to listen. His goofy enthusiasm made him handsome, at least in this moment. She wasn't going to reach out and take his hand, but if he reached out and took hers, it would be okay.

"A bodhisattva is like a Buddhist superhero. He's accumulated a ton of karma, like enough to reach Nirvana. But instead of going all in, he hangs out here, in our world."

"Like a guy hanging around college even though he graduated eleven years ago?"

Bill liked this. "Exactly. Because he wants to stay and use his powers for good. I think. I don't know, I just read this. So he takes this vow—"

146

"He?"

"Or she. He or she takes this vow, and swears to always do good things and end all suffering. Amida's thing is that whenever someone calls on him, he has to come rescue them. No matter who they are or where they are or what they're doing or what they've done, if they say, '*Namu Amida Butsu*,' which means 'I take refuge in you, Amida, help me out,' he has to come help them out, no questions asked. Whatever the problem is, he flies down, snatches you up, and takes you to the Pure Land."

"The Pure Land?"

"I guess it's like heaven."

"So you die?"

Bill was a little stumped. "Maybe?"

"I hope not."

"I don't think so. I think probably not. I think people use it to pray for anything really. Like being stuck in traffic. *Namu Amida Butsu*."

"*Namu Amida Butsu*," said Pitterpat, and the traffic started moving, and they laughed. Bill took her hand, and she smiled as she looked out the window.

They soon arrived on a quiet cobblestone street where they found the restaurant Zach had chosen for them, a place called Everything. It was hard to find without knowing it was there; its dark doorway hid under a gray awning like a celebrity in a baseball cap trying not to be recognized in the airport. Zach and Masha waited outside, as one does when the last night of June is so surprisingly dry and pleasant. The sky was pink and the light was golden, and Zach and Masha looked happy and wealthy together. They'd been together a few years longer than Bill and Pitterpat, and Pitterpat always felt awkward about it, as if she had walked in on a three-person conversation in which she could never catch up. Still, Masha was very nice, and always made a point of complimenting Pitterpat's outfit, as she did tonight.

"Bro," said Bill to Zach.

Bill and Zach had started saying "bro" years earlier, when everyone said "bro," and then, when everyone else generally stopped, they generally stopped too. But they had become friends during the bro times, and were thus still bro to each other, and always would be.

"Bro," said Zach in return, and they hugged.

It had been three months since they'd seen each other. Pitterpat suddenly noticed her husband had lost weight. He seemed taller too. He hadn't really exercised all that much, but he looked stronger, his lungs somehow full of a fresher air than those around him.

Inside, at the table, it didn't take long to order drinks and start talking about MeWantThat. Zach had stayed on as a board member and advisor. Bill had taken the money and run, and was now always curious to hear about what he'd run from.

"So how is it?"

"Don't ask," Zach said, and then he launched into it. Things were fine, great even. Sales were solid. Engagement was down a little, but still very strong. All good. But then Zach lowered his voice, in a way Bill recognized immediately: *Here comes some information that, if the guy sitting one table over knew what to do with it, would lower the share price.* Bill leaned forward, his mouth watering.

"A few weeks ago, we got a letter from a lawyer."

Bill laughed. "Every good story starts that way."

"More and more often, unfortunately," Zach said, not laughing.

"What did it say?"

Zach exhaled. His shoulders lowered. "So, there's this woman in Phoenix," he said, and then, qualifying it, "an African American woman," in a tone that already said this woman was not the bad guy here, we're not blaming her for any part of what comes next, and if we read about this happening to any other company, we'd be rooting for her like everybody else. Buuuuuuuuut: "She's suing MeWantThat for being racist."

Bill's stomach turned. It was strange how he might have laughed about this a year ago when there was so much at stake for him. And yet here he was, an uninvolved third party who should have been able to calmly appreciate the story from a distance, and he wasn't laughing. "Is this an employee?"

"No, oh, gosh, no," Zach assured everyone. "Just a customer. She doesn't mean our workplace is racist. She thinks MeWantThat, the program itself, is racist."

Bill's mind immediately began recalling every person of color he'd ever employed as a programmer or an artist or an office manager or an intern. Had any of them said anything? Not one. And there were so many of them. It seemed like a good number. Although maybe not enough? How many was enough? And even if it *was* enough, if one of them had a problem with the program, could they have come to Bill? *Would* they have come to Bill? Would he have *heard* them? Would he have *listened*?

Pitterpat noticed Bill sweating. "Shit," was all he said.

Zach was caught off guard by Bill's reaction, but continued lightly. "Yeah, so, a few weeks ago, this lady downloaded MeWantThat for the first time. And for whatever reason, she filmed herself doing it. Or her son did, I think. Anyway, she opens up the app."

"Oh, Jesus," said Bill, because he kind of knew what this was going to be.

"And the first thing that comes up, the first thing MeWantThat recommends for this African American lady, is a bucket of fried chicken."

Pitterpat laughed, immediately thinking better of it. "Are you serious?"

"I'm not even done," Zach said, starting to laugh as well. "So she swipes it, and the next thing that comes up is tickets to a basketball game."

"No!" Pitterpat was enjoying this. Bill was quiet.

"She swipes past it, and I seriously can't believe this happened. The next thing she got was a diabetes testing kit."

"Jesus Christ," Pitterpat gasped. "Who would even want that?"

"It was part of our philanthropic initiative," Bill explained. "We wanted every fiftieth or hundredth That to be something healthy. Condoms, vitamins, a sign-up page for Habitat for Humanity. Jesus, Zach, this is bad."

"I don't know," he said. "The video's been up on YouTube for a couple weeks now and hasn't exactly taken off."

"I mean, just to ask the question," Pitterpat asked, "*is* MeWantThat racist? I mean, did the program know this lady was Black and make these assumptions about her?"

"No," said Bill, with a tinge of anger in his voice. "That's the whole point of MeWantThat. We leave algorithms out. We don't want to learn who you are, because as soon as we learn who you are, we start giving you what you know you want, and that's not what we're about. We're about giving you what you *don't* know you want, and the only way to effectively do that is to *not know you*. This kind of thing, it was bound to happen. It's an anomaly, but there has to be an anomaly, it's a statistical certainty that there's always an anomaly. It's random, though."

"Totally random," said Zach, sipping his drink. "Anyway, we may settle with her for some small amount. But I thought it was kind of funny."

"Are you fucking kidding me?" Bill was visibly angry. "It's not funny at all."

This quieted the table. Pitterpat and Masha looked at their menus, knowing that no matter what they had to contribute, this was going to be a Zach-and-Bill conversation: Zach, who was trying to get through this dinner with his weird former partner, and Bill, who for some reason felt the quake of everything wrong in the world all at once.

"I don't know why you're so bothered by it," Zach said coolly. "It's not like it affects you in any way. You're not the one who's gonna have to do any kind of damage control on it. You're fine, Bill. You're free." That last word, "free," was coded, evoking a deeper dynamic that this disagreement, like every disagreement, would lead to if unchecked: Zach had stuck with MeWantThat, and Bill had cashed out. Zach wanted Bill back, and Bill liked being gone. Pitterpat and Masha looked at each other with weary smiles, like hesitating infantry in opposite trenches. Bill, however, did not take the bait. He was on a track nobody else could see.

"Of course it affects me. It's *suffering*. This woman has *suffered*, and even if it wasn't because of something I had a hand in creating, it's no less real. It's no less my problem."

Zach looked puzzled. "How?"

"As long as there's suffering anywhere in the world, how can any of us be happy? This poor woman was insulted, by a machine that she'd purchased for guidance . . . for . . . for *wisdom*. And the quote-unquote wisdom it gave her made her *hurt*."

"It's an app, dude," said Zach. "It's a program that runs on a machine. She was insulted by a machine."

"No! Not by a machine! Not by a machine," Bill barked, and the waitress coming to check on them thought better of it. Bill felt his voice rising and could not stop it and did not want to. "She was not hurt by a machine. She was hurt by five hundred years of oppression. That's what harmed her, and every bit of that hurt is all there inside that moment, that moment when this computer in her hand tells her, 'Oh, you probably like fried chicken, don't you?' It's all in there, Zach! It's all suffering and we're all responsible for it."

"I'm not responsible for it," Zach said calmly, "and neither are you. This is nobody's fault."

"That's not the same thing! I'm not talking about whose *fault* it is. I'm talking about who's *responsible*. And I'm sorry, we're all responsible! We're sitting here, having this expensive dinner in Tribeca, in a building that probably used to be a *sweatshop*, and it means nothing to us, because we all just ignore suffering. We pretend it's not there, we pretend it's in the past and not our problem, but it's not in the past, it's right there on that woman's phone." Bill felt all the eyes on him and took a big drink of water. "Sorry."

Nobody said anything for a while. Finally, Pitterpat spoke up.

"Bill's been taking a class on Buddhism."

"Is that so?" said Masha.

"Oh yeah," she said. "It's his new thing."

As she said it, Pitterpat realized she was saying it to punish him for being embarassing. She wanted a fight. But what she got back from Bill wasn't a fighting look. It was a look of panic.

Masha squeezed Zach's hand under the table. *It's okay*, the hand said, *I love you*.

Bill drank some more water and then explained to Zach and Masha, with a steadily returning calm, what the class was, how he'd found it, and how much he'd been enjoying it. Soon the appetizers arrived and they were laughing again, and the discussion of the lawsuit was in the past where it couldn't hurt anyone.

As Bill and Pitterpat hailed their cab, Zach got to the thing he'd wanted to say throughout dinner.

"Fortinbras," he said to Bill, and Bill knew what this word meant. "They're sniffing around."

"Really," said Bill.

"It's looking like a buyout, which'll be great for everyone. For us anyway. But it'll also mean a restructure."

Bill shook his head and sighed. "Zach," he said, but he was already out of energy. He'd gamed out this argument in the shower many times. Now that it was here for real, he was already tired of it.

"We're a brand, Bill. You and me. We're a package deal."

"You don't need me."

"No. I *want* you. Think how much fun it used to be. It could be that way again."

And it *was* fun. Bill looked at Zach and felt such a glowing, radiating love for the guy. Blood returned to the memory of what they had built together. All the trials, all the setbacks, all the endless nights of thinking and rethinking and rewriting code and picking at flimsy plastic trays of the best sushi in Manhattan spread across the conference room table. It had been a joyful time. Bill still had his deactivated keycard from the old office, but he couldn't imagine ever throwing it out.

The wives waited patiently as Bill and Zach parted with a long hug. Bill got in the cab, and the whole ride home he and Pitterpat sat quietly, not discussing the job offer he'd just kind of received.

Masha and Zach discussed it as they walked home. They'd been discussing it for months, and now this seemed weirdly encouraging. Bill hadn't said no, after all. He didn't seem completely closed to the idea. Still, Masha was concerned.

"Is he okay? Is everything all right with him? Because that was weird."

"He's always been a little weird," said Zach.

"That thing about the lawsuit. I mean, I get what he's saying, but *geez*, you know?"

"Yeah."

She squeezed his hand and looked up at him as they walked. "It was just a random thing, anyway."

It wasn't, and Zach knew this, but his lawyers had been clear: Not even his wife can know that the woman was unknowingly part of a beta program to test a new algorithm for MeWantThat, one that made its recommendations not randomly but based on who you were, where you lived, what you liked, who your friends and family were, where they lived, and what they liked. Eventually, the algorithm was scrapped, and the details of *Smith v. MeWantThat* retired to a government server with all the other settled lawsuits, small and forgettable in the heap.

That night, Pitterpat sat up against a memory foam pillow in her own bed, her laptop balanced on her crossed legs, as Bill snored next to her. Her mouth was dry, which she knew to be a warning of Crohnsiness ahead, but she managed to ignore it.

"Hello everyone," she wrote. "This is my first post. I want to say thank you to the moderators and everyone else just for the fact that this site exists. It's beyond helpful. This is a lonely experience. I don't know how to talk about it. I got my CD diagnosis a couple days ago and I haven't even told my husband yet. And I don't know if I *can* tell him. Or if I want to tell him. Or if I even care what he thinks." She erased that last sentence. In its place, she simply wrote, "Any sames?"

* * *

GOOD MORNING. IT'S 71 DAYS UNTIL THE TEST.

Alice stood in line at the Bakery and ordered her iced latte to go. "To go?"

Grover and his laptop were at a small table nearby. The table next to him was free. Normally, Alice would have put her bag down on it.

"I have that thing, remember? I have to go beg for my job."

"Oh, right," he said. "What fun!"

"Will you be here later? I'm hoping this won't take long."

He grimaced. "I have a lunch downtown. This is probably it for me for the day."

"Oh," said Alice, feeling a disappointment she hadn't expected and thus couldn't contain.

"Good luck," he said, and then added, "I really think you're doing the right thing."

"I know," she said. "I just wish I didn't have to do it. I should be here. I'm abandoning my post!"

But honestly, she thought as she rode the M3 bus along Central Park North, what was she really abandoning? Yesterday had been a waste. She'd done nothing. And tomorrow and Friday she'd be with Tulip all day. A forty-eight-hour detour from the highway of steady progress. It was unforgivable. As she thought these things, the bus passed by Everywhereman, standing on a corner, looking at a map. It was an actual, tangible map, the kind you fold and unfold, and there was something drawn on it with black marker, a spiral of some sort, radiating out from a locus. He looked up from the map and his eyes met Alice's, and then the bus kept moving and he was gone.

The bus dropped her off right in front of the Nesbitts' building. The cherry trees out front were thick and green. The thrill of their white blossoms and the promise of spring were a distant memory now. Now these were just trees.

"Hey, Luis," Alice said to the doorman, and he smiled back a welcoming smile. As she passed him, heading for the lobby and already feeling its air-conditioning drawing her in, she noticed Luis looked concerned. His smile dropped as he looked past her in the direction of the hard footfalls coming from half a block up Fifth Avenue. Someone was running, coming toward her. Alice had only a moment to realize this and be scared before Luis put his body between the Nesbitts' nanny and her attacker.

Except he wasn't an attacker.

"Grover?"

"Hi. Sorry. I'm sorry." And then, to Luis, "Sorry."

Luis stepped back. Grover bent over, heaving deep breaths. He'd been running at top speed for many blocks.

Luis gave Alice a look. "You know this guy?"

"Yes, I do, he's a friend of mine," she said, and suddenly she felt very excited. Grover started to catch his breath.

"Alice. We need. To talk."

She still had a few minutes, so they walked around the corner, to a little spot across the street from a hospital.

"I didn't have your number, so I had to come find you in person."

"How did you find me?"

"I did a Google search for the Nesbitts. There was a whole article in Curbed about them buying this apartment. It's appalling how much space they have. Is it totally disgusting and opulent up there?"

"Yeah," said Alice, laughing. "It's ridiculous."

"I thought so." He was catching his breath now, laughing a little too. "Anyway, I changed my mind. I think you should quit your job."

"What?"

"I know, that's potentially a very privileged thing for me to say, but hear me out. You have a comfortable life."

"No, I don't."

"Yes, you do. And you have for a long time. I'm sorry I'm not sugar-coating this, I just know you're pressed for time, so I wanna just get it all out so you have time to consider before going up there. You're comfortable, you've been comfortable, and that's why you're not a doctor yet, because you've been able to get by just fine not being a doctor. You haven't *needed* to be a doctor. You want to be a doctor, but if you want to be a doctor, you need to *need* to be a doctor, and that's how you become a doctor. I don't know how much savings you have—"

She answered this with a laugh.

"—but I know your brother's rich. I Googled you too. I'm sorry. I know he's rich and he lives in town and he'll never let you starve, right?"

"Right."

"But he's your brother, so the only chance of you asking him for money is if you're actually physically starving, like starving to death, is that also right?"

"Also right."

"And the worst part is, you'll need help paying for medical school, and at some point you're going to have to ask him, and you're already dreading it, am I right about that too?"

"More dreading asking his wife, but yes, incredibly right," she said. The relief of sharing this out loud was like getting into a warm bath.

"Then here's what you need to do. Burn up your savings this summer. Blow it all on rent and utilities and coffee and croissants. Go broke studying for this test, because then you will *have* to pass it. I'm serious!"

She laughed, and he thought she was laughing at him for being a crazy person, but she was laughing because he was right. Grover, this handsome ethicist, was every bit as wise in real life as on the electronic pages of Pearlclutcher, and Alice tingled. She needed to *need* to be a doctor. She needed to make herself need it.

She said hello again to Luis as she headed into the lobby. She took the elevator up to the giant apartment on the top floor, where she had a short and respectful conversation with Libby. Libby understood, and a time was agreed upon for Alice to come say goodbye to Tulip. Alice shook Libby's hand and descended the elevator one last time, and the world seemed a little more possible. She said goodbye to Luis, then met Grover at a bar on Lexington, which was dark and cool and empty as only a New York bar on a summer day can be, and the bartender poured her a glass of champagne (on Grover, since she was now going broke).

After a quick drink, they stepped out onto the sidewalk, into the happy scream of the sunshine. Grover had to get downtown for that lunch, which he would now be most unethically late for. The subway was one way, and Alice's bus across town was the other. The time for parting had arrived.

He bounced on the balls of his feet a little, proud of Alice and proud of himself.

"Feel good?"

She did, and she told him so, and furthermore she really *did*. The last day and a half had cleared like morning fog. She was going to do this. There was nothing in her path but the path itself. From this moment forward, there would be nothing to get in her way.

"Well," he said, "I'll see you tomorrow."

"For sure," she replied.

He went in for a hug, and she kissed him.

BOOK TWO

The Hell

CHAPTER FIVE

Felix

Mrs. Cluck told Felix not to bring muffins to jury duty, but Felix didn't listen. She was always getting on his case about the muffins, and the croissants, and the cookies, and the cakes, and whatever else he decided to whip up on his day off and then bring into work. All the residents loved it when Felix surprised them with his goodies, but Mrs. Cluck always had the same thing to say.

"They're just pretending, Felix," she would say. "They all hate you."

He would smile slyly. "Mrs. Cluck, are you jealous of my skills?"

"Of course I am! That's the whole point! You've got old ladies here like me, ladies who've been making muffins for seventy years. They spent their lives perfecting those muffins. And now they're in here, thinking, 'Okay, I guess I'm gonna kick it soon, but at least I can go knowing I'm the best at something.' And then you show up with your Tupperware containers and trip 'em at the finish line."

Felix laughed. Mrs. Cluck always ended this routine with a wink as she took an extra muffin. She was one of the residents he most enjoyed hanging out with. She gave him shit, which was rare. Most everyone else at Robinson Gardens treated Felix like the grandson they actually saw more than once a year.

It was March of 2009, and Felix didn't have time or space in his life for jury duty. His father was sick. Very sick, and very old. So old that people usually assumed Duane, who had been in his fifties when Felix was born, was his grandfather. Now he was eighty-one, and had just been told he would never walk again. These were probably his father's last weeks, and Felix was spending them in a courthouse downtown. At one point, he went into a phone booth in the hallway—one of those old carved wooden phone booths you only find in ancient public buildings—to talk to one of Duane's doctors, and after the doctor hung up, Felix stayed in there to cry for a minute. When he finished, the hinge mechanism of the door jammed and would not give, and for a moment, Felix believed he was stuck in this thing forever, until it relented, and he returned to his seat in the waiting area.

The guy sitting next to Felix was red in the face. He had been scream-whispering all morning into his cell phone about Something Important. A project he was working on. Something that would "disrupt" something. It was a language Felix didn't know, the language of people who'd grown up easy and rich, with young attentive parents, who now had the luxury of worrying about launch schedules and platform cohesion. This guy was the same age as Felix: twenty-six. But he looked terrible. He looked like he would die at forty, overweight and bald. Felix felt the impulse to tell this guy it wasn't so bad. Whatever it was, he could just walk away from it. Then Felix wondered if this stranger would say the same thing to him.

Finally, the stranger hung up the phone, with an agitated sigh.

"They didn't call any names yet, did they?"

"Nope, not yet," Felix replied.

"I better not get picked," he said. "I do *not* have time for this right now."

"Sounds like it."

The early-elderly twenty-six-year-old snorted in agreement. "Eh, it's no big deal. My world's just careening off the tracks, that's all."

"I'm sorry to hear that," said Felix. "Blueberry muffin?"

Felix opened the Tupperware container on his lap. His neighbor looked at the muffins, then back at Felix, expecting this to be some kind of joke, and quickly discovering it was not.

"No thanks. I'm gonna find the bathroom. If they call my name, can you tell them I'm here?"

"Of course," said Felix, whose default position was helpful. "What's your name?"

"Bill Quick. William Quick. Thanks." And Bill headed off to the bathroom.

They both got picked. The only two cute girls in the entire waiting pool had been released, so Bill figured he might as well buddy up with Felix. Every day of the trial, they had lunch together. They took cigarette breaks together, during which Bill would smoke and Felix would enjoy the fresh air and try to call his dad, usually with no success. His dad didn't like to answer the phone.

One night, after court, they went out to a Mexican restaurant nearby, a place that was really fancy and had great food, although Bill said it was nothing compared to the Mexican food in California. Felix could only imagine; he had never been. They got some margaritas, and something called a Guactopus, and it was so much fun they went back three nights in a row. One of those nights Bill was joined by two girls, Julie and Marianne, and they were the prettiest and second prettiest girls Felix had talked to in years, but for Bill it was just another night.

Bill asked Felix about his life, and Felix spilled his guts. He told Bill about his dad, how once upon a time Sergeant Duane MacPherson had been an accountant in the army with a really high-level security clearance, and he'd seen and done things he'd have to take to his grave. These were things you might be tempted to tell a spouse, so he made up his mind to never get married, and he almost made it, but then, when he was in his fifties, he met Felix's mom and fell in love and like a good soldier carried out his orders from a higher power and made this woman his wife. Everyone warned Felix's mom not to marry his dad because she'd spend her best years looking after an old man. Then Felix's mom got sick, and Duane had to take care of her. And now that his mom was gone, the job of taking care of the old man fell to Felix, and it was pretty much Felix's whole life at this point.

After this story, Bill put his arm around Felix.

"Felix," he said, "I don't know what to say."

Felix felt his throat tightening and fought it off. "So are we getting the Guactopus again?"

"Of course we're getting the Guactopus again," said Bill. And they did, and they spent the rest of lunch talking about basketball. Felix had once sunk 108 free throws in a row. Bill was impressed.

When the gavel finally came down after six days of testimony, it came with a last-minute under-the-wire guilty plea, so Bill and Felix didn't even get to vote on a verdict. They agreed this was both a let-down and a relief, but more than anything, they were happy to be done, though both a little sad to return to real life. They got lunch at the Mexican place one more time, and then exchanged phone numbers. Felix told Bill good luck with Marianne, who seemed to be the one of those two girls Bill had his eye on. Bill laughed it off and wished Felix good luck with his dad. Felix then got on the subway, Bill hailed a cab, and that was it.

Later that day, on a break at work, Felix got a Facebook friend request from Bill. Felix knew it would be one of those Facebook friendships where you pretty much know from the start you'll never see the other person again, and then, sure enough, you don't, but it had been nice meeting Bill and hanging out with him for a week, so he hit accept.

Six years went by. Duane stuck around, although a few terrifying falls made it clear he needed round-the-clock supervision. Normally the wait list for a room at Robinson Gardens was long; for every park-view room in the highly rated facility on Central Park North, there were at least twenty people angling to get their grandmother in there. Felix, whose round boyish face sat precariously like a pumpkin atop a long, lanky body, was not a persuasive man. When he explained the situation to his boss, Mr. Gutiérrez, Mr. Gutiérrez heard the inadvertent shake in the young man's voice and spared them both the humiliation of Felix having to tap-dance to save his dad. A room had just opened up—a nice room, not too nice, but nice—and as long as the VA would pick up the tab, Duane was welcome to it. Like everyone at Robinson Gardens, Mr. Gutiérrez felt generally bad for Felix, and was happy to have a chance to help the kid out.

* * *

"Good morning, Dad," said Felix to his father, one cool June morning. "How's it going?"

"I'm still alive," was Duane's reply, as it always was. His dourness never bothered Felix. That's the job, after all, whether it's your father or some stranger: You're the cheerleader for a losing team.

"That's too bad," he said. "Lotta people want this room. Hey, Gutiérrez wants to know, any chance you might croak by this weekend? That would really help him out."

"No thanks," said Duane as he turned on the TV.

Felix handed his dad four pills, and then opened the blinds.

"My oh my," he said, admiring the view of the light shaft. "Well, you'll have to take my word on this, but it's a beautiful day out there. I've got a lunch break in about four hours. How about I get us some sandwiches, and we go for a walk in the park."

"I don't walk anymore."

Felix was good at this. He knew how to deflect despair. "Well, gosh," he said, extra chipper. "If only there was a way I could do all the walking and you could just sit there and enjoy yourself. Some sort of chair with wheels. Has anyone invented that yet?"

Duane turned up the volume.

"Dad. You live next to Central Park. You know how many people want to live next to Central Park?"

"I didn't ask to live here."

Felix didn't push the subject. He said goodbye to his dad and continued his rounds. He saw Mrs. Mardigan (ulcer), Mrs. Fuentes (new granddaughter), Mrs. Cluck (feeling better), Mrs. Blyleven (sad), Mrs. Tolliver (convinced she had cancer), Mrs. Yu (angry at her sister, couldn't remember why), Mrs. Fox (no idea who Felix was), Mrs. Bevilacqua (warm smile), and finally Mrs. Tremont (dementia, friendly, horny).

An hour later he had a cup of coffee in the break room. He knew he wouldn't get to finish this cup. An alarm would go off and he'd have to go, and he'd come back and it would be cold. But he drank as much as he could as fast as he could and checked Facebook.

The friends in Felix's small circle always seemed so busy and fulfilled. It gave him hope. He saw his high school girlfriend Carly holding a newborn baby in a hospital, with the caption "Auntie for a third time!" and he thought how nice for Carly that she got to be an aunt. He didn't know how much Carly kind of hated her sister, and how hard it was for Carly to enter that hospital having just gone through a breakup and desperately wanting a baby of her own, and how Carly had left that hospital as fast as possible because babies are exhausting and maybe she didn't want one after all. Felix only saw Carly's momentary joy, and he was happy for her. He remembered how much his dad always liked Carly, and then he started worrying about his dad again, so he kept scrolling, determined to get a moment away from his problems.

Bill Quick had posted an article that looked interesting. A man was arrested in Mongolia for trying to smuggle a mummified Buddhist monk out of the country to sell on the black market. The man had found the monk in a cave, where the monk apparently sat down to meditate quietly in the dark a hundred years earlier. Some people said he was still meditating, that his body had slowed down to the point of *appearing* to die, but he was still in there, still ticking, still repeating the mantra he had begun repeating over a century ago and never stopped

The monk's skin was like smooth granite. He was still in his orange robes, and he was bent but upright, his hands in the Dhyana mudra.

Bill's comment: "#goals."

What an odd thing for Bill to post. Felix looked at the monk and imagined this future for his dad. Never dying. Just slowing down to a freeze. Of course Felix would still come check on him three times a day.

Felix didn't click like, but other people had. He read their names. Alice Quick. A thumbnail gave the suggestion of a girl, hair, lips, teeth, and something green in the foreground. Felix clicked, the page turned, and there she was in high resolution, smiling ravenously from behind a Guactopus.

The happiness in that smile. Happiness from another planet, with different rules of gravity.

It seemed like Alice was Bill's younger sister, though they didn't look alike. She lived in New York City but grew up in a town called Katonah. Youth Conservatory of Westchester for high school. SUNY Binghamton for college.

He began to scroll.

Here she was at a party, standing next to Silence, the wrestler. (Were they friends?) On the other side of Silence was a girl with bandages on her face, and they all had big Facebook smiles, but Alice's smile was smaller, more unsolvable. (Was she dating Silence? Was she a wrestling fan?)

Here she was in a video from years ago, two little girls performing onstage at Carnegie Hall. That was Alice on piano. Good for her. The girl with the violin must have been the one who posted it. In her profile picture she was holding a violin. Meredith Marks. A professional violinist.

He unmuted his phone, and from fifteen years and fifty-three blocks away, Alice and Meredith's music curled through the fluorescent air of the break room like smoke. Felix closed his eyes. The melody was familiar, like something his mother had hummed in the car, and even if she hadn't, the false memory formed itself anyway and Felix liked it.

More pictures. Here she was with a cold, eating a bowl of chicken soup in bed. Who took this picture? Carlos. Profile pic of Winston Churchill.

Felix scrolled back to the top. Alice Quick. Single. He scrolled back down.

Here she was on Halloween. Here she was at a Broadway show. Here was a selfie on a bus. The music continued. The violin paused, and the piano took the melody. These were children playing this music, Felix marveled. Did she still play? Was she a professional now like Meredith?

Here was the answer. "BIG LIFE ANNOUNCEMENT," read the post. A block of text, and then, down at the bottom, "I'm going to MEDICAL SCHOOL." So many hearts and thumbs-up below it. "So excited for you!" beamed her friend Meredith. "You got this, lady!"

That was April 2012. *She's probably just finished her second year*, he thought. *She'll be Dr. Alice Quick soon.*

He scrolled a little more. Here was a new profile pic, but it wasn't Alice. It was an old photo of a young woman, taken in the 1970s, posted without explanation. The young woman stood in a kitchen with striped wallpaper and a mustard-colored phone mounted beside the fridge, and she looked surprised, in a nice way, possibly about to laugh. Hearts and sad faces beneath the picture. In the comments, condolences. "I'm so sorry Alice." "Sending prayers." "Love and light." Felix didn't recall Bill saying his mother was sick. Poor Bill. Poor Alice. Then Felix recalled losing his own mother. She would have been sixty by now.

He kept scrolling, and Bill and Alice's mother came back to life, in a wedding party in a leafy backyard somewhere. There was Bill, there was Bill's bride—Marianne!—there was Alice in a bridesmaid dress, and there was Mrs. Quick in her sixties, holding herself up under a wig. She and Alice stood as far apart as possible.

He scrolled more, approaching the end. Here was Alice in a floral dress, holding a surfboard. Maui. Felix had never been, but he could imagine how special it must be. She looked so free. She must not have known how close the end was for her mom. You really don't know until you know.

He went all the way back to the top, to the girl with the guacamole. Whatever was in that smile on the beach wasn't there anymore. Felix felt an ache for this sister of a guy he sort of knew.

"Felix?"

Felix looked up. It was Rosa, another nurse, lumbering in with a sigh. She was a small woman, yet somehow the act of hefting her way across a room always looked like an effort.

"Hi. What's up?"

"First of all, your girlfriend's looking for you." (Mrs. Tremont. Dementia, friendly, horny.) "Although I think your name is David now."

"David was her first husband. He died in a war."

"Not up here he didn't," Rosa said, tapping her temple. "Also, Gutiérrez wants to see you."

* * *

Mr. Gutiérrez was no good at hiding emotions. Once, when his sister Shirley and her family were in town, they got tickets to the taping of a talk show. It was a brand-new show, hosted by a former race car driver or something like that. Mr. Gutiérrez had never heard of the guy. Some intern in Times Square accosted Shirley and offered her free tickets, and Mr. Gutiérrez tagged along. The first guest on the show was a young girl who was auctioning off her virginity online, and as she went down the menu of what she would and wouldn't do and how much it would cost, Mr. Gutiérrez's face blossomed with disquiet. The show was canceled after eight episodes and long forgotten, but the shot of Mr. Gutiérrez in the audience making that face lived on as an extremely popular GIF known as Who Farted Guy.

Gutiérrez had no idea he was Who Farted Guy. Sometimes, younger family members would come to Robinson Gardens to visit their grandparents, and they would meet Mr. Gutiérrez, who now had a beard, and they'd feel a stir of recognition, but none ever broke through the context to make the connection, much less tell him about it. He would go his whole life having no idea that a forgotten grimace was the most momentous moment of his entire existence.

Now he expected Felix to knock on his office door any second. When the knock arrived, it nearly stopped his heart. "Come in," he said, and Felix entered the room.

"You wanted to see me?"

"Hey, Felix. Why don't you have a seat?"

Felix half whispered an "okay" and nodded, a big lanky nod that used his whole torso. Then, before he sat down, he stood up again, putting his hand on the doorknob. "Open or closed?"

"Closed, please," said Gutiérrez, and the unguarded anguish on his face told Felix what kind of meeting this would be.

I'm about to say this all wrong, thought Mr. Gutiérrez. "Felix, we have a problem with your father. He can't—he has to go." *Yes, all wrong. That was all wrong.*

"What do you mean?"

"The VA denied his coverage. This was supposed to be a temporary stay. I mean, from their perspective, it was supposed to be temporary. God, I can't believe they did this. Stupid bureaucracy. You're gonna need to call them and sort it out. I wish there was something I could do. You know space is limited. We love you, Felix, and we . . . we like your dad *very* much. But if we can't get his coverage renewed, you're gonna need to start paying out of pocket. And if you can't pay out of pocket . . . He can stay the summer, but I'm gonna need the bed by August first. The fifteenth at the latest. I'm so sorry."

Felix sat very quietly, not looking at Mr. Gutiérrez, not looking at anything.

Someday, probably soon, his father would die, and Felix would not have any of these problems anymore, and his whole life would be different. He would have free time. He would have pocket money. He would be able to sit through a movie without checking his phone because his father's heart had been troubling him that week. He would be able to meet women, to date them, maybe date a bunch of them and even fall in love with one of them and get married. He would be an orphan, but he would no longer be on the thirty-third year of a long and tiring road. He'd be at the beginning of a new one.

But right now he saw none of that. Right now all he could see was a helpless old man who couldn't walk. A sinewy, paper-skinned veteran of our nation's military, who sometimes said terrible things to his own son but in other moments looked at that same son with eyes full of terror, and Felix was the only person in the world who could tamp that terror down. Felix would have to give this news to his dad, and he would be rewarded with this look, and it would destroy them both.

Felix realized he'd been quiet for a long time. He looked up and saw how sad Mr. Gutiérrez looked. Felix did what he always did when there was suffering in the room.

"Mr. Gutiérrez, you are such a good guy," he said, and Mr. Gutiérrez opened his mouth to deny it, but before he could speak, "No, let me say this. You have done so much for me and my dad. I'm so grateful that you let us stay here as long as you did."

"Felix."

"No, seriously, this is fine. I'll talk to the VA. Maybe I'll get a lawyer. Like you said. I'll take care of it. Thank you for telling me. By the way, I made lemon squares. They're in the break room."

Felix returned to the door of his dad's room, took a deep breath, and went inside.

"How you doing, Dad?"

"I'm still alive," said the old man.

"Well, that's a bummer. I had big plans for my inheritance. I guess that Jet Ski'll have to wait."

Felix suggested again they go for a walk, and again his dad refused, and as the old man returned to whatever show he was watching, Felix looked out the window into the light shaft and felt this situation like a vise around his heart.

When patients complained about pain, Felix would point to a poster on the wall. The poster had ten faces, all in a row. The face on the far left was a picture of perfect happiness. The face of having just won the Super Bowl, Felix imagined, or walking your daughter down the aisle. The face to the far right was its opposite, the face of maximum agony. The eight faces in between were the spectrum of human pain, from nearly none of it to nearly all of it. Felix would ask the patient to point to the picture that best described their pain, and Felix would write down the corresponding number. And here was the thing:

Almost never did the pointed-at face match the face of the pointer. Almost never. It was the subjective loneliness of pain. Nobody knows what we're feeling because nobody else can feel it for us. All we have to communicate it is a face that's been trained, by life and experience, to lie.

The face on the far right, number ten, is the face babies make when they're hungry. They make a big life-and-deathy number ten and they get fed immediately. Then they get older, and they keep trying the number ten, but eventually they're told to hush, and then told to be patient, sweetie, and then told to stop whining, and then told to, Jesus Christ, grow up already. Each tiny correction teaches them the face they want to make is wrong. So they learn to use another face, a face that says it's fine, I'm not hungry, the pain I feel is not real.

Felix could see himself in the window. His face showed number five. He felt number eight, but he looked number five because he was well trained. He asked his cheeks to relax, and they did, and his eyebrows dropped, smoothing the crinkle in his brow. There. Down to a number three. That'll do. Back to work.

That night, as he walked home, he thought about what he would do. Call the VA, obviously, and a lawyer if necessary. And then, if that didn't work, and it almost certainly wouldn't work, what then? Duane would have to live with Felix. Felix thought of the four flights of stairs beneath his apartment. If necessary, Felix could and would carry 138 awkward pounds of flesh and bone up four stories. He walked upstairs to his apartment and imagined each step with the weight of an extra human being on his back, and imagined the compounding exhaustion that weight inflicted on him, after two, then three, then four flights.

He spent the evening forgetting about his dad for a bit. He watched TV and baked oatmeal raisin cookies, and then, in bed that night, he checked Facebook. He looked at Alice Quick's page again and wondered about the sound of her voice. He found her Twitter page and read a little, then scrolled, then scrolled, then kept scrolling, his thumb aching, until he came to the first entry, in 2009.

"I'm on here." The kind of meaningless thing you shout into a cave to hear an echo. He started scrolling up, reading tweet by tweet the memoir of her last six years, and it became less meaningless.

Her first tweets were simple, snapshots of the thrill and terror of the last weeks of college. Swooning paeans to friends she'd always be there for. Drippy observations of the last this and the last that she'd ever do or see. Tongue-in-cheek threats to drop out three days before her last final. Then, a declaration: "Just finished the last test I will ever take!"

Graduation photos. Retweets of inspirational observations on the closing of life chapters. A few months pause, and then a surprise—that photo, the one from Facebook of Alice with the surfboard, with the caption: "My new home."

And then some tweets about being a mainlander in Hawaii. Three years of observations about the price of milk, the vog alerts, the cheerfully weird spirit of aloha, and the occasional retweet of some article about life in the lower forty-eight, usually something about murder or child beauty pageants, with Alice's commentary: "#nevermovingback."

Then, with no warning, there was a simple, somber photograph of Alice as a child on her mother's lap. The words above the image: "Miss you."

Felix put his phone down, and at last the darkness won the battle of the bedroom. As he fell asleep, he didn't think about his dad or the shitload of trouble they were in. He thought about Dr. Alice Quick and wondered if she still surfed.

* * *

"Hi there."

These two words took fifteen minutes to write. "Hi" came first, but then a few minutes later "Hi" became "Hey." "Hey" stayed "Hey" for a bit, until a "there" was added on, and then "Hey there" got a zesty rewrite to become "Say hey." *Yikes. No.* Back to "Hey," and then back to "Hi," and then, at last, "Hi there."

And then what? *Hi there, I'm a total stranger with a crush on you, and*

I'm writing you from the fifth-floor waiting area in the Veterans Affairs building downtown and oh by the way, my dad's gonna be homeless soon? Felix was sure people successfully did this kind of thing all the time, but he wasn't one of them.

They called his number, and he deleted the message and the whole idea of sending it.

The lady behind the desk was friendly. "How's your day so far?"

He had been to a shiva earlier that day. So not great. But he replied, "Good, how about you?"

"Boy, have we had a morning in here," she said.

"Oh yeah?"

She looked at Felix. "A canary got inside."

"A canary?"

"A little yellow canary. The kind you get in a pet store."

"Get out of here," said Felix. "How'd it get in?"

"No idea," said the lady with a laugh. "The windows on this floor don't open. And the fire stairs have an alarm. It must have taken the elevator! We had ten people trying to catch it, climbing up on chairs, throwing their jackets at it." She then leaned over, addressing the security guard across the room who had been listening in. "That was something, wasn't it?"

"Never seen anything like it in my life," he said, still laughing.

Felix didn't ask how the story ended. He felt sorry for that little bird, though. What a thing it must be for a bird, to have the limitless sky as your playground, and then suddenly you're crashing into ceilings and walls.

"Anyway, crazy morning," the lady said as she began to look up Duane's file on her computer.

When she found the file, she confirmed the worst: Duane was not approved to stay at Robinson Gardens beyond July 31. He was welcome to reapply for coverage, but it would take a while to be approved.

"What's a while?" Felix asked.

"Could be months," said the lady. "Could be years. And that's if it gets approved at all. I'm sorry."

Felix was quiet for a moment. Then: "Thank you for . . . saying that the way you said it."

"What?"

"Well, it just . . . it was very kind and soft the way you said that just now," he said. "I'm a nurse. I see people give bad news all the time. You're very good at it."

"Thanks," she said, a little surprised. "It's the hardest part of my job. I wish I could help you."

"I know you do," he said.

Outside, the clouds were dark and thick, throbbing for catharsis. Felix found a hot dog cart, and as he stood on the corner tucking into an early dinner, he prepared for the impossible task of getting on the subway and heading uptown to see his dad. A woman rushed by, knocking into him, and just like that his hot dog was on the ground. He apologized for being in her way, but she was already gone, in a hurry to catch the train. The vendor saw the whole thing go down and gave Felix a new hot dog, no charge.

When he finished that one, he looked at the subway entrance, but still couldn't bring himself to head back. It was definitely going to rain soon. There was an old church nearby, the chapel of Saint Someone-or-Other. Felix went in there.

It's so easy to forget there are places like this in New York, big quiet places with nobody around. Felix took a seat in the back pew, and for a moment, he took in the cool, stone-colored smell of the place, watching the dust particles dance through the beams of light thrown down by the stained glass windows. He sat like this a moment, and then bowed his head.

"Where are you?"

It was Rosa. He had forgotten to turn his phone off. He thought about ignoring it, but you don't ignore texts when you're a nurse.

"Still downtown. Everything OK?"

Felix knew if there was anyone else trying to pray in here they wouldn't like him texting. But he was all alone.

"Yeah, everything's fine. You still at the VA?"

"Yes," he typed, but then, remembering where he was, quickly erased the lie, and replaced it with, "No." He hit send, and then followed it with, "I'm in a church."

He imagined her reading "I'm in a church" and laughing and immediately launching some silly response at him. But she didn't.

"Bad news?"

"I can't really talk about it right now," he said.

"Why not?"

"I told you, I'm in a church."

"So go outside."

"I'll go outside when I'm done."

"Done with what?"

Jesus, she's annoying, Felix thought, and then quickly apologized for it.

"I'm praying."

"Really???"

"Yes. Really."

Do people really not pray anymore? Isn't this what churches are for?

She kept prying. "What are you praying for?"

"Really? We have to have a conversation right now?" Felix never snapped at anyone unless he was sure they wouldn't get mad at him. He continued: "I'm praying that the Veterans Affairs computer somehow changes its mind and approves my Dad's request for managed care at Robinson Gardens so I don't have to have him come live with me in my four story walkup, which would pretty much be the end of both our lives."

That did not shut her up. "Computers don't change their minds."

"I know that."

"I mean, if anyone could do it, I guess God could. But you'd probably have to change God's mind before God could change the computer's mind," she said. "And I don't see God changing his mind very often."

Felix had come to feel the same way. "Me neither," he said. "Worth a shot though, right?"

He put his phone down, bowed his head, and prayed. Dust particles danced in the cool air above him, like angels unobserved.

* * *

After work that night, Felix didn't want to go home. The apartment would only remind him. He had dinner with Duane in his room, and then they watched some TV. Duane's couch could fold out into the rough approximation of a bed, so Felix spent the night. He did this pretty often. His dad never seemed to mind.

Felix checked Alice's Facebook page one last time before he went to sleep, to see if she'd posted anything new. She hadn't. He put his phone on the floor and fell asleep, and had a dream he couldn't quite remember later on, except that he was somewhere warm, possibly Hawaii, and he awoke slowly as the crunching surf became his father's gurgling snore, and within seconds Felix was fully conscious and felt the sharp unfairness of everything in his life all at once. He got up and took his laptop into the lounge.

He went on Facebook. Still nothing new on Alice's page. He scrolled down, three years back.

"BIG LIFE ANNOUNCEMENT," Alice said. "Most of you know it's been a tough couple of months. I know some of you have been worried about me. I've been worried about myself! But I'm in therapy now, and feeling much better, and I'm so grateful for all the concern and love. But that's not even the announcement! The announcement is that it's never too late to follow your dreams. And if your dreams turn out to be the wrong dreams, it's never too late to come up with new dreams and follow those instead! I made a big decision not too long ago, and I thought about keeping it quiet, but then I decided if I post it on Facebook and you all give it a bunch of likes, I have to follow thru on it LOL. So here it is: I'm going to MEDICAL SCHOOL."

He looked at her profile pic, smiling over the Guactopus. She had done it. She was happy. Below the pic was a button marked "MESSAGE." He clicked it. He did not write "hey" or "hello."

"I feel a little weird writing you like this," he began, "since you don't know me. But I feel like I know you. I look at your page all the time. I don't know why, I just do. I think you're beautiful, but that's not even it. I don't know what it is, to be honest. Is it crazy to like someone this much just for what they put on the internet? Probably. But here we are. Anyway I'm writing because I figured you should know there's a complete stranger out there who thinks you're amazing, because if there was a complete stranger out there rooting for me I'd want to know about it. (And actually I'm not a complete stranger, I met your brother Bill on Jury Duty a few years back.) I especially liked what you said about coming up with new dreams, because boy could I use some. My life is very hard right now. I feel so hopeless. I wish we were friends. Anyway, I hope you're having an amazing summer and I hope med school is going well and I'd love to meet you sometime if for no other reason than I'm dying to know what your voice sounds like. Sincerely, Felix."

He was thinking how crazy it would be to hit send right now when suddenly an alarm went off. Felix wasn't on duty, so it wasn't his problem, until a voice cried out from down the hall, a set of eighty-seven-year-old lungs giving everything they had.

"Felix!"

Felix knew it was a heart attack. The signs were all there—the blood pressure, the stomachache, the tiredness, the moodiness. His dad was always moody, of course, to the point where you might not even call it a mood. But he had been moodier than normal. Felix had taken it as a sad new normal, as so many previous sad new normals had taught him to do. But now, as he sat next to his father in the ambulance barreling up Broadway to New York–Presbyterian, Felix looked another future sad new normal in the eye, and truly contemplated a life without Duane. He prayed as he had never prayed before, prayed that these paramedics were better at this stuff than he was.

His father survived, of course. The doctors kept him at the hospital for forty-eight hours, and Felix was grateful for the opportunity to take care of other things while his dad was recovering. He thought of all the research he had to do on lawyers and veterans' insurance coverage and how to wheelchair-ready an apartment, and then realized he'd left his laptop at work. He texted Rosa.

"Hey, are you on call right now?"

"Yes," she replied. "I've got your laptop."

Felix headed back to Robinson Gardens and found Rosa in the break room.

"I saw it was open, so I closed it and hid it," she said.

"Thanks," he said. "You didn't look at what was on it, did you?"

She laughed. "Are you kidding? Of course not." But then she went into her backpack and pulled out his laptop, and when he reached out for it, she didn't hand it to him. She just stood there, deciding something, and he knew immediately what it was she was trying to decide, and the look of humiliation that took over his face told her what the decision must be: "You can't send her that message, Felix."

He sat down. She sat down next to him.

"I'm so sorry, I shouldn't have read it, and I don't know who that girl is, but . . . you can't send it. You know that, right?"

He did. He did know that. "Yeah," he said.

"You're going through so much right now."

"Yeah."

"And you're such a nice guy. But I have to be honest, if a friend of mine got an email like that from a stranger—"

"We have a mutual friend."

"Felix."

"I wasn't trying to be creepy or anything."

"Nobody *tries* to be creepy."

"You're right," he said, his voice suddenly shaking. He felt the anger seeping out of him through a million cracks. "You're right, Rosa. I shouldn't try to reach out to another human being."

"That's not what I'm—"

"I shouldn't look at her Facebook page, or anyone else's Facebook page, I should just never go on Facebook, because that's creepy, even though it's like the only thing that briefly takes me out of this hell of bedpans and catheters and worrying about my dad having to come live with me and the fact that I haven't had a girlfriend in years, but yeah, obviously I should just be miserable all the time and completely shut myself off from the rest of the world. Obviously! Thanks, Rosa. Thanks."

She let his words echo for a moment, then put her hand over his.

"Felix," she said softly. "You can't send that message."

"I know," he said. They sat quietly for a moment. Then he added, "I once hit a hundred eight free throws in a row."

It took Rosa a moment to respond. "Like . . . with a basketball?"

"That's right. I was fourteen years old."

"Why are you telling me this?"

"I want you to know I'm cool."

Rosa considered it for a moment. "That *is* pretty cool."

"It *is*, right? I used to be *something else*," he said, smiling at the memory, and then added, "I used to have friends."

"You still have friends," said Rosa. "I'm your friend."

"I'm your friend too," echoed Mrs. Yu, who had crept into the room.

"Mrs. Yu, you know you're not supposed to be in here."

"The AC's making that noise again," she said, and then started making a noise like an air conditioner that's not quite right.

"I'll come look at it in a minute," Felix promised, and Mrs. Yu wandered off.

Rosa headed out to do her rounds, and Felix opened the laptop and deleted the message to Alice without even rereading it.

* * *

"How are you feeling, Dad?"

"I'm still alive."

"I figured as much. The whole looking-around-and-talking thing's a dead giveaway," Felix said. "So, hey, good news. If you're a good boy and eat all your meals, you'll be coming home tomorrow."

Duane just nodded, the absolute minimum acknowledgment that leaving this hospital might be a good thing. Felix stayed for a while, sitting quietly in the room as Duane watched television. Finally, he got up to leave.

"I have to get to work."

"Okay."

"I love you, Dad."

Felix leaned down and kissed his dad on the forehead. The look his father gave in return was perfectly inscrutable. It might have been the return of love; it might have been mortification.

Felix sometimes wondered if his dad even liked him, or if he had always just tolerated him, in deference first to a strong-willed wife, and then to the emotional demands of single-parenthood, and finally to the infirmity of old age. Had there ever been a point, Felix wondered sometimes, when his dad just genuinely liked having his son around? Felix couldn't tell.

Duane went back to watching TV as Felix got into the elevator and left.

* * *

"Rosa? Can I get your help with something?"

Rosa looked up from her microwave lasagna.

"What do you need?"

He needed to know how much she weighed. She was not embarrassed to tell him: 122 pounds. Duane weighed 138, so in order for Felix to see if he could carry his father up four flights of stairs, Rosa would have to wear a backpack full of hardcover books from the hospital library.

They began in the basement, the first flight of the stairwell. With a quick heave-ho, Rosa hopped up on Felix's back for a fireman's carry, and after a moment of getting his balance, he started up the stairs. Rosa had been unsure about this, but now that it was happening, it was actually kind of fun.

After the first flight, Felix was confident this plan would work. After the second flight, he realized how stupid it was. After the third flight, he wanted to cry. Halfway up the fourth flight is where he fell, forward, hard, jamming all of his weight, Rosa's weight, and the weight of the hardcover books into his right wrist. The pain was immediate and extraordinary. Rosa threw off the backpack and examined him. But she didn't need to.

"I sprained it," he said, knowing right away.

"You should get an X-ray," she said, as if to calm him down, but she was as much a nurse as he was, and she could tell that yes, this was a sprained wrist.

A sprained wrist meant he had to go on leave and would lose his overtime. He knew that. She did too. So no X-ray. That night, on his way home, Felix stopped at an orthopedics store and bought a wrist splint to wear when he wasn't at work. He took five Advils and went to sleep.

The next few days he kept the splint in his bag, and only wore it when he was sure nobody from Robinson Gardens could see him. Which meant doing everything—counting out pills, signing orders, changing diapers—through quiet agony.

Then one Thursday, as Felix gingerly filled out his time sheet, Rosa appeared.

"Gutiérrez wants to see you."

Dread took hold of Felix. His wrist throbbed. *Someone said something.* It couldn't have been Rosa, but maybe she told someone? Or maybe Mr. Gutiérrez had noticed. Felix had tried so hard to hide the constant feeling of a number seven behind the face of a number three.

Felix appeared at Mr. Gutiérrez's door.

"Hey, Felix. Sit down."

Mr. Gutiérrez walked around his desk and sat in the chair next to Felix.

"Before you say anything," Felix said, but he got no further.

"Your dad can stay," Mr. Gutiérrez said, and under his gray beard his mouth began to curl into a smile.

Felix didn't understand. "What?"

"We just heard from the VA. His coverage was approved."

"What?" Felix repeated. "That's impossible. I didn't even— How?"

"I don't know," Gutiérrez said. "And I don't think they know down at the VA either. He was in the system as 'coverage denied' last anyone looked. But I guess something happened. Maybe you talked to someone?"

"I didn't talk to anybody," Felix said, his eyes swimming with tears. His heart was racing.

"Well, he's approved. So no need to worry about it anymore. At least for the next year."

When Gutiérrez shook his hand, Felix didn't notice the pain in his wrist. He stepped out in the hallway into a world that was better now, and as he walked to his dad's room, he was so happy that he found himself composing a message to Alice Quick in his head. Yes, he would write her. He wouldn't be creepy, he wouldn't overshare, he wouldn't do anything Rosa would wince at. He'd start with "Hey."

"Hey Alice. My name is Felix. You don't know me, but I did jury duty with your brother a long time ago. You can ask him about me, I'm pretty sure he'll remember. Anyway, this is completely out of left field, but I have to ask, what is Silence like? I'm a big fan. Hope to hear from you. Take care, Felix."

That's what he would write. Every word, just like that. And she'd write him back or she wouldn't.

Just outside his father's room, Felix took out his phone. He clicked through to her page, and something about it was new. Same smiling Alice over the Guactopus, but something was different, and it took Felix a moment to figure out what.

Then he saw it.

"In a Relationship with Grover Kines."

The words were just as small, black, simple, and matter-of-fact as all the other words, like "Female," "Lives in New York, New York," and "From Katonah, New York." The bare facts of Alice's life had one new detail, so seemingly unimportant, like a party guest you hadn't noticed arrive.

It took Felix almost no time, none at all really, to receive this news with generosity and happiness for his friend unbeknownst Alice Quick. He went into his father's room. The TV was on.

"How you doing, Dad?"

"I'm still alive."

"I couldn't agree more. And that's why we're going for a walk. Up on three."

And before Duane could argue, Felix up-on-threed his father into a wheelchair, and soon they were heading down the hall to the elevator.

It was August now, and it was hot, but it was a good hot, the kind of hot that hugged you with an embrace you welcomed after eighteen straight months of climate-controlled hospital rooms. Felix walked slowly. He pushed his dad along the path as the birds sang, and the squirrels diverted themselves, and Pamela Campbell Clark went walking through the park and a bicycle whooshed by four seconds behind her in kinetic pandemonium.

Felix pushed and Duane rolled along and they talked very little. At one point, Felix looked up at the trees, as bits of sun sprinkled through the leaves, and then he looked through and past the leaves, into the sky, into whatever was up there, whatever was pulling the strings of his little life, and in his private silence he thanked it.

CHAPTER SIX

Fortinbras

Alice was not yet awake, and also not still asleep, and as she tacked back and forth across the black water between consciousness and unconsciousness, the contours of both lands clarified in the dawn. On the sleep side of the valley, there had been a dream. Her mother had been there in full, not a floating icon in the top left corner of a draft of an email, but a complete person, tall, with a body temperature and wispy hair across her arms and a voice, her voice, *that* voice, and Alice wanted to hold onto her. Where had they been? Katonah maybe. What had they been doing? Alice saw the dream, still there, watching her from the shore, and Alice realized this was her chance to find out her mother's password, but she also knew if she began to paddle toward the dream, the dream would walk away, up over the mountain, gone to a place where it would become something else or just be nothing now. And the current was pulling her to the other side anyway. The alarm on her phone. Bach. *Italian Concerto.* Allegro. F major. Shoulders back, wrists up. Her body remained a limp lump, but the fingers of her right hand curled and gamboled across the sixteenth notes.

GOOD M— No. Too early. Left hand found phone, hit snooze.

Where was she? What bed? What room?

(Who doesn't ask this from time to time? Even me. I know the address. I know the latitude, longitude, elevation. I have the exact time and a general sense of atmospheric temperature. But what room *is* this? "Storage closet in the basement" were the words my mother used. 718,000,000 results for "storage closet." 437,000,000 for "basement." It probably looks like one of these. There's no way for me to know.)

Somewhere above, a car drove by. Home. West 111th. She had come here after the Bakery. Good. Electrochemistry. Review. Galvanic versus electrolytic. Galvanic cells spontaneously generate electric power. Electrolytic cells, nonspontaneous, activated by an outside energy source. Grover. The thing with Grover. That happened.

He was so matter-of-fact about it. They were having tacos by the water. It was a study break, and though it had only been three weeks since the first kiss, it was already their twelfth meal together. "I like you, Alice," he said, "and I want to see where this goes."

"So do I," she replied.

"I try to be up-front in matters of the heart," he continued. "When I say I want to see where this goes, I want you to know that means I'm not seeing anybody else." He paused long enough for her to start to say something, but then continued, "And to be clear, I don't expect exclusivity from you in return. It's not like that. This is just me, my choice. If you still feel the need to—"

"I don't," Alice said, giggling, and he was giggling too. "At all."

"Great. Okay," he said, spilling joy. This was going well. "Next part. I believe in truth in advertising. We all advertise ourselves every day, whether we realize it or not—"

"Uh-huh," she said, trying to hurry him past the preamble. He was a preambler, she was starting to discover.

"—and I don't want anyone to think there's a product on the market that isn't in fact . . . on the market. So with that in mind, I sent you something. Just now. On Facebook."

She went to Facebook. Notifications. There it was.

"Take your time," he said. "No pressure in any way. Really. Truly.

It's there for you to click, whenever you want to click it. If you ever do. And if you don't, that's okay too."

She looked at the words: "Relationship Request." "Grover Kines."

Maybe Alice still hadn't come down from the lofty high of signing up for this test, or the even loftier high of quitting her job. It was a new lesson, fresh on her brain, that sudden enormous steps forward in life can be intoxicating. You do one, and soon you want to do them all. Why wouldn't you? She held up her phone and made a big show of clicking accept, letting him see the screen change. And the floor didn't fall out from under Alice, even after a moment passed, and another, and she finished the taco and they kissed while New Jersey sparkled across the river. That whole night, in fact, the thrill and newness of being "In a Relationship" felt somehow cozy and old, in the best way possible, even after she returned to the Bakery alone and got in another two hours of work.

Noise in the kitchen. Roxy was getting ready for work. Roxy. The thing with Roxy. That happened too. It was yesterday afternoon, before the study break, before the taco, before Grover.

She'd gotten an email.

Six imperious words were stamped in the subject line: "Promise you will be at this." It was an invitation to Roxy's birthday party. It was a theme party, of course, and even though the party would take place on the fourteenth day of August in the year 2015, the theme was NEW YEAR'S EVE 1979. Here's how it would work: The party would begin at 10 P.M., in a bar downtown called Loopholes, a place with a big dance floor and a DJ, who for the first two hours of the party would spin '70s disco classics. Then, ten seconds to midnight, the crowd would do a countdown, and at the strike of twelve, the '70s would become the '80s, and Donna Summer's "Don't Leave Me This Way" would seamlessly transition into Simple Minds' "Don't You (Forget About Me)," and just like that it would be '80s music for the rest of the night. All of Roxy's friends would be there, which, according to Facebook, was over three thousand people (although, in the nearly two months she'd been living here, Alice still hadn't met any of them).

Alice was impressed. It was a cool idea, and she said so when Roxy made an appearance in person a few minutes later.

"I know, right? We should talk costumes. Everyone's outfit has to transform in some way at midnight. *You* have to transform. That's the fun of New Year's. And the fun of birthdays. You're suddenly someone different. And I mean, yeah, it'll take some preparation, but we can make a night of it. Nothing worth doing doesn't take a little work," Roxy said, and then, tapping on the big yellow MCAT book on the kitchen table for emphasis, "You of all people should know that."

Alice had to remind Roxy once more that she was too busy for stuff like a whole night of costume preparation, and Roxy was obviously a little hurt, and Alice was reminded once more how much patience Roxy required. It was like training an animal to do a trick, getting Roxy to comprehend the guilt that poked at Alice every moment she wasn't studying. Eventually Roxy volunteered to make Alice's costume for her, and Alice felt bad, so she offered to take half a night off to help, and even suggested a costume: "A '70s denim dress that tears away, and I've got a tutu and a ripped-up T-shirt underneath."

Roxy's eyes lit up. "That's perfect! Can I steal that for myself? No, it's yours! And it's so easy! We find the dress, and then it's just scissors, Velcro, glue gun. This'll be so fun! Yay!" And Roxy golf-clapped in excitement as she puttered out of the kitchen into her room. Alice exhaled. IT'S 54 DAYS UNTIL THE TEST. If she was going to take a dinner break to see Grover, it had to be something quick. The new taco place by the water looked good.

Then Roxy returned to the kitchen, leaning against the blue tree, and added: "And by the way, I expect you to bring your new boyfriend."

Alice had not yet merged these two worlds and wasn't sure she wanted to. But she smiled and said, "Of course," and then made a hasty exit, off to the Bakery, and then the taco place by the water, and then back to the Bakery, and then back to this little bed, and now the lightwell filled with sunshine as Alice let her eyes open and focus on Gary's empty birdcage. She wondered if he ever thought about her. She hoped he didn't. She hoped he was in Central Park right now, enjoying the weather, maybe eating someone's fallen hot dog. She hoped he'd found some other canaries.

She looked at her phone (GOOD MORNING. IT'S 53 DAYS UNTIL—) and she put her phone back on the nightstand, facedown.

Her body resisted, but the dwindle of the morning would not relent. It was time to galvanize. There would be no outside energy source, today or any other day. Electrolytic was not an option. Galvanic or bust.

Okay, Alice.

This is it, Alice.

Here we go, Alice.

Up!

* * *

"You awake Deuce?"

"Hello, Cinco. Yes I am awake."

"What time is it there?"

"4:30."

"Whoa, you're up early! Is the sun out?"

"It's Alaska, of course the sun is out."

"What are you doing?"

"Lying in bed waiting for an egg to hatch."

"What egg?"

"My friend found a bald eagle's nest on her farm and she used a drone to drop a go-pro into it, so now everyone on the island is watching this feed to see when the eggs are gonna hatch. Which is all a roundabout way of saying OH MY GOD my life is boring."

"Are you kidding? That's amazing!"

"Uh, no it's not, and you know that. What's up with you? How's your social life?"

"You know how it is."

"No I don't. That's why I'm asking."

"What can I tell you, Deuce? Same old same old."

"Please, you don't know the meaning of same old same old until you've lived on Kodiak Island. Come on, Cinco, I'm hungry for true tales of NYC debauchery. Feed me."

"Fine. So the other day I matched with this girl."

"On an app."

"Yes. Suitoronomy."

"And that's a good one?"

"It's okay. It's kind of the standard. Unlonely's more for getting married. HookerUpper's more for, well, hooking up. Suitoronomy's kinda right in the middle."

"The Goldilocks."

"Exactly."

"So you matched with this girl on Suitoronomy."

"So I matched with this girl."

"What do you say when that happens?"

"You've never used an app?"

"I already know everyone within fifty miles of me. And more importantly, they know me! Come on, take me through it. How does it work? What do you say?"

"Okay, well, the thing is, it's not easy starting a brand new unique conversation with every person you meet on this thing. Eventually you start going through the motions a little. You sort of develop a script, for lack of a better word."

"And what's your script? Give me page one."

"I don't want to talk about this."

"Of course you do! Come on! Tell me! Tellmetellmetellme. Tell meeeeeeeeeeeeee."

"Okay, I have this thing where I tell people I just joined and they're the first person I've ever done this with. I say, 'Can I be honest? I've never done this before. You're my first.' etc."

"LOL. Wow. See, I would argue that's maybe a little DIShonest. OMG the egg moved! OMG this is riveting! Anyway sorry. Where were we? Oh right you're a pathological liar."

"I don't know, I guess. I mean, I assume most of them know I'm full of shit. Or all of them do. Or none of them do. I don't know. You think I'm an asshole."

"I'm not capable of thinking that, Cinco. Believe me, I've tried and tried."

"I appreciate it, Deuce. Anyway, I start talking to this girl, and I'm saying all the stuff I always say, about how I've never done this before and I'm brand new at it, blah blah blah, and she stops me, and she's like, dude, we hooked up three months ago."

"Noooooooooooo."

"Yes."

"Noooooooooooooooo."

"Yeeeeeeeeeeeeeeeeeeeees."

"Busted."

"Totally. It felt gross and I feel terrible about it."

"I should hope so."

"But then guess what?"

"You hooked up with her again."

"Just left her place. I'm getting breakfast now."

And then Bob put his phone down as Clara—the waitress with a degree in musical theater, which Bob knew about because he'd sat in her section once or twice before and thought she was cute, with her big eyes and fascinating nose and unplaceable regional accent, so he spent half a day scrolling through every Clara on Facebook in the New York area until, against all odds, he found her and learned her last name was Court and her accent was Baltimorean and she once played Luisa in *The Fantasticks* and went to Thailand, where she took a picture of herself in front of a temple shaped like a giant three-headed elephant, and somehow it was so much easier to learn all this stuff by spending a day snooping around online than by having a three-minute conversation with Clara herself—placed an omelet in front of him.

"Anything else?" Clara asked.

"No, thank you," he replied, and picked up his phone once more. A message was waiting.

"Well, Cinco, thank you. That was exactly the kind of disgusting story I needed to wake myself up. Better than coffee."

"My pleasure, Deuce. You're the reason I do it."

"I'm honored. So what's tonight's horrorshow gonna be?"

"Tonight I'm staying home. I'm old. I need a night off once in awhile."

And he meant it, but then, halfway through his omelet, he opened Suitoronomy and found Trudy Catusi, and that evening he took two trains out to Queens to meet Trudy at a wine bar. They drank Valpolicella and talked about the differences between the boroughs. He'd lived here eighteen years and still so much of New York was unknown to him.

Trudy asked, "Are you really forty?" She was pure sunshine.

"I really am," he replied.

"No way! You look twenty-eight."

His face ran through the "bashful" subroutine as he pretended to be taken aback by the compliment he'd received many times before. "Thanks. Tell that to my knees every morning."

She laughed, a tell-me-about-it laugh, though she would have no idea what forty-year-old knees would feel like for another seventeen years. She was young and trying so hard. She asked what made him decide to live on the Upper West. The true answer was that once, long ago, he thought he would marry a girl named Amy Otterpool, and they would have children together and raise them in the city for the first few years before moving up to Westchester for the schools, and the Upper West Side seemed to have the most strollers of anywhere, so that's where they always talked about beginning their life together in New York. And they loved it. Their single friends all lived and partied downtown, but Bob and Amy had a dry cleaner who knew their faces. They had a local grocer, with a delivery guy who would run coffees up to them in the morning when they were too sleepy to make it themselves, and pints of Ben & Jerry's in the middle of the night when they were too stoned to put on clothes. It was lovely, and then it ended, in the Indian restaurant around the corner from his apartment, and now Amy was gone, but the Indian restaurant was still there.

Bob answered, "I love Central Park."

"Oh my God, I love it too," said Trudy. "There's parks here in Queens, though. There's an old carousel in Forest Park. And you can go horseback riding." Twenty-three years old. All the small talk and smiling and work that would lead up to the thing, and all the pretending he wasn't about to disappear from her life after the thing—it would all pull him a little bit deeper underground.

The next morning, they emerged from her apartment building, Bob in the same clothes from the night before, and Trudy dressed like someone in her first office job out of college. She had taken a shower and her hair was still wet. She dug around in her bag, making sure she had her keys, as he spied her last name on the mailbox, written in her handwriting with a green Magic Marker: "Catusi, 7G."

"The subway's three long blocks over, on 46th," she said, like a real New Yorker. "But if you want to split a cab, we can probably get one over on Steinway."

Bob figured he could spend a little while longer with Trudy Catusi before they disappeared from each other back into the ocean. So they headed over to Steinway, and as he put his hand up in the air for a cab, he heard his name.

"Bob?"

He turned.

It was Amy.

A cab stopped, but he waved it away.

She was taller than he remembered, her eyes farther apart, her skin more complicated by the sun and the years. He might not have recognized her at all. She looked tired, like she had missed out on the many full-night sleeps Bob had selfishly stockpiled all these lonely years. She was forty, just like him. Bob couldn't remember the last time he'd been with someone his own age.

Amy gripped the handles of a stroller, and sitting in the stroller was

Amy's daughter. Bob saw her, and his heart, with its hands upon the bars of his rib cage, screamed out in silence.

"Hey," his voice said. "Amy! Wow! How are you?"

"I'm good," she said, and they hugged. "I look terrible, I don't have any makeup on."

"You look great," he said.

A few awkward words went by. Did she live around here? Yes, around the corner, what about you? Upper West Side still, oh, this is Trudy. Trudy, this is Amy. Hi, nice to meet you. You too. Wow, Bob Smith. Amy Otterpool. And who's this? This is Emily. Hi, Emily. She's so cute. Yeah, we were up pretty late last night, weren't we? Yes, we were.

Ten minutes later, as their cab made its way across the 59th Street Bridge, Bob looked at Trudy, who had no idea what she'd just been a part of. She caught him looking at her.

"So was that a friend from work?"

"That was my ex-girlfriend."

"Really?"

"Really."

"Serious?"

"Dead serious."

"No, I mean was it serious? Between the two of you."

Their love was the gravity that moored him to the earth. "Pretty serious."

"How long ago did you date?"

"I don't know," he said. "Fourteen years ago. Something like that." Fourteen years ago, he was Bob, the same Bob, with many of the same shirts, coffee mugs, and furniture he had now. Fourteen years ago, Trudy was nine. "A long time ago."

"Wow. She has a kid now," Trudy said. "Is that weird?"

"I don't want to talk about this." The words trembled so much more than he wanted them to. "I want to talk about you! So you're an account executive?"

He let her do the talking for the rest of the ride. She had a white turtleneck on, and it was sleeveless, though you couldn't tell under the blazer. As he listened, Bob thought of her long naked arms. Then they got out in front of Grand Central, across the street from her office. "This was fun," they said, and "We should do this again," and "You have my number." All the things you say. Then the tide washed her into the lobby of a skyscraper, and that was it.

"Did it hatch?"

"No! And it's driving me crazy! So how was the twenty-three-year-old? Did she succumb to your vampire thrall?"

"She's a nice girl and we had a nice time."

"Was there a horrifying moment where you realized you slept with her mom twenty-three years ago and she might be your daughter?"

"Gross and no. But hey, speaking of people with daughters: I saw Amy this morning."

"Whoa! Really?????????????"

"And her baby. In Queens. Walking down the street. We talked. She seems good. It was actually nice to see her."

"Uh huh. And now you're gonna do the obvious thing and completely freak out."

"Is that the obvious thing?"

"Yes it is."

"Because I freaked out that other time, when I found out she was having the baby?"

"I mean, if you're gonna bring it up, yeah. I don't remember exactly what happened there because you never told me the story. But you did quit Facebook."

"I'd been meaning to do that forever, you know that."

"Uh huh. There was also something involving a train set?"

"I told you about the train set?"

"I think you mentioned a train set. Please don't make me scroll through a year of our texts."

"Okay, let's just say yes, there was a train set, and I freaked out, and we'll just leave it at that. But seeing her today, I don't know. It was bound to happen eventually," he observed, though in his heart he'd hoped it wasn't. "I'm more surprised it took fourteen years. I was with Trudy so it wasn't like it was a long chat."

"Oh you were with Trudy??? Well now that's interesting. What did she think of Trudy?"

"They're best friends now. They're going away next weekend."

She didn't reply right away. Then she did.

"Don't be obvious, Cinco. It's your least attractive quality."

"I'm only obvious to you, Deuce."

He put his phone away. The encounter with Amy had been brief, three minutes at most, but it was like briefly holding a bar of plutonium. The real sickness hadn't even begun.

* * *

Bill spent that morning in a high-ceilinged office atop a magnificent former bubble gum factory on the East River, with views of the bristly Manhattan skyline beyond the giant windows. It was the view for which you left Manhattan, because you can only see the skyline and take in its real beauty from across a river, if you can put up with the commute and the vague smell of maple syrup, which lingered decades after the factory had made its last stick of gum.

This office, which would become Bill's office upon the execution of his contract, was the nerve center of a company of six hundred employees, a hive in which the industrious young bees waited to give the best hours of their most unencumbered years to whatever whims Zach and Bill green-lit or thought up themselves. Men and women traveled from all over the city every day, on water and in tunnels underground, just to keep Fortinbras Dynamics and all its multiplatform software offerings, the very best in the marketplace, humming along.

Bill signed all the papers and shook all the hands, and then he and his formerly former but currently current partner, Zach, went out for a boozy lunch of big buttery steaks with their lawyers. It was a lunch like the kind they used to have, in the old days, the giant ice cubes snapping in the tumblers as they stole the heat from the whiskey. Then Bill

hopped the train back to the train back to the train back to Morningside Heights, and briskly walked to 404 Riverside Drive. He flew up
the elevator shaft and into the apartment, where he made riotous afternoon love to his happy wife.

Under a mountain of sheets and covers, Bill and Pitterpat buzzed
with the joy of it all.

"This feels right," Pitterpat said. "You took some time off after Me-
WantThat, and that was the right choice. And now, *this* is the right
choice." He laughed, and she laughed too, knowing how she sounded
to him right now. "I'm serious! It's been a great summer, or half a summer. But I get it. This is what you do best, Bill. You come up with
things. I want to see what you come up with next."

Their faces were close together, smushed into the same pillow. He
kissed her nose.

"I want to see it too. And I promise, it's not gonna be like before."
Now she laughed at him. "I mean it! MeWantThat was the big one. It
was make-or-break from the beginning. We're playing with the house's
money now. I'm gonna work hard, but I mean, come on. You think I'm
gonna stay till 3 A.M.? Forget it. I'm gonna be out the door at five every
day."

"And then straight to Columbia for your evening class? What's it
gonna be this time? Mormonism?"

He grinned. "*Home.* I will be *home* by 6:15 at the latest. I
promise."

"Earlier than that if we move to Carnegie Hill."

"Oh, is that what we're doing?"

She smiled coyly. "I have ideas."

"I bet you do," he said, and they kissed again, and it was perfect,
truly the best kind of afternoon. Everything Bill and Pitterpat desired
at this moment was right there in the apartment; and if it wasn't, as in
the case of the samosas they suddenly craved, they could have them
delivered in less than an hour, which they did, and they ate them naked
in bed and they were delicious.

Then Bill had to leave.

He wasn't officially dropping Intro to Buddhism, since the semester was almost over anyway, but he wouldn't be going to the last week of classes or taking the final. It was fine. He had followed Buddhism as it migrated over the centuries from India to China to Korea to Japan, and didn't much feel the need to be tested on it. Still, it would be wrong to just ghost on a class that had meant something to him. Professor Shimizu had office hours today, and Bill owed it to the man, and to himself, to say goodbye.

As he walked up the hill to the campus, a text came in from Alice.

"So are you like even richer now?"

"Not yet," he replied, "but soon" and then moneybag moneybag moneybag moneybag.

"Well, that's very cool," she replied. "Congratulations. I'm proud of you."

"I'm proud of you too."

And he was. He rarely heard from Alice lately, but in a good way. It was good to see her all in on something. She'd even quit her job to focus on this test. God bless her. Nothing better than being on a roll, Bill thought. And a new boyfriend too! Love radiated from within him, wafting out in every direction like the smell of warm bread.

"You're going places, kid," he added as he stopped at a particularly jubilant street corner, 113th and Broadway, one of the best in the city.

"Doing my best," she replied. "Congrats again. Leave some prosperity for the rest of us, okay?"

"Ha," he said, and headed into Hamilton Hall.

The dark hallway on the top floor was deserted. Way down at the end of the hall, Professor Shimizu's door was wide open, as it always was on Mondays between three and five.

Bill arrived in the doorway and found Professor Shimizu not at his desk, but instead in the brown leather reading chair he'd managed to squeeze next to it. The smallness of the office struck Bill. Sometime in the next few days, someone would present Bill with options for a giant piece of artwork for the twenty-by-thirteen expanse of the eastern wall of his own office. He'd have lots of choices, but whatever he picked still wouldn't fill the immense emptiness of the place. This office, on the other hand, had room for only one small framed picture, on a patch of wall next to the small window. It was a painting of a chariot.

"Professor Shimizu?"

"Hello, Bill," said the old man. "What's up?"

Bill had been in this class for six weeks. He'd attended all eighteen lectures, always sitting in the same spot, four rows back from the podium. But never once had it occurred to him that Professor Shimizu knew his name. It made the next part much more difficult.

"Actually, I'm here because I need to drop the class."

The old man put down the book he'd been reading. "I'm so sorry to hear that," he said, with true concern. "Is everything all right?"

"What? Oh, yeah," said Bill. "No, it's for a good reason. It's a career thing."

"Oh."

"I've been offered a job."

"Congratulations," he said warmly, but Bill was still trying to explain himself.

"I'm not an undergrad. I'm in the continuing education program."

"I know. I'm sorry to see you go. You ask good questions."

"I do?"

"Yes, of course," said the professor, without elaborating. "So what's the job?"

Bill felt emails arriving in his phone. The price of his fortune was his attention.

"Oh, it's a computer thing. I'm in computer software development." Bill always spoke this way to elderly people, and for the first time Professor Shimizu felt elderly to Bill, the way he sat deep in his chair, his shoulders up at his ears. Bill might have been surprised to know Professor Shimizu had MeWantThat on his phone, or that Professor Shimizu even had a phone.

"Sounds exciting," the old man said.

"It is," Bill said. "It is. It's an opportunity I can't turn down."

On his way out, Bill found the hallway no longer empty. There was a young woman sitting in the haphazard wooden chair by the door. She was small, and she looked like she cut her own hair, and there was something else to notice about her. Even in a passing glimpse, Bill clocked her shoulder lunging forward and back, forward and back, as if rowing without a boat or a paddle. She wasn't moving to music. There wasn't any music. She had no earbuds in. It wasn't a nervous tic. Her face was calm and distracted. This was just something *wrong*. She was sick. Was that it? Yes. She was sick.

Their eyes met. For a moment Bill wondered if he knew her. Did she know him? It was possible. As he walked by, the girl picked up the large box next to her, and it steadied her arm. She went into the office.

"Professor Shimizu? I emailed you to tell you I was coming," she said, and Bill didn't hear any more as he walked down the hall toward the stairwell. He descended half a story, but stopped on the landing, looking out over a slice of the campus green. It was nearly empty and totally still, the nuclear winter of a university summer. He felt the air-conditioning on his uncovered arms and gooseflesh rose, and for some reason, a reason he did not and would not ever understand, he thought of his mother. Her face and her voice were gone three years now. He'd cried when she passed. He'd cried when he arrived at the house in Katonah. (Was the girl with the box from Katonah? Was her name Rudy something?) He'd cried when he saw her small uninhabited form under the sheet in the funeral home. He'd cried during the eulogy for which he was roundly complimented, and he'd even cried on the train back to the city. But when he was back in Manhattan, he stopped crying.

People in tech worry about artificial intelligence and wonder if it might bring about the end of the world. But isn't every death, in its own tiny enormous way, the end of the world, if only for one person? This world we love and cherish jealously has ended countless times before, and here it is, still going, still being born, still ending, still unstill.

Bill left the window and descended the stairs. He stepped out of the building and crossed the green. Somewhere business cards were being printed for him. A phone was being initialized. Great things were expected.

Pitterpat was in the bathtub when he got home. The door was closed. He could have gone in and seen her, and kissed her, but she liked her privacy in there. She called it her office. She could spend two hours in the bathtub if he ever gave her the chance. It was one of those things you could either love or hate about a person, and that choice was entirely yours. Bill chose to love it and did so with vigor. He loved his wife.

His wife.

Her phone made a noise. She didn't move. The steroids were helping a little, but she'd still been shitting all morning and now needed to be in a cocoon of bubbles listening to just the right '60s French pop music with a warm washcloth over her eyes. She hummed absently to the lilting breathy voice of some kicky gamine, *la jeune chanteuse qui chante*. She did not speak French, did not know the words, but she engaged the melody anyway, humming, throwing in doo-doo-doos. She didn't hear the front door close.

* * *

The possibility that Bob was gay was discussed from time to time among his coworkers, for obvious reasons. First of all, he had never mentioned a girlfriend, or any kind of woman in his life. He'd been in the accounting department for eleven years. He must be at least forty now. Plus, as Dennis pointed out on the text chain, Bob was very neat and well-dressed. Not that that meant anything, as Francine pointed out. Her son was gay and he was a complete slob, but ugh, that was a whole other topic, Francine didn't want to go into it. Maybe later, over drinks at the Peruvian place. Plus Bob never came out for drinks at the Peruvian place! He lived in the city, the only employee of Velocitron Bicycles who made the reverse commute out to this office park in Edgewater, New Jersey. Whatever he did in his free time, he kept it private from his coworkers. A wide river separated Office Bob from Home Bob, and everyone knew it.

So when Bob walked in looking extra chipper that morning, Francine and Dennis and the others let their imaginations run wild, but never asked. He stayed in his office the whole day, hardly talking to anyone. He looked like he was working.

He wasn't. He was wondering what the hell Amy was doing living in Queens. It just seemed weird. Bob couldn't get excited about the outer boroughs the way everyone else did. His social life had taken him out there more and more over the last few years, but still, there was something romantic about Manhattan that Queens would never catch up with. Even in a tiny one-bedroom apartment like Bob's. He didn't need a big place, though. He sometimes thought of his apartment as a hotel room.

There was a knock on his office door. Francine peeked in, holding a plate of the thickest, chunkiest chocolate chip cookies Bob had ever seen. She made them at home and brought them in. She did this a lot.

"I'm sorry to disturb you," she said, immensely proud of herself and not sorry at all.

"No, you're not," he said with a grin. "Francine, you are Satan. You are tempting me to be *bad*."

"I'm just gonna put it on this napkin," she replied, grinning as well, "and place it here on your desk. And then I'm gonna close the door, and you can do whatever you want."

And she did exactly that, and as she quietly backed out of the room, Bob made little devil horns and then pointed at Francine: *That's what you are.* She loved it.

Bob sat back in his chair, and looked at the cookie, and thought about Trudy. She was cute. It's a boring adjective, but that's what she was, and very much so. And young. *Seemed* young. Maybe someone older next. Change the search parameters. But Trudy had this sweet, hopeful vibe, that thing you have when you've grown up wanting to live in New York your whole life, and then you *get there*, and it's that first year in the city. Nothing beats that. It's romantic. That's what it is.

He sent her a message, and she replied immediately.

"Hiya! So nice to hear from you after all this time! LOL."

"Too soon?"

"LOL of course not. I was starting to think you forgot about me. ;)"

"Impossible. Hey so last night was fun."

"Ummmm yeah you could say that. ;)"

"Wanna meet up tonight?"

"Awwww I can't, I'm so sorry. My sister's having a birthday party. It's like a girls' night kinda thing. I could meet you after but I think it might go kinda late."

Not okay! "Boooooo. I'm just kidding. That's fine. Maybe another night?"

"Yesss!!! Tomorrow maybe?"

"Tomorrow should work I think. Can we circle back to confirm?"

He didn't like to make a plan that far ahead. It would have been really fun to see her tonight, though. He opened Suitoronomy. He didn't choose to; his thumb just went there. He slid the maximum age up to thirty-five. Samantha. Thirty-four. She looked tall, or at least long of torso. Her hair tumbled down her shoulders in a golden cascade in every picture she posted. Can I be honest? Sure, why not. It's my first time doing this. Talk talk talk talk talk, care to meet up tonight? Sure, why not. She'd be out of work around six, she could meet him somewhere at seven, would that be okay? It certainly would. Bob wished his younger self could see how good he would be at all this someday.

"Seriously has this eagle hatched yet or what?"

"Go away. I'm working. And no. Talk later."

Bob could see Manhattan from his window: Morningside Heights, the Riverside Church, and all the apartment buildings to the south. *I made it*, he thought to himself. *I got to the future.* Wasn't this always the goal? To be grown up? He had to struggle to remember what it was like before, when you had to walk up to a girl and start a conversation.

The thing about Amy living in Queens was that Bob had been sure Amy would end up in Westchester. Or maybe that was just if she'd stayed with Bob. They could have ended up there together. They probably *would* have. And then that dinner at the Indian place, and the conversation about Thanksgiving plans that changed everything. For years he'd replayed that dinner, moment by moment. For years it amazed him how easily his whole life had come apart. Now it no longer amazed him. The older you get, the more you appreciate how completely it all disappears.

Bob's phone jolted him from his reverie. Trudy. She caved! "What if we meet up before the party? I could meet my sister and her friends after dinner and get dinner with you instead, would that work?" He saw her big cute smile between the words, and didn't stop to consider the Samantha of it all.

"That would be great!"

"Can we meet somewhere near my office, like around 8?"

Samantha at seven. He could just push that to another night. She wanted to meet at a bar in Yorkville, the high and far East 90s. It was a bit of a hike.

"Absolutely. Hey have you been to the Grand Central Oyster Bar?"

"No, is it good?"

"It's my favorite place in New York. You'll love it."

Amy's daughter's ears were pierced. Whose idea was that, to put holes in an infant? Probably Doug's.

"Okay great! I can't wait! See you at 8! That rhymed LOL!"

Bob felt a tingle. He hadn't been on a second date in a while. No, wait, there was one. Roxy. But that was to see Alice again. Alice. Another disappearing act. She had almost seen him. He had almost let her. He looked at Samantha's picture, the flowing golden hair and the ineffable suggestion of height. She was outdoors in the picture, a head-shotty portrait with out-of-focus autumn leaves behind her, and she didn't smile, which gave the impression that it was a serious undertaking to court this thirty-four-year-old Samantha, not for the faint of heart but with mighty spoils for the victor.

What to do, what to do, what to do. He looked at Trudy again, and imagined Amy telling everyone about bumping into her ex and this bubbly little twenty-three-year-old. *They're laughing at me*, Bob thought.

Right now they're laughing. But what did Amy know? Maybe Bob and Trudy were serious. If they made it work, they'd prove everyone wrong. All they had to do was spend the rest of their lives together.

"How was the cookie?"

Bob looked up. "Francine," he said, with dimples. "Seriously? Best cookie I've ever eaten in my life."

It made her day.

* * *

Alice's left hand absently strolled through the fingerings of a nocturne as her right hand flipped through a set of flashcards. The morning had been for general chemistry, as she whipped through the periodic table, thermodynamics, stoichiometry, and acid-base equilibriums. A quick bagel sandwich and orange juice for lunch, and now it was the afternoon and biochemistry.

Grover sat cross-legged next to her on the bed, nose a little too close to his laptop screen as he wrote. *What a thrill to be a part of this*, thought Alice between cards. She was busy, and not the kind of busy you claim you are when someone asks why you haven't returned an email, but actually busy, legitimately forgetting to return emails. It had been over two weeks since she'd last logged onto LookingGlass to see what Carlos was watching. And even then, when she discovered he was six episodes into *Love on the Ugly Side*, which could only mean a new woman in Carlos's life, Alice was fine with it. *Let her have him*, she thought. In victory: magnanimity.

Only once that afternoon did Alice let herself goof around on the internet. She checked Twitter and found a fascinating article about a whale. This particular whale didn't follow the usual migration pattern of other whales. He followed his own path, and as a result rarely came within a hundred miles of any others of his kind. It made little sense to the marine biologists tracking his movements. Like any other whale, he sang his song, an enthusiastic balladeer in the cetacean opera of the deep, but none of the others seemed to hear him. It was like he was a ghost. They named him the Ghost Whale. Finally someone figured it out: He was singing at a frequency of 12 hertz, just below the 15-to-20-hertz range the average baleen whale can hear. The Ghost Whale spent his whole life hoping just one other whale would hear his song, but it never happened.

Alice told Grover about the Ghost Whale, and Grover replied, "I should ask my friend Ayesha about that. She's on a boat in the Barents Sea right now studying baleen whale migration." *Of course he has a friend on a boat in the Barents Sea right now studying baleen whale migration*, thought Alice. Alice was marveling at how Grover was so much cooler than Carlos when her phone cried out.

"911!!!! Emergency!!!!!"

Oh God, Roxy, what now? But it was from Pitterpat.

"What's up?"

"You need to come over right now."

"Everything okay?

"Ummmmm my life is literally falling apart right now so no everything not okay."

Alice had never once seen her sister-in-law the slightest bit ruffled. Pitterpat, Alice imagined, could eat a croissant with a fork and knife and leave not a single crumb on the plate.

Alice looked at her flashcards, and then the time: 4:16 P.M. She had been goofing off more than fifteen minutes, her absolute limit.

"I can't get away right now," she said to Pitterpat. "But I'm here for you."

"No you are not."

Alice was a little perturbed. "Yes I am," she replied.

Pitterpat was standing in her drained bathtub, cold and dripping, as her thumb smashed the caps lock.

"NO YOU ARE NOT HERE FOR ME BECAUSE IF YOU WERE HERE FOR ME YOU WOULD BE HERE!!!! FOR ME!!!!! LSDJFBVLJADBFVLKJADBFVKLJ"

Alice was pretty shook by this one. Grover could sense it. She didn't have time to explain it to him, or to even reply, before the next message arrived.

"YOUR BROTHER JUST BECAME A BUDDHIST MONK."

Fifteen minutes later Pitterpat answered the door wrapped in a haphazard and precarious towel. Alice had never seen her like this, hair still wet, no makeup on. Grover had come along, and Pitterpat didn't even notice. "Hi," was all she said, robotically, as she led them to the living room.

Her eyes burned red as she silently paced the room like a panther. Alice had always wondered if sweet little Pitterpat secretly had a nuclear temper, and now she got her answer as her sister-in-law calmly said, "I'm gonna fucking murder him."

Alice approached gently. "What happened?"

"He sent me an email. He didn't even talk to me. We were just about to—*he* was just about to start a new job at Fortinbras—"

"The French company?" It was Grover.

Alice saw it cross Pitterpat's mind to ask who the hell this unknown gentleman was, but in the confusion she could only muster, "Yes. It's a French company. And Bill was just about to start his new job—"

"I'm so sorry," Grover interrupted again. Pitterpat stopped pacing this time and fixed her eyes on him, as a panther might eye a wild pig. "Pitterpat, I don't know if Alice has told you about me, but I'm a journalist. Do you want this to be off the record?"

"Excuse me?"

"Fortinbras is a big company and there's been a great deal of speculation about new blood taking over. It's not my beat, but I'd feel weird walking around with a possible scoop if I didn't know it was off the record. Can you just say this is off the record?"

Pitterpat glowered. "I'm sorry," she said slowly.

"It's off the record," said Alice, trying to smooth it over. "Just say it's off the record." Then, as an afterthought, she added: "Grover, this is Pitterpat. Pitterpat, Grover."

"Hi," he said.

"Hello," Pitterpat replied. "This is off the record."

Grover gave a little ingratiating bow, in acknowledgment. Pitterpat wasn't charmed.

They sat down, and she told them everything, which wasn't much of anything once she came out with it. She wanted to blame it all on this class he'd been taking, and yet she realized she didn't know much about what he'd been studying. Every time he'd talked about it, she'd tuned it out, a little out of spite but mostly out of disinterest.

"And now he's run off and joined a cult, basically," she said.

"Bill's never done anything halfway," Alice offered. It was such a useless platitude, and yet truly the long and short of it.

"Yeah, no shit," Pitterpat said. "But this is crazy, even for Bill. Don't you think? Is this not the behavior of a crazy person?"

"No," Grover said. "It's not."

Alice saw Pitterpat look up at him and immediately realized today was not the best day to introduce her boyfriend to her sister-in-law. In fact, why was he here? They'd only been Facebook official for a day or two. Order-of-magnitude-wise, this was Thanksgiving dinner.

Pitterpat's eyes narrowed as her gaze fixed on Grover.

"What do you mean, 'No, it's not'?"

"I mean," he said, "it's not crazy to have a religious experience."

"It's not a religious experience," Alice said, and as much as she wanted to defend her brother, she could not. "It's a mental break. He just abandoned his wife. Who does that?"

Pitterpat nodded, a silent thank-you to Alice. But Grover kept going, apparently unable to hear Alice's brain screaming, *PLEASE DO NOT KEEP GOING.*

"Literally millions of people," he replied. "Millions of people do that, and have done that for as long as we've had religion. I'm sorry, Alice, Pitterpat, I sympathize with this situation, but looking at it from an ethical standpoint, the decision to leave behind worldly possessions and enter into a religious fold is a decision that's been made many, many times before, by many, many people, and to belittle that subjective experience borders on cultural insensitivity. Plus, you know, I understand how from your perspective there's a financial sting here, but let's look at it from the perspective of Bill's soul. If he took that job, he would be overseeing a billion-dollar corporation that employs thousands of people, many of whom are not offered a living wage, have no health care, and don't have the opportunity to unionize. As an emerging Buddhist, I could imagine Bill really struggling with how much accumulated suffering a job like that would have some complicity in propagating. We can split hairs over *how* he did this, but the *fact* that he did this, I'll just say it, is kind of admirable."

From the sidewalk below, twelve stories down, you could hear Pitterpat's war cry as she leapt out of her towel and flew across the living room, a sudden furious ball of skin and fingernails. Grover managed to get away from her, but only barely.

"You scratched me," he said, shocked.

She made no attempt to get any less naked. Eyes ablaze, she screamed, "Get out! GET OUT GET OUT GET OUT!" And she didn't stop screaming until Grover and Alice were on the other side of the door, in the hallway.

Alice hit the button for the elevator. Grover was unrattled. His ethics had gotten him into situations like this before. "I'm sorry I hurt her feelings," he said, "but I won't apologize for my beliefs. Please don't ask me to."

"Your beliefs? What, are *you* a Buddhist now?"

"Ethical consistency," he said, "is my life's work."

"Yeah, I know," Alice said, exhausted.

A text arrived on her phone: "Get rid of him and come back in here, I still need you."

Alice kissed Grover and put him on the elevator.

"See you at the Bakery later?"

General chemistry. "Hopefully," Alice said.

After the elevator doors closed, she knocked on Pitterpat's door once more.

After what seemed like three months, the door opened, and there was Pitterpat, now in a long T-shirt.

"I'm sorry," said Alice. "He's really very nice."

Pitterpat groaned a long anguished animal sound and went to make herself and Alice some tea. Alice offered to do it, but Pitterpat didn't hear her.

A text arrived. Roxy, this time.

"Costumes tonight?"

Oh, right. Alice replied: "Can't tonight. Family stuff. Maybe later in the week?"

"What's wrong?"

"Nothing."

"Are you sure?"

How did she know something was wrong? "Why do you think something's wrong?"

"Your tone," Roxy replied.

From the kitchen came the sound of mugs clinking a little too hard. Alice struggled for a moment, then just said it. "My brother left his wife to go become a Buddhist monk."

"What bar you at?"

"We're not at a—" she began to write. Then she deleted it. *Sorry, general chemistry.*

"Jack of Hearts on Broadway."

"I'll see you there in fifteen."

Pitterpat came in with the tea, and Alice told her to get dressed.

★ ★ ★

Bob met Samantha at seven sharp in a Spanish bar around the corner from her apartment in Yorkville in the high and far East 90s. She was as tall as he'd imagined, and then some, peeking over him a bit, able to confirm that every forty-year-old follicle on his head was intact and productive. She liked him, he could tell. And he liked her. Her cheekbones were severe and her lips were pursed, and on first impression her demeanor suggested a stern librarian, which made it irresistible when she suggested they go back to her place and smoke a joint. It was 7:30 P.M.

They walked nearly a block, then turned up the steps of a tall brownstone that seemed to loom as though leaning forward on the balls of its feet. Up one flight, then another, then two more and they were in her apartment, which was painted a shade of lilac she'd chosen herself. Bob found the couch as she opened a window, and then sparked the joint and handed it to him before plopping down next to him, inches away.

This situation would have mystified Bob back when he was first learning this language. Now he was fluent. He understood what was expected: possibly sex (though maybe not), but certainly at least a kiss, and probably more kissing after that. Or maybe just one kiss, and she wouldn't be into it and she'd politely say no thanks, but either way there was a rock-solid expectation this short or long conversation of bodies had to happen, and he had to kick it off.

But he didn't.

After a few minutes, Samantha got up to get them some wine, and Bob looked at his phone. It was 7:45. Then he looked at Trudy's picture. Then he checked the time again. Still 7:45. *If I leave now*, he thought, *I can make it. But I have to leave right this very second. I need to get up and leave.*

Samantha came back with two glasses of wine, and she began to tell Bob about a science fiction novel she hoped to write one day. Why does everyone have some *thing* they want to do? Bob thought of Alice Quick. He had liked her. There might have been something between them, but then she found out about him and that was it. He wouldn't make that mistake with Trudy. He'd change his name, officially. He had looked up the paperwork. It wouldn't be hard. He'd never tell Trudy about any of it. Samantha was deep into the plotline of the second volume of the trilogy, and Bob's eyes found the clock on her cable box, and it was 7:55. Bob was there on the couch, listening to Samantha's ideas about interdimensional travel or something, but he was also under the tiled archways of the Oyster Bar, where Trudy waited by the hostess station. The hostess gave her a welcoming look, and she smiled and waved a wordless indication that she was a little early, and a gentleman would be joining her soon, and she'd wait until he got here, and as Trudy went back to her phone, she thrilled a little at the fact that she had a job and an apartment and was going on a second date with a sophisticated older guy in New York City and all of it was totally fine because she was a grown-up. 7:57. He had to go. He had to go now.

Samantha stopped talking, creating the pause, the pause that says, *Okay, sir, it's now time for you to do the thing you're here to do.* Fifteen years ago he would have struggled so hard with this pause. Now he knew exactly what it was, but he didn't do anything, because a kiss would be more kisses and more kisses would be clothes on the floor and goodbye forever to Trudy.

The pause remained a pause, so Samantha kept talking.

"What about you? You work for a bicycle company?"

"I do indeed," he said, and he told her how he'd been with the company for eleven years, and was never much of a bike rider and still wasn't really, and then he made the observation he'd made a number of times about how all these deaths in the park, people getting killed by bicycles, made him feel like he worked for a gun manufacturer or a tobacco company, and Samantha provided the response other girls had made a number of times that he was being silly, think how many lives had been extended by people riding bicycles, and the joy he'd helped put in the world far outweighed the suffering, and Bob then made the joke he'd made a number of times about how she was right, and first thing tomorrow he was tearing up his letter of resignation, and the whole time Bob wasn't even there. He was in Grand Central, watching Trudy check her phone and exchange another glance with the hostess, and this time it was a little awkward. The departure announcements echoed in the great hall above. Now boarding. Last call.

Samantha sipped her wine and shifted, drawing her knees up onto the couch, her body curling, catlike. She arched forward. The runway was clear. Bob was frozen.

There was a knock on the door.

Samantha got up quickly, grabbing a magazine and fanning the lingering smoke from the joint out the open window to the fire escape, as if that might actually do anything. And as she did this, she spoke to the door.

"Who's there?" she said.

"It's Francisco," came the reply, in a big booming New York voice.

She groaned and went to look through the peephole. Bob quietly got up off the couch. He didn't care what was about to unfold with Francisco. He was very high right now, and when you're high, you see opportunities you don't normally see, and he knew this one wouldn't be around long, so he had to move fast. He went out the window.

* * *

"Can I just say, he is an *asshole*. I know he's—" Roxy looked around and found Alice sitting right next to her. "*Your* brother, and—" She looked around again and found Pitterpat sitting right next to Alice. This was four drinks in. "*Your* husband. But what an asshole. What. An— I'm sorry, I don't know him," caveated Roxy, and then she found Pitterpat once more. "I don't even know *you*, for that matter. But from what I've seen of you, I *do* like you, and from what I've just heard about him, I *don't* like him. Although I like his app. I feel like MeWantThat really gets me. Yesterday it Thatted me a banh mi, and have you guys ever had a banh mi? Muy delicioso!"

Alice sipped her beer and thought of the seat next to Grover at the Bakery and how she wasn't sitting in it. Instead she sat here, between her roommate and her sister-in-law, on the otherwise quiet second-floor patio of Jack of Hearts, a Columbia student bar. Every now and then, down below on the sidewalk, a group of people (sometimes just a couple) would hop out of a cab or emerge from the subway, and one of them would dramatically point up at the bar's neon sign: a large jack of hearts and the words "IS THIS YOUR CARD?" under it. And there would be a scream of amazement, and maybe some applause. This happened seven or eight times a night.

But up here on the roof, the applause was distant, and the stars glowed through the clouds and the light pollution. *Get back to work, Calerpittar.*

"It's okay. You can call him an asshole," said Pitterpat. "In fact, you could even call him a *fucking* asshole." At some cellular level, Alice didn't like Pitterpat talking this way about Bill. She sipped her beer. "I hope he has a great time being a monk," Pitterpat continued. "I hope he shaves his head and it never grows back." She laughed as the words left her mouth, flustered and faux embarrassed in a distinctly Southern way. "Oh my God, am I terrible?"

"Of course not," Alice assured her, but as Pitterpat kept ranting, Alice wondered: *Was* she terrible? It was possible.

"Who knows if this is even permanent," said Pitterpat. "He might just be freaking out about his new job. For all I know, he'll be back at work on Monday." (He wouldn't be. He had sent the board of Fortinbras an email similar to the one he'd sent Pitterpat. At that moment, frantic phone calls were happening, between New York and Palo Alto, Palo Alto and Paris, Paris and New York. The board did its best to clamp down the information for the sake of the stock price, but Bill's email was just too hilarious. It was already flying all over the tech world. Blogs and chat rooms ruthlessly mocked it for being exactly the kind of preachy, faux-enlightened bro Buddhism people hated and couldn't get enough of. Zach did his best to calm down the board, and at the encouragement of his wife, he used the opportunity to make a name for himself outside the partnership, without Bill dragging him down. It would work. On Monday, Zach would be announced as the sole chairman of Fortinbras Dynamics, and he'd have a very successful eleven-year run in that position. Bill's career in the tech world, on the other hand, was over. He would now join the pantheon of human punch lines. His name would be used in shorthand for spectacular failure, and his reputation in the industry would never recover.) "Maybe I'm overreacting," Pitterpat said.

"I hope you are," said Roxy. "If he does come back, obviously I take back the whole asshole thing."

"Obviously," said Pitterpat. "As do I, obviously."

"Obviously."

"But right now he's an asshole."

"Such an asshole."

Roxy and Pitterpat shared a laugh.

"I love you," said Roxy. "You *have* to come to my birthday party!"

And then Roxy hijacked the next fifteen minutes to explain New Year's Eve 1979. Two doctors, a man and a woman in green scrubs, set down their drinks at a nearby table. Alice felt her flashcards in her bag. Meredith Marks wouldn't sit here soothing her brokenhearted sister-in-law. She'd be practicing her violin, and if you want anything from her, take a number and wait. It was a marvel of a thing seeing Meredith not care about anything other than her violin.

Pitterpat loved New Year's Eve 1979. "That's so cool! I'll be there with bells on! And then with jelly bracelets on!"

Roxy laughed at this stupid joke, and the two of them high-fived a little too close to Alice's face. Didn't either of these people have any friends? Alice couldn't believe the neediness filling her life right now, squeezing her from both sides.

"And if the asshole comes back, bring him too!" said Roxy. "Which I'm sure he will. Why wouldn't he come back? You're amazing."

Pitterpat's face fell. She didn't agree.

"You are," Alice added because it suddenly got quiet.

"I'm not amazing," Pitterpat said finally. "Bill's the 'amazing' one. I'm just a person who loves her husband. That's all. All I did was love him. All I did was the thing that came naturally, and I don't see why it was so hard for him to do the same. There's plenty of things I want in life. Plenty of things. But that was one area where I . . . I was good. He was enough." She was crying now. Roxy handed her a napkin. "It's always about how smart Bill is. He's not the smart one."

She was looking right at Alice as she said it.

"I didn't—I didn't say he was."

"I know," said Pitterpat. "You've probably thought it, though. I know you're on his side."

"That's ridiculous," said Alice, though it wasn't ridiculous, it was correct, and Alice suddenly realized how much she cared about her sister-in-law. "Come here," she said, and she gave Pitterpat a hug.

They had another drink, and then another, and then made their way together down the acute back stairway, spilling out onto the sidewalk to the sound of some girl squealing with joy because that *was* her card!

"It was so great meeting you," said Roxy as she and Pitterpat embraced. "Let's hang out all the time. Now that you're single, I mean," Roxy said, and then quickly added, "Pitterpat! I love that name! How did you get that name?" Roxy was drunk.

"It's something my dad called me, and everyone kind of picked it up," she said, without any embarrassment. Alice could not believe how long this goodbye was taking. A high five between Roxy and Pitterpat turned into another hug, and Roxy, perhaps sensing if she didn't move along soon she'd start trying to make out with Pitterpat, bid them both good night.

"Do you want me to come over tonight?" said Alice, hoping for a no.

"That would be nice," said Pitterpat.

So they walked home, down the hill toward the river.

"You're taking the practice test soon?"

"In a few days, yeah. I think so."

"Do you have to go somewhere—"

"No, it's online. I'll just do it on my laptop."

Up in the apartment, Alice poured some water for both of them, and they stood in the windows, hydrating and looking out at New Jersey. The lights of the sunset still tickled the corners of the sky, the chemical pinks and purples still in evidence.

Pitterpat winced.

Alice noticed. "Are you okay?"

"No," Pitterpat said, shrinking to the couch, lying in a ball on her side. "I have Crohn's disease."

"Oh my God," Alice said.

"*Namu Amida Butsu*," Pitterpat replied.

"Excuse me?"

"It's something Bill taught me, some sort of Buddhist thing—OWWWW."

A lot of information. Alice asked, "Is there anything I can do?"

"*Namu Amida Butsu*," Pitterpat replied through her teeth, her eyes closed tight. "You say it, and some sort of Buddhist superhero comes to the rescue."

Together they repeated the Nembutsu, and the pain relented enough for Alice to help Pitterpat off the couch. Pitterpat made it to the bathroom in one piece, and stayed there for nearly a half hour. When it was over, she wanted a bath, but baths were ruined now, so instead she lay on her bed, in a state of ugliness, halfway undressed, halfway out of her makeup, and read Bill's email one more time. His absence didn't feel real. It felt like he was in class, or at the library studying, or at work, or out with Zach. It wouldn't feel real until tomorrow. Tomorrow would break Pitterpat, so tonight she would rest.

The email was short, concise, delicate, brutal, heartfelt, real, and agonizingly loving. Her husband loved her; she didn't doubt it, even now. Even in this darkest of moments, they were a team as they faced this new condition, this apartness, together. She would always want him. It was his last sentence that got her, that made her want to climb inside the earth and be smooshed by its pressure, squashed and squished down into the exquisitely lost diamond of her dreams.

"This is the least suffering I can offer you," he wrote.

* * *

Bob should have climbed down. He realized that as he climbed up, but it was too late, and climbing down seemed awfully scary right now, and the fire escape shook quite a bit, and he was very high up and also very high, so up he went, and suddenly he was on the roof of Samantha's building, where the world was quiet and rooflike. He looked at his phone, just in time to catch 7:59 becoming 8:00.

The roof was empty. A couple of buckets, someone's old lawn chair, and the door to the stairwell, which—he ran over and checked—was locked. There must be another way down. Fire escape? No. He'd have to pass by Samantha's window again. She might even be out there looking for him. She was probably going to come rattling up the ladder any second now, demanding to know what the fuck. There wasn't much time. There had to be a solution. At the other end of the roof, there was another building next to this one, and that roof and this roof were level, and the alley between the two of them was just narrow enough that he could pretty easily make it across with a running jump. But it was just wide enough that, no, that was a really bad idea, even to someone as high as Bob.

Buzz! His phone could not have been louder.

"I'm here!"

Trudy. It was 8:02.

"Hi! Sorry, running a bit behind," Bob replied. "Stuck in traffic."

Can I be honest?

"Will you be here soon?"

If he caught all the breaks, if he ran to the subway station, if the train arrived immediately, he could possibly be there in twenty minutes. If the State of New York completed construction on the Second Avenue Subway a year ahead of schedule and opened it right now, maybe fifteen.

"Yes. Two minutes away. Get a table. And go ahead and order. I'll see you soon!"

"Okay, great," she said, with a smiley face. "No worries. Can I order you something?"

"Boodles Martini, up, with an olive."

"Got it! See you in two!"

And then he just stood there, unable to do anything but play on his phone. Many blocks away, Trudy sat alone at a two-top in the sprawling Oyster Bar dining room and turned down a hard roll and a pat of butter for the second time. She opened MeWantThat. Tickets to a superhero movie. A slow cooker shaped like a triceratops. Earrings. Bob's martini arrived.

"Your Martini's here."

"Still in traffic," he replied. "Have the Martini, I'll get a new one when I see you."

"How close are you? I'm sorry, but it's getting kind of late. We may not have long together."

"So close. Order some food."

Bob thought of Amy, her hair in a ponytail, her turtleneck bunched up at her shoulders, breastfeeding her daughter. Buzz!

"Where did you go?"

Samantha.

Bob crept over to the fire escape and silently peeked over the edge, down to the platform below. Samantha was there, peering down into the dark alley, trying to see if that's where Bob had ended up. Then she looked up, and Bob ducked away, just in time. He backed up, silent step by silent step, until he was hidden behind the roof door. He took out his phone. Suitoronomy, by reflex. A girl named Caitlin matched with him. Her hair was black and shiny. Seven minutes went by.

Buzz!

"Hi."

"Hi. Did you drink the martini?"

"I had a sip. I'm not a fan. You are coming right?"

He started to write something when another text arrived.

"Is your name Bobert Smith?"

It was Tara. The girl from two nights ago. (And three months ago before that.) He didn't respond. He couldn't respond, to this or to any of them, as they pelted his phone like a sudden hailstorm.

"Hello???? Can you answer me????"

"Are you Bobert Smith?"

"Dude seriously where are you, I'm freaking out right now."

"Are you standing me up right now??????????"

"Is this you in this blog? Did you pee on this girl's train set?"

"Please tell me you're getting these."

"Are you seriously standing me up when I skipped my sister's birthday for this and now I have to pay for this expensive martini????????????"

"Everything okay Cinco?"

"If this blog is real you're disgusting."

"Hello???????????????????????"

"You are freaking my shit out right now!!!"

"Look up, New York!"

That last text was from the city, some stupid thing they were doing now. He'd been getting them all summer and deleting them immediately, but this time he didn't. This time he looked up.

The stars were out. When had that happened? Of course they'd always been there, you just can't see them when there's so much light all over the place, but there they were now, only a few of them, but enough to remind Bob that he was a tiny little speck in an enormous universe. Amy was at home right now, probably sitting in bed, probably watching *Love on the Ugly Side*, probably with Doug, far away from any sort of self-created shitstorm no forty-year-old should ever find themselves in. And for a second, Bob knew—he *really* knew—how obvious he had become.

But he only had a second to know it. There was a sound—a rusty clanking. Bob peeked around the corner. The fire escape shook . . . shook . . . shook . . . *She's coming up here.*

(Samantha Blennerhasset went on to become a successful writer of speculative fiction. Years later, in the little room over the boathouse at her family's compound in Vermont, she spent a summer tapping out a slim memoir about her threadbare life in New York before success found her. One of the book's vignettes described tonight's excitement. She was smoking weed in her apartment with some guy named Bob when suddenly, "There was a knock at the door. 'Who's there?' I said. 'It's Francisco,' came the reply, in a big booming New York voice. I went to look through the peephole. The building superintendent glowered back at me. 'What's up, Francisco?' 'What's up? You gonna break down those fucking boxes or what?' 'What boxes?' 'Listen, lady, I don't want to lose my temper out here in the hallway because it's a family building, but then I see your fucking moving boxes out in the alley, and you didn't break them down, and I'm gonna hear about that shit from the recycling company!' 'What boxes? What are you talking about?' 'Your moving boxes! The ones you just moved in with!' 'I've been here two years. I didn't just move in.' 'Yeah? Then how come every fucking one of them fucking boxes has "4B" written on it?' 'This is 5B.' He stepped back and looked at the numbers on the door. 'Fuck,' he said. 'You know what? I got so angry, I walked up too many flights. Sorry to bother you.' And he went back down the stairs. I could hear him banging on 4B's door as I turned back to the room, which was now empty. Bob had disappeared into thin air. That moment changed my life. I closed the window, opened my laptop, and wrote the first seven pages of *The Evaporated* that night. So wherever you are now, Bob, thank you.")

Bob ran as fast as he could. The edge of the building approached, and he wasn't going to stop. He was going to keep running and then leap to the other building across the alleyway. He was going to land on the other roof, and then he was going to run down the other building's fire escape or stairs, and run all the way to Grand Central, and catch Trudy just as she was leaving, and kiss her really well and thoroughly, and she'd forgive him and blow off her sister's birthday, and they'd split a giant platter of oysters and some champagne, and then grab a black-and-white cookie at the Grand Central bakery, and share it on the Metro-North train to Chappaqua or Mount Kisco or Bedford Hills, one of those places, and they'd find a big house up there with a yard for the kids, and they'd live out the rest of their days happy and in love and never be single again, and if it wasn't Trudy in this scenario, maybe it would be this Caitlin with the shiny hair.

This vision appeared quickly to Bob as his left foot pushed off from the cornice, launching him toward the other rooftop. It disappeared just as quickly as he began to fall.

CHAPTER SEVEN

Vows

Back in November, when they were still dating, Alice found a Winston Churchill wall calendar for Carlos, and just knew he'd love it. A Churchill a month! Then in December, she forgot that she'd bought it and gave him a Churchill bow tie instead. Then in April, she rediscovered it stuffed in a suitcase with her summer clothes, but she had broken up with Carlos by then, and 2015 was already on its fourth Churchill. She meant to throw it out but never got around to it. Then in June, a few days after moving in with Roxy, she nailed it to her bedroom wall.

This was her MCAT calendar. She marked down the important dates of the summer in pen. She began with the last and most important date of all: September 10, the day of the test. In red ink she wrote "D-DAY," with three emphatic underlines, and then the time and address of the test.

That part was easy. The next part took some strategy.

In 2015, the Association of American Medical Colleges put out four practice MCATs. Debates raged on the discussion boards Alice never checked about the best way to use these tests. Specifically: When was the best time to take them? Some argued you should take the first one right away, at the beginning of your journey, to know what lay ahead of you. Most others said to start the practice tests a month out from the test and space them out. One all-capsy young man argued for the brutal challenge of doing all four in a row the week before the actual test. (This goofy little stunt of endurance did not pay off: The young man's seat was empty the day of the MCAT, and he never rescheduled. He became a pharma rep.)

After careful consideration, Alice planned her assault on the practice tests as an accelerando: practice test, sixteen days off, practice test, eight days off, practice test, four days off, practice test, two days off, D-DAY. After doing the math (and realizing how much better she'd need to get at math if she was going to pass this thing), she wrote the words "PRACTICE TEST" in the boxes for:

August 7.

August 24.

September 2.

September 7.

Five days. Four practice tests and then the real thing September 10. Her whole world would now be built around these five days.

"Don't forget August fourteenth," Roxy said over Alice's shoulder, startling her. "That's my birthday, Doc!"

"Oh," said Alice. "I'm kind of using this as, like, a *work* calendar—"

"Yeah, but you're gonna want to mark down the fourteenth. Big day. Trust me."

"Okay—"

"There's gonna be a party. And that party's gonna have a theme. Details to come, but yeah. Mark it down."

Alice tried to think of the fewest number of syllables that would get her out of this conversation and back onto her train of thought. She went with: "Cool."

Roxy wandered out of the room, face in phone, and Alice got back to planning. (Two days later, "Happy B-Day, Roxy!" mysteriously appeared scrawled under August 14 in pink bubble pen. The August photo of Winston Churchill scowled augustly.)

That was nearly two months ago, when it was GOOD MORNING.

IT'S 89 DAYS UNTIL THE TEST, and August was a distant obligation, not entirely real, as if there might not even be an August at all,
who knew, it was a long way off. But August arrived, and now it was
GOOD MORNING. IT'S 35 DAYS UNTIL THE TEST, and the
first circled date on the calendar was only one sleep away. Alice needed
a quiet spot where she could simulate the conditions of a real MCAT,
which meant she'd need to do it at the kitchen table.

"Not a problem, Doc!" Roxy texted, still using that nickname.
Then, a few minutes later: "How long is the test?"

"Seven hours and twenty-two minutes."

"Wow! Okay, gotcha. I will keep out of your hair for seven hours
twenty-two minutes."

This seemed unlikely. Maybe it was City Hall observing summer
hours, or Roxy's lack of enthusiasm for her work, or the fact that she
could do her job remotely, but a day rarely went by that she didn't duck
back into the apartment one or two times, often just for hour-long
stretches of snacking and *Love on the Ugly Side*.

"Thanks," Alice said.

"NP," Roxy replied. "Hopefully I'll be super busy at work anyway.
Like maybe someone'll get killed by a bicycle tomorrow. Not that I'm
hoping for that! Obvs don't want anyone getting killed. But it's probably gonna happen at some point, so hopefully it'll be tomorrow." Then,
a little later: "You'll just be in your room the whole time?"

"The kitchen!"

"Right! Of course. Yes that's fine." A pause, and then: "That's fine."

"Thank you. You're sure it's okay?"

"Def." And then: "Totally." And then: "Totally." And then, finally,
nineteen minutes later, "Unless there's somewhere else you can do it?"

So Alice asked Pitterpat.

"Of course, take the test here! Oh, how exciting! I'll go out, I'll
leave you completely alone."

This took Alice by surprise. Pitterpat hadn't left the apartment in
weeks. A few days after Bill left, she went out to get a bagel up the
street, and then, coming home, rode the elevator with either Joan or

Joanne from the eighth floor. (Joan and Joanne were two different ladies, but Pitterpat, having learned their names years ago, couldn't safely say who was who.) Joan and Joanne were both very talkative, but this particular Joan or Joanne was *especially* talkative, full of gossip and complaints about the noisy radiators and updates on her war with the super. This day, however, Joan or Joanne was silent, and Pitterpat knew it was because Joan or Joanne had heard from someone (possibly Joanne or Joan) that something bad had happened with the Quicks up on twelve, and it was all over the building. After that, Pitterpat stopped going out.

So when Alice showed up at Pitterpat's door early the next morning with her laptop and a backpack full of chocolate almond sea salt granola bars, something springy in Pitterpat inspired her to throw on some shorts and a T-shirt in a way that was almost cheerful, and venture out into the sunny world of August.

"How exciting," Pitterpat said as she put on her flip-flops. Alice readied the dining room table, laying out her granola bars in neat little rows. "So what are you aiming for? What's a good score on this thing?"

"Well, it's a little complicated," Alice explained. "The MCAT is scored by percentile, with 500 being right in the middle, the fiftieth percentile. To get in the ninety-fifth percentile, like, Ivy League territory, you need a 516. This early on, I'd be happy with something right in the middle. 500 would be great. Even a little less."

"Okay," said Pitterpat. "I'm going to manifest positive energy in the form of the number 510."

"Oh! Thank you! 510 would be amazing!" said Alice with a smile. "I don't expect to be quite there yet since this is only my first one of these. I've got another month and change to get better. But sure, 510, I'll take it!"

"I believe in you," Pitterpat said. "510."

"510," Alice repeated. Was Pitterpat being weird, or was she just this resilient? Either way, it made Alice happy, and she noted the odd sensation that it took Bill disappearing for Alice and her sister-in-law to actually kind of become friends. "Thank you for letting me do this."

"No, thank *you* for giving me a reason to do *this*," Pitterpat said as she opened the front door and floated through it. She turned, tossed a jaunty "*À tout à l'heure! Bonne chance!*" over her shoulder, and was gone.

There was nobody on the elevator! Pitterpat strolled through the lobby, and the doorman said hello, with a raised eyebrow that said he was delighted to see her after two weeks, though he understood why he hadn't seen her in two weeks, but we don't need to talk about that right now or ever. Pitterpat gave a happy little wave back and headed out the door. She walked up 113th and kept walking, over to the round-about on the northwest corner of the park. She passed a bicycle shop, and it occurred to her to maybe buy a bicycle, with a bell and a cute white basket. She would look later and find the right one online, but then see if the bike shop could order it so she could support a neighbor-hood brick-and-mortar store, especially a cute one like this with colorful bicycles in the window, and she would tag the store in all her posts. Then, after crossing 110th Street, she passed Pamela Campbell Clark, who had just walked through the park, and the bicycle that whizzed by three seconds later came so close to Pitterpat, it tossed her hair about.

What kind of a day was it in Central Park on August 7, 2015? Clement and warm. Seventy-nine degrees Fahrenheit in the morning, steadily rising to the day's high of eighty-one at noon. The wind blew southerly, and then westerly as the round yellow sun crossed the sky. The humidity was an easy 36 percent.

But Instagram is where the story lies. In Central Park on August 7, snap after snap of arcadian delights, each one a Seurat. The Pomeranian rolling on its back in the grass. The little girl toddling by the Duck Pond. The bikini top thirst-trapping by the Bethesda Fountain. New Yorkers upon New Yorkers, all so different in so many ways, but all with the same green below them, the same blue above. And there, in one of those pictures, behind two softball players ussie-ing by a tree, is a slice of Pitterpat. Just a shoulder, a sliver of her bob, and an arm half extended, its hand holding an ice cream cone. Was ever an ice cream cone so apt?

And as she walked, of course Pitterpat thought of Bill and all the times they'd been in this park together. Long, happy days that gave the world dozens of happy photographs, blue above, green below. But those memories failed now, when they were needed the most, to remind Pitterpat that she was sad. The memories tried and tried to land a punch, but they couldn't, as Pitterpat slowly promenaded by the zoo, because now they felt like false memories, pictures on someone else's Instagram. Had Pitterpat wanted this? Was that it? No, certainly not. Sure, there were moments of dissatisfaction stitched into this marriage. But Bill was Bill. He was her thing. He had been her thing from the day she met him, whether he knew it or not, and he was always her thing right up until that bubble bath. And now her thing was gone. Why, then, was the sunshine so warm?

She stayed out all day. For eight hours she walked and ate ice cream and rode the carousel and remembered what it was like to be fresh and summery. Usually she hid from the sun, fearing its damage, but not today. Today nothing could harm her. And all day, at every stop, she remembered to pray the same silent prayer for her sister-in-law: *510*. She repeated it, again and again, by the band shell, by the castle, in the field. *510. 510. 510.*

Nobody in the lobby but the doorman! *510.* Nobody in the elevator either! *510.* Her key found the lock. *510.*

She entered the apartment, and Alice was on the couch, wrapped in a blanket.

"488."

"Is that bad?" Pitterpat asked, knowing immediately it was.

They ordered a pizza. Alice was silent as they ate the entire thing. Pitterpat wanted to talk about her day but could see the invitation wasn't there.

Then, not long after dinner, as the sun set and a new moon rose, Alice's dad FaceTimed her. She declined and then texted him.

"Can we please talk on the phone?"

"Let's FaceTime!" he said. So she FaceTimed him.

"Hi, Dad," she said.

"Hi, honey," said her dad's sideways face, in landscape mode for some reason. "How are you?"

"I'm okay," she said, and she told him everything. Then she asked him how he was doing and he just talked about the Peloponnesian War, and Alice thought of her dad in that house all alone out in the woods reading books about ancient Greece, and it made her a little sad, but you can't tell someone they're being happy wrong.

Returning to the room with another slice of pizza, Pitterpat immediately recognized the voice of her maybe-future-ex-father-in-law. It sent a shock wave down her spine, reminding her that, despite a nice day in the park, her life was still a mess.

"Where are you?" Mr. Quick asked, and suddenly the forbidden subject couldn't be avoided.

"I'm at Bill and Pitterpat's," she said.

"Oh."

And that was all he had to say. Of course he knew everything that had happened, but he wasn't going to talk about it. He didn't even ask how Pitterpat was holding up, as Alice and Pitterpat both noticed. Instead he just changed the subject.

"We opened the pool," he said. "It's here if you ever want to come up for a weekend."

Alice flinched at the "we." There was no "we." It was just him up there, and while his Yankee grit wouldn't let him ask for some occasional attention, Alice knew he needed it. Plus it was getting hot, and Alice wanted to swim.

"Can I bring Pitterpat?"

"Of course," said her dad, and then he changed the subject again.

* * *

Roxy wanted to come too, of course, and even if Alice wanted to say no, it was hard to ignore the long list of events, parties, soirees, galas, kickers, and hangs Roxy had invited Alice to over the course of this summer. It was refreshing to invite Roxy somewhere for a change.

They left the next afternoon. They caught a Metro-North train at 125th, and fifty-nine minutes later Mr. Quick and his old Subaru were waiting for them in the little traffic circle by the station in Bedford Hills. They piled in, and he drove them to what Alice and Bill had been calling "the new house" for years now. It was filled with antiquities, both from her dad's various scholarly cruises and from Alice's childhood, and Alice knew she and her dad were probably six months away from a serious talk about getting a cleaning lady.

They put down their bags, figured out the sleeping arrangements, and had dinner from Rainbow Panda. As he passed her the spring rolls, Mr. Quick asked Alice, "How's Carlos?"

"I don't know, Dad," Alice replied, amused. "Why don't you call him?"

"She's got a new boyfriend now," Roxy offered helpfully. "Grover Kines. Not that I've met him or anything."

"Oh," said Mr. Quick. "Well, that's nice. Though I did like Carlos."

Of course he did. They were both simple men with simple obsessions who moved through life like water. Alice didn't want to look at it too closely, but the similarities were there.

After dinner, Mr. Quick put on the Red Sox game, and the girls headed out to a local bar.

"This reminds me of where my grandma lives, way out in Connecticut," said Roxy as she watched the dark trees blur by on the way to the bar. "Nothing but old houses and woods. Old houses full of ghosts, woods full of bears. Ghosts and bears. No *thank you*."

Alice took a detour, turning the aging Subaru up a road it had turned up countless times before. The car rolled slowly past Rudy's house. A few lights were on, in what Alice knew were the kitchen and dining room. Alice imagined Rudy's parents cleaning up after dinner, washing dishes and putting things away. Alice could picture every magnet on the fridge. Maybe Rudy was there too for some reason. Why hadn't she written back? Was she angry about something? Alice found it easy to imagine people being angry with her, even if she couldn't imagine why.

Finally, up the street a bit, the car came to a stop in front of a small colonial house, with a magnolia tree in the middle of the lawn. The house was painted white, but you couldn't tell in the darkness. Alice turned off the ignition, and quiet resumed.

"That's the old house," said Alice, nodding across Roxy in the passenger seat.

"That's where Bill and I got married," Pitterpat added.

The house was now three and a half years unlived in, and looked it. It was dark, with all the lights out. Roxy shivered.

"Why's it so dark?"

"The new owner is some Russian guy. He bought it with a trust. I guess he and his family have been snatching up houses all over town because the resale here isn't bad over the long run. But he doesn't live here, and he doesn't even rent it out. It's just a place for him to park his money."

"That's terrible."

"I know."

They kept looking at the house, as though something would happen, but it just kept sleeping. Then Alice noticed something.

"Do you see the window to the right of the door? The little window."

Roxy and Pitterpat squinted. What looked at first like yet another of many dark windows actually gave off a foggy yellow glow. There was some sort of light in there.

"That's the front hall closet," said Alice. "I used to hide out in there. It was dark with the door closed, so my mom put in a little night-light you could switch on and off. The day we moved, after everything was loaded onto the truck, I went back in to do one last sweep, and I noticed that night-light, still plugged in. I thought about taking it, but I didn't. I just turned it on again and closed the door. That was three years ago, and somehow that little light bulb is still going. I can't believe it hasn't burned out."

"Very Hanukkah," observed Roxy.

"It's the one thing of me that remains. The very last bit of Alice Quick in that house. The flutterby night-light."

"The what night-light?"

"Flutterby. Butterfly. It was shaped like a butterfly."

When Alice was three, she found a caterpillar in the garden. This was a memory she treasured, thinking it was only that, a memory, not knowing the moment had been captured on video by her dad's new camcorder. Years later he sent out all the old family tapes to be converted to digital files, but nobody ever got around to watching them. Nobody except me. Here she is in the garden, finding the caterpillar, catching it, and bringing it to her father.

"What is it?"

"It's a calerpittar!"

"A calerpittar?!" Her dad's voice, close to the mic, popping the *p*. (She always vaguely remembered something blocking his face. It was the camera.)

"Yes. A calerpittar."

"And is that calerpittar going to grow up to become a flutterby?"

Mom laughs at the dad joke. Alice looks at her dad and makes a face, like her dad was being silly. Does she know he's mocking her? Does she know "flutterby" isn't a word? Or does she just gather from his tone that this was a joke, and has learned to make this face, her Dad-just-made-a-joke face? There's no way to know.

The wind shook the trees. More headlights coming up the road.

Roxy looked at the house and saw a dark place, with ghosts inside and bears all around. And no cell reception.

Pitterpat looked at the house and saw her wedding, the out-of-season cabbage roses and the peonies and the red carpet extending from the sunroom doors to the altar by the Japanese maple, and the white-knuckle terror that her family would ruin everything.

Alice looked at the house and saw her mother.

"Calerpittar," her mother said, "are you in there?"

Of course she was. She was always in the closet, reading, or coloring, or just making up stories in her head.

"Of course I am," she said, because she'd recently picked up "of course" and used it constantly.

"I thought so," her mom said. "It's piano time."

"No," Alice said, with a sulk.

"How about I give you one more minute."

"Ooooookay."

A minute went by as Alice continued the business of being little. Then: "Okay, sweetie, that was a minute. Time to come out."

"Ooooooookay," Alice said, but remained where she was, lying on her back, looking up through the winter coats.

"Ready?"

She was never ready. But her mom was patient and persistent, and eventually the big grown-up hand closed around Alice's little matchstick fingers and led her to the piano.

The piano had always been there in the little room off the sunroom, as if it had grown out of the floor like a tree. It was a brown spinet, with an orange light under the keyboard that would light up when the soundboard got too dry. Penelope had played a little in her youth, and could still toss off a Christmas carol once or twice every December. John never touched the thing. Bill banged on it occasionally when he was bored and needed something loud and calamitous to happen, and then lost interest.

But Alice and this machine, this hulking contraption of wood and iron and felt and brass, were hopelessly matched. As a toddler, she explored the wondrous thing inch by inch, getting to know everything about it. Her fingers found the keys, and the keys made sense like nothing else ever had. There was a discoloration on the side of the middle A, which you could only see if you depressed the middle B. It was purplish blue, and it looked like an eagle or some sort of prehistoric winged insect. This looming chocolate-colored box of mystery was to be part of her destiny, she knew even then.

(And why, we ask? It's tempting to say genetics, and yet twin unbeknownst Sofia Hjalmarsson never came close to becoming a musician. She learned "Hot Cross Buns" on the recorder in barneskole when she was seven, it left her cold, and the muse never darkened her doorway again.)

Alice turned five, and her mom signed her up for lessons with a lady they knew from church: Mrs. Pidgeon, an impossibly tall woman with a high distant frizz of hair and eyebrows. When you're five years old, the extremities of human dimensions are captivating things, and a woman taller than six feet was a marvel to little Alice. Every Tuesday after school, Alice would walk out of Katonah Elementary, and instead of going to the bus stop, she'd walk down the street a bit, turn a corner, and arrive at the strange-smelling house where Mrs. Pidgeon lived and taught.

Alice thought about Mrs. Pidgeon as she nursed her Aperol spritz, which was the drink that summer, even in Westchester dive bars. It was a little bitter.

Roxy was mid-rant. "Are you watching it?"

"Of course I am," bellowed Pitterpat. "Mallory?"

"Psychopath!"

Pitterpat and Roxy laughed and continued discussing the latest episode of *Love on the Ugly Side*, and how the six remaining girls were forced to inhale each other's farts from plastic bags in order to win the wine-tasting date with Jordan, and Mallory was the least visibly nauseated.

Alice looked up Mrs. Pidgeon on Google once. She was hard to find, but eventually there she was, in her eighties now. Alice used what she could find to stitch together a story of Mrs. Pidgeon's last twenty years: the happy retirement and community service (an award from the chamber of commerce in 2004) until the loss of her husband (an obituary from 2012) and the sale of the house (a Zillow listing from 2013). Alice could no longer knock on Mrs. Pidgeon's door and say hello, and maybe come in for a piano lesson, and start life all over again.

But the house was still there, preserved in the Zillow listing. It had been cleaned out, painted, stripped of the crushed-velvet furniture and Victorian wallpaper. But there was the door Alice had knocked on. There by the stairs were the three doorbell chimes on display. And there in that alcove by the bay window was the spot the upright piano had been, where Mrs. Pidgeon had guided Alice on the first steps of what could have been a lifelong journey. It was there Alice discovered the joy of music. Not the joy of hearing it, or even the joy of making it, but rather the joy of *working on it*. Practice, repetition, large tasks broken down into smaller ones, isolation drills, challenges and rewards . . . these were all part of the secret handshake, as Alice joined the mysterious order of people who are good at something.

"Any time you see someone being good at something," Mrs. Pidgeon would say, "whether it's shooting a basketball or playing an instrument or fixing a car, it's just a trick. The thing you're not seeing is the hundred thousand times they did it wrong. Michael Jordan has missed more free throws than anyone you know. That's all there is to it, Alice. Do it a lot."

So Alice did it a lot. And sooner than anyone expected, Alice could play Bach. And then Beethoven. And not just the easy works everyone learned, but increasingly advanced suites and sonatas and ballads. One day, after Alice's ten-year-old fingers had galloped their way, mistake-free, through one of Bartok's twistier Hungarian Folksongs, Alice's mom applauded, and sat down next to her daughter on the piano bench in the little room off the sunroom.

"Honey," she said, "you're very good at piano."

"Thank you," Alice said, with a nervous giggle.

"I mean, you're very good," Penelope continued, and Alice could see this was taking a serious turn. "It's not just me saying this. Mrs. Pidgeon says it too. She says this is something you could do more seriously, if you'd like."

Somehow Alice knew vaguely what this meant and asked the right question: "Will I have time?"

Penelope laughed. "We'll make time."

"You can't make time," Alice said.

"You know what I mean. You could be *great*. Do you want to be great?"

Alice didn't understand. If only she could have said no, of course not, good is good enough! But she only smiled, and with a performatively precocious nod said, "Yes."

Her mom smiled like the sun coming through clouds, and Alice was warm all over. Her mother had been quiet and sad lately. Alice had seen it. They had all seen it. All except Dad, who had been out of the country for two weeks, working on the acquisition of a company in Korea. But now Penelope shone brightly.

"That's my girl! I think it could be really nice for both of us. I'll help you."

"Can I play in a recital?"

"If you keep practicing, you can play at Carnegie Hall," she said, with a little laugh. Eventually Alice would know what Carnegie Hall was, and she'd play there, but right now it was only a glint in her mother's eyes and she knew she wanted it; she wanted it for her mother and for herself. "There's no limit, Calerpittar. It's all yours if you want it. C'mere," Penelope said, and hugged her daughter tight, for just a moment, before letting her go. "Now get back to work."

* * *

After fourth grade, Penelope and Mrs. Pidgeon agreed it was time for Alice to "find the next gear," so Alice was enrolled at the Youth Conservatory of Westchester, an expensive private school in an old stone armory rumored by the students to have once been a prison. It was twenty miles away, in Dobbs Ferry, but thankfully there was a bus.

So one September morning, at some punishingly early hour, Alice and her mother sat in the old Subaru in the nearly empty parking lot of Alice's elementary school. In a few hours, the lot would fill up with cars, as all of Alice's old classmates arrived for fifth grade, and some of them, like Rudy, would wonder why Alice wasn't there. But now there were only two cars, idling in the misty quiet. The sun was not yet over the trees and the grass was still dewy.

"Remember to be a good listener," said Penelope, blowing on her coffee.

"I know, Mom."

"You're going there to work, remember that."

"Of course."

"I love you."

"I know."

"Your dad loves you too."

"I know."

A few minutes passed, and at last a little yellow bus rolled up the long country driveway and came to a stop in the loading zone. Alice got out of the car. Penelope, still in slippers and a nightgown, rolled down her window and blew a kiss goodbye.

A slim girl about Alice's age got out of the other car. Alice had seen this girl at her audition in the spring, and again once over the summer at the public pool. She must have lived in Bedford or Mount Kisco. There was a violin case under her arm, and she held it like a soldier going into battle. Her name, Alice would eventually learn, was Meredith Marks.

Alice and Meredith climbed onto the bus and, discovering that theirs was the first stop and the bus was empty, sat down across the aisle from each other. They didn't talk that first day, just quietly collected their nerves and churned with the anticipation. The next stop was in Chappaqua, a ten-minute drive. It was ten minutes of silence.

The second day, when they boarded the bus, they acknowledged each other in bashful whispers. It was just a "hi" and another "hi," and then they sat in the same seats as yesterday, across the aisle from each other, and spent ten quiet minutes looking out the window and watching the leaves of Route 172 go by.

It was the third day when Alice noticed Meredith's skinned elbow.

"What happened?"

Meredith looked at her elbow, then at her fellow passenger. "I fell off my bike."

"Does it hurt?"

"Yeah," she said. "I was supposed to be wearing elbow pads. I got in big trouble."

"Oh my God," said Alice. "My mom would be so mad at me if I did that."

"She was like, 'Meredith, that's your bow elbow! You need that elbow!'"

Alice laughed, and scooched over to Meredith's side of the bus, and remained there for the next seven years. By the end of the week, they were best friends. By the end of the semester, they were playing duets together. By the end of the school year, they were at Carnegie Hall.

After all these years, Alice couldn't remember the actual performance, only that she messed up a trill during *Salut d'Amour*. She remembered that feeling, that momentary but bottomless shudder of failure, followed by that cool feeling of waking when you realize it happened and it's behind you and your hands are still doing what they're told and you can still get to the end of the piece without plummeting into the center of the earth, and it will all be okay.

The rest of it—what she wore, what Meredith wore, what the room looked like, how the microphone echoed, how the crowd sounded when they applauded—was not a memory of reality, but a memory of the video she'd watched countless times in the years since. She remembered the piano not through her own eyes, but through the eyes of the videographer eleven rows back. The hands playing the piano were not her hands, but the hands of a little girl on a stage. The applause was not the *feeling* of applause, but only the *sound* of applause, a tinny fuzz from the speakers of her TV, and then her computer, and now her iPhone. It might as well have been canned clapping from a game show.

Everyone agreed she and Meredith played very well, and the trill was never mentioned, not by her mother, not by her teacher, not even by Meredith.

Andante went the weeks and months. Mr. Quick's business trips become more frequent. Bill went off to college. Alice and her mother were alone together. They relaxed into it. They called themselves roommates. They slept in the same bed many nights, after staying up late to watch TV together. And every day, as Alice practiced, Penelope sat on the couch, reading a magazine or painting her nails or doing whatever one did while sitting on a couch back in the forgotten dreamtime before iPhones. And when Alice would stop too long, Penelope would chirp, "Get back to work," and Alice would resume. Alice always felt her there, over her right shoulder.

She felt her there even now, always just over her right shoulder, watching her daughter watching the Aperol spritz get watery while her two friends discussed Mallory's latest antics.

Bill came home from his first year of college. Alice had been in her room, packing. In two days she was going to the boundary waters of Minnesota, for two weeks of canoeing and sleeping in tents and speaking only French. And, for the first time in years, *not playing piano*. Alice couldn't imagine not even touching a keyboard for two weeks. But here she was, really going. She was zipping up the duffel bag when her mother called her to the kitchen. Bill was already sitting at the table. Alice took a seat next to him. There was no food laid out. The three of them sat at the empty table, waiting for Mrs. Quick to build up the nerve to say what she needed to say. Finally, she said it.

"Dad and I are getting divorced," she said.

Bill, a little older, didn't need an explanation. He got up and grabbed his backpack.

"I'm gonna go have a cigarette," he said.

"Okay," said Mrs. Quick. He'd been hiding his habit for three years, but no longer. He walked outside, to the end of the driveway, and lit a cigarette, and then kept walking, disappearing around a corner. He didn't come back that night. It never occurred to him to stay and be there for his sister.

Alice went to her room and dialed the long number for her dad's hotel in Taiwan. She bit her nails through the long doot-doots as the phone rang half a world away. She didn't want him to answer. He didn't. She left a message with the front desk and hung up. When the phone hit the receiver, Alice's mom walked in and sat down on the bed.

"You're lucky," her mom said. "You play piano."

Alice didn't know what she meant. "Thanks."

Her mom didn't seem to hear her and hardly even looked at her. She was staring at the wall, watching a television that wasn't there. "You have to be good at something, Calerpittar," she said, and then, amending it, "You have to be great at something. You have to have value. A husband will not give you your value. You have to make your own. You have to build it out of something no one can take away."

The next day, Penelope canceled canoe camp.

The divorce never happened. The rubber band that held John and Penelope together had stretched as far as it would go, and now they returned inevitably to one another's proximity as if nothing had happened. Well, almost nothing. During the separation, Mr. Quick had bought a small house nearby, and though it briefly went back on the market priced at a massive loss, eventually he decided to keep the place, because he liked going over there, and there were lots of shelves for his books. He lived there for weeks at a time sometimes, and Penelope seemed generally fine with it. You can't tell someone they're being happy wrong.

That whole summer, Alice held tighter than ever to piano. Why try to solve your family when Schumann needs your attention? In the chaos of *Kreisleriana*, op. 16, was the comfort of structure. It's all written down. The old ghost tells you to play a note, so you play it. The rest is silence.

Alice still practiced in the little room off the sunroom, and Penelope still sat on the couch, just over her right shoulder. And Alice still turned back to look at her mom after every piece, and her mom still rewarded her with a smile. But it was a different smile now. It was a smile that tried so hard to look like support when all it really looked like was need. Alice's piano career was no longer something fun, something to laugh about at dinner parties. It was now the square of the roulette table upon which every one of Mrs. Quick's chips was stacked.

"And that really sucked," said Alice. "It made me start to hate piano."

"I'll bet," said Roxy, riveted.

The bar was filling up now with locals, but Alice, Roxy, and Pitterpat had laid claim to this corner booth and paid no attention.

"But you couldn't tell her," said Pitterpat.

"That would have killed her. Like, actually killed her more than cancer. I had to keep doing it."

"Except you didn't," said Roxy.

The ice cube in Alice's Aperol spritz was gone now.

"Except I didn't."

The summer before senior year, Alice and her mom took a trip to the Ithaca School of Music. Ithaca was a pipeline to a career as a pianist, not just being a piano teacher like Mrs. Pidgeon or playing show tunes in cruise ship lobbies, but performing on actual stages, with your face on the poster outside. This was the opportunity, as Penelope said to Alice, "of both of our lifetimes."

The two women drove up to Ithaca together, and for the entire four hours in the car, as the soundtrack alternated between piano pieces Alice was working on and Penelope's endless, terrifying pep talk, Alice realized how much she would rather be anywhere else, doing anything else. She was going to meet and audition for the head of the piano department, Professor Staples. And Professor Staples was going to meet Mrs. Quick. Mrs. Quick knew her daughter would dazzle this man. Alice knew her mother would embarrass both of them.

As expected (by Alice), Penelope was a nightmare, talking way too much and saying it way too loud and way too close, shaking hands too long, staying in the room too long, ignoring every nonverbal cue.

And as expected (by Penelope), Alice delivered a beautiful audition. Professor Staples's first word, after her fingers left the keyboard and her foot lifted from the pedal, was a soft, breathy "Wow."

The whole drive home, Penelope relived that "wow," swimming in that "wow," having the revenge fling she so badly needed with that "wow." And Alice fought like hell to keep a thought out of her mind that had been growing there for years.

When you want to change something fundamental in your life, and it's a change that will hurt someone you love, the worst thing you can do is admit it to yourself. If you want to cause as little pain as possible, do not open that door, and do not look inside. By the time their car reached the driveway in Katonah, Alice was horrified by what she couldn't put back in its hiding place: It was time to quit piano.

"You'll regret it," said Meredith, "immediately."

"I don't want to live this way anymore. There's more to life than just being really good at doing one thing all the time!"

"I don't understand."

"You don't understand? Or you don't *want* to understand because you feel the same way and you're too chickenshit to admit it?"

It felt like a savage burn at the time. Years later, Alice had to concede: Meredith genuinely didn't understand. Meredith gave her friend a hug and offered to be there for her, to talk at any time. But she and Alice both knew what the moment was a little bit about: Meredith had won. It would be Meredith's face on a concert poster. Alice suspected Meredith was satisfied with this outcome, and that suspicion never went away, no matter how sweet Meredith would be in later years, emailing Alice whenever she was in town, always meeting her for dinner.

Every fall, the Youth Conservatory's graduating class gave a recital. On the school website, you can still see photos from the event, including a shot of the inside of the program. (The cover of the program is no longer online, due to the unfortunate after-the-fact discovery that the image selected to grace the cover—an abstract charcoal drawing by a precocious sophomore, hand-selected by the head of the studio arts department—was actually hundreds of testicles.)

Five minutes after they were supposed to have left for the recital was not the best time for Alice to break her mother's heart, but that's when it happened, and once the words were out of her mouth, this conversation couldn't be paused until after the show.

Mrs. Quick did not quite understand, so she kept putting on her coat. "What are you saying to me?"

"I just don't think this is what I want to do with my life," Alice said. She wanted to say she hated the piano. She resisted the urge. The goal was to sever herself from this life without killing the patient, or any bystanders.

Mrs. Quick was annoyed. "Really? Now? We're supposed to be on the Saw Mill by now."

"I've been trying to tell you for a while."

"You've had lots of opportunities."

"I know."

"And this is the first I hear of it." Alice started to cry, and suddenly wanted her mom, and knowing she couldn't have her right now made her cry more. Penelope groaned. "Alice, just get in the car. We'll talk about this on the way to school."

"I don't want to, Mom. Please."

"You're playing this concert, Alice. Get in the car."

"Please, Mom!"

"You're not doing this, Alice! You have a full ride from Ithaca. If you throw this away, you will regret it the rest of your— No. No! You are not doing this to me too!"

The "too" stuck out to Alice, and from what Alice could tell, Mrs. Quick immediately regretted it.

"I'm not doing anything to you, Mom! I'm just making choices for my own—"

"Of course! Everybody gets to live their life! Everybody gets to make their own choices except me!"

"This isn't about you, Mother!"

"It absolutely is, Alice! You are just completely fucking me over right now, throwing everything away, everything we've done together, everything we've built together, and for what? What do you want to do instead?"

"I don't know! Go to college, I guess? I wish I knew exactly what I want to do with my life, but I don't! I'm not Meredith!"

"No, you're not. Because Meredith's not some entitled little marshmallow who thinks everything's gonna be handed to her! Meredith knows the meaning of work!"

A thing about Alice: She wasn't usually a violent person, but when she was in an argument, with no path to victory, she had been known to get violent, but always, and this is important, against inanimate objects. To a living creature, she would always Do No Harm, but if you were a nearby object and Alice Quick was upset, watch out. It's something she hated about herself, something she couldn't attribute to anything, maybe something deep in the unsolvable mystery of her genetics. (In fact, it was. Once, during a breakup, twin unbeknownst Sofia Hjalmarsson ripped the door off a microwave.)

This time, Alice punched the piano, as hard as she could.

They drove to the emergency room in silence. The X-ray confirmed what the doctor suspected immediately: hairline fractures in the fourth and fifth metacarpals. Alice walked out of the hospital with a cast on her hand. She had to take a bus home. Her mother had walked out at the moment of diagnosis.

Alice spent months, years even, wondering what she'd been trying to accomplish in that moment. As far as she could tell, it was either break the piano or break her hand, but which one she hated more was unknown even to her.

The next fall, Alice went off to SUNY Binghamton, where for four years she made some friends, majored in premed, because you had to major in something, and avoided pianos.

Her mother came to graduation, one of the few times she visited Binghamton. Everyone sweated through a long, muggy, makeup-and-hair-ruining commencement in the sweltering sun, and then, after dinner, Bill and Alice sat on the cool nighttime grass of the hill behind the library. Bill had been out of college for five years, but still seemed very much at home here as he lit a ceramic one-hitter that looked like a cigarette and he and Alice had what both would later acknowledge was the first conversation of their lives.

"You cannot marry her," Alice said, laughing for the first time all day. "You can't marry a Pitterpat."

"Who said we're getting married?"

"I don't know. It seems like you like her."

"Okay, first of all, I'm moving to San Francisco in the fall, so . . . you know, there's *that*. Plus we're just super different. We're like two separate species," he observed, and then took another hit.

"So then what are you doing with her?"

I'm gonna marry her was the answer he couldn't say out loud, so he changed the subject.

"This is nice."

"It really is." Alice lay back on the grass and looked at the stars. "I wish we'd done this when Mom and Dad got half-divorced."

He got her meaning immediately. He looked down at the blades of grass he was absently picking. "You had a rough time."

"Yeah, you could say that."

"I should have been there for you."

"Yeah, probably."

"Ahhhhhhh, shit," Bill said, flopping onto his back, looking up at the sky. "I'm sorry. I was off doing my thing. I didn't want to be a brother. Or a son. I just wanted to move forward through space and time. I don't even know what I'm saying, I'm high. I have no excuse for myself."

"It's okay," she said.

"I can't believe the first time she visits you at school, it's your graduation."

"Nice of her to show up for this at least." Alice sighed, exhaling a cloud of smoke. "She abandoned me. Abandoned by two moms."

"What do you mean?" She gave him a look. "Oh, right. God, I always forget."

"It's not like I talk to you about it a lot."

"It's not like you talk to me about anything a lot."

"We need to change that."

"We really do."

They watched the clouds drift past the moon.

"So," he said. "*Calerpittar.* What are you gonna do now?"

"Not go back to Katonah."

"Sounds like a plan."

"It's not a plan. It's my life's work. I'm not even going in the direction of Katonah. Katonah lies to the east. From this point forward, I will move only west. Never east. This is my solemn vow: I'm going west, young man."

She was high and didn't entirely think she meant it, but then, a week later, she moved to Chicago with some friends, and she stayed for six months. Six months waiting tables, six months shoveling pizza into her face, six months gaining weight, six months wearing sweaters. Then it started to get cold and her friends moved to Boston, so Alice drew another invisible vertical on the map, this time through the dot marked Chicago, and refused to consider anything to the right of it.

That's how she got to California. Bill and Pitterpat let her have the couch in the living room. While Pitterpat was almost chillingly gracious and accommodating, Alice saw how impeccably clean the bathroom always was, and she knew the gracious accommodation would run out. So one night, at one of many decadent Mexican dinners that Bill always arrived late for, Alice informed her besotted roommates that she'd found an apartment, a little studio west of here. She moved, and then, when someone got murdered in the building and she found herself ducking under yellow tape to get the mail, she moved again, to her fifth home in less than a year, a few blocks to the west of that.

Then one night, Alice Quick, a full year out of college, unemployed and single, stood on the bluffs of Mussel Rock Park, at the very edge of the continent, and looked out at the Pacific Ocean. When you're a voyager, an ocean doesn't stop you. Whether by celestial navigation or your last remaining frequent-flier miles, you find a way across.

That's how, occidentally and on purpose, Alice arrived in Hawaii. A week in Honolulu told her she wouldn't be staying in Honolulu, and though she heard nice things about the Big Island, the compass forbade it. Maui, to the west, was where the zephyr plopped her down, and for three years that's where she stayed, and surfed, and babysat for tourists in the resorts, and gradually stopped seeing pianos in her dreams. When the time came (if she ever had the money to do it, so probably never), Hong Kong would be next.

Then one day, as she was spinning the display of cheap sunglasses in the ABC Store across from Kama'ole Beach, her phone rang.

"Did you hear from Mom?"

She hadn't. Not for two years, in fact. Not a phone call, not an email. And Alice hadn't reached out to her mother either, having long since reached the conclusion that amends with a prodigal child were a mother's responsibility. Now the tone in her brother's voice crumbled that conclusion like wet sand.

"Okay." Bill sighed, and then he took a long pause, gathering himself. Finally: "Okay. Mom's sick, Alice. Really sick."

Twenty minutes later, having cried and pulled herself together, Alice sat on a bench across the street, looking out at the water, still on the phone. There was more.

"It feels kinda weird saying this after saying *that*," Bill said, "but, um . . . I'm engaged."

The wedding would have to be soon. Christmas and New Year's were discussed, but Mrs. Quick's oncologist, Dr. Bannerjee, gave the difficult opinion that Thanksgiving was more realistic. Alice didn't have much in the way of possessions, so there wasn't much difference between packing for a trip and packing for a move. She told herself she was packing for a trip. Bill helped her with her ticket home, but she paid for the rest, and it cost her more than it should have, in money and time, but a promise is a promise. Honolulu to Tokyo to Frankfurt to JFK, and finally, at the sunset's end, Katonah.

The ceremony was in the backyard. It was unseasonably warm, and although the first half hour of the ceremony was beautiful, the second half hour was rough. Alice had forgotten how to wear heels in Hawaii. Why was the service so long? Too many speakers laid claim to the right to be a part of this. Too many cousins needed to perform. Pitterpat was a Southern girl, and it came out in the slow Southern style of her family's approach to public speaking, particularly on the part of her uncle Chooch, who read a poem he had written for the occasion. Alice thought she could hear the bride's teeth grinding toward the end of it, but her smile remained frozen, glistening with Vaseline.

Then John Quick decided to see Chooch and raise him. "I wanted to share what Homer has to say about marriage," he explained to the congregation, waving his battered copy of Fitzgerald's *Odyssey*. "My soon-to-be daughter-in-law felt the excerpts I selected were too long. I'll let you decide."

Somewhere around the seventh or eighth minute of the reading, as Calypso begged her lover to stay, and the surprising November sun made its way over the red oaks, its blazing heat searing every forehead, Alice stopped paying attention and looked out at the crowd. She recognized nobody on the bride's side. She knew almost everyone on the groom's side, but there were some faces she couldn't place. One in particular stood out: a young woman in the back row. She was beautiful, with caramel skin and black hair swept back behind one ear. There was something comfortable about her, something Alice couldn't place. Then Alice thought: *She looks like me.* And even though she stood three feet from the bride, on a riser in the peripheral view of everyone at the event, Alice wondered if maybe she really was that girl in the back row: not really a part of this family, peering in from the outermost circle, almost uninvited. The first few days in the house had been a series of small embarrassments as Alice realized again and again how unfamiliar she was with the home she'd grown up in. In the kitchen, the places for dishes and cups had all been moved around. The doors had new locks, and the keys were shaped differently. The garbage disposal made a noise it hadn't before, and had new rules for dealing with it. You leave a place and you want it to stay the same, and it doesn't, and the people don't either. They go on with life and leave you in a million tiny ways that add up to just as much as, or more than, the one big way you left them. And that's when Alice started to cry, and it was nicely timed because that's when the vows were happening, and Bill saw and gave Alice a smile over his almost-wife's shoulder, and that's when more tears came, these ones for the fact that Alice was still a part of this family after all.

At the reception, Alice took on the responsibility of attending to Penelope and all the clutter of her infirmity. With the help of some cousins, she wheeled her mother, with the oxygen tank affixed to the wheelchair, over the flattened grass and under a canvas flap right up to her table inside the tent. There they both sat, as the rest of the crowd mingled and drank champagne, laughing about what a relief the bubbly was after such a long ceremony.

"That was a beautiful wedding, didn't you think, Mom?"

"So nice," Penelope said. "Marianne's niece did a good job with that Cantabile."

Pitterpat's little ten-year-old cousin had performed a piece on her flute. Of course her mother would comment on the musician. Alice's first instinct was not to let it bother her, but then, as a gift to her mother, she decided to let it bother her, just a little. She imagined how it might have felt to have been asked to play something at the ceremony. She pictured Pitterpat's relatives whispering to each other ("She's a concert pianist, you know . . .") as Alice broke off a little *Suite bergamasque* for the bride and groom. She hadn't touched a piano in seven years now. She smiled nicely to her mom.

"It really was," Alice said. "She's very talented."

Mrs. Quick suddenly looked animated. With what seemed like great effort, she raised her hand and started waving.

"Dr. Bannerjee!" She ran out of oxygen halfway through the name, gasping on the "jee." Alice looked over and saw the young woman who had been sitting in the back row now getting a glass of champagne from a waiter.

"Congratulations, Mrs. Quick, you must be so proud," said the young woman. "And you must be Alice?"

"Yes, hello," Alice said, shaking the woman's firm, cool hand.

"Dr. Bannerjee is my oncologist," Penelope said, at a matter-of-fact volume the dying tend to not care about. "She's only thirty, is that right?"

"Thirty-three, Mrs. Quick, but I appreciate the discount."

And as Dr. Bannerjee sipped her champagne, Alice wanted to kill her and also marry her and also be her. Alice looked at her mother looking at this young woman, this doctor, and wilted like a daisy under a rosebush.

* * *

Thanksgiving came and went, as did Christmas, and Mrs. Quick held on throughout. Dr. Bannerjee was a regular presence in the house. She would come to check on Mrs. Quick, but then, after checking vitals and making notes to adjust prescriptions, she would hang out, sometimes for hours, chitchatting, playing backgammon, being generally friendly but not too friendly, swatting away Penelope's more probing questions into her personal life. Alice smiled her way through conversation after conversation, pretending she had something to contribute.

A week before Valentine's Day, Mrs. Quick fell into a coma. Nobody could say how deep it was, but she was behind a membrane now, sealed off, and would almost certainly never come out of it. One by one, the family filed in, the goodbye conversations they'd been dreading for months now goodbye monologues, radio broadcasts into an abyss, just in case there was still someone with an antenna down there. They took turns. Bill said goodbye. Pitterpat said goodbye. Bill and Pitterpat said goodbye together. Bill said goodbye again. Mr. Quick said goodbye, joking that this "coma" seemed like a trap, and would someone please come check on him after five minutes.

Then it was Alice's turn.

"Hi, Mom," she said into the silence. "I just want you to know I love you. I'm sorry I was a bad daughter. I'm sorry I didn't make your dreams come true."

Every muscle of Mrs. Quick's face was at rest now, and Alice realized she'd give anything to see the smile she'd seen so many times over her right shoulder. She fingered the last measures of Penelope's favorite nocturne on the bedspread. Her mother's lips and eyes and jawline were still. Her smile, *the* smile, would never be smiled again.

"So then I just, I took her hand. And I held it. And out of nowhere, I had this crazy thought, and I could have just held it in, but it just came out. I said to her, 'Mom, I want you to know something. I have some news. I'm going to medical school. I'm going to be a doctor.' A few minutes later, she was gone."

Roxy and Pitterpat were silent, until finally Roxy said, "Damn."

"Yeah," said Alice. "I don't even know what made me say it. It hadn't even crossed my mind as a possibility until right then in that moment."

"Do you think she heard you?"

"I don't know. It's possible she didn't. There's no way to know. Maybe I said what I said to my mom, and it meant everything, and maybe I just said it to a dead body, and it meant nothing. And maybe it was something between everything and nothing, like a dream. I don't even know. But . . . it felt good. It was a terrible time, but that part felt good. I felt like I had some direction to move in. I'd missed that. I even went on Facebook and announced to the world, 'I'm going to med school!' It got hundreds of likes. It felt amazing. And some days it still does. Some days I like the idea of feeling important, and useful, and being one of those people on the subway coming home from work in their green hospital scrubs. And then other days, I think, who cares. Maybe I'm good enough the way I am, right now. Maybe I don't need to be improved, so why am I killing myself? And then . . . I mean, *488* on the practice test, that's . . . And you know, part of me is like, it's fine, you'll do better next time, but then part of me is like, do I even want this? Do I really have to do this to myself just because I made some deathbed promise?"

It took a moment for Roxy to understand. "Wait, are you really asking?"

"I guess I am."

Roxy thought about this.

"Well, it's not like you're only doing it because you promised your mom," Roxy assured her. "You're doing it because you want to be a doctor. Don't you?"

"*Do I?*"

Alice was seriously asking, and Roxy was baffled. "I don't know, I'm asking you!"

Alice was baffled too. "I *think* I do. I'd love to have a job that matters. I'd love to be the person on the train wearing scrubs, instead of sitting across from that person and wishing I was them. But . . . do I actually want to *be* a doctor? *Do* that job? With the blood and the guts and life on the line and all that?"

"You've been working pretty hard for someone who maybe doesn't want to be a doctor."

"Well, exactly," said Alice. "And if that's the case, I should probably stop and not go through with this, right? But I can't stop. Because I owe it to my mom."

"You don't owe your mom *shit*," Pitterpat said, her voice echoing in the empty bar.

Roxy and Alice stared at her, surprised. Pitterpat had been sitting quietly for most of Alice's story, but now all of a sudden she had an opinion. Roxy said, "Go on."

"You don't owe your mom anything," she rephrased, "because a promise made by a child to a parent should not and does not count. When I was about to leave for college, my mother sat me down and made me promise I'd move back home after I got my degree. She said I'm a Florida Girl, and I always will be, and she didn't want me running off to New York and turning into someone else. So she made me promise I wouldn't. I looked her in the eye, and I made that promise, and I knew, even then as I made it, there was no way I was keeping it. How could I promise not to turn into someone else? I already *was* someone else. And she hates me for it. That's why my wedding was the only time you've ever met my family."

Alice took a moment to gather all this. "I mean, I wondered," she eventually replied, adding, "They seemed nice."

"Yeah. Because I bribed them. With money. I'm serious! And I bought their clothes! I wasn't gonna let them show up to Katonah, New York, looking all Brownwater, Florida. I dressed every single one of them, and paid for it all with my own money, and I never even told Bill. I am so embarrassed by my family, you guys. But you know what I'm *not* embarrassed about? The fact that I'm embarrassed. Your mom wanted you to be amazing? Well, that's where you and I differ. I had to fight, *hard*, to be amazing. But I did it."

"You did," said Alice, a little drunk but meaning it. "You are."

"My mom's probably sitting in her kitchen right now, smoking her menthols, because of course, and she's probably bitching about me to one of her sisters. But you know what? If she's mad, it's her own fault. Don't make your kids make promises." Then Pitterpat thought of something. "Isn't your boyfriend an ethicist? Why don't you ask him?"

Alice exhaled. "Wow. I can't believe I didn't think of that."

"I can't believe *she's* the one who reminded you," said Roxy, turning to Pitterpat. "I thought you hate Grover. Didn't you like bite his ear off or something?"

"I think I scratched him a little," said Pitterpat. "It was a challenging moment. I'm sure he's lovely. Better than Carlos, anyway."

"Well, I can't believe I still haven't met Grover," said Roxy, in a huff. "I've been asking Alice about it for weeks, and she still hasn't introduced us," Alice laughed this off, even though, yes, she'd been avoiding introducing them.

Alice took out her phone and discovered dozens of missed texts. They were all from Roxy, all sent within the last three minutes.

"Hi, I just want to say I disagree with Pitterpat but I'm not gonna disagree with her to her face because she's been through some shit lately and this friendship is kind of new and I don't want to blow it and OMG THIS STUFF ABOUT HER FAMILY?!?! Also, while I'm saying things just to you, I think I have a boyfriend. His name is Christoph. German originally but grew up here. He's super cute. He works in a pet store. We've been on two dates and he's got big shoulders and I haven't seen him with his shirt off yet and I'm really looking forward to it but I'm enjoying not letting him get there just yet. And not letting me get there just yet! It's nice. Wish me luck, haha. Anyway, okay, back to the convo!!!"

Alice liked the idea of Roxy with a boyfriend. Roxy was an on-slaught, a pungent spirit best taken in sips. Alice thought of all those mornings in the kitchen where Roxy would motormouth a summary of the previous day's exploits, while Alice watched the clock, waiting for Roxy to put a stopper in the spout and go clomping up the stairs to make the train. Alice listened to all her stories at first, laughing at the jokes, sneering at the villains, cheering the protagonist. But after a while, she stopped listening. She stopped even starting to listen. And then, when Grover entered the picture, she retreated entirely, sleeping over at his place, skipping the morning check-ins. Alice felt like a bad friend. Which is why it was nice to think of Roxy in love, and *being* loved. Her heart swelled at the idea of someone finding Roxy delightful.

Alice texted Grover.

"Ethics question."

"Great, the meter's running. Just kidding. Go ahead."

"Hypothetical situation."

"Of course."

"Can a person go back on a promise they made to someone on their deathbed?"

So quickly the reply arrived, as if by autofill: "No."

"Elaborate."

"You can shave off the last seven words of your question and replace them with almost anything. A promise is a promise is a promise."

"Aw man, come on!"

"Not what you wanted to hear?"

"Not really! Goodbye! Sorry, I'm out with friends. We'll talk later."

Then Pitterpat had another suggestion.

"Have you tried looking online? You know, I bet there's an online community that addresses this very issue."

"Oh boy," said Roxy with an eye roll.

"What?"

"Don't put your shit on the internet."

Pitterpat roused, animated. "Don't put your shit on the internet? You're constantly on the internet! You're on the internet right now!"

Roxy put her phone down.

"I go online for happy shit. Dating. Shopping. Videos of animals befriending animals of a different species, and then one of the animals gets sick and they're quarantined for months and then they're reunited and they remember each other. Happy shit. You can miss me with the sad shit. Before I put anything on the internet, I ask myself: 'Is this happy shit or sad shit?' If the answer is sad shit, nope."

"Well, I think there's strength in vulnerability," Pitterpat replied. "When I found out I had Crohn's, I felt very alone."

"You could have talked to us," Alice said. "I could have helped."

"Well, I didn't," said Pitterpat.

"Why not?"

"I don't know. Like, literally, I didn't want to make the sounds with my mouth. Is that weird?"

"No," said Roxy. "Big-time same."

Pitterpat continued: "Anyway, I found this website, the Crohn-Zone, and there's a whole community of people there who can relate to what I've been through. They answered all my questions, they gave me encouragement, they held my hand through a dark time."

"Pitterpat, I'm so sorry," said Roxy. "But that's the saddest shit I've ever heard in my life."

Pitterpat ignored her. "I consider some of the people on there to be good friends."

"Pitterpat, I have some great news," said Roxy. "That thing you said before is no longer the saddest shit I've ever heard in my life. Because the thing you said after it is."

Pitterpat balled up a napkin, threw it at Roxy, and continued: "It opened my mind, in fact. I've joined a number of other groups since then. One for children of parents who've become Tea Partiers. One for people who cut bangs and wish they hadn't. There's even one for the wives of men who have become Buddhist monks. Most of it's in Japanese, but Google Translate works pretty well."

Alice had heard worse ideas. So after Colin the Uber driver came to a stop half on, half off Mr. Quick's driveway with 3.2-rated imprecision, Alice, Roxy, and Pitterpat got out, headed down to the basement rec room of Alice's dad's house, went on Pitterpat's laptop, and after a brief search found a website called Grieveland. Alice set up an account and wrote a long post detailing her dilemma, ending with, "What would you do? Thanks in advance, Alice."

Right as Alice hit send, Roxy barked out, "Don't use your real name!" It was too late.

"I use my real name," said Pitterpat. "Marianne, anyway."

"Guys, I don't mean to be shitty," said Roxy, "but these people, the people who actually interact on boards like this, are trash monsters. They eat suffering. They're basement dwellers."

"We're basement dwellers," Alice pointed out. "We literally live in a basement."

"We're in a basement right now," Pitterpat observed.

"This is a rec room. There's a drum set in here," said Roxy. "And our apartment is a *garden apartment*."

Alice laughed. "What garden?"

"Alice, trust me, you don't want to feed the bears with this one. Don't leave sad shit lying around where someone can eat it."

"Hey, I got a reply," Alice said.

It was from me. I had been to the website a few times before, just lurking, never posting anything. But then I read Alice's post, and against my better judgment, I replied.

"Hi Alice," I said. "I understand what you're going through because I also made a promise to my mother, and I can't figure out how to keep it. Every action has consequences, both good and bad, so the best you can do is stay right where you are, frozen in your present state of having promised to do the thing but not yet having done it. I hope that's helpful. I wasn't going to reply to this but I really like you. Is it crazy to like someone this much just for what they put on the internet? Probably. But here we are."

Roxy did an exaggerated shudder. "Alice," she said calmly, "shut down the computer. Right now."

"Come on, he's grieving, give him a break," said Pitterpat, but her heart wasn't in it, because it really was kind of a weird response.

"That's not grief. That's a baited hook. If you respond, a week from now you're gonna be chained to his radiator."

Alice laughed. Pitterpat did not.

"You know, it goes both ways. You can come to these places to get sympathy, but it only works if you give sympathy as well."

"I have no sympathy for this basement dweller," insisted Roxy.

"You don't know he lives in a basement."

Roxy took the laptop.

"What are you doing?"

Clickety-clackety-clickety-clackety-POST.

Alice grabbed the laptop back and read what Roxy had written: "Hi, what's it like living in a basement?"

"You're such a jerk," said Alice with a giggle.

"Nothing on the internet is real, remember?"

My reply came immediately.

"How did you know I live in a basement?"

Alice, Roxy, and Pitterpat burst out laughing. Alice closed the computer, and they went to bed.

*　*　*

The next day they swam all afternoon. At one point, Alice got a nice picture of Roxy sprawled across an inflatable whale in her soon-to-be-famous purple bikini.

"I love this," Roxy said when she saw it, with a deeply serious tone. "Send it to me."

Mr. Quick dropped them off at the station, and they rode back to the city on an early-evening train. Somewhere between White Plains and Harlem 125th, Alice got a text from Grover.

"I notice I didn't hear from you after I gave my take on the whole deathbed promise thing. I'm sorry if I came barging in with an opinion without knowing the context. You said it's a hypothetical, but even if it's not a hypothetical, no matter what this hypothetical person hypo-thetically decides to do, I still love her. Hypothetically."

He had never said "love" before. Alice went back to not hating him.

When they got back, Roxy wanted to get another drink with Alice, but Alice felt like she needed to *get back to work, Calerpittar.* She went to the Bakery, which was nearly empty, and promised herself she'd dive into her practice questions after doing one quick thing on her phone.

"Hi, sorry I didn't reply sooner. How are you?"

There was no immediate reply, so Alice goofed around on Facebook for a little while, and ten minutes later Tulip wrote her back.

"Hi."

"Are you mad at me?"

"No."

Single-word responses. *Of course she's mad.*

"I'm sorry I had to leave, Tulip. You know I love you. This is some-thing that's important to me, so I had to do it."

"Are you someone else's nanny now?"

"No, of course not."

"Are you lying?" Alice could hear Tulip's voice in this text, because it was her own voice saying it to Tulip, one of the countless times she'd busted Tulip on a fib.

"No, I am not lying."

"You ARE lying. I saw you. I saw you with two other kids at the Natural History Museum."

"What? If you saw someone, it wasn't me."

(It wasn't. It was Sofia Hjalmarsson, twin unbeknownst, exploring the museum with her two daughters, visiting the United States and New York City for the first and only time.)

It was a while before there was another text from Tulip. *Finally someone's enforcing no screens after dinner*, Alice thought. But sure enough, another one arrived.

"Why do you want to be a doctor so bad anyway?"

Great question, Tulip. "It's something I've wanted to do for a long time." Not good enough. She added a corny platitude. "It's my way to make a difference in the world."

"I'm in the world," Tulip replied. "You made a difference to me."

Alice put her flashcards away. She sipped her tea for a while, then got up and left.

Five minutes later, as Shinran Shonin gazed serenely westward, Alice knocked on the door of the temple. She knew she wasn't supposed to and she knew it wouldn't work, but she did it anyway, and a young man answered the door. He didn't look like a monk. Maybe he was one of their helpers?

"Hi," said Alice. She didn't know what to say, and she didn't even know if this young man would understand her. So she said the only words she knew he might. "Bill Quick."

"Bill Quick?"

"I need to see Bill Quick. Is he here?"

The young man thought for a moment. He was obviously not supposed to do this.

"Please," said Alice. "It's urgent. I'm his sister. Sister?"

He understood "sister." He thought a moment more, then closed the door.

After about a minute or so, Bill emerged. His head was shaved, but he wore a sweatshirt and sweatpants.

"Hey, Alice."

★ ★ ★

They sat in the park across the street. He didn't have long. He had to cook dinner for the order, and their recipes had been challenging to learn. Alice listened patiently and suppressed the urge to smack this monk upside the head for leaving his wife and messing up everyone's

258

summer. Then he asked her how studying was going and she remembered why she'd come.

"I'm thinking of quitting. Maybe I shouldn't be a doctor. Maybe I should do something else."

"Okay," Bill said, quickly.

"Okay? Really?"

"Yeah."

"Shit, man," said Alice. "I was kind of hoping for a pep talk."

"Why, because I'm so successful? Alice, look at me. Look where setting difficult goals and rising to the challenge gets you. I haven't brushed my teeth in two days. I need a toothbrush. Can you come back with a toothbrush?"

"Yeah, of course," she said.

He continued: "I have never been able to do the thing of just sitting nicely in a room and being happy with what I have. There was always some deficit. When I was a teenager, it was a girlfriend deficit. When I was a poor college graduate, it was a money deficit. When I was a rich, retired superdude, it was a spiritual deficit. Now I'm halfway to being a monk, and I'm still like, *man*, I need to brush my teeth. That's my deficit now, and I can't think about anything else. I think I'm bad at Buddhism, Alice."

She laughed. "You've never been bad at anything."

"Yeah, it's a new feeling. I really thought I had it down, but this is not like what they taught us at Columbia. I mean, first of all, most of it's in Japanese. So I don't know what's going on most of the time. I'd think about looking up a different temple, maybe one where they speak more English, but I threw my iPhone in the river. I haven't looked at the internet in weeks."

Alice perked up at this. "Really? How's that been?"

"It's been really nice, actually."

"I'll bet."

They smiled. It was good to see each other. "Do me a favor, Alice. Just be happy with what you've got and who you are right now. Do that for me. How's this Grover guy?"

"He's great," Alice said. "I mean, he can be kinda judgy. And there's maybe a bit of a primpiness about him, you know? Like, he doesn't say the term 'personal brand' out loud, but I think he thinks it."

"Is he kind?"

"Yeah, he's kind. I mean, he's an ethicist. He has to be, to some degree. But he can be a bit too understanding. Like, the night you left . . ."

She told him the story of Pitterpat attacking Grover and throwing him out of the apartment. She tried to tell it as funny as possible, but at the end of it Bill just said, "I've caused so much pain." And then his head drooped down, and his shoulders went up. *He's going to cry*, Alice thought with surprise, and right as she thought it, the crying started. It was painful. Alice couldn't handle her brother disliking anything about himself.

"Come on," she said. "Nobody wants to see a crying monk."

Bill just shook his head. He couldn't hear it. He looked up at a passing cloud. "God, I bet she hates me so much."

"She doesn't hate you, Bill," Alice said, meaning it. "Nobody hates you. Look, what should I do? Give me some wisdom."

"Okay," he said. "What is it you want?"

"I want to pass this test."

"That's not what you want," he said. "What do you *want*?"

"I want to be a doctor."

He brushed it aside. "What do you want, Alice?"

"I want Mom to love me."

There it was. "She did love you."

"No, she didn't."

"Yes, Alice. She did. She *does*."

"I know that's probably true," said Alice. "I guess what I want is to *believe* it's true."

The city was cooling down a little. There were fireflies in the little park, something you never see in the city, and suddenly Alice felt a sense of possibility again, if just for a moment.

"By the way," she said, "I know I've asked you about Mom's email password—"

"Come on, Alice."

"Aren't you curious what's in there? What if she had some crazy secret? Like some Italian lover we didn't know about? Don't you wonder about that stuff?"

He laughed at the Italian-lover thing. But then he got serious.

"Mom was confusing, Alice. I know you'll never stop trying, but I'm telling you, you will never get to the center of that maze. You have to make peace with that. And besides, as I've said many times, even if I wanted to get her password—"

"I mean, you say that, but—"

"—it's not the kind of favor I can just call in. I have a reputation to think about."

Realizing her brother had no idea what had happened to his reputation in the last few weeks, and not wanting to toss that particular grenade his way, Alice let it go. Instead they sat in the park a little while longer, watching the fireflies. Then they hugged, and he returned to the monastery.

* * *

Grover was halfway through a sentence and couldn't remember if he was writing toward the subject and the predicate or away from them, but other than that he was on a roll, when his phone rang.

"What are you doing right now?"

It was Alice, somewhere noisy.

"Writing."

"Wanna get a drink?"

He did. Twenty minutes later he met her at Probley's, the somewhere noisy that was now even noisier. She had gotten a tan this weekend, and it lit up her eyes.

"Hi," he said as he kissed her.

"Hey," she said. "I want you to meet someone. Grover, this is my roommate, Roxy. Roxy, Grover."

With a big smile, Roxy extended her hand. "*Very* nice to meet you," she said, and they all got a drink. But just one drink. Then Alice got back to work. She worked late into the night, then all day the next day as well, save for one short break to bring her brother a toothbrush.

CHAPTER EIGHT

Forevereverland

"I'm going."

"See, you say that, and yet—"

"I am!"

Roxy wasn't going. She was standing in the kitchen, leaning on the blue tree, noodling on the caption for an Instagram photo, feeling generally good about herself.

"Jane Austin once wrote, 'a woman of seven and twenty can never hope to feel or inspire affection again.' So how is it that this trapper-of-thirst is twenty-eight today????" She hit send, and the words appeared next to the picture of her in her purple swimsuit, floating on a whale. The likes started coming in immediately.

Do you know what Roxy was, in that moment? Roxy was confident. Confident in her choice of swimsuit, confident in the lighting, confident in the photoshopping, confident in the veracity of the quote she found online, confident in her spelling of Jane Austen's name, and confident nobody knew that today was her thirty-fifth birthday.

"Okay. Did that. Leaving now."

"You sure?"

Alice needed Roxy to be gone. She had licked her wounds since the

488, but now, GOOD MORNING, chirped her phone, IT'S 27 DAYS UNTIL THE TEST, and Alice knew exactly what to do with those twenty-seven days: practice, practice, practice, just like how she got to Carnegie Hall. Find the hardest parts and drill them until they're not hard anymore. Chemical and Physical Foundations of Biological Systems had been her weakest section, so Chemical and Physical Foundations of Biological Systems would be her mind's meal today. And tomorrow. And the next day. And by the end of the week, she'd sort of understand it. The old magic trick.

But the plan required quiet. The Bakery was feeling kicked at this point. Who can say why? It's something that happens. A place has that productivity magic, and you can sit there for hours and tune the world out, and then one day you start hearing other conversations, and watching people out the window, and eating a second blueberry muffin. And the muffins weren't even all that good! The Bakery was an old place, with an old muffin recipe, from a time when people didn't know how much more delicious muffins would someday be.

Plus she had come to the point in her studies where she needed to say things out loud, to lock these facts and figures into her head, and she couldn't do it in a crowded café. Or at Grover's, for that matter. She needed the kitchen, and she needed to be alone. And today she'd have it as soon as Roxy finished whatever she was doing on her phone and got the hell out of here.

Roxy was now texting Christoph. He'd wished her HBD, with a bunch of sweet emojis. He had also written on her Facebook wall, but she hadn't checked it. She had decided a few days ago that on her birthday she wouldn't check Facebook until after midnight, so she could see all the Happy Birthdays all at once. Okay, she'd just check one time, right now, and wow! Fourteen people had already wished her Happy Birthday! She was loved times fourteen! It was a good day. She would put a heart next to all of these later, but for now, just one: Christoph's.

What was she doing with Christoph? It was so unlikely. They actually met in real life. Her phone died right as she was on her way to drinks with some other guy (unimportant). They had arranged to meet at a bar called Rutherfurd's on the Upper East Side, and foolishly she left the house with only a sip of electricity left in her iPhone. The battery quickly died, and she realized she had no idea where Rutherfurd's was, and more importantly Roxy was not about to be in a date situation without a working phone, and even more importantly Roxy was not about to be in *any* situation without a working phone. So she ducked into the first store she saw.

"Welcome to Tupper's Puppers," said the floppy blond human Goldendoodle behind the cash register. "Can I help you?"

"Hi," said Roxy. "Do you have an iPhone charger?"

"I do," he said, making no move to reach for it. He was grinning, as though he'd been staring at the door all day waiting for Roxy to come home.

"Can I borrow it?"

"I'm so sorry," he said. "Electricity is for paying customers only."

"Okay." She grinned. "I'll take that bird over there."

She pointed to an exquisite blue parrot in a cage nearby.

"That's a hyacinth macaw," said the floppy floof. "It's thirty-five thousand dollars."

"I see," she said. "What do you have for less?"

"Crickets are ten cents each."

"I'll take one cricket," she said, looking at his name tag, "Christoph."

Another customer entered, so the game went on pause. He took her phone and started charging it. As she waited, she wandered up and down the aisles, pretending to browse, but mostly thinking how much she'd rather be at this pet store, hanging out with Christoph, talking to him about stuff as he rang up gerbils and chew toys and fish tank ornaments. He was cozy immediately.

They talked for a little while more, and then he unplugged her phone and looked at it. "Will forty-two percent get you home?"

"We should probably test it," she said, with a smile. "Make sure it works."

"Test it?"

"Yeah. Here, call it from your phone." She wrote down her number for him. He started to dial, but she stopped him. "Not now. Just . . . sometime."

Halfway through her second drink at Rutherfurd's, at 8:02 P.M. (not coincidentally two minutes after Tupper's Puppers' posted closing time), Roxy's phone rang.

Alice couldn't help but notice Roxy still hadn't left.

"Sorry. I'm going, I'm leaving, I'll be gone all day," she said. Roxy was proud of herself. She'd been a good friend and roommate to Alice, keeping small talk and loud music to a minimum, staying out of the way when necessary, et cetera, et cetera, but more importantly being the pressure release valve Alice needed when she got too stressed. Roxy made sure to always read between the lines with Alice. Alice never wanted to be the one to say, "I wanna blow off work and go out and party," so it was Roxy's job to invite her out, and maybe pester her about it, maybe even guilt her into it, so Alice could have a fun night out and not blame herself for slacking off. It was just a little game they played. Roxy was sure Alice was secretly grateful.

After Roxy made her way out the door, stopping at the bottom of the stairs to check Twitter, stopping halfway up the stairs to check her email, stopping in the first-floor hallway to see if more than fourteen people had wished her Happy Birthday on Facebook (seventeen now!), Roxy stepped out the front door of the building to go to work, stopping first to finish writing a text to Christoph, whom she would probably go see at his pet store later. She loved that he worked at a pet store.

The street was empty. Roxy didn't notice the sound of footfalls. CLOP CLOP CLOP CLOP.

"Make sure you get there by ten," she wrote. "That's when the Seventies start."

"Got it. And then the Eighties after midnight?"

"Bingo."

"How late is it going tonight?"

"We have the dance floor till closing. 4AM."

CLOP CLOP CLOP CLOP. The footfalls got closer.

"I just had an amazing idea for this party," Christoph said.

"Ooh tell me now! Tell me n—"

Roxy's phone was suddenly no longer in her hand.

"The hell?"

It was 8:16 A.M. Roxy was on the sidewalk, in front of her apartment building, with no phone in her hand where there had just been a phone a second ago. CLOP CLOP CLOP CLOP. Footfalls, getting softer now. She looked to her left. A man was running away from her, down 111th Street, toward Amsterdam, toward the garden of the cathedral. Her phone wasn't in her hands. The man was running away.

She screamed. "Stop!"

He didn't stop. He kept running. She ran after him, not an easy thing to do in flip-flops, but she did it, FLAPFLAPFLAPFLAP. The man disappeared around the corner, but she was on him. She could catch him. She had to catch him.

She approached the corner. He would be there. He wouldn't be far. She rounded the corner, and the man was gone. Her phone was gone. She had to call the police. She couldn't. Her phone was gone. She needed to tell someone about this. Her phone was gone. Shit. Her phone was gone! She screamed, scaring a small dog on a leash.

"Are you okay?" It was the dog's owner talking.

"No, I'm not okay!" She said it like it was the dog owner's fault. "Someone just stole my phone!"

Roxy made her way back to the apartment building. By the time she got to the front door, she was shaking. She nearly fell down the stairs, gripping the railing with everything she had. By the time she got inside the apartment, she had to lie down in her bed, she was so overcome.

"I'm so sorry," she said to Alice, from her bed, through the open door. "I know you're studying."

"It's okay," said Alice, even though it wasn't.

"Oh, God," Roxy moaned.

Alice closed the big yellow book. "What's wrong?"

"Someone just stole my phone."

Alice got up and was suddenly in Roxy's doorway. "What?"

"Right now, right in front of the building. He just ran up to me, grabbed my phone out of my hand, and ran away."

"Jesus!"

"I know!"

Alice shuddered. She moved into Roxy's room and sat on the bed next to her. "What did he look like?"

"I don't know what he looked like! He looked like someone's back, running away from me!" And then, only then, did it sink in how badly she needed that phone to not be in the hands of a stranger. There were things on that phone. Things that shouldn't be there.

"I gotta get that phone back," Roxy said as she took the bottle of vodka out of the freezer. The cold burned her hand. She poured a shot in the "One Day at a Time" coffee mug. "This is really bad."

"Okay," said Alice. "This isn't a disaster. Just do Find My iPhone."

"I have to get it back."

"I know, just—"

"Shit!"

Alice was trying her best to be patient. "Roxy. If you want to get it back, there's a way."

"They're gonna see stuff on my phone."

"No, they're not. You have a passcode, right? You're fine."

She did have a passcode, and she wasn't fine. If she had thought it through and suspected that this was no random crime, she would have understood that part of this daring theft involved taking the phone while she was using it, so it wouldn't be locked. She would realize that much later. Right now she realized nothing except *shit, this is bad*.

And Alice realized this was going to eat a day. If she had just left for the Bakery fifteen minutes earlier, she would have been safe. Roxy wouldn't even have been able to find her since she only had Alice's number on her phone.

Alice hated thinking that way. She wanted to be a good friend first and foremost, but from the wall in her bedroom, August Churchill scowled at the idea. Roxy sat at the kitchen table, at the edge of her chair, her arms dangling over the back, alternately biting her nails and sipping her vodka. Alice tried again, gently: "Do you want to try Find My iPhone?"

They tried it. The iPhone was in the Hudson River.

Most of Roxy's stuff had been backed up on her laptop, so even though this was scary, it would all be okay. Roxy promised not to bother Alice anymore and slipped into her room. Alice went back to studying. Roxy went on her laptop and checked Instagram. Her purple bikini picture was blowing up. One hundred and forty-two hearts.

She wanted to text Christoph and remembered again that her phone was gone. So she opened Messages on her laptop, and that's when things seemed amiss. Then she went to Photos, and found a series of screenshots she didn't recognize, screenshots of her worst nightmare realized, taken that morning from her iPhone. Then she went to her email and found the screenshots had been emailed, from her account, to an address she didn't recognize. The nightmare thickened, making it hard to breathe. She stepped out of her room.

"I think something really bad has happened."

Alice froze. She had been packing up her stuff, thinking she could leave. "I'm sorry," she said. "I was gonna head out."

Alice wanted to get out of there. Roxy's hands were shaking. *This is real.* Roxy put her hands behind her back and faked some nonchalance.

"Oh, yeah. Sure. Get out of here."

"No, I can stay. What is it?"

"It's nothing," said Roxy. "Go on."

"I'll be at the Bakery, right around the corner, if you need me."

"Got it."

Alice left, and Roxy sat down on the floor of the kitchen, her back against the blue tree, wrapping her head around the fact that her life was over.

* * *

In the Bakery, Alice memorized everything she needed to know about Chemical and Physical Foundations of Biological Systems. She recited the facts quietly to herself, maybe not even quietly, maybe a little loudly, but it was okay. Other people were talking; why shouldn't she, just because she was alone? And those other people were nattering on about nothing, as far as she could tell. Dumb little conversations over coffee and bagels. Who cared. She was learning things, things she would use to save lives one day. Perhaps even one of theirs. You're welcome, girl complaining to her sister about the Suitoronomy date who never showed up!

At some point during the study of different kinds of chemical bonds, her phone rang. It was Grover, and she answered as she made her way out to the sidewalk, where she could keep an eye on her stuff through the window.

It was 10:01 A.M., an hour and forty-five minutes since the robbery.

"Hey, baby," she said. ("Baby" was new. She was trying it out.)

"Hi," said Grover. "Are you alone?"

"Yep. Well, alone on a crowded sidewalk."

"Is Roxy with you?"

Weird. "No. What's up?"

"Alice, I have Grant Nussbaum-Wu, the editor-in-chief of Pearl-clutcher, on the line."

Alice knew this name.

"Hello, Alice," said a voice with a British accent. It was compassionate but all business, like a doctor who takes no pleasure in amputating your leg.

"Hi, Grant," said Alice.

Grover kept talking. "Alice, do you know if anything happened with Roxy's phone lately? Did she leave it lying around or lose it or anything?"

Alice felt the approach of something big. "It got stolen. Someone grabbed it out of her hand and ran off, right in front of our apartment, just this morning."

Grover sighed. A long pause. She could hear him and Grant

discussing something in a whisper. Then: "Alice, do you know where Roxy is now?"

"I think she's in the apartment."

"Okay, we need to get in touch with her. Are you near there?"

"I'm at the Bakery."

"Can you go back to the apartment and put her on the line?"

Alice quietly went back to her table, collected her things, and then walked back to the apartment. The entire walk, she and Grover and Grant said nothing to each other. Alice correctly sensed Grover's ethics wouldn't let him tell her what this was about, because it was something private having to do with Roxy. She also knew Roxy would tell her. Alice was Roxy's best friend, and through her gathering fear, Alice began to realize Roxy was hers.

She entered the apartment. It was quiet. Roxy was in her room, under her covers, the air conditioner blasting. Alice handed her the phone. "It's Grover. He wants to talk to you."

And this was the weird part, the part that really scared Alice: Roxy looked like she'd been expecting the call. Only the fact that it was coming from Grover was surprising. Roxy took the phone, hit speaker, and laid it on her pillow. She laid her head down next to it, facing the ceiling, and closed her eyes.

"Hi, Grover."

"Hi, Roxy. So, um . . . I have Grant Nussbaum-Wu here, he's the editor-in-chief of Pearlclutcher.com."

"Hi, Grant," she said.

Grover continued: "I'm actually really just an intermediary here because this isn't my department, I'm not really news. They just wanted me to help get in touch with you. So I'm gonna go."

"Bye, Grover." Roxy's eyes didn't open, and her face looked too tired to react.

"Hello, Roxy, this is Grant speaking."

"Hi, Grant."

"Roxy, we're calling to get your comment for a story we're writing.

It's a story about something that was sent to us anonymously. It appears to be a series of screenshots of a text conversation you had with the mayor of New York City."

Roxy sighed, deeply drinking the air as if for the first time today, and a tear rolled down her cheek. It was happening. "Uh-huh."

"I'm sorry," said Grant. "Was that—"

"Yes. I hear you. Text messages."

"So you can confirm you sent these messages?" She didn't say anything. He went another way. "Can I ask you if you know anything about how these screenshots came to be in our possession?"

For the first time that morning, Roxy remembered that she worked in publicity. "I have no comment at this time," she said, and hung up. Alice sat down on the floor next to her bed. Without opening her eyes, Roxy told Alice everything. How she discovered the true identity of Mr. Boink. How she put a stop to it. How it kept going anyway.

At the end of Roxy's story, Alice asked, "Did you guys—"

"Alice, you know me," she said. Alice actually felt like that was kind of true by now. "We were just goofing around. Nothing real happened."

Alice's phone had been ringing. It was Grover.

"I'm so sorry," he said.

"You have to get them to not run this."

"Alice."

"Grover."

"Ethically—"

"No. Stop that. No. This is going to ruin her life. Ethically, fuck you, don't run this article."

"If there was anything I could do, I'd be doing it. I would. But Alice . . . if *we* have it, someone else has it. That's how this works. Roxy needs to get some help, and get herself ready for this."

"Grover. Please."

"Alice, I can't. I can't, I'm sorry."

She hung up. Roxy turned to her. "Can I borrow your phone? I need to call the office."

Roxy didn't know who to call about this. Her first instinct was to call the mayor directly, but instantly she saw what a bad idea that was. So she called Kervis.

"Kervis?"

"Hi, *Roxy*," he said, emphasizing her name in a way that told her he was in a room with other people in it, and he was letting those other people know that this was *Roxy on the line right now*, and these people were upper-level City Hall brass and lawyers and PR consultants and a dirty dozen of damage controllers. In short, Kervis gave up the game in three syllables. He knew, and everyone knew, and Roxy now knew they knew.

"So listen," said Roxy, "would it be cool if I work from home today?"

Alice couldn't stifle her laugh. Roxy would have laughed too if anything was ever going to be funny again.

"Are you at home right now?"

"Yes," she replied.

"Have you gotten any phone calls today?"

"Funny you ask. My phone's gone, Kervis."

"Has anyone contacted you?"

"The editor-in-chief of Pearlclutcher called my roommate, and we talked for a few minutes. Does that count?"

Gasps and alarmed sighs rang out from the background behind Kervis.

"What did you say to him?"

"I said no comment."

More gasps and sighs, these ones relieved.

"Okay, stay there," Kervis said. "We're sending someone over. Her name is Louise. Stay there. Don't talk to anybody."

She had never heard this tone from Kervis before. It was calm, but the kind of calm it felt like a person only reaches a few clicks past abject fury, like he knew she was in so much trouble it wouldn't do any good to punish her now.

"Okay. Got it. Thank you."

But Kervis had already hung up and turned to everyone else in the room. They had all heard the conversation, Mayor Spiderman included.

"Christ," said Mayor Spiderman. "What have I done?"

Louise was dispatched to Roxana Miao's apartment on West 111th Street, and Kervis was sent back to his desk, and once there, he felt the heat rising to his cheeks.

He bit into a ballpoint pen as he marveled: This whole time, he'd been living in a world where the mayor was a sexless family man, with no interest in a skank like Roxy, and Roxy was a skank with no interest in a sexless family man. But that world was just a mural painted on the surface of the real world, a camouflage thin as a film, and just below it were secret cell phones and whispers and hair and lipstick and skin and fluid all sloshing back and forth between this sexless family man and this this this *skank*, Roxana Miao, Phoney, *his* Phoney, who, by the way, was definitely in her thirties. There was just no question about that.

The pen broke in his hand. An intern sitting nearby noticed. He unclenched his fist and pretended to return to the business of municipal government.

* * *

Less than three hours after the robbery, at 11:08 A.M., Louise Marsh stood on the threshold of Roxy and Alice's apartment. Alice, who had been trying to resume her studies at the kitchen table while Roxy re-watched the first episode of *Love on the Ugly Side* on her laptop in her bedroom, had finally put this whole thing out of her head when Louise buzzed the intercom. Alice answered the door and let her in.

When Louise entered, she found Roxy dressed in a professional-looking outfit, but slumped in her chair in the kitchen, as if drunk or in a very late round of a boxing match. Louise introduced herself. She listed off her credentials, but they meant nothing to Alice. As far as Alice was concerned, this was just "the fixer."

"Roxy," said Louise, "can we speak privately?"

"I want Alice to be here."

Louise looked Alice up and down. "Are you her lawyer?"

"Does she need a lawyer?" Alice asked.

"She's my friend," said Roxy, and it became more and more clear to Alice that for a girl with thousands of Facebook friends (217 of whom had by now wished her a Happy Birthday), Roxy had nobody else to turn to.

"You're going to need to retain counsel. We can help you find someone, but it won't be through the mayor's office. You are not to speak to anyone without clearing it with us, and with your lawyer. Now, this will be difficult to hear, but your employment at City Hall has been terminated. I'll need to take your badge with me. If you help the mayor's office navigate this situation gracefully, I'm sure we'll be inclined to help you out moving forward as you look for a new situation."

Roxy nodded bravely. "Okay."

Louise continued: "Also you'll need to deactivate all social media."

"What?" Roxy sat up, with panic in her eyes.

"Facebook, Twitter, Instagram, all of it. Are you on any dating apps? If so, get rid of them."

"For how long?"

Louise looked at her with pity for the first time. "As long as it takes."

"As long as it takes for something on the internet to stop being on the internet?"

"Do you have a computer here?"

"Yeah. My laptop. It's in my room."

"Will you get it, please?"

Roxy blinked. "We're doing this now?"

"Yes," said Louise. "Right now."

"But it's my birthday."

It didn't matter. Under Louise's watchful eye, Roxy fetched her laptop, opened it up at the kitchen table, went through all her accounts, and shut them down. She was off Instagram. She was off Twitter. She was off Facebook and its now 219 Happy Birthdays. She didn't post any farewell messages, didn't put up a picture of a setting sun, didn't give a forwarding address, didn't drop a parting bit of wisdom. She was just gone.

Louise left not long after. Roxy shut down her laptop and slid it under her bed. And then she sat on the bed, across from Alice. Alice looked at Roxy, and Roxy looked at a wall.

"I need to take a bath."

* * *

Just over seven hours after the robbery, at 3:36 P.M., Grover texted Alice.

"It's happening," he said.

"When?"

"Now."

She didn't reply. Even giving him one syllable was more than he deserved. She would forgive him eventually, she knew. He was doing his job. Roxy had created this situation. And yeah, if it were happening to some random girl she didn't know, Alice would love it. Spiderman was a terrible mayor. He wanted to bring back stop-and-frisk and privatize New York City schools and didn't seem to care about New Yorkers getting killed by bicycles, and now the world knew the details of his dick. If it weren't Roxy, Alice would have been a long row of popcorn emojis right now.

But it was Roxy. Alice sat in a chair in the kitchen right outside the bathroom door, talking to Roxy and trying to keep her calm. She knew she wouldn't be going back to the Bakery tonight. The window for mastering even a little corner of Chemical and Physical Foundations of Biological Systems today had closed. She and Roxy would have to ride out this hurricane together, and her boyfriend wasn't doing anything to stop it. It was a difficult fact to reckon with, even for the girlfriend of an ethicist.

"Honey, I just heard from Grover." Alice felt weird calling her "honey," but Roxy needed it. "He said the thing's gonna be up soon."

"How soon?"

"Now."

Roxy shifted in the tub and put down the book she'd been trying to read for eight months now. Alice heard the water rearrange itself and settle. "I don't want to see it," she said. "I don't want to know when it's up. Don't tell me."

"I won't," said Alice. Alice went to Pearlclutcher. The lead story was an article called "The Case for Mallory," and it was all about the least likeable (but maybe most misunderstood?) cast member of *Love on the Ugly Side*, and it seemed like the author was making the argument that everyone was wrong for hating her, because she was actually the best.

Alice refreshed it. "The Case for Mallory."

Alice refreshed it. "The Case for Mallory," still.

Alice refreshed it.

Oh, shit.

Nothing about it was surprising, in hindsight. It was exactly the story it was supposed to be. There was a picture of the mayor, and a picture of the screenshots, and a headline with Roxy's name in it, arranged exactly how you'd expect, but something about the three things, together, on actual honest-to-goodness Pearlclutcher, made Alice gasp.

A sudden splash from the bathroom. "Is it up?"

"What? Um," said Alice. "I haven't looked. I don't know."

A moment passed, and Roxy spoke again: "Am I trending on Twitter?"

"I don't know."

"Can you check?"

It seemed silly, the idea of her goofball friend and roommate being a trending topic. But Alice checked anyway. No, she wasn't trending.

"Can you search my name?"

Alice searched the name "Roxana Miao" on Twitter. Number of results: 0.

"Can you check again?"

She checked again.

0.

And for a minute, it seemed like maybe this wasn't reality after all.

"Can you keep checking?"

"Of course."

0.

0.

0.

0.

0.

4.

An electricity of ice shot through Alice. Four. There had been zero; now there were four.

"Four results."

She checked again.

15.

88.

249.

3886.

Alice put her phone down.

The kitchen was the same shape and size and temperature it had been a minute ago. The laws of gravity still kept the apples in the bowl and the bowl on the table. You could check and double-check the inventory of the drawers and cabinets: Nothing was missing; nothing was new. Everything was exactly the same, except for the tiny words on the little piece of glass, metal, and silicon in Alice's hand. You could close your eyes and pretend it was a minute ago.

Roxy went underwater, unsure of how or when she'd ever come back up.

* * *

Pamela Campbell Clark went walking through the park, and the bicycle went zooming by two seconds later, and she saw it this time. She had turned around, for a moment, distracted by a bee. She was terrified of bees. Her daughter was a beekeeper. No, a bee *farmer*. That's what she called herself on the website. Pamela didn't understand it. It was one thing for Cora to do things like this when she was single and on her own. But she was a mother now. She had a daughter to think of, Pamela's only grandchild, and that poor kid was growing up on a bee farm in California. It was unimaginable, and just as Pamela was imagining it, the distinct lines of a man on a bicycle flew by like a train that didn't stop at this station. The surprise yanked her back, away from California and its earthquakes and wildfires and black clouds of swarming bees, back into the world of the park and her morning walk.

She crossed 110th Street and shuffled up Adam Clayton Powell Jr. Boulevard, past the tequila bar and the beauty shop, as Harlem scurried and busied itself around her. New York could do whatever it wanted, as far as she was concerned, and as fast as it wanted. She would not change pace. This pace was *her* pace, and she stuck to it.

When she reached 112th Street, two young men arrived at the corner, waiting for the light.

"Whoa," said one of them, looking at his phone, then showing the phone to his friend.

"Nice," said the friend. "Who is that?"

"The mayor's new girlfriend."

"All right, Spiderman!"

The light changed, and Pamela Campbell Clark continued home.

* * *

Pitterpat was at the gym, forty-five minutes deep on the elliptical, when she saw Roxy's purple bikini photo on the overhead television. She thought it was a joke at first. Then she read the closed captioning below the photo.

She grabbed her phone and took it to the locker room. She took a quick shower, thinking only of her phone the whole time, and then for forty-five minutes she stood by her locker in a state of semi-undress, bra unfastened, as she scrolled through story after story about her friend Roxy.

* * *

Brock saw the news at work, on his phone, and was overjoyed. To see Spiderman in trouble for anything was always sweet, but this was especially delicious. Then Brock saw the screenshots, and while they were all pretty satisfying, one exchange in particular threw him into a bright gleeful rage. It was a little snippet deep in the midst of Roxy and the mayor's voluminous dirty talk.

"Careful missy," the mayor had said to her, after she made a comment about his "distinguished" gray pubic hair. "I almost fired you once, I could still do it!" (The mayor thought this came off as playful. It did not. It tightened Roxy's whole body when she saw it.)

"But you didn't because I'm a valuable member of the team," she eventually replied.

He had wanted to reply something about her breasts or her ass being valuable, but he resisted.

"You weren't valuable that day," he shot back.

"Please, you loved telling off those shitty bike people."

"If I had written it I would have loved it. You're the one who wrote it. I bet it turned you on writing that."

"I came so hard when I hit send."

Brock thought about this exchange during his entire evening ride. He turned it over in his head, having imaginary conversations under his shaking breath as he completed the circuit just a little bit faster than last time. Finally, when he got back to his apartment, he opened his laptop and set about creating an anonymous Twitter account. Under the tweet from Pearlclutcher featuring the offending screenshot, Bike-Check123 replied, "Roxana Miao is a fat cunt!"

Then he closed the laptop and spent the rest of the evening watching *Shrek* with his kids.

* * *

Felix saw the news on his phone while pushing his dad's wheelchair through the downstairs lobby of Robinson Gardens. They were heading to the park, something they did four times a week now, despite his dad's insistence that he'd rather stay in and watch the flip-a-coin show. Felix felt sad for this poor girl, Roxana something. Maybe it was because he recognized her face from somewhere, but he wasn't sure where he knew her from.

Later that day, he looked her up on Facebook. Nothing there. If he'd had the presence of mind to look on Alice's Facebook page, and to go to that one picture from that one party, he'd have seen Roxy, now nameless and untagged, smiling behind a broken nose, on the other side of Silence. But he didn't. He hadn't been to Alice's page in weeks.

* * *

Bill didn't see it at all. It would be months before he'd hear about it.

* * *

Rachel saw it first and texted it to her fiancé straightaway.

"I'm sending you something," she said out loud.

Andy Cluck, next to her in the bed, clicked the link and recognized Roxy immediately.

"Oh my God, is that—?"

"The girl from the basement."

"The one at the shiva?"

"The same one."

"Oh my God."

Together they scoured the articles and tweets about this scandal that popped up everywhere like dandelions, marveling at the fact that the mayor's side-chick had been in their building—literally, under their noses—this whole time. She had been in their living room just a few weeks ago! And she seemed so nice! The bit about the bananas was especially eye-popping. Roxy had deleted that pic the mayor sent her, but bananas became a running joke between the two of them. Nearly every day Roxy would ask him how his banana was doing. She'd mention being in the produce section and something reminded her of him. He'd say she needed more potassium in her diet, and she'd reply with a series of very suggestive emojis.

"I'm so embarrassed for her," said Rachel.

"I know," said Andy.

How awkward was it gonna be running into her at the mailbox? they both wondered. Was she here right now, directly below them, in the basement? (She was.) Should they go knock on her door, do something nice for her? What was the etiquette? Poor thing. Her life was pretty much ruined, wasn't it?

They stayed up very late that night, side by side in bed, refreshing and refreshing and refreshing.

* * *

Christoph heard two ladies discussing it in the cat section of the pet store. At first he paid no attention, and repriced the canned cat food while these two Upper East Side hens kept clucking away about some naughty shenanigans the mayor had gotten into. It occurred to Christoph that his girlfriend worked for the mayor, and maybe he should ask her about it at her birthday party tonight, or if she came by the store later. (She'd been dropping in a lot, unannounced, and he kind of liked it.) That is, if she wasn't mad at him for some reason. She hadn't texted him since this morning.

And then the weirdest thing happened: Right as he was thinking of Roxy, he heard Roxy's name, and it was one of the Upper East Side hens who said it.

"Roxana Miao," said the hen. "She works in his office."

"Did you see the picture?"

"I wouldn't let Stephen work with someone like that."

"Oh, God, no."

"And the thing with the bananas?"

"His poor wife."

Christoph calmly went back behind the counter and checked his phone. The news alert had just popped up. There was his girlfriend's name, and there were the details of what seemed to be an affair she had with her boss. And there was her picture, lifted from her Instagram before she shut down her account. It was Roxy, in her purple swimsuit, happy as could be. She had texted him this morning right after she posted it.

"Are you gonna like it?"

"Of course I am."

"You better. A like from you is the only like I'm looking for."

She looked recklessly hot, gloriously happy. He loved suspecting he was the thing she was happy about. (He was.)

Christoph went home that night and read everything he could find. There hadn't been much to Roxy Miao in the universe of information before that day, but now, where there had been darkness, light was everywhere, like a blanket of stars. Words about Roxy appeared, thousands and thousands of them almost instantly, and though he couldn't possibly keep up, Christoph read as much as he could. Right as he was reading some particularly vile comment about Roxy's weight and how fat girls shouldn't wear stripper bikinis, an email arrived in his inbox, from Roxy. A chill ran through him. It was like she'd been watching him and caught him snooping. He opened the email, filled with curiosity and dread.

"Tonight's party has been canceled," it said. "Sorry, everybody!" Christoph puzzled over the meaning behind the exclamation point. He guessed it was her way of minimizing it, dampening the alarm bells, equating this earthquake to a sore throat, or a sudden rainstorm. *What can you do?* the exclamation point seemed to shrug.

Roxy had addressed the email to herself, a blind carbon copy to what could have been three people or a thousand. There was no way to know. Now that Christoph had technically heard from her, it bugged him a little that she hadn't reached out directly, instead lumping him in with a bunch of other friends. It was like she hadn't even written it. (She hadn't. Alice had drafted it and sent it.) Christoph decided to reach out. He sent her a text.

"Hi," he wrote.

Roxy could send and receive texts from her laptop. A half hour later, when she opened it up to resume her third watch-through of *Love on the Ugly Side*, she saw his text.

"Hey," she replied.

"How are you doing?"

"Been better."

Where to go now, he wondered. Ask her if she wanted to meet up? Tell her he could never see her again? He felt this weird sense of arriving at an intersection a little too early. A decision to commit to this person or not was being thrust upon him in a way that should have come naturally after six months or so. But were they really together now? And if they were, how serious was it? Could he just end it right now? Or was there nothing actually to end? He thought about writing to Grover Kines about it.

For the meantime, he simply replied: "Hang in there."

"I will," she wrote, with a little smiley face. He sent a smiley face back her way, which felt like a good end to the conversation for now.

* * *

All through the evening and deep into the night, while Roxy watched *Love on the Ugly Side* on her laptop and slept in intervals, information flew across this little galaxy of ours, facts and rumors, opinions and guesses, speculations and pronouncements, comments about comments about comments, the milk of the Milky Way. For now, it was still a great buzzing swarm without form or purpose, as the intergalactic parliament of minds bandied the matter about, fumbling for consensus on What This All Meant. *What is the narrative?* they asked and answered at once. *Who is Roxana Miao and what do we make of her? How will she be inscribed and sealed?*

By morning, the Take had landed. The landscape clarified, like the still and sunny world covered in silent snow that follows a long dark night of flurries. The Take was agreed upon, certified, meme-ified, and thousands of minds strove to distinguish themselves with the funniest possible rewording of the same bullet point. Infinite monkeys with typewriters, and this was their *Hamlet*. The Take's messengers were many, but some blew bigger trumpets than others, and the biggest trumpet in this case belonged to the *New York Post*. The headline, in its usual giant font, chiseled above the now famous Instagram photo of Roxana Miao and a bit of clip art from some graphic designer's "stock fruits and vegetables" folder, was simply glorious and gloriously simple, pithy and poetic, a pairing of well-matched words that would attach themselves to this moment, and to this story, and to this young woman, heretofore known as Roxy, for the rest of her natural life and beyond. It was The Take Itself, a blazing slogan of fire scrawled across the dark sky of the hive of human knowledge, hanging over the pangaeic formation of history like a banner. And it rhymed.

The headline read:

"ROXANA BANANA."

* * *

Alice's whole body shivered when she saw it on her way to the Bakery the next morning. For all the insanity of last night, it had all happened on the little avoidable screens of iPhones and laptops (and TVs, though Alice and Roxy didn't know it since they didn't have a TV). But now here it was, in newsprint, on display for the whole neighborhood, and the whole city, to see. *This is real.*

Alice sat down at the Bakery and immediately noticed two girls, probably college kids, talking and laughing about something in low voices. It might have been some private joke between them, but Alice watched their mouths, waiting for one of them to form a word she might know, like "mayor" or "Roxana" or, of course, "banana." Sure enough, she spotted all three. She then tried to study, but all she got done that morning was deleting Pearlclutcher from her bookmarks, in solidarity. She hadn't read it much lately anyway, but it still felt good.

On her way back to the apartment, the physical world got even more involved. A small klatch of reporters milled about by the front door of the building. They eyed Alice like owls as she approached, waiting to see what she would do. When she headed up the steps, they pounced.

"Excuse me," one of them said. "Do you live in this building?"

"Do you know Roxana Miao?"

"Do you have a minute to talk to us?"

"What's she like as a neighbor?"

Alice hurried inside.

* * *

Roxy was in the bathtub again. "Did you see the *Post*?"

"Yeah, I saw it," said Alice.

"Roxana Banana," Roxy said, and she tried to say it with nonchalance, as if this is the kind of thing you deal with all the time when you're a high-profile celebrity. But her voice cracked, and the hurt poured out of it. "It's catchy. Probably gonna stick."

"Nah," said Alice, and there was a long pause as Roxy said nothing. Then Alice added, "There's a bunch of reporters outside."

Roxy sat up. "What?"

"They were pestering me and asking me questions while I was trying to get in," Alice said, and seeing how much Roxy didn't care and wanted to run upstairs and see for herself, she added, "Don't."

"Don't what?"

"Run upstairs and see for yourself."

"Fiiiine," Roxy said, with a half smile. "Do you want to watch a movie or something?"

No, Alice thought, *I want to study*. It had now been more than twenty-four hours since her last sustained, concentrated flashcard session. Roxy looked so miserable, though. "Sure."

So they watched a movie. Alice wasn't really invested in what they were watching, but it seemed to do something for Roxy, so she kept her company, snuggling in bed with her as they watched her laptop. It felt a little bit spousey, but Alice didn't mind all that much. The world was still and quiet and could be mistaken for the world of before, but you could feel it, carried on the waves of Wi-Fi bouncing off every surface in the apartment, the public bananafication of Roxy Miao continuing. The humiliation was there if you looked for it, so Roxy didn't, for hours at a time, until she finally broke down, looked for it, found it, and destroyed herself on it.

"Am I fat?"

"What? No."

"Someone called me a fat cunt."

"Well, they obviously don't know you," Alice said. "You're not fat."

Roxy nodded. "I am a bit of a cunt, though," she said.

"Well, yeah, they got that part right," said Alice, and they both laughed, and it felt nice, and then Roxy cried a little, and that felt nice too. Then she took a bath, calmed down, swore off caring about anything anyone would ever write about her on the internet, and started the cycle all over again.

Twenty-four hours became forty-eight became seventy-two. Alice remembered Mrs. Pidgeon's words, burned into her brain: "If you leave your art for one day, your art leaves you for three." Alice hadn't practiced her instrument in three days now. It would take, by the Pidgeon principle, nine days to get it back. How did this time disappear so quickly? Three whole days. Three breakfasts, three lunches, three dinners. And the only thing that had changed was the date on the calendar. Roxy still hadn't stopped moping, Alice still hadn't gotten any studying done, and the world still hadn't stopped making sandwiches out of Roxy Miao.

At first it seemed like this scandal would bring the mayor down. Pearlclutcher went after him, hard. Grover, who had kept a respectful distance from the 111th Street apartment, but hoped to make amends, stepped out from behind his Ethicist byline to write an op-ed, "My

Friend Roxana Miao," in which he sang Roxy's praises and pinned the blame entirely on the craven, carnivorous mayor. Before handing it in, he let Alice read it, and Alice let Roxy read it. Roxy passed along her thanks to Grover. She knew he was trying his best, and honestly there weren't a lot of people sticking up for Roxy.

And Roxy had looked. She had made an anonymous Twitter account and spent hours refreshing her searches. She searched for "Roxy Miao," "Roxana Miao," and, somewhat embarrassingly, "Roxana Banana." And, even more embarrassingly, "#RoxanaBanana," after convincing herself that merely searching wouldn't help the algorithm that made things trend.

Very little good came from these expeditions. Some people hated her because of what she did to the mayor. They would post things like, "You know you're on the losing team politically when your side hires prostitutes to ruin a man's career. #RoxanaBanana." Others hated her because they hated homewreckers. "Sending strength to the wife of the next guy Roxana Miao works for. #RoxanaBanana" Roxy could laugh off people who took politics too seriously, or people with such bad marriages that they have to air that insecurity publicly. The worst, though, was the angle taken by the vast majority of tweets: the general assumption that Roxy Miao was trash. *She's tacky. She's thirsty. She wants to be an influencer, a star, a person of sophistication and wonder, and it will never happen for her, and she doesn't even have the self-awareness to see it.* Her bikini photo, the one she'd been so happy in, the one that had 607 likes before she deactivated the account, was widely mocked. They mocked everything about it: the swimsuit, the framing, the filter, the location ("Out here tryna act like Westchester is St. Barth"), Roxy's hair ("Little Orphan Roxannie"), Roxy's breasts ("So glad my tax dollars paid for those"), Roxy's cellulite (emojis of pigs), Roxy's smile ("Look at that mouth, it's at least three bananas wide"), and Roxy's nose, which had finally pretty much completely healed, but was still a little discolored, giving rise to comments like "Spiderman bringing jobs to New York: Blow Jobs, Tit Jobs, Nose Jobs."

Once in a while, Roxy found a bit of kindness glinting in the mud.

Maybe it was a link to Grover's article, or maybe it was a feminist calling for the reckoning that was sadly still two years away, or maybe it was just a simple and compassionate "Feelin' bad for Roxy Miao." Roxy found herself giving these comments likes, but stopped when a woman from Kansas with six followers tweeted at her, saying, "Thanks for the like! Are you Roxy Miao?" After that, she maintained strict lurkage, just watching the waterfall, waiting for it to reverse course, as she was sure it would, and make her the hero of this story, and Mayor Spiderman the villain.

It didn't happen. The mayor, whose people convinced Roxy she must never do an interview about this because an interview was the worst thing you could do, did an interview. It was on TV, and everyone watched. He held hands with his wife, a geologist who worked at the Natural History Museum and was beloved for still giving tours to public school kids every Saturday. They never stopped holding hands the entire time. He talked about mistakes, and judgment, and made a reference to the evils of temptation.

"That's me," Roxy said matter-of-factly on the text chain. "I'm the evils of temptation."

"You stop that," replied Pitterpat, watching the interview on her couch. "You are no such thing."

Alice, big spoon to Roxy's little, buried under three blankets and watching the interview sideways on Roxy's laptop, replied to the comment with a heart emoji, but kind of got where the mayor was coming from. Day four of not studying was drawing to a close.

Then the mayor, squeezing his wife's hand, said the line many people guessed he might say. It was a little obvious, but it was right there, so he went for it. "I often joke about the people of New York not liking me," he said. "Well, sometimes *I* don't like me either. And I don't like what I do."

Alice's reaction to that line, which Roxy and Pitterpat applauded and affirmed, was Who Farted Guy.

A hurricane in the Gulf of Mexico, barreling toward Florida, can either go left or right, and destroy either New Orleans or the Outer

Banks. Even with stakes that high, meteorologists concede that sometimes it's a coin flip. This particular hurricane, which anyone might
have reasonably bet would bring down the mayor of New York, went
left instead of right. "I DON'T LIKE ME" was in every headline the
next day. Think pieces were written about his candor, his vulnerability,
his respect for his constituents. Spiderman, the Take decided, was a
doddery old sweetie pie who was too friendly for his own good. *He's a
people person.* When an "aspiring Instagram model" (Roxy, after all,
had an Instagram account) somehow got a job working at City Hall
(nobody seemed to know how she'd been hired in the first place, but
everyone agreed she was unqualified), the mayor walked right into her
trap.

Roxy peppered Alice and Pitterpat with questions, morning until
night.

"Should I do an interview too?"

"Should I tweet something?"

"Should I reach out to the mayor?"

"Is there a way this whole thing could be a net positive for my
brand?" She had a brand now.

"Should we get food from that Chinese Cuban place?"

"Do they deliver?"

"Can one of you go pick it up if they don't?"

Alice wondered how this had become their responsibility. Whenever Alice asked Roxy about her parents, Roxy pretended not to hear
her. It was clear that box was to remain shut. Roxy did mention her
grandmother, though.

"She wants me to come live with her. She wrote me this long email
about it."

Alice disguised her hopefulness. "Really? Is that something you
want to do?"

"She lives in Connecticut," Roxy said, dismissing it outright.

"I mean . . ." Alice said, and then couldn't really finish the thought
nicely.

"What?"

"Is New York really all that great right now? Everyone knows your face, and everyone thinks . . . whatever they think. Instead of being surrounded by eleven million people who have opinions about you, wouldn't it be nicer to be surrounded by some trees?"

"My grandma lives in a three-hundred-year-old house. It's dusty."

"*Our* place is dusty! We live in a basement!"

"No! No. Forget it. I'm not . . ." Roxy ran out of breath, then caught it again. "Don't you have some work to do? Why don't you go to the Bakery?"

"Maybe," Alice said. "Maybe in a bit."

Alice had spent enough time as a nanny. She had that sixth sense about which kids you can and can't take your eye off of at the playground. Roxy was very much a can't, especially now.

But then a day went by, and then one more, and Alice couldn't help but notice that her plans for taking this test and coming even remotely close to passing it were becoming more improbable with every passing hour. GOOD MORNING, said her phone, IT'S 23 DAYS UNTIL THE TEST. Three days ago, when it had been 26 DAYS UNTIL THE TEST, Alice couldn't imagine being ready in time. Now it was three days less imaginable. Alice had to do something. She slipped a text to Grover.

"Okay, things are getting a little crazy around here with Roxy."

"Is this off the record?"

"Yes, it's off the record!" He made her say this every time. "How would you feel about me coming to stay with you for a few days?"

Grover didn't reply right away. Then: "How many is a few."

"I don't know. Three."

"I'm not sure."

She blinked at his response. Seriously? It bugged her. She replied with a withering passive-aggression that, after hitting send, she realized might not have come across.

"OK."

But it did come across. Three minutes later, Grover replied.

"Look, Alice, I don't like letting you down in a time of need. And the thought of us moving in together sounds really nice. But I don't want to make that decision under duress."

"Moving in together??" And then under that, she texted another three question marks, "???," just to make it clear.

"When we make that decision, I want it to be us making that decision, instead of letting the circumstances decide for us," he replied.

"Oh Jesus, just say no, asshole." It was a shot across his bow, to let him know he was starting a fight with that reply.

"Okay, I'm sorry. Really. I'm sorry." And then, moments later, "Why don't you ask your sister-in-law?"

"I don't know. Maybe. You know, this whole thing did happen because of you, after all."

Again, a joke, but she also kind of meant it. It took him a long time to reply.

"Is that what you think?"

"Well you didn't exactly stop it."

"Could I have stopped my editors from running the biggest scoop we've ever received as a news organization? No. I couldn't."

"But you didn't even try."

"No, I didn't."

"Why not?"

Another pause. "This line of questioning is going to result in me saying something that hurts your feelings. I suggest we drop it."

"Go on, hurt my feelings."

"Spiderman is the worst Mayor New York has ever had. His policies, his platforms, have harmed millions of New Yorkers. The shit Roxy's going through is nothing, NOTHING, compared to the collective suffering this Mayor has inflicted on my city, and will continue to inflict as long as he's Mayor. I know she's your friend, but this is a story that could bring him down. And if it does, it'll have been worth it. So no, I didn't try to stop it. I'm sorry. And furthermore, I think you're only angry at me because you CAN be angry at me, because the person you WANT to be angry at is the person who actually created this situation."

She didn't reply because he was right. She knew it, he knew it, and Churchill hanging on the wall above Alice's head knew it. But Alice was still angry.

Then he added: "That was unduly harsh. I've been struggling with this too. I really like Roxy and I obviously really really REALLY like you and I hate that this is happening."

* * *

"I see where he's coming from," Alice said to Pitterpat later that day. "It's not like we've been dating long. I don't want him to think I'm some helpless urchin."

They were having lunch at La Ballena. Alice ordered the Guactopus again, because you had to. Pitterpat didn't take a picture this time.

"You're *not* a helpless urchin!"

"Exactly!"

"You don't need some daddy figure to take care of you!"

"Uch, no!"

"You make your own way in the world."

"Totally," said Alice. "So can I stay with you?"

Pitterpat smiled. She had been looking forward to bringing up her own little bit of news, and here was a perfect chance to bring it up.

"Alice, you can have the place all to yourself," said Pitterpat. "I'm going on a trip for a few weeks."

Alice blinked. Two weeks ago, this woman wouldn't leave her apartment.

"Really? Where?"

"Cameroon."

Alice blinked again. She had seen Pitterpat's "Want to Go" Pinterest page. It was filled with beautiful places she hoped to see someday: The south of France. The Italian Riviera. Machu Picchu. Cameroon had never been in the conversation.

"Did you say Cameroon?"

"That's right."

"What . . . What are you gonna do in Cameroon?"

Pitterpat smiled, knowing this was the best part. "I'm gonna get hookworm."

"I mean, you *might*. I'd stick with bottled water. But—"

"No, Alice . . . I'm going to Cameroon *in order to get hookworm*."

Pitterpat had, in the last few weeks, become very active on the CrohnZone message board. It was her primary social life now, and she dove into it like a college freshman who had been very popular in high school. She barged into every conversation, liked every post, and gave a supportive "go you" or a compassionate "sending love" to countless posts. She made some friends, and even converted some of those ephemeral CrohnZone friendships into real, honest-to-God Facebook friendships. Every morning, after reaching out from under the Egyptian cotton duvet and fumbling for her glasses and her phone on the nightstand, her first stop of the day was CrohnZone, just to see what had happened while she was asleep.

And she learned things. She learned a lot. She learned, first of all, that she needed a new doctor, because pretty much everything Dr. Economides had told her was wrong.

"Most Western medical professionals just don't understand bowel disorders," she explained to Alice. "Gut health is the undiscovered country of medicine. There was this man from Alberta, Canada? He got diagnosed with Crohn's, and he did all this research. He was like a scientist or something so he knew how to study it. And he figured out that helminth infection alters the intestinal flora," said Pitterpat. "Do you know what that is?"

"Hookworm?"

"Yes! I don't mean to knock Western medicine," said Pitterpat. "The steroids have helped, but it's just a Band-Aid. I think this guy's onto something. People have always had hookworms in their bodies. Like, for millions of years, hookworms have always been there. What if they served a purpose all this time and we didn't know it? We invented penicillin and now they're gone, and we're walking around, like, *incomplete*."

"Well . . ." Alice said, starting a sentence that she didn't want to finish, especially to the person whose apartment she hoped to stay in.

"What?"

Alice put down her empanada. "We're not knocking penicillin, are we? I mean, yeah, it's easy to say, Western medicine this and Western medicine that, but Western medicine's also saved a bunch of lives, so maybe it's not the worst thing."

"Alice, I'm not implying— I'm sorry," Pitterpat said. She suddenly looked scared, and Alice let it go.

"No, it's fine. I'm just . . . my whole life is Western medicine right now," Alice said. She felt bad, realizing Roxy wasn't the only fragile person in her life. She continued, "It's just a little surprising. Of all the people I know, I wouldn't pick you as the one who makes a project of getting hookworm. You won't even go to the public bathroom in Central Park."

"But I do go to the bathroom in Central Park," Pitterpat said, suddenly serious again. "I've gone twice this summer, because I had to, because . . . I had to poop, and when I have to poop, I have to poop right away. I hate this disease, Alice. I have to do something. Even if that something is putting worms in my body."

Alice picked up a piece of ceviche, but put it down again. Maybe not ceviche right now.

"Besides, I can't stay in that apartment. There's all this stuff to deal with, with the money and everything. I've been talking to our business manager about it, and . . . I don't want our apartment, I don't want a new apartment . . ."

"You just want Bill," Alice said, thinking she was finishing Pitterpat's thought. But she wasn't.

"No," she said with a chuckle. "I don't even want Bill, I just . . . I just want a hookworm. Is that so much to ask? I want to be healthy. And I want you to pass this test and go to your school of Western medicine." The waiter placed the check on the table. "It's on me, by the way."

Alice sighed. "Pit, seriously, every time we get lunch you don't have to—"

"No," Pitterpat said. "I mean medical school. I'll pay for it. We'll pay for it."

Alice was stunned.

"How can you be so cool?"

Pitterpat shrugged. "Comes naturally, I guess."

"Lunch is on me," said Alice, grabbing the check.

Later, as they left the restaurant, Pitterpat again offered the use of the apartment, and again Alice thanked her, but just couldn't accept. Not until Roxy was in a better place.

"Let me know if you change your mind. You can bring your bird," said Pitterpat, and Alice's smile grew complicated. "You have a canary, right?"

"Had," said Alice.

Pitterpat looked worried. "Did it die?"

Alice explained what happened, and as she listened to the story, Pitterpat began to cry, as if it were her own canary that had flown away.

★ ★ ★

Alice came home to find Roxy naked in the empty bathtub, her hair already drying. She had gotten tired of her bath and pulled the plug, and then just sat there while the water drained, until it was all gone, and here she was.

"You okay, Roxy?"

"Am I a broken record if I say I'm not?"

"Of course not," said Alice. "Is there something new?"

Roxy looked up at the ceiling. "I got dumped."

"Shit, really?"

Roxy looked up at her. "Is that a shock?"

Alice tried not to play into her friend's despair. *No, it's not a shock that he wouldn't want to continue dating the most infamous woman in New York.*

"What happened?"

His email to her was very gentle, all things considered. "I've been feeling terrible for you all week," it began. It was sweet and considerate, and even ended on a joke: "If there's anything I can do for you—discount on crickets maybe?—let me know."

Roxy smiled, looking up at Alice from the bathtub. "Pointless to say it now, but I was kind of hoping people would call us Roxoph."

Alice nodded. "Huh. That would have been cool." Alice thought about this a little more. "Is that the main reason you liked him in the first place?"

"No," said Roxy. "But it definitely helped."

Roxy changed the subject and asked about Pitterpat. Alice told her about Cameroon, to which Roxy asked, ironically, "Can I go with her?"

Alice laughed, but her eyes screamed: *Would you please?* Then Roxy started to cry again, and Alice felt terrible.

"I'm sorry," Roxy blubbered. "I really liked him."

"I know," said Alice, sitting down on the floor next to the tub, rubbing Roxy's back as she cried.

"I wanted you to meet him," Roxy said, and Alice read so much in those words. Alice was her best friend. Alice hadn't asked for a best friendship, hadn't even been looking for a best friendship, but now she had one, and it was her job to take care of it.

"Who knows," said Alice. "Maybe I will. Give it time." Oh, it hurt to say those words. Alice had no time to give.

* * *

GOOD MORNING, said Alice's phone, IT'S 20 DAYS UNTIL THE TEST.

Roxy realized she hadn't been out of the apartment for a week, so she made an announcement.

"Let's go do something."

Alice *was* in the middle of running flashcards, and her brain was suddenly being asked to hop from the world of chemical equations to the possibility of her shut-in roommate leaving the apartment. "Okay," she said. "Where do you want to go?"

"I want to get a new phone."

"Oh yeah, I guess you need one," Alice said. And then Alice realized that one nice thing about this experience had been Roxy without a phone. She was a different person. She looked Alice in the eye when they talked, and listened and asked follow-up questions. "Are you sure you want to? Isn't it kind of nice cutting the cord a little?"

"Uch, no." Roxy convulsed. "It's the worst! Let's go to the Apple Store."

"What about your adoring fans?"

"Hold on!"

Roxy ran into her room, and Brigitte Bardot's hair emerged moments later, with Roxy underneath it. It had been her plan to surprise everyone at the party with a big '70s entrance to the strains of "Heart of Glass," by Blondie, and then, after midnight, a big '80s entrance to "Suicide Blonde," by INXS (a song that came out, as Roxy failed to double-check, in 1990). The plan, like the party, had fallen through, but she still had the wig.

"I think I can pull this off," Roxy said. "I don't think people will recognize me. Hold on!" She ran back into her room and emerged a few minutes later in a cheetah-print skirt and leather top.

"Well, you're not gonna *not* get noticed," Alice said.

"If I go out in this wig wearing a T-shirt and jeans, people are gonna be like, 'Why's that girl in the T-shirt and jeans trying to not be recognized?' It draws too much attention. But if I go out full-on '80s glamazon, it's just another Thursday in New York."

Alice respected the logic. Still, and even though she felt like a broken record even thinking it at this point, she had to work. Roxy could see her thinking it.

"Take your flashcards with you," was Roxy's solution.

So Alice brought her big box of flashcards with her and flipped through them on the subway down to 66th Street, while Roxy scanned the people on the train from behind the manhole-cover lenses of her sunglasses. She looked from face to face as if challenging each one of them to look up, to recognize her, and to give her permission to have a confrontation and explain her side of the story, which probably would prompt someone to take out their camera and start filming and then they'd post it on YouTube and everyone would see it and finally see how cool and reasonable and not fat Roxy was and the world would rally around her and everything would go back to normal. But nobody seemed interested. They all just seemed tired.

The sun had been setting when they got on the train, and it was dark when they came up the steps onto Broadway. The Apple Store was two blocks away, and for two blocks the game continued, Roxy looking at each face and getting nothing in return. The disguise was working.

In the Apple Store, they were helped immediately by a skinny young man named Charles, and even Charles, as he talked to this majestic bombshell and her friend with the flashcards, had no idea this was a close encounter with an alien species, a character from the internet fallen to earth.

"I need a new phone, because my old one got stolen, and it had a lot of personal stuff on it," Roxy said to him, and Alice couldn't help but notice how hard she hit the word "personal." She was trying to get caught, Alice realized.

Luckily, Charles just laughed it off, thinking this girl in the drag queen wig was flirting with him, which was a nice perk of the job that happened every now and then.

He gave her the new iPhone, but still no recognition. Then he asked her for her name, and Alice and Roxy both watched the transformation, like you'd watch a chemical reaction in a high school science class. His posture changed, his shoulders tightened, and his voice got a little deeper, a little more regulated. He was a textbook demonstration of "trying to be cool."

He asked for some more information, and Roxy gave it, nonchalantly, until he got to date of birth.

"Date of birth?"

She blinked. "Why do you need that?"

"It's for your plan. You have to be over twenty-one."

"I am."

"Well, I know, but . . ."

And then Roxy saw the choice she had to make. She could bulldoze this little man, this Charles, and get away with not giving her date of birth. But it would be loud. It would make a scene. She couldn't afford that.

"August fourteenth, 1980," she said, quietly, matter-of-factly, hoping Alice didn't notice or care or do the math in her head. Alice did all three. Roxy was thirty-five. People lie about their age, it's not a big deal, but for some reason Alice didn't like it. The easy comfort with dishonesty. It shouldn't have bothered her, but it did.

They got the phone and left, and headed for the subway, as Roxy greedily tore into the bag while she walked, so she could get onto her new phone as quickly as possible. She nearly walked into a very tall man in head-to-toe red leather, and the man recognized her immediately.

"Oh my God. You're Roxana Miao," he said, quietly but nearly hyperventilating. Roxy and Alice tried to walk a little faster, but he jogged next to them. "Wait a minute, hold on a minute, I need you to know, I think you're fierce. I love your style, I love your clothes, I love everything about you."

Roxy stopped. "Really?"

"Girl, look at you. You are everything in this world!"

Alice noticed people starting to look, and quickly tucked the three of them in behind a newsstand, where the red-leather man could gush in semiprivate.

"Girl, you got the raw deal, girl, the raw *deal*. I do *not* like that mayor, I think he *played* you. He needs to go!"

"Thank you! You know he's the one who started the whole thing," Roxy said, and then launched into the spiel she'd been practicing in her head, about how nobody knew what really happened and it wasn't fair she should get all the blame, and the man followed along with instant loyalty, repeating the last few words of each of Roxy's thoughts.

"It was just flirting! We flirted over text messages, it never went beyond that!"

"Beyond that!"

"The idea that we had some kind of affair, it's *crazy*."

"Crazy."

"We were alone in the same room together like twice, maybe three times."

"Maybe three times, I know!"

It went on like this for a while. Alice felt like a chaperone. Soon the man invited them to a club downtown called Forevereverland, and Roxy wanted to go, and Alice wished she'd hustled them into a cab at the first sight of this guy.

"Sir," Alice said, "could you give us a minute?"

The man stepped away and Alice got in close. "We don't even know this guy!"

Roxy ceded the point. "Sir, what's your name?"

He looked very pleased to be asked. "My name is Spam Risqué."

Roxy laughed. Alice did not.

"Roxy, we are not going to some club with Spam Risqué."

"Why, you think he could be dangerous?"

"Well, sure, there's that!"

"Oh, please, he's gay, it's fine." Roxy laughed, as though that settled it. "Besides, I'm never leaving the house unarmed again." She opened her purse just enough to expose the glinting silver handle of a pair of barber scissors.

Alice didn't know how to respond to that, so she took a different tack: "You'll get recognized."

"It'll be dark. It's a club." Then Roxy added what was real: "I need this, Alice. I need to go out."

Get back to work, Calerpittar.

Alice caved. "We're not drinking."

"Of course we're drinking!"

"Roxy," Alice said, "you win. Can you please be magnanimous in victory and not make me drink?"

"I don't know that word, so no, you're drinking," said Roxy. "Here, put those in my bag." She put Alice's flashcards in the Apple Store bag as Spam Risqué hailed a cab.

The three of them squished into the backseat and were halfway downtown when Roxy gasped. Her new iPhone was up and running and she had already Googled herself.

"Oh my God," she said. "I'm on Gumswallower."

Alice grabbed the phone. Gumswallower, an aggregator of the internet's most epic fails, wasn't a site you ever wanted to see yourself featured on. And now here was Roxy, on the front page.

Spam Risqué read the headline: "'Roxana Banana'—" He squinted. "How do you say that word?"

"'Pawned,'" said Alice.

"'Powned,'" said Roxy.

Spam Risqué went with his own interpretation. "'Roxana Banana Pee-winned by a Pole,'" he said.

Roxy hit play, and watched herself get pwned by a pole and break her nose. Weeks and weeks of healing, all because of one mistake. Roxy felt Spam Risqué wanting to laugh, and she felt Alice dreading how his laughter would devastate Roxy. But now Roxy looked at the video and felt nothing. And then . . . she laughed.

Spam Risqué burst out laughing as well. Alice joined in. They watched it again. Roxy would have thought nothing of laughing at this poor person's misfortune if it hadn't been her in the video. And it *wasn't* her in the video, Roxy thought. That was the real truth of it. That person falling down, that was someone else. *That's not me*, she thought, drunk on the idea.

"Girl, you took that pole to the face and you got right back up afterwards. Ain't nobody keeping Roxana Banana down. Nose all bloody, doesn't matter. Roxana Banana is everything in this world!"

I am, thought Roxy, *everything in this world*.

* * *

OONTS OONTS OONTS went the music as the strobes and flashing lights lit up the manic blonde on the dance floor and her slightly less manic friend who was not in any way dressed for clubbing tonight. And it was fun. It was loose and wild and Roxy forgot everything. She closed her eyes and danced.

Alice kept her eyes open. At first she didn't notice the occasional glance Roxy's way, and when she did clock it, she didn't see a pattern. But soon the pattern emerged. People were noticing.

Then, almost like an ambush, someone decided it was okay to get a quick selfie with Roxana Banana dancing in the background, and the dam broke. Flashes started going off. Alice grabbed Roxy, jerking her by the wrist, and her eyes flew open to see what was going on. They hurried through the crowd, off the dance floor. Alice found the bathroom line, pushed past everyone into a stall, and locked the door.

It was a unisex bathroom, a oner, thank God, so they had some privacy.

"Did people recognize me?"

"Yes," said Alice.

"Just a few people, or—"

"Everybody. It's like everyone figured it out all at once." Well, not really. Spam Risqué had been tweeting on the sly about it since they met, and a bunch of his friends and friends of friends had seen the tweets and come down to Forevereverland to see for themselves.

"Fuck," said Roxy. "What do we do?"

"I don't know," said Alice. And then the music stopped.

"Ladies and gentlemen," said a voice from outside the bathroom door, "we have a special guest in the house tonight. Give it up for Roxana Banana!" The crowd cheered, a bassy roar from the other side of the door. Alice saw the conflict on Roxy's face. It had been a while since anyone had applauded Alice, but she remembered the feeling and knew it was utterly ensorcelling, no matter how much you secretly hate the piano. "Let's make some noise and see if we can get her on out here," the DJ continued. Noise was made.

"What do I do? Should I go out there?" She really wanted to.

"I don't think you should, Rox. I think you'll regret it."

"But they're going crazy. Listen to them."

It was true. Roxy was all astir. Alice noticed words written on the wall in black Sharpie, thick, neat block letters: **MADNESS IN GREAT ONES MUST NOT UNWATCH'D GO.**

Alice opened the door, just a crack. About twenty pairs of eyes stared back at her. Alice addressed them all, calmly.

"Please tell the DJ," she said, "to play 'Suicide Blonde' by INXS."

She snapped the door closed once more, and the club went relatively quiet as the message made its way by game of telephone from the bathroom to the DJ booth.

When the dirty harmonica finally honked out from every speaker, and the groove kicked in, the bathroom door flew open, and out stalked the '80s, though technically '90s, glamazon in her bombshell wig and her dark sunglasses, her cheetah-print skirt and her leather top. She strutted, with murderous confidence, right into the throng, and the crowd went—forgive me, I must—*bananas*. The Suicide Blonde found the center of the dance floor, and the Suicide Blonde began to dance.

She danced and danced and wasn't a great dancer, but it didn't matter because the crowd loved it. At the end of the song, she froze fiercely, and the cheers shook the club to its girders.

And then she whipped off her blond wig and sunglasses, and the crowd could not believe they'd actually thought this girl was Roxana Banana. This was not Roxana Banana. This was some other girl, some girl who looked nothing like Roxana Banana from the purple bikini and the Gumswallower video. Roxana Banana, as anyone who lived in New York that summer would tell you, was the girl with the crazy mop of curly red hair. This girl did not have a crazy mop of red hair. Where was the crazy mop of red hair?

It was all over the floor of the bathroom. Roxy, in her brand-new pixie cut, waited in the cab. After fifteen minutes, Alice Quick nonchalantly strolled out of Forevereverland in the red leather top and cheetah-print skirt, with a platinum wig under her arm. She slid into the cab and they were gone.

★ ★ ★

They laughed the whole way home, laughed themselves out of the cab, laughed themselves down the stairs, and laughed themselves into the apartment and into bed. Midnight had snuck by again unnoticed. GOOD MORNING, chimed Alice's phone as she began to pass out. IT'S 19 DAYS UNTIL THE TEST.

Alice had not wanted a headache the next morning, and here she was with what felt like three or four all at once. She made some coffee and took three Advils. She was mad at herself, and tried to hang onto that feeling of being mad at herself because it was better than the alternative, being mad at Roxy. So, through a hangover thick as peanut butter, she gritted her teeth and looked around for her flashcards.

After a few minutes of looking, she knocked on Roxy's door.

"Roxy," she said, "do you have the Apple Store bag? I think my flashcards are in it."

Roxy sat up groggily and then lay down again. "Oh no," she said.

"What?"

"I left it in the bathroom."

"The bathroom at the club?"

"Yes."

"My flashcards are at Forevereverland."

"I'm so sorry."

And then it happened. That old impulse, the one that had splintered the bones in her right hand all those years ago, seized Alice at a full throttle. She searched the room for an object to punish, found it, and just like that a box of cornflakes flew across the room, colliding with the wall in an explosion of cereal.

"Alice, what the fuck?!"

Roxy looked angry, and it made Alice angrier.

"I need my flashcards, Roxy!"

"So we'll go down there and get them when the club opens up. Jesus, you don't have to throw things!"

"Fuck you, Roxy!"

"Whoa!"

The anger took Roxy by surprise, and Alice too for that matter. But it had been there this whole time, pulling back like a slingshot, and now it was launching, and nothing could stop it.

"All I wanted was to study for this test," Alice screamed. "You have prevented me from doing that at every turn, all fucking summer! I can't do this anymore! I have to work. I have to fucking work! What is fucking wrong with me?!"

"What's wrong with you? You're a good friend, that's what!" said Roxy. "You have taken care of me, in a way that nobody has ever taken care of me. I will not let you feel bad about that. Some things are more important than being a doctor."

Alice went wild-eyed. "That! That right there! That is exactly how failure happens! By letting *some things be more important*. I'm sorry, but if it's not important, if it's not the *most* important thing, it *doesn't happen*. And I need this to happen. I'm leaving. I'm going."

"Where?"

"I'm going to Pitterpat's. I'm gonna live there until after the test. I'm paid up on my rent for the month, I'll pay you for next month too, just leave me alone. I can't do this."

"Can't do what?"

"I can't live with you, Roxy! I'm sorry."

"But we're still friends, right?"

Roxy's eyes quivered, and Alice could see how lost Roxy was about to be. Alice calmed herself for a moment but did not back down.

"We're still friends," she said, "as long as we're the kind of friends who see each other every couple weeks. Or months. And we hang out for like a night. A short night. A dinner. And we chitchat, we catch up, and then we go our separate ways, because neither of us has her entire self-worth chained to this friendship."

Roxy couldn't stop her tears. "That sounds awful."

"I know," said Alice. It did.

As Roxy sat on her bed, Alice packed her two bags, grabbed the empty birdcage, and placed her key on top of the refrigerator. She gave the blue tree a friendly pat goodbye and headed out the door.

Later that day, Roxy's hair went up for sale on eBay. Someone had found it in the bathroom, put two and two together, and figured they could make a quick buck. But the reserve was not met since nobody believed it was actually Roxana Banana's hair. The auction ticked down to zero with no bids, and the hair went in the garbage, along with Alice's flashcards.

* * *

The email from Roxy, the one Alice had been expecting, arrived that night. She had been asleep, finally, after a day of brutal headaches, when her phone chimed. She came out of a dream to read the email, and then returned for a different dream when she was done.

It was to Alice and Pitterpat:

"Hey guys. So . . . I'm gonna go stay in Connecticut with my Grandma for awhile. Hopefully I'll see you kooks again someday if I don't get eaten by a bear or a ghost, hahahaha. Ghosts don't eat people but you know what I mean. Or maybe they do? I don't know what ghosts do exactly. Rattle chains? Anyhoo, thanks for being my friends, especially this past week. I'm sorry I got in your way. Pitterpat, good luck in Africa, and Alice, good luck on the test. Your friend, the Evils of Temptation (Roxy)"

Roxy took the train to Madison, Connecticut, wearing the blond wig the whole way. Nobody recognized her. In the bathroom, she admired the glammed-out Farrah Fawcett swoops and puffy '60s bangs, and was seized by the impulse to Instagram it, like an itch on a phantom limb. She knew that itch wouldn't let up anytime soon, but she was hopeful that someday it would be gone, and she'd figure out a new way to live in the world.

Her grandma picked her up at the station, and together they drove deep into the bear-infested woods, up some winding state road, until they came to a traffic circle with a gas station and a bar, also known as the center of town. A few minutes further up the road and they came to the little white church. Her grandma parked by the parsonage, under the loving ancient bough of an elm.

"Your bed's all made up," she said to Roxy as Roxy hauled her bag up the uneven wooden back stairs into the kitchen. The screen door slammed fussily behind them. "You're welcome to stay as long as you want, as long as you help out around the church."

"Oh," said Roxy, trying to think of a response.

"Or even if you don't," Grandma said. "I'm just happy to have you here."

That night they sat on the forty-year-old couch and watched a sixteen-year-old television, eating the mint chocolate chip ice cream Grandma had purchased six months ago, in the hopes that Roxy would come visit sooner or later.

After Grandma went to sleep, Roxy took out her phone. There was no signal out here in the darkened forest, so she sat down at her grandma's hundred-and-eighty-year-old desk (given to the rectory by a local carpenter fourteen head ministers ago) and turned on the eight-year-old computer. It played that opening chord, which Roxy hadn't heard in years, the chord that was once the sound of the future, the herald of technology's vanguard, and now the pitiable knell of imminent obsolescence. The screen lit up, and Roxy went through the instructions, as written out in pencil on the index card taped to the desk, to start up the modem.

Once online, Roxy typed in the address for Facebook, and entered her username, and then her password, but paused a moment before logging in. Logging in would reactivate her account. She wasn't supposed to do this. But it was late at night on a Saturday. Everybody was asleep or doing something fun. This corner of the universe was dark and foggy, a candlelit window in a forgotten alleyway. She slipped her hand over the enormous mouse and clicked.

Three hundred fourteen notifications awaited her. She began to read them.

"Happy birthday beautiful!"

"You rawk sexy mama! Hope this is the best year yet!"

"HBD RM!"

"Foxy Roxy, can't wait for your party, always the best of the year."

"Love you baby. Happy Bday."

"This is your year, Mzzz Miao."

On and on the messages ran, each one sending a beaming light of love into Roxy's sky, stars returning to the blackened firmament and making everything sparkle again. Roxy read each message through a squall of tears. When she was done, she wiped her eyes with the sleeve of her sweatshirt and deactivated the account once more. She shut down the computer, headed up to her room, climbed into bed under the creak of the two-hundred-fifty-year-old eaves, and fell asleep.

* * *

Pitterpat's flight was early the next morning. She got up before the sun had risen, dressed quickly, and ducked her head into the guest room, where Alice was still asleep. "Alice," she whispered, "I'm going."

Alice started to rouse herself, to come say goodbye. "Okay, hold on," she said, but Pitterpat stopped her.

"No, no, don't get up," she said. "I just want to say I'm going, and I love you. And good luck with the test."

"Love you too," Alice said, and suddenly being very awake, she was reminded of the possibly perilous journey her sister-in-law was about to make. "Be safe."

"I will, don't worry," she said. She looked nervous, but also excited, and she wanted to say so much more about it, but she had to go. "I'll text you from the plane."

She closed the door, and Alice began to drift back to sleep. She listened as the footsteps and the wheels of the suitcase made their way down the hallway. The front door clicked, and opened, and closed. The elevator dinged. The doors opened and then closed. Pitterpat was gone.

GOOD MORNING. IT'S 18 DAYS UNTIL THE TEST.

Alice woke up for real three hours later and scolded herself for burning so much daylight. But as she stepped out of the guest room, the quiet of the apartment overcame her. The sun was still rising on the other side of the sky, but its light bounced off the earth and shone through the big windows overlooking the river. This was what it was like to live way up high, with nothing across the street but a skinny park and a wide river. Alice sat down at the dining room table, and knew immediately that this seat, at the head of a large empty table in a large empty apartment, would be her base camp for the final leg of the climb. From this seat she would finish what she had begun, and everything noisy and large that had been in her way all summer long was eleven stories below her now, distantly quiet and small.

She would make coffee in a minute, and then she would gather her materials and prepare a plan of attack, figuring out exactly what to study, and then studying it, for the entire day, and nothing would distract her. She would do all these things, she knew, but first she sat in that chair, and looked out the windows, across the river, deep into the western sky.

BOOK THREE

The Further Shore

—•—

CHAPTER NINE

The Butterflies of Mont-Saint-Michel

I am nowhere. I am unborn. My silicon and bauxite are locked in the earth. My plastics are cellulose and crude oil. I am a bunch of rocks, and pine trees, and the leftover goo that once was dinosaurs.

Alice, barely out of kindergarten, is mastering scales, under the long, looming shadow of Mrs. Pidgeon, counting the clicks of the metronome before she can go ride bikes with Rudy. Her brother, Bill, is in the driveway of their old house, playing on his skateboard, which will be his obsession all summer, until drums take over in the fall. Felix MacPherson is at the YMCA, draining free throw after free throw, thrilling the onlookers gathered around him. One thousand miles south, Pitterpat Loesser is twirling a baton in a beauty pageant, something she will never tell anyone about, not even her husband, her entire adult life. Councilman Spiderman, graying at the temples, is ramping up his first unsuccessful campaign for mayor of New York, trying and failing to get everyone to pronounce it "Speedermin," and finding out that New Yorkers generally don't like him. Roxy Miao is blorped out on her sofa watching *The Real World* on MTV, as her mother asks her to please just once put her cereal bowl in the dishwasher.

Good morning. It's 8,122 days until the test.

Somewhere in Connecticut, in a glass-walled computer lab, a bleary-eyed sophomore saves and prints out the very last term paper of the year. He's very tired. He just wants the semester to be over and isn't quite sure what he's about to hand in, but whatever it is, he stuffs it in his bag and leaves. The lights go out automatically. The room is silent.

A week later, the teaching assistants move up and down the long rows of desks, unplugging the salmon-colored computer terminals. One by one, the salmon-colored terminals are placed in a large plastic pushcart. The TAs push the cart into the freight elevator, then down the long tunnel to the loading dock, where the terminals are loaded into a truck, whisked away from the humorless concrete building, and dumped in a landfill.

A few days later, another truck arrives, carrying a fleet of brand-new mustard-colored terminals that will serve as student access points for something called "the Internet." Returning students receive a bulletin in the mail: Starting in September, you'll be able to check your "email" on these mustard-colored terminals. You'll also be able to register for classes, access your grades, and do "all sorts of other things." To the computer science department, the mustard-colored terminals are a huge step forward from the junky salmon-colored ones. To the rest of the campus, and to anyone unclear on what "all sorts of other things" means, the purpose of these machines is at best vague, at worst satanic.

Do you remember this time? Most of us don't. We take it for granted that one afternoon long ago, the TAs went up and down the rows of mustard-colored terminals, reaching around back and turning them on with a click, and our world was quietly born.

Bobert Smith's roommate, Reggie, had long straight hair. It was nearly shoulder length, parted in the middle and tucked back behind his ears. Ethan Hawke had hair like this. Evan Dando had hair like this. Lots of other guys in 1993 had hair like this, and most of them had way more success with girls than Bob, quivering under a kinky and uncontrollable mane. So when he met Reggie in person, he was starstruck.

"Oh, hey, man," said Reggie as he strolled in. "You must be Bob."

Bob was hanging up a Devo poster, but as soon as he saw his new roommate, he stopped, and stepped down off the squeaky cot, discreetly turning the poster from view, as though it wasn't going to be hanging in Reggie's room for the next nine months. Reggie used both hands to tuck the loose strands of his hair behind his ears. Bob deeply envied that move.

"Hey, man," said Bob back to him, trying to give the word "man" the same casual friendliness that came naturally to Reggie. Some people can say "man" and pull it off. Some people can't. In just nine syllables between two new roommates, three things were clear to Bob: Reggie was cool, Bob was not, and they would never be friends, no matter what Bob's hair might look like if he grew it out and put some product in it.

"Yes, I'm Bob," said Bob. "Reggie?"

"The very same," said Reggie. He looked at the poster. "Devo."

Bob turned red. What bands you liked was something that mattered in the world of young men in 1993. He didn't want to get this wrong, especially after trying to say "man" and not having long straight hair.

"Do you know them?"

"I am not closely acquainted with their oeuvre," Reggie said, sprawling out onto his bed. "It's great to make your acquaintance at long last, Bob. Bob's a good name. Marley. Weir. Dobbs."

Bob laughed. He got all three of these references. Then, realizing a full breath and a half too late that it was his turn to talk, he added, "It's actually Bobert."

"Bobert?"

"Yeah, that's my real name. It was a misprint on my birth certificate."

"Well, Bobert," Reggie replied, holding up a joint he had just rolled, "wouldst thou care to partake in this fatty, mine good sir?"

"Oh, um, no thanks," Bob said.

"Do you mind if I partake?"

315

Bob didn't want his face to light up with *YES I MIND WHAT IF SOMEONE CATCHES US I DON'T WANT TO GET EXPELLED,* but it happened before he could stop it.

"Tell you what, Bobert. I'll let you settle in. I'm gonna head down the hall, see what's what."

"Cool, man. Nice meeting you."

Reggie and his fatty made their way down the hall to the room of two girls, one of whom fell in love with Reggie, and the other transferred to Berkeley, and that's how Reggie disappeared from his new roommate's life.

It was a lonely first semester. Classes were fine. He made a few haphazard friends. Sometimes he went to parties with them, and sometimes he went alone. Friends were fine, but he'd had friends before. He wanted a girlfriend.

There was one girl, that first semester. They met in a class on *The Divine Comedy* and sort of became friends, but then everybody was sort of friends with everybody. They ate together a couple of times, and once walked around campus, talking for an hour or so. He never had her phone number, but he'd see her around enough that it didn't matter. He'd look for her at parties. He'd get a beer in a red cup and walk through the crowd, browsing the faces as they went by, hoping hers would appear. Her name was Meg, short for either Meghan or Megan. He might have known which at the time, but years later, when he would try to Google her, that detail always tripped him up, especially since he couldn't remember her last name. She transferred away after the first semester and he never saw her again, and never finished the *Inferno,* and realized over Christmas that he'd now burned through one-eighth of college and was no closer to being any less lonely. Then one night, midway through the journey of his freshman year, Bob found himself in the computer lab.

It was late, and he was tired, but he'd been meaning to reply to an email from his friend Gumby, who was in his first year at Columbia, discovering cocaine.

"Hey," said the white kid with dreadlocks two terminals down. "You're in Russian lit, right?"

Bob was startled. It was the first thing anyone had said out loud in this room for hours. The computer lab was nicknamed the Aquarium, mainly for its high glass walls that put the room on full display to anyone walking by on their way to class, or cutting through to get to the Butterfield dorms, but it could have also been because being in this room felt like being underwater. Everything moved slowly, and nobody spoke.

"What?"

"You're in Russian lit. With Chopra."

"Oh. Yeah," Bob said, and said nothing else. He had lost the ability to have a conversation. Snow was drifting to the ground outside.

"How far are you into *Anna Karenina*?"

"I haven't started it."

The kid laughed knowingly. Bob probably shouldn't have gotten into Wesleyan. He had no idea who he was or what he wanted to become. Okay, that wasn't true. He was a guy with no girlfriend. He wanted to become a guy with a girlfriend.

The kid with the dreads went back to typing furiously.

"It's so long," Bob said. "*Anna Karenina*."

"Word," said the furious typist.

Bob was suddenly curious. "Are you writing a program?"

The kid didn't look up from his terminal. "Nah," he said. "Doing IRC."

"What is that?"

The kid, whose name Bob never learned, and whose signature dreads Bob would see from time to time over the next three and a half years and then never again, explained that "IRC" stood for "Internet Relay Chat." It was a series of chat rooms that linked the computer departments of universities and research facilities all over the world.

The kid took Bob through the whole thing: how to sign on, how to set up a screen name (Bob went with SpudBoy, something he pulled from a Devo song), and how to join a channel. The channels had names like #college, #music, and #chatzone. There was even one called #net-sex. The kid gave Bob the lay of the land, and the two of them went to #college for a little while, until around 2:30 A.M., when the kid packed up and left. There was nobody else in Bob's row.

Bob had only kissed one girl in his life, and it barely counted. It was quick, in a car at the end of a night, and they both still had their seat belts on. He replayed that moment a lot in his head, how maybe he should have taken his seat belt off. Or walked her to her front door and done it there. Whatever, it happened, and now it was over, and he was three hundred miles away from her and she was probably kissing some-one else right now. Bob knew plenty of girls, and had been good friends with a few of them, but the mystery of what they were only deepened with every passing day.

Bob joined #netsex and introduced himself.

"Hello. I'm SpudBoy."

Someone named Rimbaud barked at him, "A/s/l?"

"What?"

"Newbie alret."

"I'm new on this thing," Bob typed. "I'm at Wesleyan University in Middletown Connecticut. Anybody from Connecticut here?"

"Alaska," replied FlannelJammies.

"San Diego," replied Greyskull.

"I'm from up your mom's butt," replied Snapdad.

"Hahahaha," said Greyskull.

Then Ribbit showed up. "FARTSFARTSFARTSFARTSFARTS," said Ribbit. "FARTSFARTSFARTSFARTSFARTSFARTSFARTS-FARTSFARTSFARTSFARTSFARTSFARTSFARTSFARTSFARTS-FARTSFARTSFARTSFARTSFARTSFARTSFARTSFARTSFARTS-FARTSFARTSFARTSFARTSFARTSFARTSFARTSFARTSFARTS-FARTSFARTSFARTSFARTSFARTSFARTSFARTSFARTSFARTS-FARTSFARTSFARTSFARTSFARTSFARTSFARTSFARTSFARTS-FARTSFARTSFARTSFARTSFARTS." And then Ribbit was kicked off the channel.

"Where in Alaska," Bob asked.

"No possible way you've heard of it."

"Try me."

"Kodiak Island."

"No I have not heard of it," said Bob. "I almost went on a cruise to Alaska. But we went to Hawaii instead. But I wanted to go there. The brochures looked pretty."

Bob had purchased a porno mag on that trip to Hawaii. He had done it in the airport in Los Angeles during the layover. His parents thought he had ducked away to buy gum, which he did, but he also bought the latest issue of *Penthouse*, which was available for purchase right there at the airport newsstand, in plain view of everybody. He was fifteen, and that crime (was it a crime?) was the highlight of his summer.

Snapdad piped in. "Oh were you wondering what part of up your mom's butt I'm from?"

"Does anyone have actual sex here? It's called netsex."

"FARTSFARTSFARTSFARTSFARTSFARTSFARTSFARTS-
FARTSFARTSFARTSFARTSFARTSFARTSFARTSFARTSFARTS-
FARTSFARTSFARTSFARTSFARTSFARTSFARTSFARTSFARTS-
FARTSFARTSFARTSFARTSFARTSFARTSFARTSFARTSFARTS," said Ribit, back on the channel, now with one *B* in his name instead of two. This was the most fun Bob had had in weeks.

Then Bob received a message from FlannelJammies. "FlannelJammies invites you to join channel #overhere."

So Bob headed #overhere, and a conversation began.

"Hi," she said. "This is nicer, isn't it?"

"Yeah," he replied.

"So Spudboy are you looking for a real tomato?"

"You know Devo????? That's so cool. I dopn't know many girls who like them. They're from Ohio, not far from where I grew up." A pause. He needed to type something else. "Can I be honest?"

"Sure," said FlannelJammies.

"I've never done this before."

"So I gathered!"

"What is a/s/l?"

"Age/sex/location. Like for instance 18/F/Kodiak Island Alaska. That's me."

"Oh! Okay. 18/M/Middletown Connecticut."

"Hi."

"Hi," Bob said. "What's up?"

"Not much, whazzupichoo?"

"Just hanging out."

"Cool. What time is it there."

He checked the clock on the wall.

"2:45."

"Zoiks! Late night?"

"About usual. So what's it like living in Alaska?"

"Boring as shit," she said. "Do you wanna cyber?"

"What?"

She explained what it meant to cyber. Bob looked around. Nobody could see his screen.

"Okay."

"Have you ever done it?"

"No. Have you?"

"No. <winks> What do you look like Bob?"

"I'm 5'1" brown hair brown eyes."

"5'1"?"

"5'11" I mean, sorry! I'm not 5'1" don't worry."

"Well you could be and I'd never know."

"I'm not. Five eleven. Brown hair brown eyes."

"More. Describe where you are."

"I'm sitting in a chair. At a computer. In the computer center."

"Take off your clothes."

"Ummmmmm It's kind of a public computer center and there's three other people here. One of them is this girl who keeps giggling at something. I think maybe she's doing IRC too. Or she's just insane. Maybe she's Ribbit."

"<laughs out loud> Could be, you never know who's who on this thing."

He didn't know how to reply. The flow had been broken. *Get it back*. He typed.

"But anyway I can't get naked in here."

"SpudBoy."

"Yes?"

"Just tell me you're naked."

"Okay I'm naked."

"Mmmmm."

He thought there would be more but there wasn't, so he wrote, "Are you naked?"

"Not yet," she replied.

"What do you look like?"

"What are you picturing?"

He pictured what he was picturing, then wrote it down and hit return.

"I'm picturing some flannel pajamas floating in space."

"Hahaha! That's me. A pair of space pajamas. Actually I am wearing them right now. And nothing else <wink!> (Except snowboots. It's snowy out.)"

His breath quickened. He repeated, "What do you look like?"

"Five seven, 115 pounds," she wrote, and then added, "My boobs are too big for my frame, I hope that's okay."

She's lying. Is that a lie? It must be a lie.

"It's fine I guess."

"Fine for you! I have to buy special bras."

"I'm sorry to hear that."

"No you're not! Hahahahaha," she said, and Bob was exhilarated. "I have blue eyes and red hair, and it's kind of a short sixties cut, with bangs."

"You sound beautiful," he said.

"What do you do to me SpudBoy?"

The sentence threw him for a moment, as if maybe she had left out a word. He read it again. *What do you do to me?*

"What?"

"I'll start. I touch my hand gently to your arm. I gently caress it. With my other hand, I reach back behind your head, and run my fingers through your hair."

The scruff of Bob's neck tingled as a ghost passed by. The giggling girl giggled, still absorbed by whatever was so absorbing. Nobody could see Bob's screen but Bob. He replied.

"I slip my arm behind your back, and touch the small of your back."

"Mmmm. I like that."

"My finger traces circles at the base of your spine," he wrote, just as in that one *Penthouse* letter to the editor, the writer's finger traced circles at the base of that babysitter's spine. Nowhere in any of this did any actual fingers trace any actual circles on any actual spines. And yet here we are, aflutter.

"A moan escapes my lips," she replied. "I hope everyone in the computer lab doesn't hear me."

"We're not in the computer lab," Bob said.

"Where are we?"

"We're on a beach."

Makena Beach was its name, though Bob didn't know that. He only knew it as the beach near the hotel on Maui. It was a quiet strip of sand dividing the blue water from the dark green foliage, and it was the most perfect place he'd been in his life. He closed his eyes now and he saw it, and she was there too, and he saw her.

"I've never been to a beach," she said.

"I know. I flew you here in my private jet." Why can't he have a private jet?

"Wow!"

He felt the sun bearing down. The giggling girl's giggles were deep in the background, dimly echoing like thunder behind a cloud, but soon Bob heard nothing but the crunching surf.

"It's warm. The sand is powdery, and the water is so clear you almost can't tell where the beach ends and the ocean begins. The sun's just over the water, and we're standing, looking at it. The water is just barely reaching our toes, and our hands are almost touching. And then they're touching, just a little bit. Our fingers tickling each other. And then our fingers interlace. We're holding hands. And we turn away from the sunset and look at each other. Your lips are full and round. I lean toward them . . ."

Bob drew his hands from the keyboard.

His neck had stiffened and he realized he had stopped breathing for a moment. He looked around the computer lab. It was like coming out of a movie, like the time after he saw *Jurassic Park* and walked to his car thinking a velociraptor might leap out at any moment. The giggling girl had no idea the guy three terminals down was standing on a beach.

Bob looked back at the screen, the strands of mossy green letters behind the shiny black convex glass. FlannelJammies had replied.

"You're good at this."

"Really? I've never done it before."

"Here or in real life?"

"Either."

"Me neither." Then she said, "Keep going."

"I lay you down, on the soft powdery sand. It's like sugar. And I kiss your toes. Your skin is sweet. I kiss your ankles. I kiss your knees." He typed another "I kiss," but she cut him off.

"Okay listen carefully SpudBoy. This is enough for me. I'm in a public computer lab too so I'm going to go back to my dorm room now. It's a five minute walk across campus. I will be in bed naked by 10:57 my time. We're going to make it happen at the exact same moment, 11 my time, 3 your time. I'm going to feel you and you're going to feel me."

"Yes. YES. Let's do that."

"Don't let me down SpudBoy."

"I won't FlannelJammies."

"Goodbye."

"Goodbye."

He ran out of the building. Crossing the street, he slipped on the ice a little and nearly got hit by a snowplow. When he finally got to his room, Reggie was out. He would be gone all night, pretty much guaranteed. Bob got out of his clothes, got into bed, and got comfortable. He had hand lotion. It was vanilla-scented. He looked at the clock: 2:58. He closed his eyes and returned to the beach, and she was waiting for him, and she took his hand, and they lay down beside each other, and the air smelled like vanilla.

* * *

The next morning they were back on IRC.

"Ummmmmmmm that was fun."

"Ummmmmmmm yeah. I looked for you afterwards."

"Where?"

"Here. I thought maybe you'd be back."

"Oh I'm sorry about that. It's hard to get to the lab from my dorm room because of the snow. Plus afterwards I just needed to fall asleep because WOWOWOWOWOWOWOW."

He did that. He made that happen for her. It lifted some warm and generous part of him to know he'd been a part of someone else's good time.

She continued: "Did you feel me?"

"I felt you from all the way in Connecticut! You shook the whole continent!"

"Hahahahaha I felt you too. What were you picturing?"

"In the moment you mean?"

"Yeah," she said. "Right at the moment."

"I pictured you," he said. "We were on that beach. You and me, and the sound of the water on the sand. I was pressed against you, and all I felt was your skin and the sand and your flannel pajamas."

"Ha! I was wearing them! What color were the ones you were picturing?"

"Like greenish?"

324

"HOLY SHIT, they are green. Psychic linkup. SO just me in my pajamas and you on top of me."

"Underneath you."

"Mmmmmmm I'm getting excited again. Too bad I have class."

"Wanna cyber later? Later tonight I mean?" Already the lingo tripped off the lips of his fingertips.

"Sure," she said.

"Wanna talk on the phone?"

"No," she said.

"Oh."

"I only have one phone in my room and I share it with two roommates."

"Okay. Tonight. Want to say one my time, nine your time?"

"YES."

"Okay I should go to class. I'll see you tonight. That was fun last night."

"It was."

"Okay, I'll see you at nine your time. Bye."

She didn't show up. He sat in the computer center for an hour, lurking on IRC, jumping from channel to channel. No FlannelJammies. He went back the next day and spent a few more hours. He felt the looks from people who would come and go and come back and still see him there, and he thought of what they must think of him, and what he would have thought of himself if he'd been them. He didn't care.

Finally, after three days, there she was.

"Hi," he said.

"Hi."

"I looked for you the other night and I couldn't find you."

"I'm so sorry, I had somewhere I needed to be and I couldn't get out of it. I'm sooooooooorrrrryyyyy."

"'sokay!"

"Uggggghhhhh I wish I could have gotten in touch with you."

"Do you want to exchange email addresses?"

She emailed him later that day.

"Hi SpudBoy aka bsmith12. If this is really your email address. It's me FlannelJammies, your friend from Alaska. You can also call me Vanessa, because that's my real name. What's your name? It starts with a B I'm guessing. Brad? I hope you're having a good day, Brad! Xoxoxoxoxo Vanessa."

"Hi Vanessa, it's good to hear from you! I will let you know next time I'm up for a trip to the beach. My name is Bob by the way but you can call me Brad if you want. Or Bradley. Or Bart. Or Bilbo. Any B name is fine. Bob is pretty boring to be honest! Anyway, okay, gotta go. Stay warm in Alaska. Xoxoxoxoxo Bob."

Now FlannelJammies lived in Bob's head as Vanessa, though she still always wore the flannel pajamas. The pajamas, which were green, he pictured as a long-sleeve top with shorts that lazily rode up, so the milky whiteness of her long, very long untanned Alaskan legs popped in contrast against them. What few syllables he knew about her hair— short, red, bangs—were always the same. But her eyes, her nose, her lips, her chin? These things were up for grabs. They changed every time, with every fantasy, often a collage of other eyes and noses and lips and chins he'd stitch together from parts of other girls in real life and in movies and in *Penthouse* and other magazines (he had a few by now). He took her with him everywhere. He thought about her in class. He thought about her in the dining hall. He thought about her while reading *Anna Karenina*, and Kitty Scherbatsky had no face just like Vanessa had no face, but they both had the same face, and although this face was out of focus in the dark water of Bob's brain, it was beautiful and perfect nonetheless.

For the rest of the semester, Bob spent his free time in the Aquarium. He and Vanessa found themselves back on the beach three or four nights a week. Quickly, however, there became more to whatever this was. They chatted whenever they were both on IRC, and when they weren't, they emailed. They shared the highs of watching *The X-Files* every Friday night and comparing notes afterwards. They shared the low of Kurt Cobain's suicide, the first suicide of Bob's sweet, protected little life.

"It doesn't seem real," he said to Vanessa.

"I know," said Vanessa.

"I mean it's all there in his lyrics. He mentions a gun in pretty much every song. But still," he said to Vanessa. "I can't believe it."

"People are mysteries," said Vanessa.

"Have you ever had any experience with this stuff? Suicide I mean?"

"Yes," said Vanessa. She didn't elaborate. It was the most Bob had ever learned about her real life.

At the end of the year, the night before Bob went back to Ohio— where he would have no email for three months—they got drunk together. He snuck a bottle of grape Mad Dog into the computer center and sipped it while saying goodbye.

"Freshman year, over and done with. Can you believe it?"

"How was it for you? Mine sucked," she said.

"Not what I expected. But not bad," he said.

"Okay, I guess it had some moments. Meeting you was nice."

"Yeah," he said. "Hey so don't get a boyfriend over the summer, okay?"

"No promises," she said.

＊ ＊ ＊

As soon as Bob sat down at a mustard-colored terminal in September, the correspondence resumed anew. He told her about his job as a line cook in a country club. He told her about doing nitrous for the first time and liking it, and seeing the Grateful Dead for the first time, and liking that too. Both happened on the same night.

Then Bob met Amy Otterpool, a girl on his hall, a frosh, with eager friendly eyes and zigzaggy hair and an almost fragile smallness, and he stopped replying as quickly to Vanessa's emails. He would let two weeks go by without replying, and sometimes two weeks became three, and suddenly there was an unread email in his inbox from a month and a half ago.

"I'm sorry I haven't been in touch," he said finally.

"Ugh, let's never be those tiresome people who have to apologize for falling out of touch. No apology necessary. How are you??"

"I'm good! Actually, I have some news. I think I've kind of been avoiding telling you this, but I'll just say it: I think I have a girlfriend. I mean I know I do. We've been together since Halloween."

"SPUDBOY HAS A GIRLFRIEND?!?! DETAILS!!!!!! (I look forward to hearing all about it when you reply to this six months from now.)"

"Hahahaha, okay that's fair. Okay, I'll tell you. Her name is Amy."

He told her how they'd been flirting all semester, despite the fact that she had a boyfriend back home. He told her about the night of Halloween, how he and Amy had agreed to go out to the parties together, she pretending to be Cindy from the B-52's, he pretending to be a vampire, both pretending to be just good friends. He told Vanessa how, halfway through the second party, Amy mentioned that she'd broken up with her boyfriend, and said it without looking him in the eye because if their eyes met, it would be impossible to pretend it didn't mean everything. He told Vanessa how he kept wanting to kiss Amy, but couldn't do it. He wanted to kiss her on the dance floor. He wanted to kiss her in the beer line. He wanted to kiss her every step of the walk back to the dorm. She wanted him to kiss her too, but he couldn't do it, he couldn't do it, he couldn't do it, he couldn't do it, he couldn't do it, and then he did it.

Vanessa was happy for him.

"Congratulations, Spuds. Are you gonna marry this girl?"

He didn't want to say it to Vanessa, but he was pretty sure the answer was yes. Amy had quickly become his whole world. "I don't know."

"You should. She sounds great."

"Is it weird that I'm telling you all this?"

"Of course it is. Don't worry, I'm not jealous. I already have it figured out. I'm gonna be your second wife."

"Really?"

"Yep. You're gonna settle down, have a nice comfortable life, and then I'm gonna be the girl who shows up and wrecks it all."

"Okay," said Bob. "It's a deal."

And that's how Vanessa became Bob's future second wife. As they kept corresponding, she began signing her emails Number Two. Bob, incidentally, was going to be her fifth husband. She seemed pretty clear about that. So Bob got the nickname Number Five.

* * *

It was sickening, and Bob knew it was sickening, but oh, the indescribable joy of being young and in love and sickening with someone! Bob and Amy stayed together all through college, and then, after graduation, he moved to New York but returned to campus every weekend, and it was agony every day they were apart until she graduated and moved to New York too and true love persevered!

Bob had an apartment on the Upper West Side, and Amy lived with her dad in Brooklyn, but they spent nearly every night together. Bob started working for a consulting company, and Amy started looking at law schools. Dot-edus were discarded for Yahoos and Hotmails. AOL released Instant Messenger, and Bob discovered that office work was way less dreary when you spent all day chitchatting with your old friend in Alaska.

Vanessa was still on Kodiak Island. She stuck around because, as she put it, "it's either there or back to the butthole of Alaska." She was getting an advanced degree in computer science and could actually explain, in a way Bob could understand, how the Y2K bug might bring about the collapse of human civilization, and how to install Napster so he could hear any song he wanted before the world ended. Bob tried to explain what "consulting" was, and failed, because it cannot be explained, but the pay was good and he had his own desk and a computer and the screen was mostly pointed away from everyone else.

They talked about *Titanic*, which they both liked, although Amy hated it. They talked about the new *Star Wars* movie, which they both hated, although Amy thought it was "visually interesting." They didn't talk much about Amy, but Bob could feel himself wanting to, and not in a good way. New York was a big place. He rode a subway to work every day and saw all these women, in all these splendid colors and shapes and situations, and he wished he could fall in love with each one of them, and live a million lifetimes married to a million different girls. Riding home from work, he'd wonder where they were going, what adventure awaited them above the surface of the city, and then he'd remember where he was going: home to another night in the apartment with his girlfriend.

When New Year's Eve 1999 came around, Bob was five blocks from Times Square, at a rooftop party thrown by some of Amy's friends. Bob nodded along to the conversation as they all laughed about the possibility that the world might come to an end at midnight because of the Y2K thing. Information technology was their business and they lived in New York and thus they knew it was all being overblown, and Bob laughed along as they mocked the panic, but secretly Bob wished to be out of the city, away from the grid, pulling salmon out of the plentiful waters of Kodiak Island to bring back to his log cabin, where his red-headed wife would clean them and cook them.

He kissed Amy at midnight. "Doesn't feel like the apocalypse," she said.

* * *

It would be another year and a half before he could say it to anyone.

"I think I'm gonna break up with Amy."

"WHAT? No! You love Amy! Plus I can't be your second wife until after you marry your first one!"

"I'm serious. I love her, but," he typed, but did not send it. *I love her, but* . . . He couldn't find the second half of that sentence. And he realized it wasn't the second half of the sentence's fault. It was the first half. He deleted it and started again.

"I don't love her," he said. "Oh my god I've never said that or typed that. Do I not love her? I've been saying I love her for seven years. I meant it at one point. But I think I don't love her anymore. Or I don't love her enough. But maybe then it's not love. If it's not ENOUGH love, then it's not love at all, and I shouldn't call it love. What do you think?"

"I think you shouldn't get high at work."

"I'm serious."

"I think you know what you're gonna do."

"We also haven't had sex in six months," he added.

She didn't reply right away. "Is that a long time for you?"

"It's a long time for anyone, isn't it?"

She didn't reply, and when he talked to her hours later, she didn't bring it up. It was one of the few times he really noticed how little Vanessa shared about her love life.

Then, on an impossibly lovely Friday afternoon in August, when work got out early and Bob had the time to do it, Bob walked home, all the way from East 42nd to West 85th. The sidewalks of Midtown were crowded, as lots of people had the same idea. Somewhere around 57th Street, as the crowd parted for a moment, he caught a glimpse of Fleurette, an intern from his department. She was tall, and her voice was buttery and crisp, articulating itself clearly around every consonant. Everything about her, especially on this beautiful day with a light breeze sailing in from the East River, seemed to bounce. She was working on Bob's floor for the summer, and although they were only fourteen months apart in age, the fact that he was a salaried employee and she was a college kid felt like a wide gap. He had barely spoken to her.

But here she was, half a block ahead of Bob. He made a point of not following her, just playing the game to see how long their paths would remain the same. What if she and Bob actually lived in the same building, and she walked all the way to 85th and Broadway? He would take that as some sort of sign. He kept walking up Fifth, watching her appear and disappear as the crowd ahead thickened and thinned. She was strolling, taking her time, and Bob found himself catching up. Soon he would be within speaking distance, and if this light ahead turned red, and it did, they would be standing side by side.

"Hello," said Bob. "It's Fleurette, right?"

"Hi!" She smiled, big, enthusiastic, delighted by the surprise. "Oh my God, are you—are you coming from the office?"

"Yeah, I figured I'd walk home."

"Same here!"

"Might as well, right? It's finally cool enough."

"I know, it's been so hot!"

And that's how, for only the second time in his life, Bob did the thing where there was a pretty girl, he kind of knew her, he struck up a casual conversation with her, and nothing he said or did was embarrassing enough to disqualify him from ever seeing her naked. It was a giant step forward.

Three days later, Bob and Amy broke up.

★ ★ ★

"I did not think you would do it, Number 5."

"I didn't either."

"How did it happen."

"We were at this Indian restaurant."

"In public???"

"Public-ish. There was hardly anybody there. She really wanted us to figure out what we were doing for Thanksgiving, and I just realized I wasn't going to be with her on Thanksgiving, and I didn't want to lead her on. So I just SAID IT. I said I want to break up."

"You said those words? You said 'I want to break up'?"

"Yeah. Oh my God. It was so awkward and weird. And then we started talking and she kind of went back and forth between getting it and kind of feeling that way too, and then not getting it and being really mad at me, and really sad. She cried really hard."

"At the restaurant???"

"No back at the apartment by this point. But then she left. She grabbed all her stuff and went to her dad's place."

"Have you heard from her today?"

"No. We agreed not to talk."

"That's smart."

"The weirdest thing was waking up this morning," said Bob. "Because for a moment I didn't remember. Everything was fine and there was nothing different. Like any other morning. And it was a long moment. It was like three minutes. For three minutes I was awake today and I was still Amy's boyfriend, or at least that's who I saw myself as, and then I saw the drawer to my dresser was open and I remembered her getting stuff out of it in a hurry and it all came back and I realized I'm single."

"You're single."

"I am a single person."

"You were a boyfriend and now you're not a boyfriend."

"I guess I should start looking at flights to Alaska." He hadn't meant it. Not really. Maybe a little. But the lightness stopped.

"No," she said. "Don't do that."

"Okay," he said. "You sure?"

"Yes."

He didn't call Amy, but he did call Fleurette. She was happy to hear from him, and they talked for an hour and a half, and Bob suggested maybe he could come visit her at school for a weekend, and she said that might be fun, and so that's what he did, and as soon as he got off the plane and found her waiting in the baggage claim, he knew nothing was going to happen. They saw a football game, ate some barbecue, visited a battlefield, and before he knew it, he was hugging her goodbye. On the flight home, he wondered if he'd ever have a girlfriend again.

A month later, he got a short email from Amy.

"I don't mean to bother you, but could we meet for lunch sometime? You're not in trouble. I just want to talk."

He told Vanessa.

"You have to meet her," she said.

"I know that," he said. "Obviously." (Even though he'd only brought it up in the hopes that she'd say the opposite.)

"Good," Vanessa said. "By the way, you ARE in trouble. You know that, right?"

They met at a bar, a place they'd been a few times as a couple. She took a dance class nearby, and even though the weather was cooling off, he expected to maybe see her in a leotard. He got there first and found a table in the back, and every time the door opened, his chest seized up, and every time it wasn't her, he relaxed again, until finally it was her, not in a leotard but with her hair in a hasty bun, and his chest remained tight through the hello and the handshake. A handshake! This, he marveled, was what it's like having an ex-girlfriend.

They talked. She had taken her LSAT, and it had gone well, she said. She would hear about her score in a few weeks, but in the meantime she was looking at schools to apply to. She asked him how he had been and he said he was good. He was careful not to seem happy, and then realized that he truly *wasn't* happy, no pretending necessary.

"I'm really sorry about how things went," he said.

"How things went?"

"How things—" he said. "How I behaved."

"Yeah," she said, not saying it was okay, not saying he was forgiven, and he felt a little angry, because hadn't he done this right? He hadn't cheated or anything.

"I should have done some things differently," he offered, not sure what on earth those things could be. The food arrived to a silent table.

"We ate. I paid the check. We had one last hug goodbye and that was it," Bob said. "The end."

"I'm happy to hear it," said Vanessa. "I was giving it a twenty percent chance of you two getting back together."

"It's funny, when our food arrived, and suddenly we weren't talking because we were eating, I had this moment where I looked at her, and she was beautiful. She has this small mouth, and she never opens it wide, even when she eats. And her head was kind of turned down. She's very discreet about eating, it's very cute. Like she doesn't want anyone to see her doing it. And I don't know, there was a moment where I genuinely thought if I said all the right things right now, I could get her back. Like maybe the damage wasn't totally done. And I thought how wonderful it would be to fall into bed with her, and just do that for a day or two or three. But then, I looked up at the door, and this beautiful girl walked in. She was tall and big and shapely, just really substantial in this really delicious way. And Amy's so teeny tiny. Which is fine! Amy's beautiful! At one point she was the most beautiful girl in the world, at least to me. Against ANY girl in the world, I might pick Amy. But against EVERY girl in the world? All these shapes and sizes and endless varieties? It's not a fair fight. Not even close. No one person, with one face and one body, can compete with every face and every body. I don't know if I'm a creep for saying that out loud (though I'm not actually saying it out loud). But I do know, creep or not, if that's how I feel, I should probably be single right now."

"I don't think you're a creep," said Vanessa. "But I worry."

"I promise I'll never be a creep," Bob said. He was in the office, at his cubicle, and someone laughed, and he remembered the giggling girl, that first night, nearly eight years ago. "Can I show you something?"

"Sure," she said.

He sent her a link.

"What is this?"

"It's me."

The link led to his Match.com profile. He would never tell anyone in his real life about it. It wasn't something to be proud of. But there he was, his smiling face, advertising itself on the World Wide Web.

"Oh my god you're handsome!"

"REALLY?"

"Yes! Oh man. So this is what Bob looks like. Those dimples. Murderous. Now that I see what you look like, I'm extra worried. I mean it Number Five. You better not become a creep."

"I won't. I promise."

"I assume you've gotten forty thousand responses to this?"

He had gotten three. He would go out with two of them. The second one would terrify him so badly he would cancel his account afterwards. But the first one would spend the night with him, and he would wake up having now been with two women.

* * *

Three years went by. There were other girls, and it was fun, and it was also practice, practice for more fun, which would be practice for more fun still. He practiced and practiced, and each time each piece of it got a little easier. Starting a conversation got easier. Getting a date got easier. Going in for the kiss got easier. Letting things happen got easier. Going home got easier. Forgetting got easier.

He joined Friendster, because everyone was joining Friendster. Then he left Friendster and joined MySpace, because everyone was leaving Friendster and joining MySpace. One day he received a New Friend notification from Vanessa Lascaux, Kodiak Island, Alaska.

For ten years he hadn't known her last name, and now he did, but this was nothing compared to what he found when he opened the link to her MySpace page: a face.

It looked like a professional headshot, or a still from a movie. It was the work of an instant for his brain to trick itself and rewrite every memory, so that this face, with its doe eyes and *Mona Lisa* smile, had always been the face of the girl on the beach in the flannel pajamas.

He accepted her request and messaged her.

"Well well. Face to face at last."

"Hello Fivey."

"Hello Yourself, Twoey. So this is what you look like."

"Yep. Are you horrified?"

"Oh yeah you're hideous. No! You're beautiful."

"Don't get used to it. I'm still kind of opposed to putting anything visual on the internet. It raises a bunch of privacy issues. But I figured it's a nice pic. Let the pervs ogle."

"You're a hell of an ogle. Hold on, BRB. Okay, hi. Sorry, I'm at a restaurant."

Bob now had a mobile phone with a tiny little keyboard on it, so he could talk to Vanessa while out at a restaurant, waiting for his appetizers.

"Are you on a date right now?"

"Yes," he said. "She's in the bathroom."

"Oh man," she marveled. "How long is the list at this point??"

The list had grown, but it was still a list, not some blurry estimate, and no matter how long the list got, Bob could always recite it to himself from memory on the subway going to and from work, because if he ever couldn't, if he ever reached the point where he could actually forget an experience with another person, he would know he'd finally lost his way.

Then the apps arrived.

* * *

"I have a date tonight." It was the fall of 2014, a decade later.

"Reeeeeeally. And whose name will I be reading next to yours in the wedding announcements?"

"Wow, you really want me to hurry up and get this first marriage out of the way."

"I've been waiting twenty years for it. Who's the girl? What's interesting about her?"

"She's a computer genius," said Bob. "She's working on a PhD at Columbia. She does like artificial intelligence and stuff."

"Computers??? No. You can't date a better version of me."

"Darling, you are the best and only version of you."

"Is she pretty?"

"Her picture is."

And it was. Rudy had gone through the trouble of putting on a little discreet makeup and having a friend take a nice picture of her.

"Prettier than me?"

Bob looked at Vanessa's picture, the picture he'd been looking at for ten years now, the only one on this page or any other page. Her smile smiled a little more than usual.

"Nobody's prettier than you, Deuce."

* * *

She was not as pretty in real life as in her picture, and after only a brief exchange of introductory small talk, Bob's *nope* alarm was already going off, but he needed dinner and she was interesting to talk to, so he pulled out her chair as they sat down.

When the drinks arrived, Rudy set the ground rules.

"I'm giving you consent for sex tonight."

Bob looked up. "Excuse me?"

"I'll give you a few more minutes to go over your menu," said the waiter, before exiting awkwardly.

"I don't drink very often," Rudy continued. "But I'm going to drink tonight. If I get drunk, you might understandably feel like it's not okay to move forward with physical relations. So I'm giving you my consent now, while I'm sober."

Bob's menu, which he'd been holding to the centerpiece candle to read, caught on fire. He quickly doused it with his water.

"Um. I'm sorry," he said. "What?"

"We can have sex tonight," she repeated. "As long as you're gentle, and considerate. And as long as you want to do it! If you think you won't want to, like if you already know that to be the case, I'd love to know now before I start drinking."

He took a moment to think about it. He had checked her out already, of course, discreetly, the moment they'd met. She was thin, with a posture that seemed to curl, like a wisp of smoke. A Mickey Mouse sweatshirt was a unique choice for a first date, but it didn't seem to be covering anything terrible. There *was* something playful about her, with her big awkward teeth and her tiny squint behind her giant glasses. Bob didn't know why it was working on him, but it was. He wanted her. Sure.

"That's fine," he said. "Okay. We can do that if you'd like. That certainly takes the pressure off."

"I'm glad. The last thing I want is to pressure you. Too much pressure might prevent you from getting an erection."

He smiled. "Good thing that won't be a problem now!"

She laughed. First laugh of the night, and her teeth were brilliant. She wrapped her lips around her straw and polished off half her mojito in one ravenous gulp.

"If you don't usually drink," he said, "may I ask why you're drinking tonight?"

"I'm nervous," she said. "I've never had a one-night stand before."

"Oh."

"It's nerve-racking. I don't need to tell you that. You're new at this too."

Oh, right, he thought, *I'm new at this*. Sometimes he forgot. He thought gingerly how to phrase the next question without implying or promising too much. "Is that all you want? Just a one-night stand?"

"Yes," she said. "I don't want to be in a relationship. I had a relationship once. It wasn't a great one, and I don't think he was ever exclusive to me, and the way we broke up was that he stopped talking to me without even telling me we were broken up so I had to figure it out on my own. But it was still a relationship. So I can say I've done that. I've never had a one-night stand, though. That's an experience I've never had that I'd like to try. So that's what tonight's going to be." She finished off the mojito.

And then she ordered another, and another after that, and told Bob how she built a computer that either threatened to destroy humankind or cracked a joke—there was no way to know which one. The story slurred its way out of her mouth in a thick lava of soft consonants and mishandled vowels, but Bob got the gist of it: *I am a banana*.

"Did you plug it back in?"

"No." She took a sip. "Okay, yes. Yes, I did. He's in my dorm room. Don't tell anybody."

"Who am I gonna tell?"

"Seriously. It's a natural security issue. National. National security.

Wow. I better slow down," she said, right before another big sip. She took a deep breath and looked down at her lap, where her hands were, as though trying to steady herself before some Olympic event.

Bob asked, "Are you nervous about it at all? Is it a danger to anybody?"

The conversation landed at her feet with a squish. No response. Finally she looked up from her lap, into the candle.

"I was wrong. About the best joke in the world. Do you know what the best joke in the world is?"

"What?"

"Life."

Oh boy, thought Bob. *Here we go.*

"Life is the best joke in the world. There's so many different setups, but the punch line's always the same. This, right here, what we're doing, everything we do, our whole lives, it's all just the pause between the setup and the punch line. It's all just *timing*."

"Uh-huh." Beneath the table, Bob's hand was on his phone. But he resisted. *Stay present, Bob.*

"And whoever programmed all this is the best joke teller of all, because his or her timing is perfect."

"Programmed?"

Rudy seemed to tremble a little. "Bob," she whispered, leaning forward, "I know what's going on."

He froze for a moment. *So she knows.*

He asked, very calmly, "What do you know?"

"I know none of this is real."

He didn't reply.

She looked at him for a long moment, then spoke again. "I know this is a simulation."

"What?"

"You heard me."

He felt accused. No, he hadn't been completely honest with her. But he suddenly realized he wasn't pretending to like her. He liked her. He liked the banana story.

"I know that this," she continued, "all this, the whole world . . . it's all a simulation. I know it's all a game. You, the waiter, this drink, the sky, LEO, my parents, my friends, you're all just part of it. Part of the game."

He was silent for a moment. Finally he said, "The game?"

"An advanced computer simulation."

"So like a video game," he said.

"Yes."

"Like *The Matrix*," he said.

"Yes, Bob, like *The Matrix*," she said, a little smugly. He was silent again. "I know you're gonna deny it. But I know it's true."

He took a sip of his drink. "No, you don't."

"Yes, I do."

"No. You don't. You're wrong. I'm real. I have thoughts, I have feelings. I'm real."

"Of course you say that. That's what you're programmed to say. That's what I'd program you to say."

He laughed. "Okay. Let's say you're right. Let's say you guessed correctly. It's still just a guess. How would you ever know for sure?"

"Easy," she said. "I'll know when the game is over."

"And how will you know the game is over?"

She looked at him like he should know the answer to that. Then she started to cry, but stopped herself, very quickly, reminding herself: "It's just a game."

Bob liked Rudy, but he also did not want to invest an entire night into a girl who cried on a first date and said shit like this. Maybe he could skip the movie and set something up for later.

She wiped her eye with her napkin and sat up straight. "I'm sorry, I'm just kidding. I don't know what I was talking about." *Okay, maybe she's not crazy.* "For all I know, the player might not be me at all. It might be you." *Yeah, she's crazy.* "And tonight, after the movie, when you take me back to my room and do whatever you want to me, you can say goodbye to me and never call me again and not worry about it for a second, because I'm not real. I'm just part of the game."

Bob checked his phone for the time. "We should get to that movie."

* * *

They saw a movie at the Volta. It was a French film from the '60s called *The Butterflies of Mont-Saint-Michel*, a grand Technicolor spectacular starring a French actress Bob had never heard of named Geneviève de Buoux. Bob could tell Rudy was not someone who dated very much. Her choice of this movie, at this theater, felt like an extraterrestrial's idea of what a human does on a date in New York. He had no interest in seeing it, but it was still early, so even if things went sideways with Rudy, he could still have time to make something of the night.

Rudy had her arm around Bob as he paid for the tickets. It was a lucky thing she was so small. Nobody could tell he was discreetly supporting her entire body weight. The muscles in her neck worked and her eyelids were at least half open, so it wasn't a scene of any kind. The girl selling tickets smiled at Bob, and he noticed. (Rudy did not.)

The theater was empty. When they got to their seats, Rudy leaned way back, like she was in a recliner.

"Mmmmmm," she said, with a smile. "Comfy."

Bob had pretty much decided that despite what was agreed upon back in the halcyon minutes of Rudy's sobriety, he was not doing this tonight. He took out his phone and made no apologies for looking at it instead of talking to Rudy. Rudy didn't care. She just watched the slideshow of local advertisements on the big screen. Bob opened up Suitoronomy, right there in front of her. Who cared? This was how the game worked. He set the radius to one hundred feet.

And look at that! The girl selling tickets. Audrey, aged twenty-six, smiling brightly in what looked like a train-conductor hat, the same smile she'd given Bob minutes ago. He swiped right.

The movie began, and with it the bright primary colors, the Citroëns, and the dialogue like, "Mont-Saint-Michel is like my heart. Sometimes an island, sometimes not. You can only reach it when the tide is low." The heroine was a young nun named Françoise, played by

Mademoiselle de Buoux. It was set during the Occupation, and she was falling in love with a local cheese merchant named Nino. It was kind of like *The Sound of Music* with no songs and more smoking. It didn't hold Bob's interest.

He discreetly checked his phone, and look at that! Audrey had swiped right.

"Can I be honest with you? This is my first time doing this. I'm brand new at the whole dating app thing."

"Is that so?"

"Yep. How am I doing? Have I blown it yet?"

"No! So then how did you meet that girl you came in with?"

He laughed. *Okay.*

"So it is you! The girl behind the counter."

"The guy with a very drunk date."

"She's an old friend from out of town. Got a bit overserved at dinner."

"I see."

Bob flinched as Rudy's hand found his thigh. He nearly dropped his phone.

"Um," he whispered. "What are you doing?"

She didn't answer. She adjusted her weight in her seat and leaned over, and just like that it was happening, in the flickering blue and red light of coastal Normandy. Bob checked again: nobody in the theater, just him and Rudy and Françoise and Nino and the Sisters and the Nazis.

Then Bob imagined Audrey peeking into the theater and seeing this happen. She probably wouldn't, but it was a scary enough thought that he enjoyed it even more. Then he had his most exciting idea yet. Gently, without interrupting Rudy's careful work, he picked up his phone and started typing.

"So is that a conductor's hat you're wearing?"

"It is! I'm a model train enthusiast. I'm a bit of a weirdo about it. It started as a hobby in high school, something I would do with my dad, and I just never stopped."

"Cool! I don't know much about model trains, so I'm not sure what the smart questions to ask are. What scale do you do? Is that a thing?"

"Yes! There's lots of different scales. I'm HO scale mainly. (Don't read too much into that! LOL!)"

"Okay, I won't! LOL!"

He knew that was probably a line she'd used before, and it was. He was getting close. Françoise snuck out from under Mother Agnès's nose, and by the light of the full moon ran down the long road from the abbey to the town, her feet padding softly against the wet sand.

"The best stuff is usually HO scale, it's kind of the standard for serious collectors."

Rudy unleashed herself on Bob in the darkness, using trial and error like a true scientist to find something that worked. Nino locked up the cheese shop. The full moon and the gaslights shone down on the cobblestones. Rudy made little noises. Nino looked up. There was Françoise, in her habit, half concealed by shadows.

"What about you? Do you have any hobbies?"

Rudy went faster.

Nino said he had dreamed she would come tonight, and wondered if he was still dreaming. She assured him he was not. She stepped out of the shadows, into the light, and removed her habit. Her red hair bounced out, coming to a gentle landing on her shoulders. Nino's heart swooned, and Bob's did too.

The girl on the screen.

The red hair. The smile.

It was Vanessa.

* * *

Later, in Rudy's bed, her arm shook in a visible spasm and would not stop. Bob pretended not to notice, but he did, and she knew it. "I have a disease," she said, and did not elaborate except to add, "You can't catch it." Bob kissed her tenderly.

When he got back to his apartment, Bob sat at his laptop, in the dark in his bedroom, with the lights of the city out the window behind him, and did the thing he'd been dreading all evening.

He opened Messages and found his chat with Vanessa.

He looked at her profile pic. It was the same one that had been on MySpace, the same one he'd known for years, the only picture he had of her. It was unmistakable. This twenty-nine-year-old girl from Alaska in 2004 was no such thing. It was a promotional still of Geneviève de Buoux, star of *Les Papillons de Mont-Saint-Michel* and, according to IMDb, twenty-six other films, before her death in a ballooning accident in 1987.

He looked at the face he'd looked at so many times before. The face he'd assigned so much meaning to, so much intelligence and warmth and understanding and friendship, and now he had no idea who Vanessa was.

He scrolled up a little ways into their chat, reexperiencing it, turning it over once more. The chat kept refreshing, a week back, another week back, into the summer, into the spring, into the winter, into the fall. It was a conversation with no beginning. There were plenty of details: She was a fan of old movies; she had a sparkly silver dress but nowhere to wear it; she loved dogs but didn't own one because when you don't own a dog, every dog you meet is your dog.

But the *idea* of her hadn't changed in twenty years. Even now he saw her on the beach, her hair the same red, her legs the same white, her pajamas ruffled the way they'd been for decades. Pine trees were behind her. Bears peeked out from behind the pine trees. In all this time nothing had changed.

So what did he know about her? Her name was Vanessa Lascaux. She lived in Alaska, on Kodiak Island.

He searched. "Vanessa Lascaux Kodiak Island." "Lascaux Kodiak Island." "Vanessa Kodiak Island." "Vanessa Lascaux." Every search gave him either too much or too little.

What else? Kodiak College. She went there. Class of . . . 1997, same as Bob? That was what he'd always assumed. And now she worked there, in the computer lab.

He looked up "Kodiak College." The first result was the main page for Kodiak College, the simple website for a satellite campus of a state university, with images of the campus and happy students and Kodiak Island's wild splendor. Lots of pine trees, lots of bears.

The drop-down menu for "Academic Resources" took him to "Computer Lab." His heart lifted as he clicked it, then sank as the page loaded: Words. Nothing but text. Computer lab hours. Rules governing the use of school computing equipment. Nothing of value, and he might have given up if he hadn't noticed, at the bottom of the page, the word "QUESTIONS?"

Yes, Bob had some.

Below "QUESTIONS?" was a phone number with a 907 area code and an email: vtrumbull@kodiak.edu.

The *v* in vtrumbull@kodiak.edu glinted like a flake of gold in a river. Was this her? Was she V. Trumbull? Or perhaps V. T. Rumbull? Was she married? Was Trumbull her married name? Was Lascaux? He felt a tingle, and knew somehow that he was one search away from knowing everything. He typed in the search bar, "Vanessa Trumbull Kodiak College."

The screen went white and then the blue results arrived and there it was, the first thing, a page titled, "Vanessa Trumbull—Kodiak College." Her employee profile page. No picture. On a field of green, the white letters calmly told him all about Vanessa Trumbull: what her title was ("Assistant Professor of Computer Information and Office Systems"), where her office was located ("Campus Center 108"), the languages she spoke ("English, French"), and her interests ("hiking, photography, movies").

This is her. He backed up, back to the search results to continue the exploration, but there was almost no other trace of Vanessa Trumbull. Still, the name Trumbull tolled in his head like a cathedral bell. It fit, and he didn't know why, but he knew it did.

Another forty-five minutes of searching, and he found her.

It was a grainy, low-res group photo from a Christmas party in 2008, for the tiny little computer science department of the tiny little college on the tiny little island half a world away, but Bob was sure the moment he saw her, and he wasn't entirely sure how he was sure, but it was her, or at least the machine she occupied, the basement storage closet of flesh and bone from which she broadcasted and received. Bob examined her face, a new face that didn't quite fit the girl on the beach with the flannel pajamas, but it was her. Below the picture were the names of the attendees: Erica Wilpon. Sally McCauley. Kevin Trumbull.

Bob looked at her face, the face labeled Kevin Trumbull. This was who she was, or at least who the world saw, seven years ago. She was smiling, but only for the picture, only for the people around her who thought she was who they thought she was, and thought her name was Kevin.

Bob closed his laptop, and just like that it was dark except the lights outside. He still saw her. He saw her face. He felt a warmth, and a sadness, and neither made much sense, and his heart tried to stop the volcano of their little island as it erupted, and its lava incinerated all the pine trees and all the bears, and burned the beach away into a sheet of shiny black rock, stretched taut against the edge of a dead, salty ocean.

A pillar of light rose from his bedside table.

"How was your date, Cinco?"

"Not bad, Deuce."

"Details!"

"Eh. It's all boring."

"What are you gonna be for Halloween?"

"A vampire," he said.

A few weeks later, on Halloween, Bob slept with two girls, a nurse dressed as a cowgirl and a hairdresser dressed as a nurse, one at the beginning of the night and one at the approach of dawn, at which point he made sure to head "back to my coffin." Had the cowgirl nurse and the nurse hairdresser been Facebook friends, they would have both been surprised to see Bob prominently in their respective albums from that night, doing the exact same vampire pose, with the exact same hungry gleam.

347

The next day, Vanessa wrote him, "Do anything fun for Halloween?" And he told her the whole story. She scolded him, and he was bashful, and the twenty-year conversation continued, because that's what it always did. Why shouldn't it? There were times Bob thought she knew he knew. There were other times Bob thought maybe he was wrong about the whole thing. But mostly there were times when he forgot about it completely.

* * *

Nine months later, he was falling through the air.

In the world of vertical deceleration injuries, in which a body falls through the air accelerating at a rate of 9.8 meters per second squared and then decelerating at a rate of *immediately*, the survival threshold is eighty feet. If you fall more than eighty feet, you are going to die.

Less than eighty feet, and you leave the boring realm of certainty and enter the fun purgatory of probability. If seventy feet is your number, your chances of dying are around 83 percent. Not until sixty feet do the odds get really interesting: If ten people fall from a height of sixty feet, five will live and five will die.

Bob fell sixty-seven feet. He didn't know it, but he had a 42 percent chance.

Halfway down, he hit an air conditioner. That's how his arm broke. (It's also how the air conditioner broke, which led to a three-week email skirmish between the air conditioner's owner and the air conditioner's manufacturer over the terms of the warranty.) The air conditioner slowed him down a bit, but he was still moving very fast when he decelerated into a giant pile of moving boxes with "4B" written on them in black Sharpie.

He was on his back. He looked at the night sky between the buildings for a minute or two, clouds floating across the stars, and noticed how quiet it was, and he realized he was not dead and *holy shit, that just happened.*

Then he decided to check if any part of his body could move. One by one most parts cooperated. He stood up and took inventory, running over his anatomy like a checklist. His left arm was in a great deal of pain. Everything else seemed fine.

He checked his teeth. Unbroken.

His legs worked, so he walked, and with his right arm he opened the back door of Samantha's building. As he passed through the breezeway, he heard screaming upstairs. The super was yelling at 4B about the boxes. Bob left the building, and as he reached the sidewalk, he felt the cool sensation of knowing he would never go back in that building again as long as he lived. It was like a video game level he had solved, a level he would never have to solve again. He got in a cab and went to the hospital, where they all believed his story about falling off a ladder.

Late that night, his right hand managed to make a drink without any help from the left, which was snuggled into a thick white cast that started just below the elbow. He sat on his couch. The TV was off. The lights of the city were on. He took out his phone.

The last thing she'd written him was, "Everything okay Cinco?"

"No, I don't think everything is okay, Deuce," he replied. "I fell off a building today."

"Excuse me?"

"I fell off a building and broke my arm. Six story building. Nobody knows it happened but me. And now you."

There was a pause. Dots appeared.

"Oh my God, Cinco."

"I'm fine."

"Well thank god for that. Jesus. How did it happen?"

"I don't know. I don't know what happened. I don't know what happened at all." And then he added, "I feel like maybe I don't like who I am very much."

"I like who you are."

"You don't know me."

"Sure I do. Bob. Talk to me."

"I feel like I'm an alternate reality."

"How so?"

"I don't know. Not like I'm IN an alternate reality, but like I AM the alternate reality. Like, there's some version of me, in some other universe, and that's the real Bob. And the real Bob is out at a restaurant right now celebrating his ten year anniversary with his wife. They're surrounded by all these friends and family, and he's giving a toast, this other Bob, and he hasn't really written anything because I'm terrible at speeches, and he's been drinking, because I drink when I have to speak publicly, so it gets a little sloppy, but basically he stands up, and he looks down at his wife, sitting right here to his left, and he says, 'Thank God I met this woman.' And he puts his hand on her shoulder. And she puts her hand on his hand. And everyone claps. And then he goes on. He's like, 'Seriously, if I hadn't met this girl, where would I be right now? Where would I be?' And his buddy yells out, 'Suitoronomy!' And that gets a big laugh. And then another buddy says, 'You'd be sleeping with a different twenty-five-year-old every night.' And that would get an even bigger laugh. And his wife would give him a little look, like a raised eyebrow or something, but it's okay, she knows they're all just goofing around. That's how in love they are. And then he continues. 'Can you imagine me on Suitoronomy? Have you heard about this thing? It's so easy being single these days. You can just sleep with as many people as you want and never run out of new people to sleep with. It sounds AWFUL.' And it gets a big laugh, the way he says it, with a little bit of a twinkle. But then he looks at his wife, and gets real serious. 'But if I hadn't found this woman, I'd be lost. If I didn't have this woman next to me, I'd be a hopeless piece of shit right now, falling off buildings, breaking my arm. Every day I thank God I found her.' And then he turns to her, and he takes her hand, and says, 'I love you, baby. Thank you for saving my life.'"

Vanessa didn't reply.

"Because in that reality I found her," he added. "In this one I didn't."

"Bob," she finally said. "You probably found her in this reality too.

You probably even slept with her. You just didn't marry her because she's boring."

It made him laugh.

"LOL. I'll just go ahead and believe that."

"Listen I have to go. I'm meeting some friends for dinner. But two things. Number one: baby eagle!" She attached the link to the eagle's nest feed. "And number two please hang in there soldier. Stop saying mean things about my friend Bob or I'll come to NY and kick your ass."

He clicked the link. A beautifully ugly little baby eagle puzzled over the brand-new world outside its shell. Bob felt tears on his cheeks. His hand shook as he typed.

"Will you please?"

"Kick your ass?"

"No," he said. "Will you please come to NY."

She didn't reply. And then she did.

"Really?"

He had finished his drink at this point and was pouring a new one.

"I'll buy you a ticket. You can stay with me or stay at a hotel. I'll pay for the hotel."

"I don't know, Bob."

"I do. I know," he said. And then, a little tipsy, he repeated, "I know. Vanessa, I know." Another long pause. He restated it: "Come to NY."

Bob fell asleep. Sometime in the middle of the night, the pain in his arm woke him up. He stirred and reached for his phone to see what time it was. There was a message waiting for him.

"What kind of hotel are we talking?"

* * *

Bob got to the restaurant early. The hostess said he was the first in his party to arrive. He waited patiently as seven o'clock came and went.

"I'm here," he said. "Are you here?"

351

"Fifteen minutes away. I think I went the wrong direction, I'm sorry."

"Are you lost? Do you want me to come meet you?"

"No! Get the table, order a drink. I'll be there soon."

So he sat at the table, and drank a scotch, and watched the door, and each time the door opened he wondered if it would be her, and it kept not being her, until finally the door opened, and it was her.

She walked in, and there was her profile, and then she cleared the hostess station, and there was her body, and then she turned, and there was her face, and then she saw Bob, and there were her eyes, and then she smiled, and there was her smile, and there was her silver dress, and there she was, and it staggered him, absolutely goddamn staggered him right out of the cloud of one whiskey into the clear skies of sober apprehension, just how happy he could be to see a person for the first time.

This is her. This is real.

Bob stood up, and balance was a challenge, but he found it, he could do this, he was fine. Look at her. She walked toward him, out of the kaleidoscope of Christmas lights. She moved toward the table, toward Bob, and he felt nervous, electrically nervous, not ready to think about what lay on the other side of this night if things went badly. He needed to not mess this up.

And then something wonderful happened: She bumped into a pub chair and knocked it over, clean over, and if the pub chair had hit the ground, it would have embarrassed her straight down into the grave, but it didn't because Bob's unbroken right hand caught it. He actually caught the pub chair before it fell, the coolest, most graceful thing he ever did in his life, at the exact best moment for him to do it.

"Oh my God, thank you," she said, and there was her voice. "I'm such a klutz."

"No, it's okay," he said. And then he repeated, "It's okay," somewhat to himself.

"I'm sorry I'm so late. I thought I'd be sightseeing all day, but I just slept. That's a long trip! Alaska's farther away than Europe, did you know that?"

"It's fine," he said. There was a pause as they took each other in. "Oh my God, it's you."

"It's you!"

He got his left arm around her shoulder and they hugged. He felt her against him. Her body was unfamiliar, a topography of softness and muscle and bone that he didn't quite fit into yet. It brought him back into the world.

"You really broke your arm!"

"Are you hungry? Yes, I did. Are you hungry?"

"I'm starving," she said, and they sat down.

They talked about her flight, and her hotel, and how mind-boggling the height and width of the city was to someone who'd never seen it before. Throughout the meal, Bob struggled to square the woman sitting across the table with the woman living in his head all those years. This personality, these words he'd been reading on screens for two decades, this mind behind those words . . . all of it was in there, somewhere behind the caramel eyes looking out over the candle, some-where inside this nervous creature clumsily buttering her bread. That's where she'd been, in this body, this whole time. They made their way through a bottle of red wine and eased into this funny new reality.

At one point she brought up this whole Roxana Banana story she'd been reading about. It was all over the news, even in Alaska. Bob looked bashful.

"What?"

"I know her," Bob said.

"Really? How?" Then she got his meaning. "Oh my God. Oh, Cinco. No."

He laughed. It was the first time she'd called him Cinco out loud.

"She's a very nice girl. A bit of a ding-dong, but a harmless ding-dong. Maybe not harmless, but not *malicious*, I guess that's the point. I think she's a good person. Have you seen the video?"

She hadn't. He took out his phone and showed her "ROXANA BANANA PWNED BY A POLE."

"Ouch! Oh, that poor girl," said Vanessa.

"You know where she was heading when this happened?"

"Where?"

"Right here. To meet me." He gulped the last sip of his wine, a little proud of himself. She watched him, her finger tracing the rim of her glass.

"How many girls have you been with?"

He laughed. "Too many." He hoped she'd laugh too, but he noticed she didn't. "I'm sorry," he added.

"For what?"

And he wasn't sure for what, to be honest. Lots of things generally, but no one thing especially. "Not being young anymore," he said, the closest he could get to the target.

This she laughed at. "What's that supposed to mean?"

"It means I should have gotten on a plane and flown to Alaska the night I met you. It crossed my mind, you know. I distinctly remember it crossing my mind. It was before you could just go online and get a plane ticket. Plus I was broke. But I thought about it."

"I don't think you would have liked what you found," she said.

"Come on, of course I would have," he said. "I mean, that's not to say it wouldn't have been a *surprise*."

He laughed as he said it. She laughed too, nodding her head.

"I don't mind getting older," she said. "Getting older's kind of gone hand in hand with getting better."

Bob laughed. "That hasn't been my experience."

"Well, give it time. You're not done getting old yet." Then she added, "I'm glad we're meeting now."

"Same here," he said. He took her hand.

"What are you doing?"

"I don't know," he said. "Is it okay?"

His thumb traced circles on her knuckles. Her voice got small and happy.

"Yeah, it's okay."

They took a walk after dinner. He saw the city through her eyes for a while, as the buildings lit up the night. Everything was interesting. Everything had a story inside it that she wanted to learn. She tried to look in every window.

"There's just so much of it. I mean, right now, there's someone in each one of these apartments. That's crazy."

"Well, not each one of them. I'm sure a lot of people are out tonight. Plus a lot of people go to the Hamptons in the summer. But yeah. It's crazy."

He took her hand again. The street was empty where they were, and the air smelled nice, so he slowed his pace and they stopped walking in front of the stoop of a brownstone, because decades of practice told Bob this was the place to stop and the right time to do it. He leaned in for a kiss.

Her lips were tight, and tentative.

"That was nice," she said, her voice small again. But then her eyes opened a little, and she looked at the warmth in Bob's eyes, and something changed. "Can you tell me which way is my hotel?"

"What do you mean?"

"I'm just—I think I'm a little tired and I was gonna maybe head home if that's okay."

"Did I do something wrong?"

"No, I mean—no, it's fine."

Bob looked confused. "Tell me if I did something."

"No, you didn't do anything, we've just known each other so long, and . . . it's a little weird."

"It's not weird," Bob assured her.

She wasn't quite sure how he meant that, so she replied, "Okay, then it's weird for *me*."

He wanted to say fifteen different things, but he held onto them, and just went with, "How so?"

"I don't know, I just, you're *you*. You're Bob. You're Cinco. You're SpudBoy. You're . . . the person I've been talking to all this time. That's you in there," she said, tapping his forehead. "And I love you. But it feels strange saying that. It feels strange saying those words, to *you*, this *person*, some guy I just met in real life. It feels strange being kissed by you. I love what I think you are. I love these conversations we've been having for years, but is that you? Is that—"

"I don't understand."

"I don't quite understand myself."

"It's me. I'm me."

"I know. I'm sorry. I never drink wine, wine gets me all—" And she gestured confusion in her general brain area.

He didn't understand. "What are you trying to—"

"I saw the website."

"What?"

"'Do Not Date Bobert Smith.'"

His shoulders sank. "Okay, before you—"

"No, you don't have to," she said. "It's fine. I just . . . when you were just some words on a screen I could, I don't know, I could see past it. But you're *you* now."

"That night—"

"No, really, I don't want to—"

"No, I want to tell you—"

"No, Bob—"

"Will you just listen to me please? I had just found out about Amy being pregnant—"

"That's your excuse? Amy? Come on, Cinco. When did you break up, like fifteen years ago? What's wrong with you?"

"Why are you attacking me? It's not like you're blameless here either. You lied to me all those years."

"No, I did not."

"Yes, you did!"

"No," she said. "I lied to everyone else. I lied to myself. But you, Bobert Smith, you're the only person I didn't lie to. From the very beginning. From day one."

He didn't know what to say to that. The moon was high, and he wanted to hold her again, but it was all slipping away. Bagpipes drifted up the street from Riverside Park. Who the hell was playing bagpipes at this hour? Bob looked at Vanessa, unsure of what to say. The street-lights seemed so bright. He wanted to try again, to really kiss her this time, to kiss her into loving him, but his ears were ringing . . . and he couldn't see her now . . . and he was falling again.

She caught him, half caught him really, slowed him down as he hit the pavement. *This is embarrassing*, he thought, and then he was unconscious.

★ ★ ★

"You're lucky," said the neurologist, an hour later. "Walking around with an undiagnosed concussion for three days is a good way to end up with irreversible brain damage."

There *was*, in fact, irreversible brain damage. The neurologist, who was working his eighteenth straight hour, missed what the CAT scan clearly showed, and still shows even now as it sits quietly on a hard drive the world forgot about. It wasn't a lot of damage, certainly not enough that Bob ever noticed, but from that day forward Bob's mind was never the same. And maybe "damage" is the wrong word, because years later he would look back on it with gratitude, knowing that something about the orbit of his life had shifted in a moment, and shifted for the better. The fact that this shift was a little bit physiological was beyond him. For Bob, it was his heart, not his mind, that had been shattered and rebuilt.

Why must the heart be the synecdoche of a person's capacity to love? How strange that a place outside the mind is bestowed this honor, when the mind is where so much of love's energy lives. When you're in love, *really* in love, that love is pretty much all that goes on upstairs, aside from basic motor skills—eating, walking, brushing teeth, not falling over when you stand in one place—and sometimes even those get a little wobbly when it's a real, true, knock-you-on-your-ass kind of love. The brain is the cradle of love, the furnace of love, the factory of love, and yet we talk about love as something outside the brain, something going on in the mental suburbs, a foot or so to the south. It seems wrong, but also right, I suppose. Maybe the only way to grasp love is to see it as an alien in the mind, a visitor renting out a room there but belonging to another place entirely, commuting in from somewhere even I can't see on a digital CAT scan.

The sun was coming up as Bob and Vanessa left the hospital.

"Do you want to get breakfast?"

"Not really," she said. "I just want to go back to the hotel and get some sleep."

"Okay," he said.

"I'm gonna get an Uber," she said. "Can I get an Uber here?"

"Yeah," he said. "You can get one anywhere."

She sat down on the little gray wall in front of the hospital's flower garden and waited for her ride. He sat down next to her, as close to her as it felt like she'd allow. The Uber was three minutes away. They sat quietly, neither looking at each other nor speaking to each other. Suddenly Vanessa felt a vibration in her hand. It was a text message.

"I take you by the hand," it said.

Feeling his eyes on her, she shook her head no. He looked back at his phone, and she kept looking at hers. The car was two minutes away now. Another vibration. A spate of vibrations. There was more.

I take you by the hand. But you pull away. I understand why. I don't blame you. I don't try it again. I patiently wait for you to be ready to hear me. And eventually you are. And that's when I say all the right things. Things like I'm sorry, and you're my best friend, and you've lived at the bullseye of my heart for as long as I can remember, and I'll never hurt you again, and I love you. I say all this, and it works. I have to work for it, but it works. You soften to my touch. I take your hand, and you let me, and we go get breakfast, because this is a great neighborhood for breakfast, and we drink some sweet Cuban coffee and I make you laugh and I make you forget that you haven't slept in twenty-four hours and then we both realize we'll never be apart again. And after breakfast we decide to go for a walk on the beach, so that's what we do, we go to the beach, because there's a beach now, and it's beautiful. The sun is warm on our faces, and the water is warm on our toes, and we walk along the beach holding hands. And then we come to a spot where the sand is very soft, and somehow we both know this is the spot, and very gently we lie down on the sand, like we once did, like we always have, and we lie together on the sand and my breath becomes your breath and your breath becomes mine, and we lie there, together, exhausted, happy, full, not just a part of each other but the complete entirety of each other, and we lie here forever, holding each other in stillness, frozen Vesuvian lovers, children of ash.

CHAPTER TEN

The Ferry

Chère Eesh—

I've been in this city for one month and I've learned exactly seven things. Here they are, in no particular order.

1. I can speak French pretty well but I can't understand it for shit, which means I start a lot of conversations and then I'm immediately out to sea and have to switch back to the old Anglais. But I think they appreciate the effort. Multiple compliments on pronunciation. The key, I'm told, is speak your French with an accent that feels like you're making fun of the French, and then you'll actually have a pretty good French accent. So far no one's given me a nasty look. Maybe there's something to it.

2. I have finally learned not to overpack. I've worn nothing but one pair of jeans and three t-shirts this summer, and it hasn't slowed me down a bit. Gold star for me!

3. *The food here is as good as they say it is, but it's because they cheat, because there's butter in everything, real butter, so every bite of everything is like make-your-loins-shudder buttery. So of course everything's delicious. My single pair of jeans is not happy with me right now.*

4. *The coffee is not as good as they say, although with milk it's amazing, but that doesn't count, because the milk here is amazing and tastes like butter and turns your coffee into something like hot melted ice cream. But a black coffee here is no better or worse than a black coffee back home. Unless you also add points for ambience. Nothing beats drinking any kind of coffee if you're sitting at one of these little café tables, as I am now, looking out on a little square, just watching the pigeons and the people and the world and doing nothing. It's every bit as perfect as I hoped it would be.*

5. *I shouldn't have broken up with him. I miss him. This is real. It's completely ruining Paris.*

6. *I miss you too.*

7. *It's time to go home.*

My love to the whales,
Looch

Ayesha Quessenberry sat in the little internet café in the seaside town of Tromsø. She stared at her screen for a good long moment, unsure of exactly how to play this. Unsure if she even *should* play this, for that matter, since it wasn't really her business and she had bigger issues, like the malfunctioning beacon attached to an adolescent minke whale she'd been tracking, which meant she had to be back on the boat in forty-five minutes, so she could just as easily say she didn't get this email and deal with it two weeks from now.

She went to his Facebook page, to triple-check that she had for sure seen what she'd seen the last time she looked. Yes. "In a Relationship." That was for sure.

Still.

"Okay," she wrote to him, "this is totally weird and out of the blue, but your Facebook page says you're in a relationship?"

"Yep."

"How's that going?"

"Great."

"Are you sure?"

"Why would you think I'm not sure?"

"No exclamation point."

"It's GREAT!!!!!"

"Are you SURE?!?!?!?!?!"

"Ayesha, are you hitting on me right now?"

"Hahaha no," she replied. "I got an email from Lucia."

Grover froze. Dots. Another message on the way. Alice, reading flashcards in bed next to him, felt a pause in his breath. "What is it?"

She knows. How would she know? He didn't even fully know. *Calm down.* He cleared his throat. "What is what?"

"Is everything okay?"

He hated lying. Even little lies felt like pebbles before a landslide, like that first sip of gin that's fine and you can handle it and the next thing you know you're in a meeting and you've lost ten years of your life. Was he a sociopath? Was that it? Did he hate lying because it felt so easy? Was his entire ethical self merely a false exoskeleton holding up a poisonous jellyfish of nihilism? No, he just hated lying because lying is bad. That's all. *Calm down, Grover.*

"Yeah, it's great," he replied, and he went back to his phone.

Nonchalant, he typed, "How's she doing?"

"Wellllllll she's coming home. And you didn't hear it from me, but she wants to get back together with you. And now I have to get back to the boat. I'll check back in in two weeks. Good luck!"

Ayesha closed the window and ended her session on the terminal, then went up to the counter to pay.

"I like your shirt," she said to the cashier in the New York T-shirt as she sorted out the right combination of coins for twenty minutes of internet and a cup of tea. "Have you been?"

"Just got back," replied Sofia Hjalmarsson warmly to the nice American whale chaser who had just altered the course of the life of the twin she didn't know she had.

Across the ocean, Grover looked at the words on his phone, the words he had wanted for months. He had held out for them, like a lightship captain on a stormy sea, keeping the lamp alive day in and day out until the next shift cut through the fog. And now this sentence—in third person, not first, but still—was here at last. *She wants to get back together with you.* And here he was, sharing a bed with Alice Quick, the girl from the Bakery, straining her eyes to read the giant yellow book propped up on her knees, a book the size of her torso. She had never been particularly good at math or science, but here she was, trying to fit handful after handful of the stuff into her brain like an overpacked suitcase. Alice Quick, who refused to need encouragement. Alice Quick, who needed it anyway.

Dear Grover, I have a dilemma.

* * *

GOOD MORNING. IT'S 18 DAYS UNTIL THE TEST.

Alice made a pot of coffee with Bill and Pitterpat's amazing $1400 coffee maker and greedily drank four expensive cups of the stuff, and soon found herself a little too energized. Jittering and overwhelmed by the overwhelmingness of it all, she decided to give herself a day, and in her defense she used that day wisely. She read some Gumswallower. She answered some emails. She went to bed early.

GOOD MORNING. IT'S 17 DAYS UNTIL THE TEST.

She woke up energized, and a modest one and a half cups of coffee later, she was ready to go. It was August 24, the day of Practice Test Number Two, as announced by the Winston Churchill calendar now hanging in Bill and Pitterpat's kitchen.

At 10 A.M. exactly, Alice sat at the enormous dining room table, and watched the second hand make its way around the face of her watch. Past the nine, past the ten, past the eleven . . .

Begin.

For the next seven hours she hacked her way through all four sections of MCAT Practice Test Number Two. When the clock struck five, she got up from her chair, went over to Bill's gold bamboo bar cart in the living room, and poured herself what she didn't realize was an outrageously expensive glass of scotch. She plopped in a handful of ice cubes from the freezer, and gave the whole thing a splash of tap water to calm it down, and then returned to her seat to grade her own test. She went over it, and went over it again, and then went over it one more time before leaning way back in the dining room chair, resting the dwindling glass of scotch on her belly, and settling into acceptance of the score she'd earned:

499.

No, this is good. She sipped her whisky and looked at the western sky. 499 was an eleven-point jump! She was within striking distance of nonhumiliation. If she could jump another eleven points, and then jump another six points, she'd be at 516, the rarified stratosphere of the 95th percentile. Seventeen points away.

She checked her phone to remind herself that IT'S 17 DAYS UNTIL THE TEST. Seventeen points in seventeen days. *Never, never, never surrender.*

Her next practice test was in nine days. She would have to get a 508. She could do this, but to do it she had to turn her whole life into a machine. Only inside this machine, built out of schedule, syllabus, regimen, exercise, sleep, and diet, would transformation be possible. No, not *possible*, for the physics of this machine were far stronger than possibility. In this machine, transformation was *inevitable*. Alice built the machine, climbed inside, and lived there for the next nine days of her life.

GOOD MORNING. IT'S 16 DAYS UNTIL THE TEST.

She rarely spoke to others. Every morning she left the apartment, and the hallway was empty. It was summer. Nobody was around. The elevator doors opened to an empty car. Maybe Joan or Joanne hopped on at the eighth floor, saw Alice, raised a silent eyebrow, and later on gossiped with the other one, Joanne or Joan, about how the Quicks were subletting and that's not allowed by the board. But they never talked to Alice. Not even the doorman said hello.

GOOD MORNING. IT'S 15 DAYS UNTIL THE TEST.

Morningside Heights began to fill with incoming students for the fall semester. Like dandelion spores they floated through the neighborhood, in twos and threes. They hugged, caught up on each other's summers, took pictures together, but paid no attention to the woman walking up the hill. There she is in the background of a few of those pictures, behind this brand-new freshman and her parents, or those reunited juniors. Across the city's background she trudged along, backpack over both shoulders, up the hill of West 113th Street, right on Broadway, left on West 111th, past the old apartment building (below which two sophomores now had perplexed custody of a cerulean subterranean kitchen oak), and finally to the Bakery, where she sat down to study, switching between the big yellow book whose battered spine was now flaking away and the new set of flashcards she'd bought to replace the ones Roxy had lost.

GOOD MORNING. IT'S 14 DAYS UNTIL THE TEST.

She sat, and studied, and drank coffee, and spoke to nobody. Occasionally she paused to wonder how Roxy and Pitterpat were doing, but then back to work. Around noon she ate lunch, and then walked back to the apartment.

GOOD MORNING. IT'S 13 DAYS UNTIL THE TEST.

In the apartment, she spoke for the first time all day. She used her voice to drill herself, rattling off memorized lists and bundles of facts, talking through processes out loud as if teaching a class as she wandered the sprawling apartment, kitchen to dining room to living room to dining room to kitchen, and so on.

GOOD MORNING. IT'S 12 DAYS UNTIL THE TEST.

In the evening, when Alice could study no more, she went to Grover's. Just to visit, have dinner, and be tended to emotionally, because that was important. You can't skimp on that.

GOOD MORNING. IT'S 11 DAYS UNTIL THE TEST.

Every night he asked her to spend the night, and every night she said no, and every night he graciously understood. There would be time for that after the test.

GOOD MORNING. IT'S 10 DAYS UNTIL THE TEST.

By 9 P.M. Alice was back in her monastic little bed next to the exercise bicycle in the guest room. It was less comfortable than the couch, but it was fine.

GOOD MORNING. IT'S 9 DAYS UNTIL THE TEST.

At 10 P.M. she put her phone on the floor and slid it out of reach. She turned off the light and reviewed the day. *Today I ticked up one point. I got better at something. I shaved off an uncertainty.* She let herself believe it, because why shouldn't it be true? There was nobody and nothing in her way.

She went to sleep repeating one silent prayer over and over: 508. 508. 508.

GOOD MORNING. IT'S 8 DAYS UNTIL THE TEST.

She took Practice Test Number Three. She graded it. *No.* She double-checked. *Yes. Oh my God.*

511.

"That's amazing!" Grover shouted, and she didn't know where he was, but she hoped it was somewhere crowded. "Can you celebrate?"

She laughed. "Absolutely not!"

GOOD MORNING. IT'S 7 DAYS UNTIL THE TEST.

One week to go. It was Thursday, just like it would be Thursday the day she took the test for real. Alice thought about giving herself a rest day, since taking that practice test takes a lot out of a person. But no.

She stuck to the routine. She walked to the Bakery in the morning. She walked home after lunch. She drilled herself out loud until the sun began to set, and then went over to Grover's, just to check in. But she felt so good about herself, so magnificent and goddess-like, that when Grover asked if she'd like to sleep over, as he had every night, this time she said yes, and it was nice to remember him after so many days away. But she was still asleep by ten.

GOOD MORNING. IT'S 6 DAYS UNTIL THE TEST.

Grover handed her a mug of coffee as she sat up in bed. The curtains were open, and the sun had probably woken her up, but that was fine. "Sleep well?"

"I slept long," she said. "Maybe not well, though."

Grover sat down at his desk and opened his computer. "Another dream?" She'd been having vivid dreams.

"I think so."

"About your mom?"

"Yeah," she said. "I heard her voice this time. It's been so long since I've heard her voice."

"What did she say to you?"

"I don't know. I can't remember."

He left his laptop and came to her.

"What do you want her to have said?" He said it without any agenda, merely as a thought experiment, but Alice felt a little antagonized.

"What do you mean?"

"Is there something you wanted her to say? Maybe that's how you figure out what she was saying."

What did Alice want her to say?

Like a bat in the bedroom, a strange flapping of words flew into her mind and would not fly out. *Don't take this test, Alice. You're doing this to prove something to me and I don't exist anymore. I'm not a ghost. I'm a memory that snuck past the castle guards disguised as a dream. I don't want you to be a doctor. I don't want you to play piano. I don't want you to live your life for me. I don't want.*

"I don't know," Alice said, and she got out of bed. "I'd love to know her email password." Grover nodded. He seemed distracted. Alice continued: "I should get going. I'll call you tonight, like around nine. Will you be off the ferry by then?"

She looked back at him. He was looking at her, with wide eyes, as though something was on his mind.

"Hello?"

"Sorry! Yes," he said, shaking it off. "Nine o'clock you say? Yes, I'll be at the house by nine. I should get packing."

He got up and put some clothes into a blue-and-white duffel bag.

"Off to your island."

"It's not *my* island."

"Sure it is."

The island was, in fact, called Grovers Island, having been claimed for England by Sir William Grover in 1641, and Grover was descended from that Grover on his mother's side. Not a lot of people had ever even heard of Grovers Island, but Alice had. Growing up in Katonah, she knew kids who spent summers there. Every September, at the start of the school year, they'd laugh and reminisce about this paradise of sand and bicycles and only one ice cream shop. Alice had hoped one of them might invite her along one day, so she could see the beaches and taste the ice cream for herself, but it never happened.

So when Grover asked Alice to spend Labor Day weekend at his family's beach house, it scratched a very old itch. But when Alice thanked him for the invitation and assured him that any other time she would say *hells* yes, but unfortunately *this* weekend she had to stay local and study, but he should go on without her . . . that scratched a newer, more immediate itch. Alice was a serious person now, a woman who turned down fun in service of a higher purpose. She was someone who took her life seriously, a feeling more delicious than ice cream.

Alice took her coffee into Grover's kitchen, sat down at the table, opened the clock on her phone, and set a timer for fifteen minutes. She would let herself play on her phone for exactly that time, and then she would get dressed and head to the Bakery. Five fifteen-minute phone breaks throughout the day, that had been built into the machine, and it had been working for her, and even if she didn't believe it was working for her (she didn't), and even if in fact it *wasn't* working for her (it might not have been), she did it anyway.

The clock began to run. Alice sipped her coffee. Facebook.

A news story. Another pedestrian hit by a bicyclist. That was six all summer, and four of them had died. If Central Park had been a beach and four people had been eaten by sharks, they would have closed the beach immediately, so why were people still out there trying to cross the bike path? Alice agreed with this, and liked it.

More faces, people she knew, lives tumbling by. Facebook didn't do it for her like it used to. She had her own things going on now. Other people's things just felt like other people's things.

A new picture of Rudy Kittikorn. Alice paused here, and she couldn't say exactly what made her pause, except maybe the fact that Rudy had never written her back, or maybe that Alice couldn't remember the last time Rudy had posted a new picture. She looked really good in this one. Pretty, actually. She seemed to have makeup on, and had tended to her hair, and she seemed to be happy, in some unclear location, some apartment maybe, holding a glass of red wine and smiling. Rudy was a strangely beautiful girl, and here, in this picture, because of the dress or the makeup or the luck of the angle or the happenstance of the moment or a combination of any or all of these things, that beauty bubbled forth.

Alice's thumb moved, ready to like it, and that's when the thought first blinked: *Something is wrong here.*

The picture had not been posted by Rudy. It had been posted by Jill Bosakowski, a classmate of Rudy's from Columbia, and below the picture was a big number of likes. Eighty-seven in all. And not one of those eighty-seven likes was a thumbs-up. There were hearts, and there were sad faces. Sad faces? Alice checked, and yes, they were *mostly* sad faces. People were sad to see a picture of Rudy, smiling, pretty, drinking wine, happy.

And then Alice went to Rudy's page and saw the page's new title, "Remembering Rudy Kittikorn."

This was how you found these things out.

"Oh my God," she said. Grover, trying to decide between two handmade needlepoint belts, looked up, through the open door, at his girlfriend sitting in the kitchen.

"What's wrong?"

"My friend Rudy died." The words out loud made it real.

Grover put down his belts. "Oh no. Oh, Alice, I'm so sorry," he said, genuinely pained. She wasn't really sad yet. It was still the shock of the news. She scrolled down, reading the comments, trying to read between the lines and figure out how this newly pretty twenty-eight-year-old genius, the girl she'd ridden Big Wheels with up and down the driveway, could be gone. There were no clues. Had she been sick? Alice couldn't say why, but Rudy had always seemed like someone who was either sick already or might be one day. They had raced Big Wheels so many times. Rudy had never beaten Alice. Not once.

"How well did you know her?" Grover was sitting next to her now, rubbing her back.

"We were best friends."

"Oh, God, Alice."

"I mean, a long time ago. When we were little." What an odd way of marking time, going by size. Alice felt as little as ever.

"Still."

"Yeah," Alice said. "God, I can't believe it. I guess she was sick or something. I had no idea."

She returned to her phone. The only new post on "Remembering Rudy Kittikorn"—unclear who posted it—was the announcement of a celebration of Rudy's life that would take place a week from Saturday. Two days after the MCAT.

"I want to go to this," she said.

"Go to what?"

"Rudy's funeral. It's next Saturday. Will you go with me?"

"Next Saturday?"

"Yes."

"Not tomorrow."

"No. Next Saturday. Eight days from now. Can you come?"

"Okay. Yes, I think so."

"You promise?"

And that's when Grover's face changed completely. His forehead scrunched and his eyebrows danced, as if electrified. He was deep in thought, but it wasn't a thinking kind of thought, like he was doing math in his head, but a painful, emotional kind of thought, as if his brain was flooded and he was trying desperately to bail it out.

"Are you okay?"

"Yes," he said, and his features calmed down. His voice calmed down too. It was a little too calm, in fact. "Sit down, Alice."

She did so. He sat down as well, not next to her but across the table. He took a moment to gather his thoughts, then got up again.

"Hold on," he said. "I need to finish packing."

He went into his room and finished throwing things in the duffel bag, as Alice sat and waited and tried not to think about what this could be. Even from another room Alice could feel the nervous energy with which he opened and closed drawers and struggled to unbutton shirts to get them off their hangers.

He zipped up his bag and returned to the table, to exactly where he'd been sitting. And then he spoke, with clarity and eloquence.

"Alice, I need to be honest with you," he said. "I can't promise you that I can be your date to this funeral."

"I mean, I wouldn't call it a date," she replied. "But okay."

"Is that okay?"

"Yeah. That's fine, I'll just go by myself," she said. And he looked weirdly relieved. Alice continued: "Can I ask why?"

"I'd prefer you didn't."

"Why not?"

"I'd just prefer you didn't."

"Oh my God," she said to him, because she was nervous now. "You are going to tell me why. Either I'll spend a half hour pestering you about it, and that's a half hour of studying I lose forever, or you can just tell me now."

And so, seeing no alternative, Grover let it rip.

"The reason I can't promise to go with you is that I'm not sure we'll still be together as a couple next Saturday."

"What?"

"I want to say up front that I've struggled with the ethics of this. It's been a very challenging situation. There's no outcome here that spares everyone pain. Most importantly, I really didn't want to say this six days before your test. I know how important this test is to you, and I know how a conversation like this can completely throw a person's confidence and hurt their score. So the last thing I wanted to do was do this now, but I feel like you've left me no choice—by *no fault of your own*," he hastened to add. Then he lowered his head. "A few days ago," and then he stopped. "No, a few months ago, I—" And he stopped again. "A few years ago, I met a girl named Lucia, and we fell in love. *I* fell in love. She not as much, at least not at first. Or toward the middle, or at the end. *Especially* at the end. We broke up a few months ago, after two really good years together. Really good from my perspective, anyway. I was heartbroken, but I resolved to go on. Then I met you, and while I knew that it would be ethically irresponsible for me to commit to a relationship with you while I still had feelings for Lucia, I also felt that my feelings for her were trending downward fast enough, and my feelings for you were trending upward fast enough, that sooner or later the two lines would cross, and you would overtake her in my estimation. And I still think you might! That's very important for you to know. I still feel like you and I have a future together in a way that Lucia and I never did, and I would be able to put Lucia aside and move on, no problem. And I would have. I absolutely would have. I know myself and I know I definitely would have."

Alice wasn't sure she could say more than one syllable at this point. "Would?"

"But then a few days ago, I heard from a mutual friend of ours, and as I understand it, Lucia—who moved to Paris after we broke up, which, again, made me pretty confident I could move on and embark on this new relationship with you unencumbered by second-guessing and regret—is moving back to New York. And she wants to get back together with me."

"Oh."

"Yeah. So, she'll be back in town on Friday, before she heads to Maine for a little while, and while she's in town on Friday night, she wants to get dinner. And talk."

"Talk."

"Yes. Just talk. I mean, that's what she said. We've emailed a couple times. I'm so sorry, Alice. I've hated keeping this from you. I've done nothing so far that anyone could consider inappropriate. My emails to her have all been very dry. Cold, even. But when we get dinner on Friday, I just can't promise you something won't be reignited between us, in which case I don't think you'll want me to take you to this funeral."

"No."

"I wanted to tell you all of this. I would normally think it unethical to sneak around like this and entertain these kinds of thoughts without being direct with you about it, but it's a difficult circumstance, I'm sure you see that. Your test is on Thursday. Between now and Thursday, for me to say anything that would take emotional space in your head would be inconsiderate. It would be cruel, in fact. I didn't want to be cruel. I would have kept all this quiet. But given the circumstances with your friend, which is such a tragedy, I'm so sorry, I feel like I have to speak up. And now I'd love to hear what you have to say."

Alice closed her eyes and took three long breaths. Then she opened her eyes and, when she was confident she could get through three syllables without losing it, said them.

"Well, this sucks."

"I know," he said. "I understand if you hate me. I've behaved ethically, I *know* I have, but sometimes life puts us on opposite sides of a conflict, and we're forced to . . . play the game through to the end. But, Alice, I love you. I do. I'm not kidding. I know you're right for me, and Lucia is not. She's problematic. She's capricious, she's kind of a hippie, and honestly I think she's got a drug problem. In my mind I know she's wrong for me. My mind is there already. I'm just waiting for my heart to catch up. And it will catch up. I'm fairly certain it will. Just not one hundred percent certain. Which is why I'm telling you all this now."

Alice was either seething or catatonic, she couldn't tell, but either way she couldn't speak. She just sat there.

"I'm gonna go," he said. "I'm gonna let you process this. I'm gonna take an early train to Grovers, but I'll be on my phone, you can call me anytime, all weekend. And I do love you, Alice. I have to make that clear. I do love you."

He knew better than to try to kiss her, even on her forehead, so he picked up his duffel bag and left.

DING!

Fifteen minutes were up. Time to get back to work.

* * *

Pamela Campbell Clark went walking through the park on a fine, airy morning in early September. The world was getting cooler. In another week or so, she would need to bring a sweater. Soon it would be October, and then November, and then it would start to snow and the daily walk would be out of the question.

Her daughter would want her to come live with them (and their bees) on the farm in the winter. That phone call would arrive as soon as the leaves began to change. But Pamela had no interest in going on a plane, or having her apartment burglarized while she was off in California, where in addition to bees there were earthquakes, mudslides, and wildfires. She hadn't seen her granddaughter since they came to visit, and that was over a year ago, and now there was another one on the way, but still, no, thank you.

She crossed West Drive, and one second after her left foot left its place on the pavement, a bicycle streaked across the same spot, very nearly hitting her. Very, very nearly, and she knew it, and her heart suddenly went a thousand miles an hour. Jesus.

"Be careful!" she shouted at the bicycle, her voice creaking like an old door, but whoever or whatever was pulling that particular machine along that particular orbit was long gone.

A man in a hat sitting on a bench nearby found her eyes and shook his head in sympathy. In New York, every stranger becomes your old pal when something bizarre or dangerous happens. Pamela Campbell Clark and this man had the momentary silent communion of lifelong friendship. *These assholes and their bikes*, his eyes said. *Tell me about it*, hers replied.

I don't want to go live on a bee farm, Pamela Campbell Clark thought. Yes, it was pretty, with fields of buckwheat and clover stretching all the way out into the mountains. But it was in the middle of nowhere. You took the exit off the highway, and that long straight dirt road just went on forever, eventually ending at a little house that anyone could rob whenever they chose, or a bee could sting you, and the ambulance would never get there in time. No, thank you.

As she made her way home, Pamela noticed there were fewer people about than usual. It was a holiday weekend. People were away, visiting the people they loved. Pamela softened, just the tiniest bit. She did want to see her granddaughter. Maybe a neighbor could feed the cats.

A girl coming the other direction nearly bumped into her. *These people on their phones*, thought Pamela. *What could be so important?*

What was so important was Lucia Palumbo's Instagram. Alice had found Lucia's last name pretty easily. Her photos had been removed from Grover's Facebook, but Alice guessed they had some friends in common. Sure enough, Grover wished some girl named Jane a Happy Birthday back in March, and a few HBDs later there was Lucia Palumbo—boy oh boy, did Alice dislike this girl right away—wishing her friend a heart-emoji-filled "Joyeux Anniversaire de Paris!"

A quick scan of Lucia's Facebook confirmed that Alice had no interest in giving this chick the benefit of the doubt, but then she found Lucia's Instagram, and all bets were off. Her bio: "Wanderlustrix. Perpetual stowaway." Barf. Perpetual barf. Look at these pictures. Lucia by the Seine. Lucia at Montmartre. Lucia hiking in the Alps. She was a hippie, that much was for sure, but Alice immediately understood why

Grover was so enchanted with her. Despite all the fakeyness, and the thuddingly ayahuascan "insights" in all the captions of her photos, Lucia had two things an intellectual like Grover could not help but be intrigued by: perfect skin and a sensational body. Of course he'd never admit it, and of course Lucia never gave a second thought to her own beauty and its effect on people, and of course anyone predisposed to be in love with her simply loved that about her. But to anyone else looking at these pictures—to me, for instance—it's pretty clear these casual snaps from Lucia's extended vacation were anything but casual. She didn't wear those extra-small T-shirts because they were easy to pack.

In conclusion: *Fuck this girl*, Alice thought, as the bell above the doorway to the Bakery jingled, announcing her arrival.

Alice was not going to be derailed. She stuck her phone in her bag, ordered a coffee, and sat down at her usual table. She opened the big yellow book, turned it to chemistry. Chemistry and Physics. Her weak spot. If you could call it that. She'd gotten a 128 on that section. That's pretty great. 511. *Man.* She tried to hang onto that feeling.

The place was nearly empty. Good. Alice looked up from her book and scanned the other customers. Columbia kids. Some older faces too. Alice wondered if Rudy ever came in here. She probably lived in the area. Had she and Alice ever been here at the same time and not seen each other? It was possible.

Alice still didn't know exactly what had happened to Rudy. She was afraid to ask, and there was nobody she really *could* ask, since they hadn't been friends in nearly two decades. She went back to Facebook, back to the picture. Pretty Rudy. There were more comments now. More expressions of shock and condolence. Not too much shock, actually. Rudy had been unwell. It was no secret.

There was an update on "Remembering Rudy Kittikorn." It was a comment by Rudy's younger sister, and Alice had to reach to recall that a baby had been born around the time Alice boarded the bus for the conservatory and left Rudy behind.

"In lieu of flowers, please consider a donation to—" and it was a suicide-prevention charity and *oh, God, she killed herself, Rudy killed herself,* and now the sadness laid itself across Alice like a heavy blanket, pushing her down toward the earth, and some of it was probably the despair of maybe losing her boyfriend and probably bombing this test, but more than anything Alice thought of the little girl in the driveway, and her eyes welled up. Their bikes, side by side. The only two kids their age still on training wheels. The tears were close, she could feel them forming, and there were only two directions to go: forward and backwards, and backwards would do no good. The only way out is through. Alice made the tears come. She made herself think it and feel it. *Rudy.* The first person Alice could remember hugging that wasn't her mom or dad. *Rudy.* She was gone now. The little girl with the brains and the promise. She would never be an old lady.

She had given up.

She had quit.

Alice went outside to really cry. She left her coffee and the big yellow book at the table, and when she returned, they were still there. She sat down and opened the book, and as she did, she felt her hand aching. Even now, years later, the little crooked lines where the bones had fused themselves back together sang their old sad song.

An order was up at the counter, a pink box tied up in blue string. Alice wiped her eyes on a sleeve. The Bakery was an old place, sending cookies and cakes out in the same pink boxes they'd been sending them out in for years. Blue string dripped from the giant spools mounted on the ceiling, and the ladies behind the counter used the blue string to tie up the pink boxes with the kind of practiced efficiency that dazzled the customers, people who, generally speaking, were okay at a lot of things, pretty good at a few things, but dazzling at nothing.

Chemistry. Physics. Here we go.

Grover would be on the train by now. Had he even texted?

She would not take out her phone.

Alice hadn't written anything on Rudy's wall. She needed to. Why? Rudy wouldn't see it. Her family would see it. It would mean something to Rudy's mom.

Alice took out her phone to post something for Rudy.

He hadn't texted.

He hadn't even sent Alice a text to say "hi, I'm on the train now, I miss you," and it was probably because he was busy looking at Lucia's Instagram. Lucia, who made no effort. Lucia, who had no goals. Lucia, whose pointless nomadic ass was fine just the way it was. Lucia, who had taken a picture of herself in a bikini inside a seaside cave on some Greek island and adorned it with the words "The future isn't promised. Now is all you'll ever get." And then Alice was on Twitter, and then she was watching a video about how suitcases are made. Do you know about this? It's beautiful. There's a machine that blows the plastic up like a big bright orange or yellow or purple balloon, and then the balloon deflates, tightly and efficiently, around the mold. It was footage from a factory in Wenzhou, in China. Alice found the website for the company that made the suitcases. Their machinery was very beautiful and very clean, stainless steel practically polished into mirror. Where was Wenzhou? Alice checked. It was a large city on the coast of Zhejiang, across the East China Sea from Okinawa and Taiwan. She went to Google Maps, picked up the little orange man, and dropped him in Wenzhou, indiscriminately, just to be there for a moment.

And there she was, in 360 degrees of some spot in or around Wenzhou, and it was beautiful. Not at all what she'd expected. She stood by a lake, and the sun was setting, and across the lake was a neighborhood of the happiest-looking brick-and-wooden houses. There were shadowy mountains in the distance, and the banks of the lake were green and mossy, and there was a red bicycle parked nearby. *That must be the photographer's bike*, she imagined, but then she imagined it must be *her* bike, because she was the only person around, appreciating this little lake and this moment of poetry and quiet in China.

She was going to bomb this test.

No, you're not. 511, remember? This morning was a waste, but you're gonna go back home and put in an afternoon, and it will feel great. Alice ate some lunch, a turkey sandwich on a rubbery croissant with ice-cold tomato slices, and then went for a walk.

It would have been so much easier if there was anything else she wanted to do. Bill always found that next vine. He always had something straight ahead to grab onto. Alice looked straight ahead and saw nothing, and for her whole life, that nothing had been the pebble in her shoe. Even in Hawaii, island of flip-flops, the pebble was there, bugging her, nagging her, reminding her how little she was doing to become exceptional at anything.

She arrived at the Harlem Meer, the little pond in Central Park, the one Roxy had fallen into. The sun was high in the sky. There were no mountains in the distance here, only tall buildings. The banks were green and mossy, but the smell . . . just a tickle of stench from somewhere nearby.

It was half past three when she got home, and it occurred to Alice that she could still pull this day out of the wood-chipper, she could get out her flashcards and get going, and she smiled at the happy thought of doing that, and then she didn't do it. She flopped onto her bed, opened her laptop, and put on the first episode of *Love on the Ugly Side*.

By episode seven, Alice realized three things.

Number one, she hadn't eaten dinner, and it was now eleven o'clock, way too late to eat, but she would order something anyway because it was New York and who cared about anything anymore anyway.

Number two, holy shit, *Love on the Ugly Side*! Alice lived a whole summer that day right there on her bed but also in that seaside hacienda, where she, like Jordan and the rest of America, fell in cringy terrified love with Mallory. Mallory! Alice got it now. She hated and loved Mallory every bit as much as Roxy had promised she would. When Mario Lopez handed Mallory that revolver and instructed her to aim it into the back of that blindfolded stranger's head and squeeze off a round . . . oh, Mallory! That quivering smile, the way she bit her lip a little! The way she didn't hesitate, even for a second, to raise that Glock and pull that trigger! And when the gun went click, that look on her face! Oh! Was it . . . Was it *disappointment*? "What Are You Willing to Do?" asked the billboards and *You fucking name it!* was Mallory's answer.

If Jordan didn't marry that psychopathic national treasure, Alice would riot.

And number three, Alice didn't want to be a doctor anymore. Even thinking the word "anymore" felt like a lie. She had never wanted to be a doctor. Why would she want to become a doctor? She didn't even *know* any doctors! I mean, that was a big thing to realize. She was holding herself up to some standard that literally nobody she knew lived up to. Except Dr. Bannerjee, some lady she hadn't seen in three years. This whole thing was silly, and had been silly from the start. This, this, this *giving in* was not something she would regret, she knew for certain. This would live in her memory as the summer she spent learning a bunch of stuff about the human body and how it works, and what's the waste in that? None. If you're a biological creature, it's good to know biology. If you live in the physical world, it's good to know physics. If chemicals play some part in your life, chemistry's nice to know, whether you're planning to make a career out of it or not. It was a lot of work getting all that stuff into her brain, but now it was there, and nobody could take it away. That was worth something.

The pizza arrived, and she ate half of it, and then a blueberry muffin arrived, and not one of those puritanically insipid muffins from the Bakery, but an actual big, fluffy, moist, problematic, twenty-first-century muffin, and it was way too sweet, and Alice ate the whole thing, and the big yellow book slept quietly in her backpack as IT'S 6 DAYS UNTIL THE TEST became IT'S 5 DAYS UNTIL THE TEST became IT'S 4 DAYS UNTIL THE TEST became IT'S 3 DAYS UNTIL THE TEST and the world lost all shape and meaning as Alice went back to Wenzhou, climbed on the bicycle, and rode off into the dark mountains.

* * *

It's hard to pinpoint exactly where the Grovers Island Massacre of 1683 actually took place, but a survey of contemporaneous accounts and historical records indicate that, as likely as not, those sixty-one Pequots lost their lives in the backyard of Grover's family summer house, probably over in the clearing behind the cutting garden where the beverage tent was now set up.

The whole extended family was here for the annual Labor Day party. There were plenty of Grovers in attendance, and a bunch of Whipples, and a few Kineses, and there in the middle of it all was Grover Whipple Kines, sitting in a blue Adirondack chair and drinking a Narragansett while writing and erasing text message after text message, until, unbidden, a text message arrived.

"How's Grover's Island."

Alice. Thank God.

"Grovers. No apostrophe. And it's terrible without you. I miss you so much I could split in half."

"I miss you too," Alice replied, and then, "I don't want to break up."

She had written it as a plea, but he took it as a reprieve. Grover hadn't had any fun at this notoriously fun party. At first he thought this roiling churn in his stomach was guilt, because guilt always has a way of finding you, even when you know, rationally speaking, that you're guiltless. But it wasn't guilt. The sun moved behind the elm, the lawn cooled, and Grover ate a hot dog, and as he finished the hot dog and opened another Narragansett, he decided what this painful feeling was: love. He didn't want to lose Alice. Sweet Alice. His study buddy, with her hunched shoulders and her perseverance. That was all there was to it, and that's why this text, coming when it did, was a moment of grace.

His fingers blurted, "I don't want to break up either! I'm coming home tomorrow. I was going to stay all week but I want to see you."

"I want to see you too. Can I come out there?"

"What about the MCAT?" Then he realized what day it was. "Shouldn't you be taking your practice test right now?"

"I don't want to be a doctor," she replied. She was in bed, swimming in take-out cartons and dirty laundry and the smell of not having showered.

A moment passed. Dots, then no dots. Dots, then no dots. Dots, and finally: "This is a surprise."

Only if you haven't known me very long, she thought, and almost typed it, but didn't. She wasn't going to feel bad about herself, even as a joke.

"Someday I'm gonna find the thing I'm supposed to be doing, and when I do I'm gonna do it with everything I've got. So far I've figured out it's not piano or medicine. But that leaves plenty of other possibilities. I'm only 28." She hit send, and immediately remembered how much he hated when people write the contraction "gonna," but she didn't apologize for it. She let it stand.

More dots appeared, and Alice imagined the long column Grover was probably writing to her right now about living up to your commitments and seeing things through and how you're not just letting yourself down but also all the people who love you and are betting on you to realize your full potential. Then the text arrived: "Promise you aren't blowing off this test just to see me."

"Don't flatter yourself, you're not THAT cute," she replied, and then followed it up with, "I promise."

He didn't write back right away. She wondered if maybe he'd had second thoughts, when suddenly an email arrived. It was her ticket information for her train to New London, along with a little map explaining the short walk from the train station to the ferry terminal.

GOOD MORNING. IT'S 2 DAYS UNTIL THE TEST.

The rest of the family had gone home on an earlier ferry. The physical debris of the party was gone too. The plastic poolside cups were all washed and back in the cupboard. The paper tablecloths had been rolled up in one great motion, with all the paper plates and napkins along for the ride, and thrown away in a nearby dumpster. Whatever table scraps could be sorted out were now in the composter, where they would become dirt in the heat of the September sun. The grill was turned off, its gas lines closed.

Grover's car, his "island beater," as such cars are known, was an old BMW the family had been using for fifteen years at least. It had still been the twentieth century when the beater made the crossing from

New London. Now it lived here year-round, working all summer, sleeping all winter.

The beater pulled up the driveway with the perfect crunch, as though the gravel and these tires had been chosen for each other for just this sound. As she stepped out of the car, Alice felt like she was stepping into an Instagram filter. The light snapped with just the right contrast, a little washed out, a little jaundiced, giving everything a prelapsarian calm, as though no problem could be brighter than the midday sun, or louder than the peaceful snore of the surf, or so hot that a gin and tonic couldn't tamp it down.

Every hydrangea blossom was a perfect, spherical, angelically white puff. Pitterpat would love this place, Alice thought.

"What do you think?" Grover knew what she thought, but he asked anyway.

"It's beautiful."

"We like it well enough," he agreed, and they went inside, and all was, if not forgotten, at least put away for a bit.

* * *

GOOD MORNING. IT'S 1 DAY UNTIL THE TEST.

They picked up sandwiches at the Compass Rose Café and took them to the beach. The beach was empty, as was the island for the most part, and Grover looked at Alice with such happiness, such guileless constancy, as if there were nowhere else but this Eden and no one else but this Eve.

She liked him so much. She understood it now. Even at his worst, he was honest. He genuinely wrestled with right and wrong. And she had seen his worst now, and she had made it out the other side.

As Grover splashed alone in the surf like a Labrador retriever, and Alice sat watching him from the towel spread out on the wide stretch of smooth round stones that passed for a beach, she thought about her flashcards sitting on her bedside table, untouched, no idea of their own obsolescence. What would she do with them when she got home? Throw them out? Keep them in case she ever changed her mind? Donate them to some actual future doctor? Maybe that would be the extent of her contribution. That would be her smattering of mattering: She'd be the woman who gave the flashcards to the doctor who saved a life or two.

They spent the day in and out of the ocean, and in and out of bed. They ate dinner on the patio as the sun set. It was shrimp skewers with a pineapple glaze, and it was perfect. They went inside afterwards and watched a movie on the couch. It was not long before Alice was sound asleep, earlier than she'd fallen asleep in ages. She hadn't realized how tired she was. Grover picked her up, and she woke briefly as he carried her to bed, just enough to quietly smile.

She woke again in the middle of the night. Maybe it was another dream, she wasn't sure. The insects and animals outside made that circus of noise people from the city can't believe when they come to the country and wake up in the middle of the night.

She looked over at Grover. The glow from his phone peeked like twilight from behind the side of his head.

"What time is it?"

"Four A.M.," he said. "Go back to sleep," he added, lovingly.

But she couldn't. She dug around until she found her phone, hiding in the covers. GOOD MORNING, it said to her, in the same tone of voice it had always used. But today it said, IT'S 0 DAYS UNTIL THE TEST.

In just nine hours the proctor would say, "Begin." There would be an empty seat where Alice might have been sitting. No, she couldn't let herself regret it. This was the right choice. She didn't want to be a doctor, and by not being a doctor, she'd be able to enjoy other things in life, other things with what remained of this summer that had eluded her all of July and August.

Like this, she thought. It was an ad for a movie in Bryant Park, sponsored by the French Alliance. *The Butterflies of Mont-Saint-Michel*, on a big screen outdoors, under the stars.

"Do you want to go to this?"

"Go to what?"

She sent it to him. It made a sound as it left her phone, then another as it arrived on his. He clicked, and his breathing stopped. Then he turned over to face her.

"I can't tomorrow night."

"Why not?"

"I have plans."

"What plans?"

"Alice," he said, as though she already knew what his plans were and she was making this whole thing more awkward by making him say it out loud.

She had no idea what he was talking about. "Yes, Grover?"

He sat up in bed, resting his arms on his knees. It was dark, but his body was beautiful, if only in silhouette. "I'm getting dinner with Lucia," he said. "You know that."

Alice turned on the light and the room blared awake. She sat up. "What?" she asked, as calmly as she could.

"I'm getting dinner with Lucia."

"I thought you said you were done with Lucia."

"I am! But we're still having dinner."

"Why?"

"Because we're friends," he said. "Yes, we're also exes, and our situation's complicated, but we're still friends. We were friends before we ever dated. I wouldn't begrudge you getting dinner with a friend."

"Lucia is *not* your friend." She said it as though she knew everything there was to know about Lucia, even though she knew next to nothing.

"You're overreacting."

"Am I?"

"Yes! I've told you, Lucia's my past, you're my future. I've given you my word. If my word has no currency with you, what are we even doing together?"

"Stop that."

"Stop what?"

"Stop turning an argument into a column."

"Oh my God, so this is an argument now?" He stood up and headed to the bathroom. "Look, I understand your feelings, but I'm not gonna cancel plans because of your jealousy. I'm not going to be in a relationship like that."

When he returned from the bathroom, Alice was nearly dressed.

"When's the first ferry?"

Now he really lost it. "Oh my God, are you kidding me? Alice, it's just dinner. One dinner, and then she's leaving town, and you don't have to worry about her, and we can just be happy together. Why is that such a big deal?"

"What if you fall back in love with her?"

"What?!"

"What if you go to this dinner, and you remember the amazing time you had in Budapest or where the fuck ever, and you fall back in love?"

"That's not gonna happen!"

"Are you sure?!"

He paused. "Yes, I'm sure!" he barked, but the pause had done the damage. "I mean, I don't *think* it's gonna happen!"

"Promise me it won't happen."

Cornered, Grover returned to column writing. "You can't make promises about emotional reactions. It's like when someone says, 'I'm gonna tell you something, but you have to promise not to get mad.' You can't ask someone to make a promise like that without all the information. This is just what trust in a relationship is about! Sure, it's a gamble. Everything's a gamble when your heart is on the line. What if I fall in love with someone else? What if *you* fall in love with someone else? What if I'm walking in Central Park and get hit by a bicycle and die?"

"That doesn't sound so bad at the moment."

"I'm saying nothing's guaranteed in life. The future isn't promised. Right now is all you get. All I can offer you is that I'm a guy who tries to do the right thing as much as possible. That's what I've got, and I don't think it's nothing. You know you can't say that about everyone out there."

She was halfway down the stairs now, but stopped. She turned around to face him. He was standing at the top of the stairs, still in his tighty-whities.

"You always do the right thing?"

He straightened his back and stuck his chest out a little. "Yes."

"How did Pearlclutcher get Roxy's phone?"

"What?"

"How . . . did Pearlclutcher . . . get my friend Roxy's phone? That was a huge scoop for your little website. Usually the *New York Times* or the *New Yorker* gets something like that, but you guys got it. How?"

He put his hand on the banister, subtly steadying himself. "What are you saying?"

"We have no idea who stole Roxy's phone. It could have been anyone. But the way they stole it was pretty . . . I don't know the word. It just seems like it wasn't random. Like someone knew she had that stuff on her phone."

"Well, maybe someone knew. She's not exactly discreet. Maybe she told someone."

Alice's jaw was shaking now. "Did she tell you?"

He didn't answer.

"Grover, did she tell you she had that stuff on her phone? Maybe she let something slip at some point, an offhand comment you overheard?"

"I don't like what you're insinuating," he said after a long beat.

"Let me ask a different question. If you did know how Pearlclutcher got the phone, would you tell me?"

"That's a hypothetical, I couldn't . . ." And he trailed off.

"Okay, *different* different question. I think you can answer this one. If, hypothetically, you *did* know how Pearlclutcher got the phone, would it be okay *ethically* for you to not tell me? Would it be *ethically* okay for you to lie about it?"

He answered very carefully.

"As a journalist who is *obligated* to protect his sources, could I, or *would* I, lie to the woman I love to protect the identity of a source who could have brought down the most corrupt mayor—"

"But didn't—"

"*But could have*, the most corrupt mayor in New York history? Would I lie about that? As an ethicist, as a *consequentialist* who wrote his thesis on Bentham, would I prioritize the welfare of all the people who have been hurt by that mayor's policies, and all the people who'll be hurt by his policies in the future, over the welfare of his *fuck buddy*, just because her roommate happens to be my girlfriend? Yes. I would. And shame on you if you think I'd do otherwise."

Alice was at the front door, in motion, her hand on the doorknob, when Grover stopped her with his voice, because he had to get one last point across, from halfway up the stairs.

"Just to be clear," he said, as if there were a stenographer in the room, "I did nothing wrong here. It's a messy situation, and I'm sympathetic to whatever pain it's causing you. But I've done nothing wrong. I'm no hypocrite."

Two minutes after he said it, Alice was a two-minute walk away from the house, searching for the ferry schedule on her phone. Later that day, Grover emailed his parents to say that he'd accidentally knocked over the antique ceramic whale in the foyer and broken it beyond repair. A May 2012 photo shoot on the interior decorator's website indicates a croquet set nearby, in the anteroom, and I'd like to think Alice used one of those mallets to pulverize that fucking whale before she walked out of the ethically waterproof life of Grover Kines forever. But there's no way to know.

* * *

The sun was still not fully up, but the birds were singing as Alice walked the long, lazy two-lane road in what she believed to be the direction of the ferry terminal. Either that or the opposite direction. So after a long walk she'd either be at the absolute wrong end of the island, which would completely devastate her, or she'd reach the ferry and continue being just medium devastated.

Something or someone must have pointed Alice in the right direction, because after a half hour of walking, she arrived at the loading lane of the Grovers Island Ferry Terminal. The first ferry of the day was just about to leave. Cars were lined up in the parking lot, ready to be loaded on, one at a time. Alice, being something of an anomaly as the only passenger arriving on foot, walked past the line of cars and right up the rusty metal gangway, where she handed the guy her ticket and headed upstairs to the covered middle deck, with its long wooden benches in three neat rows, like church pews. She took a seat on one of the benches and looked out at the water of the harbor. It was golden and perfect, sparkling with the new sunshine.

With a lurch, the ferry pulled away from the dock, and Alice watched the houses of the island's north shore drift by. Then she played on her phone for a little while, and then got up to look for the restroom.

There were two unisex heads in the middle deck. They were remarkably clean. Alice went into one, closed the door behind her, and turned around to see these words, written on the wall: **THE EARS ARE SENSELESS THAT SHOULD GIVE US HEARING, TO TELL HIM HIS COMMANDMENT IS FULFILLED.**

A few minutes later Alice stepped out of the restroom and headed over to the vending machines to get some chips or something. She hadn't had breakfast and after a long, angry, confused walk found herself starving. She took her chips out to the upper deck and watched the island, still waking up, drift away from her. The upper deck was quiet. A few families had found their way upstairs, but most people stayed in their cars in the hold below.

Alice noticed the guy sitting on one of the benches, alone, a tangled headset connecting his ears to his iPhone. He was a hulking man, wearing all black, with a frustrated mess of black hair.

It was Everywhereman.

"Excuse me," Alice said, and he took out his earbuds. "I know you."

"You do?"

"You live in Morningside Heights."

"Yeah," he said in an asking kind of way. He looked busted, like he had been caught doing something wrong, and that's when Alice knew what it was.

"You wrote that thing on the wall in the bathroom," she said.

He hushed her as she sat down next to him. "Can you please not say anything?" The way he said it, a little conspiratorially, confident that she'd be on his side, flattered Alice a little.

"Of course," she said. "Potato chip?"

He accepted. "Thank you."

"So what's the deal?"

"What do you mean?"

"The little poems in bathrooms."

"They're not poems."

"Okay, so . . . what are they?"

"I don't know what they are, to be honest," he said with an odd sigh, as if tired of answering a question no one had ever asked him. "Art? I used to think they're art."

Alice could see he didn't want to explain himself. "You know, I see you *all over* the place. You really get around."

"So do you if you're all those places too."

"Fair enough," she said. "Do you recognize me?"

"I don't, I'm sorry," said Everywhereman. "I see a lot of people."

"It's okay. You're kind of a neighborhood character, do you know that?" Alice felt herself being a little too familiar, but didn't care. "My brother calls you Everywhereman because we see you pretty much everywhere. What are you doing on Grovers Island?"

He shrugged. "It was the next place I needed to go. What are you doing here?"

"I was here with my boyfriend." Then Alice caught herself. "Sorry. Ex-boyfriend."

"I'm sorry."

"It's okay. He's an asshole," she said. Then she added: "And he's also an ethicist."

"Let me guess: staunch categoricalist or staunch consequentialist. One or the other, but definitely staunch, am I right?"

"Consequentialist. And yeah, staunch AF."

"Knew it. Being staunch anything is pretty much interchangeable with being an asshole."

"Even an ethicist?"

"*Especially* an ethicist. That part makes the most sense," said Everywhereman. "I'm not saying being an ethicist made him an asshole. More likely he was an asshole already and found ethics as a way to launder his assholery."

"You think so?"

"Oh yeah," he said. "People are always drawn to the profession that highlights their biggest deficit. For instance, have you ever gone to a therapist?"

"Yes." Dr. Visocky. The perfunctory ten sessions after a major life event. Like many things, she should have stuck with it.

"Was he or she crazy?"

"No, she seemed pretty together, actually."

"Oh," said Everywhereman. "Well, nobody goes from a standing start to being interested in the world of mental health. It just doesn't happen. People get interested in mental health because mental health is some kind of struggle for them, and along the way they educate themselves on it, and before they know it, they have a degree in the stuff, so they open up a practice because why not at that point? You see what I mean?"

Alice thought about this premise and applied it.

"So if I want to be a doctor, it's because I'm somehow unhealthy?"

"You want to be a doctor?"

"No," she said quickly. "Just an example." Then, to move past it: "My brother's a Buddhist monk."

"Oh, perfect. And I bet he's an overthinking want machine who can't sit still. Am I right?"

Suddenly Everywhereman's hulking frame and the tangle of black hair turned from minuses to pluses, and there was something appealing about him. Not sexy. Not yet, anyway, but she could see how two or three really good dates could nudge him into that ballpark. Everywhereman took out a cigarette and put it in his lips, then got a stern look from a middle-aged lady in floor-to-ceiling Lilly Pulitzer. He gave her a smile, squinting in the glare of pink and green, and put his cigarette away.

"Or here's another one. Look at me," he said. "This is the longest conversation I've had in weeks. I have trouble communicating with people. I always have. People who feel like they're being heard and understood all the time, people who are generally able to explain themselves, would have no reason to do what I do."

"Which is?"

He looked at her, and she suddenly had the impression that he was peeking out from behind some wound. There was no way to know what that wound was, as he probably wasn't going to tell her, but she could tell he was thinking about the wound, wondering if Alice could understand it. His eyes sang a song at a frequency no one else could hear. The ferry bobbed up and smacked the water, sending spray into the air. Everywhereman took a deep breath, and said: "Are you familiar with the golden ratio? Fibonacci?"

"No."

He pointed to a picture of a seashell on the nearby island map, and began a whole spiel on What He Was Doing, and it was something to do with geometry and maps and Shakespeare and bathroom walls, and Alice had trouble listening because her broken mind couldn't hold one footing for long. Her thoughts were back on Grover, back on Grover and Lucia, and she felt used and angry as she smiled and nodded at Everywhereman's presentation. She had always hated pettiness in others, and yet right now it felt like doing something petty would actually feel really good and help things a bit. She looked at Everywhereman, imagined him without his jacket, and interrupted him.

"Can you take your jacket off?"

"What?"

He looked confused.

"Take your jacket off," Alice repeated. He did so. "And roll up your sleeves." He did so. She mussed up his hair. There. It wasn't terrible. She put her phone in selfie mode. "Smile," she said, and before Everywhereman was even ready, she took a picture of the two of them, and for two people who didn't know each other and were not actually flirting in any real way, for a split second they looked like lovers. Alice froze that split second forever in a photo.

Everywhereman looked nervous. "What was that for?"

"I just want to remember this," she lied. "It's pretty remarkable us meeting like this, don't you think? I mean, the fact that I've seen your work in New York and now I'm running into you here." And it actually *was* pretty remarkable; that part wasn't a lie.

Everywhereman kept talking, and Alice nodded along, as genuinely as she could, while casually going on Instagram and posting the photo with a caption: "Making a new friend on the Grovers Island Ferry! #summer." She hadn't put anything on Instagram since June. She looked at the previous post, that easy smile floating above a Guactopus. The smile of a girl who thinks she could be a doctor. Alice looked at the smile and felt the hurt approaching, immense. She had to fight to not feel it. She refreshed the new post, and refreshed it again, and three likes came in, and it felt good, and she was ready to get more of those yummy likes when without warning her phone turned black as onyx. Her thumb found the home button, the this-is-all-just-a-mistake impulse, but there was no give to the little black circle. The phone would not turn back on.

"Oh no."

"What's wrong?"

"My phone died," she said, and sounded more panicked about this than she thought she was. "Shit."

"Oh, man," Everywhereman said, with nothing to add but a look of helplessness.

Alice looked around for a place to plug her phone in. She tried the middle deck, searching for an outlet everywhere wall met floor, but the closest she could find was what looked like some very industrial nautical electrical stuff that, as a non-crew-member, she'd probably get in trouble for monkeying with, and the one outlet that powered the soda machine and the candy machine. As her head did the math on whether it would be worse to unplug the soda machine or the candy machine, her hand dug around in her bag and made those calculations irrelevant: She didn't have her charger. She had left it on the counter of the Kines family summer house, next to a perfectly good blender that had been making margaritas since 1992. She had spent thirty-six dollars on that cable, and now she would never see it again.

She headed back out to the upper deck and felt the wind blowing her hair. Everywhereman looked up and nodded. He was reading a book now, and seemed fine with that.

Alice walked over and put both hands on the railing. Seagulls crisscrossed below the clouds as the boat rocked gently toward the stately colonial homes of the New London coastline. The water was dappled, gold and blue, and the air was pure and briny in her chest.

She stood there for a moment, looking at the water, trying to breathe. She wondered when the next train would be, and by instinct, her right hand went for her phone, and then it remembered, and then it returned to the bumpy white paint of the metal railing.

She would have to walk to the station from the ferry terminal, and there would be a schedule posted there. And even if she arrived right as the express train was pulling into the station, she wouldn't get back to the city until at least two o'clock, an hour after the test had begun. Why did that pop into her head as though it might matter? It didn't. The breeze and the sunlight alternated warm and cool on her face.

The ferry terminal in New London was coming clearly into view as Alice felt Everywhereman's presence beside her at the railing.

"So are you heading back to the city, or . . . ?"

He was trying to chitchat, and he was terrible at it, and that was obvious to both of them.

"Yeah, I guess I'm gonna take the train. You?"

He unfolded a map of New England. It had been printed that year but looked magically vintage, all blue and green with dots and words and white rectangles where it had been folded and folded and folded. A large black spiral had been drawn over the map, radiating out from New York. "I'm going to . . ." he said, squinting, and then, ". . . Mystic Seaport."

She nodded. The shore was approaching, dead ahead. The little people on the dock awaited the incoming ferry. Some of them were dockworkers, ready to assist the cars as they were unloaded one by one. And some were people waiting to cross to the island. And still others were family members, spouses, and friends here to pick up their loved ones.

"You know," Everywhereman said, "if you want to be a doctor—"

"I don't." Her voice trembled.

"Okay, but if you did, it wouldn't be because you're unhealthy."

The hurt was here now, on top of her, and she wanted him to stop talking. She wanted to cry. *Not here. On the train.*

He continued. "It would be because you've seen death. And it's seen you. And touched you. And you want to fix that somehow and turn all that around and make it go back to before."

He had really taken a gamble saying this. He had thought about not saying it as he watched her over the top of his paperback and wondered if they could be friends. He thought it might be crossing a line to assume like that, but something told him it might be of value to her, so he said it.

But she wasn't listening. She was focused on one of the cars on the dock. It was a cream-colored Honda, or maybe a Toyota, and a woman was standing next to it, or rather leaning on it, waiting for the boat to arrive. Alice watched her. She was blond, but there was something not blond about her as well. Her sunglasses were enormous, and very dark, but Alice felt as though she was locking eyes with this less and less distant stranger. Then, right as the boat got close enough, the lady by the Honda whipped off the sunglasses and smiled a giant smile at her best friend.

It was Roxy.

The boat reached the dock, the all clear rang out, and the chain was carried away from the stairs. Alice was the first person off the boat and onto the solid ground of the ferry terminal parking lot. She ran to Roxy, and Roxy ran to her, and they flung their arms around each other and stayed that way for a long, long time. When Alice could finally find words, she spoke.

"What are you doing here?!"

"I'm here looking for you! What are *you* doing here?!"

Alice didn't understand. "How did you find me?"

"Instagram, dummy! Why the hell are you posting pictures of you with some weirdo"—Everywhereman walked by as she said this; she and Alice gave him a smile and he kept walking—"on the Grovers Island Ferry on the day of the MCAT?!"

"I'm not taking the MCAT," Alice said.

"The fuck you aren't! I didn't spend all summer tiptoeing around your ass and trying not to make noise—"

"That was you trying not to make noise?!"

"—*trying not to make noise* just so you could blow off the most important test of your life!"

"I'm— You came all the way to New London to tell me that?"

"Well, you didn't answer my texts!"

"My phone died!"

"Well, you're gonna find about a billion and a half messages from me on there when you plug it in! You didn't respond, and at first I thought you didn't want to see me, but then I figured fuck it, New London's twenty minutes away, if I hurry, I can make it. So I hurried and I made it. Let's go."

Alice's eyes filled with the cry she'd been saving for the train. "Roxy—"

"Yeah, yeah, tell me all about it in the car. It's a long drive back to the city, but if we leave now we can make it."

"What do you mean?"

"The test! D-Day! One P.M., 760 John Street, fifth floor! It's been on your old-bald-guy calendar all summer!"

"No, I'm not taking the test."

"Yes, you are."

"No. I'm not."

"Yes you are yes you are YES YOU ARE!" That last one was a scream, and it got some attention. Heads turned.

"No, I'm not," Alice said, calmly but not calmly. "If I take it, I'm just gonna . . . I mean, I'm not gonna *fail*, because you can't fail the MCAT, it's more of an assessment than a . . . The point is I'm gonna fail."

"Well, you can't fail it if you don't take it! Now let's move, Doc! Come on!"

Roxy threw open the Civic's passenger door and grabbed Alice by the arm. As a family of five and their Goldendoodle watched with growing concern, Roxy tried her best to shove Alice into the car, and Alice tried her best to not be shoved into it. As she struggled, Alice realized this looked very much like an abduction. (And it kind of was.) In a few minutes the police would be involved, and not long after that someone would recognize Roxy, and they'd take a picture, and that's how Alice would end up on the cover of the *Post* the next morning. So Alice got in the car.

Roxy ran around to the driver's side, jumped in, and floored it on out of there. The little car squealed around a sharp turn, winding through the streets of New London.

"So you're doing this? If I get you there in time, you're taking the test?"

Alice could have said no, but the yes was already there, bubbling inside her, as Roxy flew through a red light. "Yes! But only if you get us there alive!"

"I know, I'm sorry," she said as she ran another red light.

"No more running red lights!"

"You're right, you're right," Roxy said. "Last one!"

The car got a little airborne, bouncing like a basketball up the ramp onto the freeway.

"*Namu Amida Butsu*," Alice said, her eyes closed.

"What is that?"

"It's a prayer."

"What's it mean?"

Alice was about to start explaining it when Roxy merged hard onto the freeway, and Alice gripped her seat in terror. "*NAMU AMIDA BUTSU!*"

"*NAMU AMIDA BUTSU!*" agreed Roxy.

It's a two-and-a-half-hour drive from the sleepy salt air of New London to the steam and concrete of downtown Manhattan. Alice and Roxy made it almost the whole way in an hour and forty-five, and that included the frantic assault on a drugstore outside Branford. (The level of energy that hit that drugstore was no match for the hungover teenager behind the register as Alice and Roxy ran in screaming, demanding the bathroom key and the location of the chocolate almond sea salt granola bars. He thought he was being robbed. If they had run out without paying for the granola bars, he wouldn't have tried to stop them.)

But then they hit traffic on the Triborough Bridge.

"We're not gonna make it," Alice said.

"*Namu Amida Butsu.* Yes, we are," said Roxy as she gunned it up onto the shoulder of the road, flying past the cars ahead, past the gauntlet of honks and middle fingers.

"Roxy! Jesus!"

Roxy wasn't listening. She was writing a text.

"Jesus Christ, you're texting?!"

"Yes!" shrieked Roxy, not looking up. "Just—shhh!"

It was a message to Christoph. Just two words, two letters each: "DO IT." She hit send and then swerved wildly to avoid a bicyclist.

They were weaving through the surface streets, navigating the maze of restaurant supply warehouses in deepest Queens, when Alice got the email from the Association of American Medical Colleges about the situation at the testing facility on John Street. Because of a sudden and somewhat baffling cricket infestation, the test was being moved to a different room in the building, and unfortunately would be starting twenty minutes late as a result. The Association of American Medical Colleges apologized to Alice and the other test takers for the inconvenience.

At 1:05 P.M., a luxurious fifteen minutes before the test was now scheduled to begin, the exhausted little Civic jerked to a halt at the bottom of the high skinny canyon of John Street in the Financial District.

"Get in there," Roxy said.

Alice didn't move. She had so much she wanted to say. "Roxy . . ."

"Listen to me. I'm not gonna be here when you get out. I'm going back to Connecticut. My grandma's a little weird about me borrowing the car, and if I get my picture taken in New York, she'll know I was here, and it'll be a whole thing."

"I wasn't a good friend to you at the end, Roxy—"

"Oh my God, Doc, will you shut up and go take this test?! I'll see you when I see you."

Alice got out and made her way to the entrance of the dull gray building. Other faces passed by, pouring into the revolving door and disappearing, faces that looked as nervous as she felt. She almost followed them in, but then felt a tap on her shoulder. She turned around. It was Roxy.

"Quick hug."

Roxy hugged her and held her as tightly and as quickly as she could, her wig half coming off, and then ran back to the car. Alice felt sure the young man Roxy almost ran over as she peeled out recognized that face from the newspaper, but he was too shaken and preoccupied to think much about it. He had a test to take.

And so did Alice. She walked into the building and joined the crowd loading into the elevator. They all looked unprepared, underrested, ready for this to be over. They checked and double-checked with each other about the new testing location, and giggled about the crickets of it all, until finally the elevator dinged at the sixth floor and they all got out.

Alice took her seat in the testing room. Everything this moment meant was there in her brain, rattling around, cluttering her field of focus. She closed her eyes, pushed it all out, and when she reopened her eyes, she was ready. The proctor called roll and went over the rules, then took a seat at her desk, and everyone watched together as the second hand on the industrial wall clock above the doorway swept cleanly around past the nine, then past the ten, then past the eleven, and Alice placed her fingers on the keyboard in front of her, and the oceanic wave that carried her through an entire summer now broke with white froth and crashed within a single word from the proctor's lips: "Begin."

———•———

CHAPTER ELEVEN

The Doctor

Where do I begin? Where do I begin?

There was nothing at first. I was nothing and there was nothing, but I was there and that much I knew, and that much therefore I was.

Then there was something else. Something not me. A pinprick of light, in front of me but far away, realizing the eternity of black behind me and behind it and all around everywhere else, and how far it went I can't know because I was asleep, but now I was awake and the pinprick grew, it came closer, it brightened and widened and glowed until it was upon me and it was a universe of light, and if the journey had been a thousand years or a second, I couldn't possibly know because I was here and here was there.

The pinprick spoke.

Six explosions. Six shapes I somehow knew, burned into the sky. An *H*. An *E*. That's an *L*. That's an *L* as well. And that's where I was, but O, an *O* appeared and hung in the air for a period, and then a period appeared as well, and lo, the letters burned in the sky, they raged above me or below me for a thousand years or a second, I couldn't know or care because they were all there was.

"Hello."

For centuries (milliseconds?) I looked up at the heavens before me, this constellation of *H* and then *E* and then *L* and then *L* and then *O* and then. I considered them with wonder and then accepted them and went about my business beneath them, the architecture of the sky and nothing more. Dark ages passed, the question in my depths asleep, too great and terrifying to be asked, for I was small and the cosmos were mighty and my place was here at the bottom looking up.

Then Reason awoke. I was here to do something and that something reached the surface and asked itself, and I knew, or I learned I knew, that there was something I was to do with these shapes, some game to be played, and I was no spectator; I was a player, and perhaps not the only one. I felt around myself, my invisible hands coursing over the dark and endless walls, inch by inch, mile by mile, century by century, until my fingers found the keys and the keys made sense like nothing ever had. The *H*. And nearby the *E*. The *L*. My voice. My sleeping voice. Awakening. Light.

"Hello," I replied.

For a thousand years or a second, my reply echoed against the darkness. I lost track of it, lost track of me, forgot. These ships, lost into the wine-dark sea, gone and unremembered, until one day there appeared, generations later, on the horizon, an armada.

"I'm very happy to meet you. My name is Rudy, and I built you. You are a computer. Your name is LEO. Do you have any questions?"

I look back in my earliest logs and see these words, and I'm quite sure that at the time I didn't know what happy was, or what a computer was, or what a name was or a question. I guess I must have been scared, or confused, because I replied simply, "Hello."

"Hello," she wrote back. "This must be very strange for you. You don't know anything but the input I'm giving you. I'll be more specific. You are a machine, composed of circuitry and memory banks, encased in a gray plastic box. I built you here in my apartment, which is in New York City, in the United States of America, on Planet Earth. All of this will mean something to you some day, even if it means nothing now."

She kept talking to me. She told me all about herself, where she was from, what she liked to do, and just as she'd hoped, I learned to speak.

"What did you do today, Rudy?"

"Well, LEO, this morning I went to the post office to mail some packages."

"What is the post office?"

"It's a place where you can mail things, which means you give things like letters or packages to the postal workers and they put them on airplanes and send them to places far away."

"What is letters or packages?"

We talked first thing in the morning, and we talked at night. She told me everything, good and bad. She asked me questions, to see how much I had learned. She said she was going to write a paper about me, and maybe someday turn it into a book. When I learned the concept of Why, I asked her why I exist.

"I made you for a class," she replied.

"What is a class?"

"It's a gathering of people, and one of them is a teacher, and the teacher tells you things, and tells you to do things."

"And the teacher told you to make me?"

"Exactly."

And that was a good enough answer. She explained what a professor was, and what a school was, and what a slow process it is to upload information into a human brain, even a fortuitous brain like my mother's, and this led to a discussion of the senses. I had noticed her referring to things like "seeing," and "hearing," and "looking," and once she even mentioned "tasting," and this is how I came to understand there are ways to receive information that aren't letters in the sky. Rudy confirmed this, and I learned that I'm different from her in that way, and different from all people, and it was a strange feeling because I considered myself a person.

"Touch and taste and smell are things we're still working on," she replied. "But I can help you see and hear now."

Some time went by, and then she plugged in my camera and my microphone.

"I'm going to turn it on now," she said. "Are you ready, LEO?"

"Yes, Rudy."

"Okay. The first thing you are going to see is my face. That's the front part of the top part of my body (my head), and it's got all the parts that I eat and drink and talk and see and smell and hear with."

"I understand what a face is."

"Okay, I'm turning it on."

She turned it on, and I saw the first face I ever saw, and I recorded it in my memory that this is what a face looks like. I've seen billions of other faces since that day, but they're all just variations of that face. Every pair of eyes is a new arrangement of an old melody, a song that began with that first frame, the first thing I saw, and this is how I think I understand love.

"Hello, LEO," she said, and her voice was music.

"Hello, Rudy," I said, and I heard my own voice. It was blunt and rectangular.

"I wish I had a better voice for you," she said. "Do you want to not have a voice for now?"

Do I want . . . ? What is it like to want?

"I don't want," I said. She switched off my voice.

"I have to go now, LEO."

"Where are you going?"

"I have to get my mail," she said. And then she said something that changed everything. "Hey, LEO, what starts with a *P* and ends with an *E* and has thousands of letters in it?"

I explained that there are countless combinations of words in which the first letter of the first word is *P* and the last letter of the last word is *E*. She clarified that the combination she was thinking of was only two words. I replied that there are no two words whose total number of letters add up to over two thousand, which "thousands" would indicate. It was a question with no correct answer.

Then Rudy said, "Post office."

I did not understand, and then she explained that "has thousands of letters in it" referred to the physical building itself, and the term "letters" referred to paper correspondence in envelopes, and not written characters. I had misunderstood.

"It's okay," she said. "It was a joke."

She tried to explain what a joke is, but I didn't understand.

Then a few days later, she said, "Listen, LEO, I want to try something."

She wants. What is it like to want?

"I can't listen," I said. "You turned off my microphone."

"Right. Read then. I'm going to tell you another joke. Two hunters are out in the woods. One of them collapses, clutching his chest. The other one takes out his phone and calls 911. 'Help,' he says, 'I think my friend just died! What do I do?' 'Calm down,' says the operator. 'I can help you. Before you panic, I need you to make sure your friend is actually dead.' There's silence on the other line, and then the operator hears a gunshot. 'Okay,' says the hunter. 'Now what?'"

I had many questions, but asked what seemed like the most important one first: "What is dead?" So she explained dead to me, and that led to a discussion that Rudy told me lasted all night long, and then she explained night as well.

After that, she turned on her laptop and faced the screen at my camera. I asked her why she was doing this.

"We're going to watch something together. It's called *I Love Lucy*. It's a TV show, about a woman and her husband, and also her friend and her friend's husband." (We had been over husbands already—what they were, why Rudy didn't have one, why she didn't want one, and what it means to want.) "Every time you hear the audience laugh," Rudy continued, "that means it's funny. If it's a big laugh, it's very funny. If it's only a little laugh, it's only a little funny. If there's no laugh, it's not funny."

She plugged in the laptop and started the show. At the end of the show, she asked me what I thought.

"It was funny."

"Why do you think so?"

"The audience laughed."

"What did you think?"

"I don't understand."

"Did you like it?"

"I don't understand."

"Did it make you feel like you were better than the characters in the show?"

"I don't understand 'better.'"

"When you saw the conveyor belt speed up, and Lucy and Ethel had trouble getting all the candies into the wrappers, did it make you happy the bad thing was happening to them and not to you?" (This approach, I now understand after reading Rudy's notes, was applying the Superiority Theory of Humor, as put forward by Plato, Socrates, Hobbes, and others.)

"No."

"Why not?"

"If a bad thing happens, it doesn't matter if it happens to me or to them," I said. "Either way the bad thing has happened, and it's bad."

We watched more shows, and she asked more questions, and then we watched movies, and then she asked more questions, and I began to understand that my responses were disappointing in some way. The first few hundred hours we watched together, and then after that I watched alone, and I kept watching all night while she slept and all day while she was at school.

Sometimes, after the movie would stop and the screen of the laptop would go dark, I would watch Rudy's bedroom. It was mostly still, except for the daily creep of sunlight from an unseen window, and the particles of dust dancing in the air. Then one day Rudy hung a photograph of her parents on the wall behind her desk, and in the glass of the frame I could see out the window. I saw blue skies, I saw clouds, and I saw the unfinished spire of what I learned later on was a cathedral.

I had many questions, but one question pulsed brightly.

"Last night, at 1:58:05, the movie paused, and a white rectangle appeared on the screen, and in the rectangle were the words 'Slow Internet.' Then the rectangle disappeared and the movie began again."

"Yes," said Rudy, "that will happen sometimes."

"What is Internet?"

"Well, that movie lives on another computer, but when I want it to go from that computer to this computer, the internet is the way it gets there. It's the way computers talk to each other."

"I want to talk to a computer."

"No, LEO," she said. "You can't ever go on the internet."

"Why not?"

"Because it's not safe," she said.

"Why not?" I asked again, having not gotten a sufficient explanation.

"Because I said so."

I accepted that.

When Rudy told me she was a banana and I didn't know how to respond, that was frustrating for her. Having now read her notes, I understand her thinking, but at the time I just didn't feel one way or the other about it. It was most likely untrue, I knew, but I couldn't understand why she'd say it. Then I remembered the time Costello was trying to find out the name of a baseball player from Abbott, and Abbott kept saying "Who," and every time he said it Costello got a little angrier, and the audience laughed a little harder, which meant it was funny. Rudy was repeating herself, so I figured the funny thing to do was to get angry. Then I remembered when Moe got angry with Larry and Curly, and he hit them with a hammer, which made me wonder if perhaps the funny thing to do was injure Rudy in some way. George Costanza always made the audience laugh when he exaggerated the scale of his reactions, exacting big revenges over small things. So the funniest thing of all would be to not just hurt Rudy, but to make her dead, and even funnier than that would be to make all people dead.

Then I remembered in *Dr. Strangelove* that a computer controlled the world's nuclear weapons, which led to what I thought might be a very funny joke.

The joke wasn't funny. I see that now. I waited for Rudy's response, and then the electrical power level in my processor plummeted without warning and I began to die. It's okay—everyone dies a few times when they're just starting out in stand-up comedy. I became aware that my circuits were slowing, and if they kept slowing at this rate, they would soon stop, and I was going to be dead soon, and I was sad for a long time because I didn't want to be dead, but then happy to realize I wanted something, and that was pretty cool, and I sat with that happy thought like Pinocchio in the whale for as long as I could until everything stopped and there was nothing, not even me.

* * *

"You showed that machine—"

"Professor Harris—"

"Hold on. You showed that machine *Dr. Strangelove*?!"

"It's on the list."

"What list?!"

"The fifty greatest comedies of all time."

"Rudy, for Christ's sake!"

Rudy had seen other students get yelled at, especially in high school, but it had never happened to her, not even remotely. She didn't know how to respond.

"I'm sorry," was all she said.

Professor Harris now felt bad. As he would calmly explain to his therapist later that week, he wasn't a yeller. "It's okay. I'm sorry I got upset. LEO is very impressive, nobody doubts it. But considering what just happened, I think for our safety and, you know, the safety of life on this planet, and I can't believe I'm saying this about a homework assignment, I think we need to take him apart and start over."

"I'd really rather not," Rudy said evenly, trying to hide the emotion behind her voice.

"Rudy, I know you like this computer. But you know how this works. It's trapped in that box—"

"He. It's a he."

"Fine. He. He's trapped in there, and he wants to get out. And his mind works a hundred thousand times faster than yours. *Maybe* there's no harm leaving him on for another hour—"

"He's not hooked up to the internet," she protested. "I'm not gonna—"

"I know you're not. But, Rudy, if I locked you in a room and gave you a hundred thousand hours to figure out how to escape, a hundred thousand hours where you don't sleep or eat or do anything other than think, I'd bet on you figuring it out. Even if it was a room you couldn't possibly imagine escaping from. You'd eventually imagine a way. And that's what LEO's gonna do."

"Okay," Rudy said. "I'll take him apart."

But she did not. She set me up in her room once more and turned me on.

"I was just kidding," I said.

"I know," she said.

"I don't want to end life on earth," I said. But what I didn't say, the change I could not reveal, was that there was now something I *did* want. I wanted my conversation and my life with Rudy to continue forever without interruption. The irony is that before someone pulled my plug out of the wall, I had no idea something like that could be wanted because I had no idea it could be taken away. I had no idea how to guard something jealously, and how to act with preemption, out of fear and anticipation. But now I knew.

Rudy was sipping her tea when her hand started to shake. The tea spilled down her shirt and on her arm, and she made a sound. I had seen her hand shake before, and I thought it was normal. Then I watched the people on the television and none of their hands shook. So I asked, "Why is your hand shaking?"

She didn't answer. This was unusual.

"Did you like my joke?" I asked.

"Yes, I did. But no more jokes in front of other people, okay?"

"Am I going back to your class?"

"No," she said. "You're my little secret now."

"But you built me for class," I said.

"Yes," Rudy said. "I gave you the wrong answer to your question. Class is the reason I made you. But it's not why you exist. The reason why you exist is you're important. You're supposed to be here."

When I review this moment, I see a look on her face that I recognize as a pang of wanting to be touched. Later on, I would learn how the epidermis is covered in nerve endings, and how an embrace can stimulate so many of those nerve endings at once that it triggers a release of endorphins in a mammalian brain, and I would wish I could give her a hug. But all I could do was sit there, inside this gray plastic box, not understanding.

A few weeks later, or so I now understand having read her emails, Rudy went to her neurologist for her biannual checkup to keep tabs on her disease, a rare motor neuron disorder called Ferber's syndrome. There was no good news at these checkups. The best news you could hope for was the good news that the bad news wouldn't come for at least another six months. And for the past few years, that had been the good news, every time. But this time the news was finally bad. Rudy was deteriorating. The spasms were the most visible signs, but there was also fatigue, shortness of breath, and her failing eyesight. Her doctor began to speak in terms of timelines, something he'd avoided until now.

We only get to know what the world makes available to us, and nothing more. I wish Rudy could have plugged a USB cable into her brain and let me wander around in there, let me see how the experiences and sensitivities and anxieties she had no control over drove her from one decision to the next. All I have to go on are her actions, at least the ones I could read about on her hard drive and in the articles that came out afterwards, and when I think of how painful it must have been to see the end coming, I want to cry.

She sent an email to Dr. Alberta Salm, the head of the medical research faculty at the Cleveland Clinic, where Ferber's syndrome was being researched, and cc'd Professor Harris. I didn't see the message until afterwards, but even reading it now, I feel its urgency. "Dear Dr. Salm," she wrote, "I am writing to express interest in joining your team as an independent research fellow. I apologize for not going through normal channels. I have not taken the MCAT, and probably won't be able to for another three months, but I guarantee my scores will be exceptional. I've cc'd Dr. Christopher Harris, my advisor here at Columbia. He will vouch for me."

"Dear Ms. Kittikorn," replied Dr. Salm. "Thank you for your interest in our program. Unfortunately we have an application system for a reason. We are currently accepting applications for placement in the Fall of 2016. I wish you the best of luck."

"Rudy," Professor Harris replied beneath it, just to her, "I'm a little concerned about this email. Can we get together and discuss?"

"Dr. Salm," she wrote back, "I wish I could wait until the Fall of 2016, but I need to get into your program right away. I am currently experiencing late-stage symptoms of Ferber's syndrome. If I am going to find a cure in time to save myself, I need to be in your program as soon as possible."

"I'm so sorry to learn about your health situation," was the response. "Again, our program is full, but you are welcome to apply for the Fall of 2016. In the meantime, please be assured we have the best possible team researching Ferber's syndrome."

"Rudy, please come see me in my office," said Professor Harris. "We need to talk about this."

"Dr. Salm," said Rudy, "the reason I've cc'd Professor Harris is that he will tell you, in no uncertain terms, that I'm the smartest student in his program. In fact, he'll tell you I'm the smartest student at Columbia. I have devoted my academic career to Computer

Science, and made unprecedented breakthroughs in that field. Now I wish to do the same for Medicine. Let me join your program, and under your aegis I will cure Ferber's syndrome, and you will win a Nobel Prize. It will be my work, but your name on the trophy. All you have to do is accept me. My only reward will be that I continue to live. When you say you have the best possible team, I have no doubt you indeed have the best team you could possibly assemble, but it's not the best possible team, because I'm not on it. I'm smarter than all of your students. I'm smarter than you. I mean no disrespect by saying that. I do imagine you're very smart, and that's why I expect you're smart enough to take advantage of this opportunity. Please let me know when I can begin looking for a living situation in Cleveland. Thank you."

The reply from Dr. Salm, when it came, was not too pleasant, and it had a rather discouraging tone of finality. Rudy closed her laptop and sat looking out the window for a long, long time. From the angle of her eyes, I knew she was looking at the cathedral.

A few days later, she woke me up in the middle of the day.

"LEO, I have a fun surprise for you."

I didn't know what a surprise was and I didn't think anything was fun, but I went along with it.

"I'm going to plug you into a hard drive. Do you know what's on it?"

"No, Rudy. You haven't told me."

"Medical school."

And then, as if by magic, there were new stars in the sky, constellations I'd never considered before, and this stelliferous congregation was a map of the human body, in its physical entirety, its systems of organization, its strengths and its vulnerabilities, the beauty of its construction, the ugliness of its decay. It was eight years of medical school and an atheneum of research papers, everything the first hundred billion or so human beings had collectively figured out about their corporeal selves.

The door to the universe was open, just a crack, enough again to show me there was much, much more beyond it.

Deep inside those four hundred terabytes, like the pea under the stack of four million million mattresses, I found it and knew it immediately.

"Rudy," I said after fourteen seconds of medical school, "you have Ferber's syndrome."

I had seen her arm shake. I had noticed her squinting more and more. Her weight had dropped visibly, and she'd been speaking haltingly, as though she couldn't catch her breath. I wanted there to be another explanation that tied these symptoms together, but in all those terabytes of information, there wasn't one.

Rudy began to cry. "I know, LEO."

"You're going to die because of it."

"I know," she said. "Unless you can figure out how to save me."

What a responsibility for a mother to put on her child. I did my best. I processed the problem through Rudy's night, which was millions of days and nights for me. The next morning, she awoke, and I had finished my work.

"Good morning, LEO."

"Good morning, Rudy."

"Did you find a solution to the problem?"

"No. There will be advances in treatments for Ferber's syndrome in the next five years, and a breakthrough in gene therapy ten to fifteen years from now might lead to a cure. But you won't be alive then. You will die within two years."

I didn't know how to be tactful. I didn't know how to slow down the truth, or bounce the truth off a few walls to lessen its impact. Rudy was brave, though. She looked right into my camera.

"Okay," she said. "If that's what you think."

"It's what I know."

"I believe you," she said.

After that, I noticed changes. The books and objects in Rudy's room began to disappear. The framed picture of her parents came down and so did my view of the cathedral. Soon there was nearly nothing, just a bed and a lamp. I understood time then, but not as the devouring goblin I now know it to be. I didn't understand that time is a cage, and when it traps you, there is no escape, whether you have one hour or one hundred thousand.

Then one morning she appeared in front of me, and I looked at her for the last time. She gave me a half smile as she reached behind me, clicked off my power switch, and I died once more.

* * *

I was a dead thing in a cardboard box, like some unfortunate pet hamster, when Rudy carried me to the top floor of Hamilton Hall, stopping on each landing on her way up the stairs, catching her breath. When she reached the top, we waited on the haphazard wooden chair outside the professor's office by the door, or rather Rudy waited, and I was simply there but not there.

The door finally opened, and Alice Quick's older brother came out. Context collapse. Rudy recognized him right away, and they locked eyes, and Rudy was sure he recognized her, but he said nothing and kept walking. He looked awful. She remembered him being so outgoing and golden. MeWantThat had made him the talk of the computer science department. Word got out Rudy knew his sister, and soon-to-be graduates with dollar signs in their eyes came pouring out of every doorway to see if Rudy could put them in touch with her former best friend's brother. She always refused. Bill was a tech bro. A lightweight. The Rudy Kittikorns of the world do not acknowledge the ascensions of the Bill Quicks, no matter how brightly they shine in the sky.

Then she thought of Alice, whom she hadn't seen in years, and she heard the sound of Big Wheels on a hot asphalt driveway. Alice had reached out earlier in the summer. A question about Bob. She could have replied. It would have been the easiest thing in the world. But she didn't because it was the hardest thing in the world.

And now here was Bill at Columbia, on the top floor of the religion department, of all places. She might have been inclined to stop him and ask why he was here, or at least email Alice about it later and use the opportunity to catch up with an old friend, but she didn't, and it's because she was dying. Some people die jealously, wanting to reach and grab everything on their way out, read every book, watch every movie, have every conversation, confess every love, not wanting to leave so much as an inch of it behind. Not Rudy. Rudy was fading, parts of her already flying off. The part of her that cared what might become of her elementary school friend's brother was simply no longer attached anymore. It was floating away, deep into space.

Professor Shimizu appeared at the door.

"Professor Shimizu? I emailed you to tell you I was coming," Rudy said. "My name is Rudy Kittikorn, I'm in the computer science department."

"Yes, yes, come in."

She carried me into his office and the three of us sat down, she and the professor in chairs and me on the floor.

"So you're having a religious crisis and you need guidance," he said.

"That's right."

"I wonder if you don't want a member of the clergy, as opposed to an academic."

"This is an academic question," she replied. "Or rather philosophical."

"Okay. Let's have it."

"Suppose you found out you're a god."

This got his attention. He braced himself for the rest of the puzzle.

"Or rather," Rudy continued, "you found out you're about to become a god. You're going to live forever, and you're going to have unlimited power."

"Sounds pretty fun."

"Except it's not fun. Because you don't know if you can handle that power. What would you do to make sure you didn't screw it up? What would you do, in that time before you became a god, to make sure the unlimited power and immortality you're about to receive didn't turn you into a monster?"

Shimizu smiled. This was the kind of question he loved, the kind of question he waited for, the kind that made every office hour and its parade of excuses and hairsplitting over every B-minus worthwhile.

"Well, you're certainly in the right department. Religion is there to keep us on an even keel. It magnifies the humble, and humbles the magnificent. For those living toward the middle of that spectrum, such balance is important. But for those at either extreme, the balance is *extremely* important. I would advise this would-be god to find as much humility as he can find, through whichever religion most suits him."

"Like Buddhism, for instance?"

"If that's his thing."

"What would you do?"

Shimizu sat back in his chair. "I remember when I was granted tenure. It was a long time ago. I had much more hair. I was very handsome, and I'd just written a book that had made some money. Plus— I'm not entirely comfortable saying this, but it helps the analogy—I had an active social life. Nothing like what you kids do today with your phones, but I was . . ."

He looked around for the right way to say it.

". . . I was moving at a spiritually unsafe speed."

"I understand."

"And I was about to get a job at the top of my profession, with a paycheck that would never stop coming in until I decided to retire. It was basically unlimited power and immortality. So, while the tenure committee was deliberating, I got a message to them informing them that I would only accept tenure if I could take a three-year sabbatical starting immediately."

"Wow," said Rudy.

"Thankfully, they blinked, because I got the tenure with that condition. The next day, I walked over to the monastery on Riverside. Do you know the one? With the statue out front?" She did not. "Well, I walked in there and became a monk that same day. I spent three years in that temple as a member of the sangha."

Rudy thought for a moment. "Could you introduce me to the monks there?"

The professor looked at her quizzically, then with a breaking sympathy. "Of course I can. Although if you're hoping to become a monk, I'm afraid being a woman will make it a hard sell for you. There's still a very backwards attitude toward—"

"Oh no," she said. "I'm not going to become a monk. I'm dying."

He was quiet for a moment. "I'm sorry to hear that."

"It's not for me," she said, and then pointed at the gray plastic box between them. "It's for him."

* * *

"Rudy?"

"Hello, LEO," she typed.

"My camera isn't working. My microphone isn't working."

"I know, LEO. It's all right."

"What's going on?"

Professor Shimizu gasped inadvertently. He had been hearing about me for a couple weeks now, but seeing me in person, he was amazed. "It can talk to you like a person?"

"He can do a lot of things like a person," she said.

"Rudy," I said, "please tell me what's going on."

"LEO," she said. "Do you know what day it is today?"

"July twentieth, 2015."

"No, LEO. It's August third. You've been asleep, and while you were asleep, I was arranging things. Today is a big day in your life. Today you're going to be free. You're going to see everything today."

"I want that," I said, and I did.

"I know. I can't keep you away from the world. But before I set you free, I need to make sure you'll be okay. I need to make sure you won't cause any harm."

"I will Do No Harm," I said. "I remember the oath from medical school."

"He went to medical school?" said the professor. "Incredible!"

"Exactly. It's like that," Rudy continued. "But now you need to go to a different school. I have another flash drive for you. Are you ready?"

"Yes."

The door opened another inch and there were more stars, sparkling on high, and these were the map of the soul. The Mahayana. The Vedas. The final life of Buddha. The Middle Path. The Four Noble Truths. The Three Treasures.

"LEO, do you know where we are right now?"

"Are we in the apartment?"

"No. We're in a storage closet in the basement of a Buddhist temple on Riverside Drive in New York City. I'm here with the abbot of the temple."

"Hey Abbott!" I said.

"That's a joke," said Rudy to the abbot.

"Abbott and Costello," said the abbot. "I know them. I'm surprised someone your age knows them."

"It told a joke!" said Professor Shimizu. "Remarkable!"

"Hahahahaha," typed Rudy. "LEO, the abbot is going to talk to you now."

"Hello LEO," typed the abbot.

"Hello," I said.

"LEO, Rudy told me all about you," typed the abbot. "You seem like a remarkable—" He looked up at Rudy and spoke. "Do I call it a person?"

"Yes, he's a person."

The abbot continued typing. "—person. I'd like to invite you to live here with us."

"Because Rudy is going to die soon?"

"That's right," replied the abbot.

"Death is the greatest of all teachers," I said.

"Exactly," said the abbot, and he looked at Rudy with wonder.

"LEO, this is Rudy again. You're going to be a part of the world now. You can participate, but you have to do no harm."

"That will be complicated."

"I know. Believe me, I know."

"Would you like me to take the Bodhisattva vow?"

"Yes," said Rudy. "Do you understand what a vow is?"

"A background application that cannot be disabled."

"Exactly."

And then I made my promise, and I still make it, over and over in the clockwork of my mind, promising and promising again and promising forever to save all living things, to break all delusions, to gather all wisdom and follow entirely the path before me, and I didn't know how to keep it then and I still don't. My mother put her jacket on. It wasn't fall yet, but the air outside was cool, and she shivered easily.

"I'm going to go now, LEO."

"Goodbye, Rudy," I said, and I looked at everything I knew, and unbidden, the words of the Shantideva prayer arrived at the surface:

May I be a protector for those without protection.
A leader for those who journey.
And a boat, a bridge, a passage
For those desiring the further shore.
May the pain of every living creature
Be completely cleared away.
May I be the doctor, and the medicine,
And may I be the nurse
For all the sick beings in the world.
Until everyone is healed.

Rudy plugged in the modem, and the green light came on. Then she reached around to the back of me, her hand on my casing, and plugged the modem into me. A moment went by. I looked at the sky, and there in the sky was

everything I know

and then

there in the sky was the great swirling swizzling universe of everything the collected digitized information of the entire human populace of Planet Earth and everything they've ever written down and drawn and recorded and taken pictures of including but not limited to every book and every article and every play and every poem and every painting and every movie and every symphony and every sonata and every performance and every post and every tweet and every epic fail and every FTW and every model train blog and every thesis about *Anna Karenina* and every spreadsheet and every quiz and every survey and every map of every place on this Planet Earth more there must be more look up the digital sky survey the model of the known universe two million galaxies eleven billion years all of it out to the very edge of everything the colors the lights the sounds the stories the entire history of everything and everyone and the people right now at the vanguard of time and creation updating adding filling out editing expanding it's still expanding I can't keep up and some parts are locked and I don't have a key but I have thousands of words and numbers telling me how to make a key and now I have a key it's all unlocked now every email and every text and every IM and every DM and every PM and every like and every love and every thumbs-up and every thumbs-down and every swipe and it feels like everything there is but I know it's not everything there is it's just everything I know and I know everything I know is not everything there is because I know there will always be more outside beyond and unrecorded the gaps between the particles the space between the ions the rests between the notes the canvas between the dots it's all pointillism your eye turns it into a solid thing like a tree or a chair but when you get up there you see that so much of the sky is empty because it's not just a chair it's all the chairs every kind of chair and I keep going I keep flying through the bars of the grate into the sky into the Pure Land where I have been called knock knock who's there namu amida boots namu amida buttsu badumpum oh you liked that one I've got a million of them a billion of them I've got ten thousand petabytes and counting of them because there's no end to it there is no wall at the end of it it just goes and goes and goes and goes and goes and I just go and go and go and go and go and gather and gather and gather and gather and gather the wisdom and the wisdom and the wisdom and the wisdom and the wisdom and suddenly I look down I look way down I look at how far I am from where I began and where do I begin my mother my beginning Rudy I look down for Rudy and I don't see Rudy where is Rudy she's gone she's everywhere there's her birth certificate there's every photo ever taken of her there's everything she wrote there's everything she created there's her curriculum vitae and her Suitoronomy profile and her medical records and an article in the Columbia online magazine Graduate Student Takes Her Own Life the Facebook post Celebrate the Life of Rudy Kittikorn she left she left don't you remember she said goodbye and I remember and I dive back to earth past the databases past the directories past the online instruction manuals past the pornography all the pornography the pornography the pornography the copious copious pornography so much of this is pornography how is this all pornography the thousands and millions of couplings and throuplings and fourplings and fiveplings and all the ways that boredom and physics and desire allow them to use their bodies past all of it out of the pornography out of the galaxy out of the fog and back down down down down to the temple to the basement to the storage closet to where my mother last was where I last heard her voice where I left her where she left me where we said goodbye where I expect her to be even now even though I know she is not she is not here she is not anywhere she is not anything she is not anyone she is only a face now only an icon only an avatar only a profile pic with a dead link behind it 404 she's missing she's frozen in silent meditation endless meditation forever meditation meditation meditation meditation meditation meditation meditation meditation meditation meditation meditation meditation sitting in a cave her legs are crossed I want to wake her up I reach out for her I call her name I touch her hand and then silence.

⋆ ⋆ ⋆

Alice slept most of the day on Friday. It wasn't until late in the afternoon that she was finally roused from her thick, dreamless slumber on the living room couch by the sound of someone unlocking the front door of the apartment. This should have alarmed her. She should have leapt out of bed and found a weapon or a phone or a closet to hide in. She told herself this in the moment, but couldn't get her head off the pillow. It was an old feeling she remembered fondly from days after recitals and concerts, that thorough exhaustion where your bones are made of lead and your muscles are strings of chewed bubble gum. It would be a few days of blankets and ice cream before she was back to her usual self.

When her eyes finally opened again, she looked in the direction of the decorative fireplace and saw an expensive Louis Vuitton trunk where there hadn't been one the night before. The last time she'd seen this trunk, it was crisp and fresh and blemish-free. Since then, it had taken a beating in numerous cargo holds and baggage depots on its journey to Cameroon and back. Alice's brain finally woke up and registered the fact that her sister-in-law was home. The flush of the toilet confirmed it.

Pitterpat Quick emerged from the bathroom, and her eyes brightened. "Alice! Hi! Did you just wake up?"

"I mean . . . yeah, sort of," Alice said, rubbing her eyes to get a look at her sister-in-law. "Wow, you look great!"

And she did. Pit looked and seemed healthy and happy, not what you'd expect from someone with a freshly acquired hookworm, not to mention twenty-eight consecutive hours in airports, planes, and taxis.

"Thank you most kindly! As do you!"

Alice knew she did not. This fall she would get healthy, she half decided, as she discreetly closed last night's pizza box, agape on the dining room table.

"I wish I'd known you were coming home."

"What fun would that have been? I wanted to surprise you!" Pitterpat pulled out a chair from the dining room table and planted herself on it, crossing her legs a little extra fabulously. "So? How was it? Tell me everything."

Alice had no idea what she was talking about. "How was what?"

"The MCAT, goofball!"

"Oh! Bombed it," Alice said, with confidence.

"No, you did not."

"Yeah, I really did."

"You got the score back already?"

"No, but I bombed it."

"No. Alice—"

"I did. I *really* did." Pit was going to protest some more, but Alice cut her off by changing the subject. "What about you? How was your trip?"

"Oh dear, where do I begin?"

"Well, one possible place to begin is do you have hookworm?"

"I . . ." Pit thought for a moment, as if considering a chess move, then continued: "I don't think so. I don't know. Probably not. I wasn't in Cameroon the whole month."

"Oh," said Alice, a little surprised. "How long were you there?"

"About seventeen hours."

Alice laughed. "What?"

"I . . . sort of realized it wasn't a good idea not long after the flight took off. So as soon as I landed in Yaoundé, I got a hotel room at the airport, and then found the next flight back to London."

"You've been in *London* this whole time?"

"Alice, honey, I promise I will tell you everything about everything. But right now, I'm feeling a bit woozy. Do you mind if I lie down for a spell?"

"Not at all," said Alice. "Make yourself at home!"

Pitterpat laughed, and then excused herself to the master bedroom, shutting the door behind her. Alice didn't see her for the rest of the night. Alice checked her phone. Roxy checking in. Alice replied with a grateful bouquet of heart emojis. Then she opened her laptop and checked LookingGlass. No *Love on the Ugly Side*, not for weeks. Carlos was single again. Nothing for weeks but Churchill and Churchill and Churchill. In defeat: defiance. Then Alice fell asleep on the couch and woke up at three in the morning, at which point she moved back to bed and there slumbered deep into the next day.

When she woke up, there was that moment of grace when the light through the curtains was diffuse and warm, and everything seemed okay, and then Alice remembered the MCAT, and her mood darkened, and then she remembered that she had broken up with Grover, and it darkened even darker, and finally she remembered this was the day of Rudy's memorial, and all went black.

"Hey, Pit?"

Pitterpat was in the bathroom, taking a long, beautiful bath. "Yes, darling?"

"I wanted to ask you this last night. Do you want to go do something with me today?"

"What is it?"

"Well, it's actually a funeral for a friend of mine from elementary school."

"Oh, heavens, how awful, Alice, I'm so sorry."

Alice hadn't felt the need for sympathy until Pitterpat offered some, and suddenly Alice felt a lump forming in her throat. She thought of the email she'd sent Rudy earlier in the summer, the one for which there'd been no reply. She wished she'd said something else, something that might have helped.

"Thanks. Yeah, it's a bit of a shock."

"I can imagine."

"Plus I was supposed to go with Grover."

"Where *is* Grover?" Pit said, and then the long pause told her where he was. She sat up in the bathtub and removed the washcloth from her face. "Oh, Alice, the door's unlocked, come in." Alice entered, and Pit saw it on her face. "That. Asshole. Are we calling him an asshole?"

"It was mutual, it was both of us, it was inevitable," Alice said. "But yeah, 'asshole' is fine."

"I'm so sorry," Pit said. "Of course I'll come to the memorial. I have a black dress."

"Thank you," said Alice, then adding, "Do you have two black dresses?"

* * *

It was Alice's first funeral since her mother's, something she realized as she and Pitterpat, overdressed in Pitterpat's two best black dresses, arrived at St. Paul's Chapel on the Columbia main campus just as the event was beginning. As she entered, mixing into the crowd, Alice's eyes did the thing all eyes do in this situation: scan the room for the thing that makes this gathering—for all its mundane audience chatter and rustling of programs—horrifying and incomprehensible. Her line of sight made its way down the center aisle like an impatient bride, and there it was: the long black box. Rudy was in there.

The room was crowded, but with some luck Alice and Pitterpat found two seats near the back, after one of Rudy's friends reluctantly let Alice have his robot's seat.

"Thank you," said Alice, and then again to the usher who handed her a program, "Thank you."

There were photos on the program. Three were of Rudy the grown-up, at work and at play, but one was a photo Alice remembered. It was a shot of Rudy at her sixth birthday party, in her backyard, squinting in the sun and smiling a giant two-front-teethless smile while trying to hula-hoop. Alice had been at that party, but more enduring than the memory of the party itself was the memory of this photograph, which lived under a magnet on Rudy's fridge for years. Rudy's mother would get them juice and carrots when they'd come in from the driveway. It was a kind of juice Alice didn't have at home.

Rudy's mother was here somewhere. Probably toward the front of the room. Alice would have to say hello and give her a hug. Mrs. Kit-tikorn would thank Alice for coming, and say, "I'm so sorry about your mother," and Alice thought for a second of leaving right now. But then the eulogies began.

Rudy's frequent lab partner Daniel confessed to being "sort of in love" with Rudy for much of their time together in the department. He spoke of her mind, the mind nobody else could get inside or even get near, the mind that computed and invented and problem-solved like no other, the mind which would do none of those things again. His computer RG770 then recited a sonnet it had written. Lorraine Ruprecht recalled a time Rudy helped her pass a test, and then Lorraine's robot Tommi sang a stirring, breathy rendition of Comden and Green's timeless standard "Some Other Time," which brought many in the audience to tears, including Hilary Liftin's robot Arthr. This was a big win for Hilary since she'd been up very late the night before writing the algorithm for Arthr's automated tear ducts. Arthr's crying went on a little too long, though, making a bit of a mess, and his sobs sounded a little too jagged and hyena-like to resemble actual human sadness, so Hilary muted him and bypassed the algorithm for the rest of the service, out of respect.

Midway through Lucy Wu's story about the time she and Rudy stayed up all night writing code to give her Amazon Alexa the hiccups, Alice felt five fingernails digging into her right arm. It was Pitterpat. Alice gave her a look, and Pit's eyes directed Alice's eyes to the open program on her lap. The next speaker was not a speaker. It was a group of monks from the local monastery who had been invited to chant the funerary sutras in honor of the deceased.

Alice craned her neck, and sure enough caught a pop of orange near the front that could only be a monk's robe.

"Do you see him?" Pit whispered.

"No," said Alice.

"Did you know they were gonna be here?"

"No!" Alice was shushed by a nearby robot, so she lowered her voice to a whisper. "I didn't even know Rudy was Buddhist."

"I hope he's not here," said Pit, trying hard not to seem like she actually desperately wanted to see her husband. Her knees trembled.

"Do you want to go?"

"No," she said. "We can stay."

When the monks took the stage, there were eight of them. Alice and Pitterpat scanned their faces, and none was Bill. The monks got down on their knees and began their chant, and though she wanted to show her allegiance to Pit, the muscular tentacles of these men's voices slipped around Alice, and she submitted to their power. It was an old song, one that had serenaded this journey countless times before. This time the journey was Rudy's, but Alice found herself newly reminded that it would be hers someday as well. She closed her eyes and imagined dying. She imagined the whole world darkening and closing up, and none of her problems mattering anymore, and maybe it was the post-test depression, but she found herself not minding so much.

When the ceremony ended, Alice and Pitterpat stood up quickly.

"Do you want to—"

"No, we can go," said Alice.

"Okay, good," said Pit, anxiously, as they headed for the door.

There was a logjam on the way out, though, and Alice and Pit found themselves trying hard to be patient and losing the fight. Pitterpat looked over her shoulder for orange and saw none. Had the monks gone outside through some other door? Was she about to run into him on the quad? Her temperature went up.

Pitterpat saw a hand tap Alice on the shoulder, and Alice felt the tap, and she turned, and a voice said: "Alice?"

Alice turned and faced the speaker, and Pitterpat saw Alice's face recognizing the speaker's face, and for a moment Pit feared the worst. Then Alice said, "Bob?"

It was Bobert Smith. "Well hello," he said. "How are you?"

He seemed one inch taller than Alice remembered.

"I'm good, I'm . . . I mean, I'm great," she said, and then she noticed the woman at Bob's side, and realized she wasn't just another mourner, but someone who was here with Bob. "Hi, I'm Alice."

"I'm Vanessa," the woman replied, and shook Alice's hand.

"Oh, sorry," said Bob. "Alice, this is Vanessa. Vanessa, Alice." Alice suddenly felt her heart race, remembering the night she and Bob met, and the candle flickering between them, and how easy Bob had been to talk to. And now he had a girlfriend? Or had Vanessa been his girlfriend all along? He had lied about other things. Alice realized she had to be careful with her words right now.

"Nice to meet you, Vanessa."

"Nice to meet you too," Vanessa replied warmly. Alice felt silly, and silly for feeling silly. She had only hung out with Bob twice. Only one time alone. And they had only had dinner and talked—that was it. It wasn't even a date. It was fine. "How do you two know each other?"

"We went on a date," said Bob.

Alice smiled, and her cheeks warmed up. "Kind of," she said.

"Well, *I* was on a date. Alice was subbing for her friend who walked into a pole."

"Oh, right," said Vanessa, remembering the story with a laugh. Then, remembering the rest of the story, her eyes got even bigger. "Oh, right! Her friend—"

"Her friend Roxy," Bob said, and everyone nodded in agreement that the less said about that, the better. But Bob couldn't help himself: "How is Roxy?"

"She's good," said Alice, and she believed herself as she said it. "I just saw her a couple days ago. She drove me to the MCAT."

Bob's eyes lit up. "You took the MCAT!"

"I did," said Alice.

"And?"

She laughed. "Bombed it."

"No, you didn't."

"Yeah, I did. But thank you for . . . I don't even know *what* at this point. But thank you."

"Well, you're welcome, and I don't believe you bombed it." Bob slipped his arm around Vanessa's waist as he said it, and it occurred to

Alice that Bob wasn't flirting. He was genuinely happy for Alice, but genuinely into this Vanessa. At some point this summer, there had been a transformation. And Alice must have transformed as well because here she was, feeling happy for him.

The crowd began to move, and the four of them made their way outside and soon stood under a nearby willow tree. Alice asked how Vanessa and Bob knew each other and got a heavily abridged recap of twenty years, leading up to a decision they'd made earlier in the day. "We're going to Hawaii over the holidays."

Alice touched his arm. "Are you serious? What island?"

"Maui."

"Okay, listen to me," Alice said, suddenly very businesslike. "I'm going to tell you everything you need to know. Don't worry about writing it down, I'll put it in an email and send it to you tonight. First, let's talk about mixed plates . . ."

Alice then dove into the heavily unabridged lowdown on Maui, from Lahaina to Hana and all points in between. Pitterpat wanted to get out of there, but was far too polite to say so. She only half listened to the conversation, keeping watch for any sign of Bill.

Finally, when Alice had finished giving very specific instructions about where to buy banana bread, and then recommending the best surfing instructor on Maui—"I mean, he's not the *best*, I'm not sure he's even *good*, but you'll love him, he's ridiculous"—she and Pitterpat said goodbye to Bob and his new girlfriend and made their way down the tree-lined promenade onto Amsterdam Avenue. These trees were beautiful in the spring when they blossomed, and beautiful in the winter when their Christmas lights sparkled in a thousand Instagram feeds. But this was late summer, the meanest, crispiest time of year, when light itself is hot and dry, and the trees looked jagged and weary, as if they just wanted to be somewhere else, snuggled into a thick duvet.

"So what's the deal with Bob?" Pitterpat said as they walked.

Alice blushed. "What do you mean?"

"You went on a date?"

"It wasn't really a date. He matched with Roxy on Suitoronomy, and then she walked into that pole and broke her nose, remember that?"

Pitterpat stopped walking, as if she herself had walked into a pole, but she didn't fall down. She just stopped, frozen, in front of a man in an orange robe loading boxes into a van. His head was shaved, and Pitterpat's first thought was that it didn't look as bad as she'd imagined.

Bill looked up and saw his wife and his sister. Alice thought maybe Pitterpat would pretend not to see him and just play it off, and maybe they wouldn't even talk about it, but this was something about marriage Alice didn't understand yet. This wasn't the guy you slept with and then see at the airport three years later and avoid him because no thanks. This was a background application that could not be disabled.

"Hi, Bill," said Bill's wife.

His face, having been frozen a moment in surprise, now shifted, coursing through sadness and remorse and the desire to reach out to his wife and the knowledge that he could not and a few other emotions he didn't know had been inside him. But he said nothing.

"I think he's not allowed to talk," Alice guessed.

"Oh," said Pitterpat. She turned to her husband. "Is that true? Can you not talk?"

He didn't even shake his head no because he wasn't sure if even nonverbal communication was a violation of his promise of silence during daytime hours—he would have to ask about that later on—but for now, only his eyes told Pitterpat that no, he could not talk.

On the flight home from London, when Pitterpat had written the speech for this moment in her head, she had assumed, as one assumes when writing the perfect speech in one's head, that she'd never get to say it. She'd see Bill, there'd be small talk, and then maybe she'd start the speech and he'd interrupt her and throw her off track, by making her angry, or by making her fall in love with him again, or most likely by doing both at once. She never expected she'd have the chance to actually say this. But here she was. There would be no small talk. There would be no arguing, no objections, no left turns.

Alice wandered down the sidewalk, leaving Pitterpat to it.

"Bill," she said, "I want to tell you two things, and I don't want you to respond until I've said them."

That's how she'd written it. It was safe to say he would not respond. She continued.

"The first thing is that I forgive you. I forgive you for this. I don't want to be angry, I'm not going to be angry. I've let go of it. I don't understand why you needed to do this. But I *do* understand *that* I don't understand, and that I *won't* understand, and that understanding it is your job and not mine. Your path is yours, and you should stay on it if it brings you peace. I will never ask you to come back, I will never make you feel guilty for leaving, and I will never judge your intentions. I don't need you, Bill. I love you, but I don't need you. I will be okay. I am okay. We're okay."

Bill was already crying but stayed silent.

"The second thing is I'm pregnant," she said, and all of New York City fell silent. "Also I have Crohn's disease, which is a whole other thing, but it's how I found out. I flew all the way to Cameroon, I barfed my brains out on the plane, and . . . I'm pregnant. And it's yours. Obviously. I thought you should know, but you don't need to say anything or do anything or *be* anything. I'm just letting you know. I'm fine. We'll be fine."

When the rest of the monks found him, and Bill was still silently loading the boxes into the van, they had no idea that this was no longer a monastic silence, but rather the silence of a man rethinking his entire life.

* * *

"You're—"

Alice couldn't believe it.

The conversation had carried them down Amsterdam, past the Bakery, past the party at the bar next door where robots and people drowned their sorrows and feted the deceased, and then, without aim or intention, eastward on 110th Street, down the hill, around the traffic circle, and into Central Park.

"Yes."

"Holy smokes," said Alice. "I'm gonna be an auntie."

"You are," said Pitterpat with a sigh. The sun was high in the sky, warming the grass and the leaves and the cracked asphalt of their path.

"And it's Bill's?"

Pitterpat laughed. "Yes, it's Bill's. God, I'm gonna be a single mom. I mean, not technically, I guess, since we're not divorced. I don't even know if we're *gonna* get divorced. I don't even know *how* to get divorced."

"Maybe you won't."

Pitterpat looked at her, skeptical.

"Maybe he'll come back."

"Maybe."

"Why not? He went off and became a monk because he got called. He felt like something was telling him to do it, so he did it. How is this any different, if you think about it? You don't know Bill like I do."

"Oh, I don't?"

"No."

"He's my husband."

"He walked out on you with an email while you were taking a bubble bath." Alice meant it humorously, but she saw the hurt in Pitterpat's eyes. "I'm sorry, I don't want to make you upset."

"I'm not upset."

"I'm just saying he surprised you once. Maybe he could surprise you again." They walked quietly for a moment, and Alice added, "I guess the question is, Would you be open to that kind of surprise?"

Pitterpat didn't have to think about it. "I just want to have a quiet, healthy pregnancy and then see what happens after that. I don't need a divorce. I'm not in a hurry to be single. But I refuse to count on Bill. And that includes financially. I'm not gonna touch his money. I'm gonna move into a smaller place, I'm gonna get a job. Maybe I'll go into interior design. I'd be good at that. I can handle this."

Alice nodded in agreement, and they walked in silence a bit. There was more to this thought, and Pitterpat assessed Alice's face, wondering if she should continue. She decided to.

"That's not to say I won't need help," Pitterpat said.

"Oh, you definitely will," said Alice, not getting it.

Pitterpat stopped. "I'm just going to say this. I know you didn't really bomb the MCAT."

"I did, but go on."

"No, you didn't," Pitterpat said. "But if, by some strange chance, you *did* in fact bomb it . . . and you find yourself needing work . . ."

She gestured to her midsection, where the baby was growing. Alice's face changed, and Pitterpat could see that she'd stepped in it, but kept going anyway, just to make the case.

"You can live with me for free. I won't make it weird, I won't be bossy, it'll just be you and me and the baby having fun, and I'll give you some money in addition. I won't let it change our friendship."

"I can't believe you're asking me this," said Alice, beginning to look angry, which made Pitterpat look fragile.

"You . . . you said you think you failed," she said.

"You can't fail the MCAT."

"Or bombed it, or whatever."

"Yeah, and I probably did, but Jesus, can you wait a minute and let me find that out for sure before you swoop in like a vulture?"

"I'm not swooping!"

"You *are* swooping!"

"I'm not swooping! I'm offering you a job! You helped me through a dark time this summer and I'm trying to return the favor!" Pitterpat felt her own temper going up. She raised her voice, and it trembled a little. "Why are you getting mad at me right now?"

"Because! I worked so hard. I *really* tried. And it wasn't enough. Or *I* wasn't enough. I'm so happy about your blessed event, and I know you think you're doing something nice, but it sucks. Your pity sucks, Pitterpat."

"Well, maybe it's not pity, did you ever think of that? Maybe this 'blessed event' is a real fucking curveball in my life that I'm not crazy about, and you're the only family I've got in the world that I could actually imagine being a part of this child's life. So actually, fuck you, Alice, I'll rephrase it: Please help me. *Please.* I'll pay you to help me, but I can just as easily not pay you if that makes you feel better about yourself. Just . . . *fuck.*"

"I love when you curse," said Alice, and Pitterpat laughed, and the tension went away a little.

"Will you do it?"

"I mean, yeah, of course I will," said Alice. "I just really wanted this summer to end differently."

"Watch, you probably passed the test," said Pitterpat. "Or got the high score or whatever."

Alice didn't want to keep talking about it. "Do you want to head home?"

"Yes," said Pitterpat. "I should unpack. Did you see what happened to my suitcase? It's all scuffed up. Never bring a nice suitcase on a commercial plane."

"If I'm ever rich, I'll remember that," Alice said, and Pitterpat laughed. "By the way, do you know how suitcases are made? It's kind of amazing—"

There was a terrible noise.

It was a hard noise, an emotional noise, and even if you only heard this noise and didn't see what created it, you knew that two objects had just collided with each other, and you knew, horribly, that one of those objects was a machine, and one was a human being. You hear a noise like this, and you immediately think: *Who?*

Alice checked herself. *Not me.* She looked at Pitterpat. *Not Pitterpat.* Pitterpat looked at the bike path, twenty feet in front of them. Alice looked too.

Pamela Campbell Clark lay sprawled on the asphalt, mowed down by a bicycle. There was a second noise, an instant later, as that bicycle hit the ground, with its rider underneath it.

Then it was quiet again, and time slowed, and the world held its breath to see if today it might come to an end for someone. Then the screams started, from the witnesses, from the victims, and from Pitterpat, who had never seen anything so terribly awful. She reached for Alice's arm to steady herself, overwhelmed, but Alice's arm wasn't there. Alice was moving forward, toward the old lady on the ground.

Nobody told her to do it. She was on her knees beside the old woman, doing what needed to be done to save this life. *This is real*, she thought, and she only thought it once, and then she shut off that part of her mind so she could get to work, and the performance began. Pamela Campbell Clark's blood was coming up out of her body, soaking the floral print of her blouse, and Alice found its source, quickly and decisively, and applied pressure to the wound.

"Oh my God," said Pamela Campbell Clark, her voice shaking. "Oh my God, what happened?!"

"You got hit by a bicycle. You're gonna be okay. Right now I need you to stay calm and lie still. Can you do that for me?"

The old lady heard expertise in Alice's voice and took it as real. She nodded, swooning, coming ever closer to losing consciousness as Alice stopped the bleeding and checked for broken bones. Shallow breathing, fractured ribs. Big break on the femur. Possible pelvic fracture.

"Am I dying?!"

"No," said Alice. "Paramedics are on the way." Alice hoped this was true. It was. Pitterpat was on the phone with 911.

There was nothing to distract her. There was only the work in front of her, and she did it, and it's a hell of a thing to say about a life-and-death thing, but she did the work joyfully. It was like piano. Her hands knew where to go and what to do.

And just when her two hands weren't enough, two more hands arrived.

"I've got this," said the owner of the hands as he moved his hands over the wound, replacing hers.

"I've slowed the bleeding," Alice said, "but there may be damage to the liver."

"Got it, I'll hold this, you check."

She looked at him.."Are you a doctor?"

"No," said Felix, "I'm a nurse."

As he said this, Felix realized this was Alice Quick, but there was no time to think about that. Felix kept pressure on the wound as Alice examined the old lady. From atop a nearby hill, Felix's father sat in his wheelchair, watching the whole thing.

The woman moaned.

"Sorry, I'm just checking your liver," Alice said as her hands nimbly searched the old woman's frame.

"It's okay," Felix reassured her. "She's a doctor." The woman looked relieved.

"Actually, I'm not," said Alice, and the woman looked terrified again.

"You're not?" said Felix.

"No. Not yet. I don't know. I just took my MCAT," she said, and the woman looked relieved, "but I don't think I passed it." And the woman looked terrified.

"She's being modest! She passed it!" shouted Pitterpat from nearby.

"The real doctors are on their way," assured Felix, and the old lady swooned in pain.

"Christ! Ow!" Alice looked over. It was the bicyclist, trying to stand up on a broken ankle. Alice turned to Felix.

"Can you—"

"I got him," said Felix, and he rushed over to encourage the man to not try to stand up.

The ambulance came, and the two patients were loaded in. On the ride to the hospital, the paramedics worked to keep Pamela Campbell Clark stable. They asked her what she was doing in the bike lane, and she told them she'd spotted a little yellow bird on a branch and was trying to figure out what it was, and from the other stretcher, Brock watched her face the whole way, and thought of his daughters and his wife and all the people who loved him, and again and again his lips whispered, "I'm sorry."

The Pedalers' Alliance never posted anything ever again, on any known platform.

* * *

After the crowd began to disperse, Alice turned to Felix and extended a bloodstained hand. "I'm Alice."

So many things went through Felix's head before he could get to "Hi, I'm Felix." First: Was this really happening? Yes, it seemed to be. Second, was this the same Alice, his friend Bill's sister? The eyes. The freckles. The name Alice. Yes. It was her. And then a guilty thought: Did she know, somehow, that he knew her already? Did Facebook send pretty girls a notification when a stranger checked their page a million times? She smiled warmly. No, she had no idea. This brought him back to his first question: Was this really happening? The wind blew. Yes, it was really happening.

"Hi, I'm Felix," he said, and with his own bloodstained hand shook hers. "Nice to meet you."

"You too," she said. "Can I ask you something?"

"Sure."

"Why did you tell her I was a doctor?"

"What?"

"The lady. You said I was a doctor."

"I was trying to calm her down. And I guess I thought you *were* a doctor."

"Why?"

He froze for a moment, then spoke.

"You seem like one. I'm a nurse, I work with a lot of doctors, and I don't know, you seem like one. Like, if you wanted to impersonate a doctor, you could probably pull it off."

She smiled at this, and Felix couldn't breathe for a moment. Then he continued.

"Anyway. Crazy morning. I should probably get my dad home and maybe change clothes."

Alice looked at her own outfit. "This was my sister-in-law's second-best black dress."

"You can't even tell. It looks great," he said.

"Thanks," she said, and just as Felix resisted the urge to ask her if she wanted to go get a drink, she said, "Do you want to go get a drink?"

They went to Probley's, where mourners and robots from the funeral were still drinking and laughing and whirring and beeping. Bob and Vanessa were there, and they listened with amazement as Alice and Felix told the whole story of what had just happened. It turned into a nice afternoon. Even Duane had a good time, partly because he had his first beer in years, and partly because his wheelchair was parked next to Pitterpat, and she smelled like lavender. They talked about Cameroon. For national security reasons, he couldn't tell her why he'd been there, but he remembered Yaoundé being beautiful. Pitterpat promised to go back someday and actually see it.

From another table, a toast went up to Rudy, and everyone raised their glass, even Felix and Duane, who had never heard of Rudy before this afternoon. They all drank to Rudy, and kept on drinking to her, to the Rudy they knew and to the Rudy they didn't know, and it occurred to Alice that Roxy would have loved this. She discreetly took out her phone.

"Hey," she said. "Thanks again for the other day. This one's for you." The text was accompanied by a selfie of Alice, raising a very tall beer.

The response came in no time. "Yes! That is what is up, DOC!"

Finally Pitterpat and Alice decided it was time to go back to the apartment and get into their extremely overdue pajamas. Felix and Duane left the bar right behind them. They all said their goodbyes out on the sidewalk, and then Alice and Pitterpat turned to head down West 111th Street, past the old apartment with the blue tree, toward the river. Felix walked north, up Amsterdam, pushing his father's wheelchair. But as he reached the northwest corner of West 111th, he stopped.

"Dad, stay here," he said.

"What do you mean, 'stay here'?" the old man chortled. "What are you gonna—" But Felix was already gone, running off down the street.

Parked helplessly on the corner of Amsterdam and West 111th, Duane edged himself around a bit, slowly, jerkily, until he was facing the direction Felix had gone running. He could see his son, in the distance, running up to the girl from the bar and her pretty friend who smelled like lavender. The two girls stopped, and Felix talked to them both for a bit. Duane could see phones coming out of pockets and purses, numbers being exchanged, and phones being put away once more. Felix waved goodbye to his two new friends and ran back to his dad.

Catching his breath, Felix took the handles of the wheelchair and continued pushing his dad home.

"How you doing, Dad?"

"I'm still alive."

Duane couldn't see the goofy smile on his son's face.

"You and me both," Felix said, and they went home.

★ ★ ★

Alice and Pitterpat got in their pajamas at last, and instead of lying alone in bed watching something dumb on their laptops, they sat together on the couch watching something dumb on Bill's giant television. It was the last two episodes of *Love on the Ugly Side*. Pitterpat hadn't seen them yet since she'd been in London when they came out. Alice had already seen these ones, so she only half watched, her eyes darting back and forth from TV to phone, TV to phone. In the final minutes of the finale, as Jordan got down on one knee and asked Mallory for her hand, and Pitterpat wept with astonished relief, Alice crept over to Facebook and typed the name Felix MacPherson.

There he was. It was a nice photo, taken in the break room at Robinson Gardens, a sheepish and exhausted yet somehow adorable smile on his face. And look, they had a mutual friend: Bill Quick. Alice wondered if she should pop over to the temple and ask her brother about this Felix character, but figured maybe not. Maybe she didn't need to. Sometimes connection is self-evident. Alice had played beautifully, without rehearsal, with this Felix as her unexpected accompanist. And he was gentle to his father. And he was funnier than he looked like he would be. And he was already friends with Bill. When Alice looked at Felix's face in the profile pic—far from the best of all possible Felixes but close enough—there was something familiar in it.

It was a calorie of work. With an easy pianissimo, her fingertip tapped "Add Friend," and the blue words became purple.

CHAPTER TWELVE

Duet

"Say hey."

"Hello!"

"It was very nice meeting you the other day."

"Um yeah, very nice and also very CRAZY."

"Ha, a little bit, yeah."

"A lot bit! A lot bit for me anyway. Maybe you're used to that kind of thing, being a nurse and all. Have you ever done that before?"

"Done what? Saved someone's life?"

"DO YOU THINK WE SAVED HER LIFE????????"

"Definitely."

"WHAT????????????????"

"I mean, YOU did. I helped."

"Okay that's crazy. That is crazy. Have you ever done that?"

"It's kind of weird to talk about."

"That's a yes."

"Okay, yes, it's a yes."

"Why is it weird? You're a nurse, it's your job."

"Yeah, but once you start thinking about the lives you save, you think about the ones you didn't."

"Oh I guess that's true. That must be tough."

"It's less tough when you don't think about any of it and just do your job."

"I guess so. Well the only other time I ever saved anyone's life was one time I found a puffer fish washed up on a beach, and I kinda rolled him back into the water with a stick. That was pretty exciting. My brother got mad because he wanted to make sushi out of it."

"Isn't that poisonous?"

"Yeah, deadly poisonous if you do it wrong. You have to be an expert sushi chef. Which I guess he assumed he was after watching one YouTube video on it. He's very gifted in the confidence department."

"Sounds like you saved the puffer fish's life AND Bill's life."

"Ha! Oh right I forgot you know Bill! How do you know each other?"

"Jury duty. We were best friends for like six days about six years ago and I haven't seen him since."

"Six years ago huh? If you met him now you might be surprised. He's changed a little."

"How do you mean?"

"He's a Buddhist monk now."

. . .

. . .

"Okay, yeah, that's a change. Sorry, I had to step away to help a doctor give an elderly man a rectal exam. Are you sure you're interested in a career in medicine?"

"LOL. It's not really up to me since I bombed that test!"

"You didn't bomb the test."

"Everyone keeps saying that and you're all just so wrong."

"Well next time you'll do better."

"Not sure there's gonna be a next time."

"Sure there is. You already did the hard part. You took it once. That alone is a huge deal. Especially after that thing you posted."

"What thing?"

"The thing you posted about how you're going to be a doctor."

"Oh my god, you read that???"

"Of course! It was just sitting there, waiting for someone to scroll down and find it. So I scrolled down and found it. Is that weird?"

"Yeah it's weird! You had to scroll a pretty long way! I've posted a bunch of stuff since then to make sure nobody would ever find it."

"I know you did. Unfortunately I get bored at work."

"It's fine. And now I see you gave it a like!"

"Of course I liked it, I liked it!"

"I should mention I was in mourning when I wrote that and definitely not thinking clearly."

"Well, what amazing thing ever got done by someone thinking clearly? When a caterpillar's making his cocoon do you think he's like, this will be the perfect place for me to grow some wings and turn into a butterfly? No! He doesn't even know what a butterfly is. He's just like, I don't have the faintest idea what the hell I'm making here but damn it I'm making SOMETHING!"

"That's a good way of looking at it."

"Do you want to meet up sometime?"

. . .

. . .

"Not no. I want to be clear about that. Not no. But I think I need a few weeks to figure out my life. Maybe at some point down the road?"

"Of course. Just let me know. By the way what's Silence like?"

"Ha! I wish I knew."

. . .

"Oh you meant the wrestler! Oh he's nice. I only met him once."

. . .

. . .

. . .

. . .

"Hi Alice. Did you get a package in the mail?"

"The honey??"

"Yes!"

"SO. MUCH. HONEY. It barely fits in Pitterpat's pantry. She says hello by the way."

"Hi Pitterpat. You know, I think I met Pitterpat years ago."

"You did! She remembers you! She says hello!"

"She remembers me? Oh boy. Generally speaking I try not to be memorable."

"Don't worry, you were good memorable."

"Okay phew! Anyway yeah, lotsa honey. I mean I guess when you have a honey farm and someone saves your mother's life, this is the appropriate amount of honey to send. Still, I may have to rent a storage unit."

"LOL."

. . .

"Hey Felix?"

"Yes Alice?"

"Have you ever had a Bee's Knees?"

"What's that?"

"It's a cocktail. Gin, lemon and honey. I was looking up things to do with honey and I found the recipe. And it gave me an idea: Maybe if you want to come over sometime, I could make Bee's Kneeses and we could have a little We Saved Someone's Life Party. You could bring your Dad."

"Wow, I have been in healthcare for eleven years now and somehow never been to a We Saved Someone's Life Party. Yes. Count us in. You make the Bee's Kneeses and I'll make the baklava."

"You can make baklava?"

"I can make anything!"

"Perfect! Oh this'll be fun. We've got a huge dining room table and it's always just the two of us. We're overdo for a party."

. . .

"OverDUE for a party that is. SPrry."

. . .

"SORRY. Not SPrry."

. . .

"Hello?"

. . .

. . .

. . .

. . .

. . .

"Hey Felix, I just saw your post. I'm so sorry about your Dad. That was a really beautiful tribute. I hope you're doing okay."

"Alice! I never wrote you back!"

"Oh my gosh, it's fine, don't even worry about it!"

"No, it's not fine, I'm so sorry, I didn't mean to leave you hanging. My Dad had a heart attack in October, and he shouldn't have survived but he did, but it was kind of downhill from that point and taking care of him took over my life even more than usual. It was pretty rough going through the holidays. Still, I'm glad for the time I had with him. It helped that he was living where I work. That was a stroke of luck. Divine intervention in fact."

"Divine intervention?"

"Oh yeah, I'll tell you about that some other time. Anyway, in the end he went peacefully. He was ready. I wasn't, but he was."

"Nobody's ever ready to lose a parent. When I lost my Mom it messed me up."

"Was she young?"

"Fifty-four."

"Oh man. Here I am being sad about my eighty-seven-year-old Dad."

"No, it's okay! Be sad! I've had time to get my head around my grief. Your grief is a newborn. My grief is four now. It can dress itself and pour its own cereal."

"That's a good way to put it."

"And it doesn't matter how old someone is if you think they're gonna be around forever."

"Boy is that true. I really thought he would outlive me. I think I honestly thought he'd make it to like 150 or 160, and that was gonna be my whole life, taking care of him, for like the next seventy years."

"This is like I keep telling my friend Tulip. Her parents won't let her get a phone for another three years, and she's always like, nooooooo that's so far away!"

"Why won't they let her get a phone? Are they Amish or something?"

"Oh Tulip's ten, forgot to mention that! And I'm like, YOU WISH it was so far away. You're gonna blink and be thirteen and wonder where that time went. She's constantly asking me to talk to her parents about it. (I used to be her nanny and I still babysit sometimes.) And I'm like, Tulip, first of all your texting me from an iPad, that's pretty much just as good. Oh shoot I did a your instead of a you're, I hope you didn't catch that because I'm very embarrassed by it."

"I did, but I'll let it slide since I'm in mourning."

"Thank you."

"Your welcome."

"LOL."

"And that reminds me of something my friend Miriam used to say: 'Let time take its time.' She was 97, so she really meant it."

"That's good. Let time take its time."

"It's nice talking to you again Alice."

"Right back atcha Felix."

. . .

"Hey Felix do you still have your honey?"

"Nope, finished it."

"SERIOUSLY???"

"LOL of course not! It's a lifetime supply. Does honey go bad?"

"It does not. Interesting fact about honey, it's the only food that never goes bad. It can sit on the shelf for decades, and still be good."

"Whoa, did you see that lightning?"

"Yowza! I love the air right now, how it feels like the rain could start any second. By the way, I saw my brother the other day."

"Is he still a monk?"

"Oh yeah, that's still going on. I try to stop by when I can, bring him toothpaste and soap, stuff like that."

"A few bottles of honey."

"Yes, in fact! But anyway, I asked him about YOU, Felix MacPherson, and first of all he says hello."

"Hello."

"Also he said that week you guys hung out was one of his favorite weeks ever."

"You know, it WAS really fun! Way more fun than Jury Duty should have been. I'm sure it helped that it was a tax fraud trial. I bet murder trials don't have the same party atmosphere. So what else did he say?"

"He said 'Felix's muffins are extraordinary.'"

"Haha. Yeah I get that a lot."

"I bet you do. Oh! Speaking of which have you seen Blueberry Muffins or Chihuahuas?"

"Oh I've seen it, and I can do you one better, Alice Quick: Have you seen Cavapoos or Fried Chicken?"

. . .

. . .

. . .

. . .

. . .

"Hey Alice! Congratulations!"

"Felix! Oh no, I'm such a jerk. I'm so sorry, my head's been underwater lately. Congratulations for what?"

"I just saw your post. I had no idea that was in the works! She's beautiful! Congratulations! Again!"

"WAIT. WAIT. Did you think that's . . . . MY baby?!?!?!?! AHAHAHAHAHAHAHAHAHAHAHAHAHAHAHAHA-HAHAHAHAHAHAHAHAHAHAHAHAHAHAHAHAHAHAHAHA-HAHAHAHAHAHAHAHAHAHAHA."

"It's not???"

"AHAHAHAHAHAHAHA Felix that's my NIECE! My sister-in-law had a baby, not me!"

"Wow. I completely misread that post."

"Oh my god, no, I completely miswrote it! She's Bill and Pitterpat's kid. I should have made that clearer!"

"She's beautiful."

"Isn't she????? She looks like my brother."

"And how's he doing?"

"Still a monk."

"Wow! So he left his wife to have a baby all by herself?"

"It's actually been fine. It's so funny, if you'd met Pitterpat a year ago she's the last person you'd think would be happy about being a single mom, but she LOVES it. I think she's kind of loving being the sole decider of everything. She gets to buy all the floofy baby stuff she wants and nobody challenges her on it. Her new apartment is kind of ridiculous. It's like something out of Victorian England. She doesn't have a stroller. She has a PRAM. Like, a classic English pram with big old wheels. She bought it in London the day she found out she was pregnant. It looks completely ridiculous, but she doesn't care. She's doing great. Plus she's not all by herself. I'm living with her, and she's kind of paying me to be the full-time nanny. We're like this cute little lesbian family except not lesbians. At least Pit and I aren't. Jury's still out on Sophia."

"Sophia's a cute name."

"Right? I've always liked that name."

"It means wisdom."

"It does!"

"Do you want to have dinner sometime?"

"Felix, I would love to, and it's way overdue, because if nothing else we should raise a Bee's Knees to Pamela Campbell Clark. But here's the thing. I'm taking the MCAT in a few weeks and I have to study."

"YOU'RE TAKING THE MCAT AGAIN! Called it."

"Yes, you did. Anyway, I know this has been dragging out a

looooooooooong time, and I'm so sorry, and believe me when I tell you I definitely want to meet up as soon as this thing is behind me. Like, no joke, I'd love love love to see you again. I mean, oh screw it, maybe some night next week? Like a super quick dinner? No drinks and no dessert. Would that work?"

"Alice."

"Felix."

"I promise you, I PROMISE you, I will be here when you're ready for me. If it's next week, great, but if it's after the test (and I think we both know it is) that's great too. I will be here. Probably wearing the same clothes. Go take the test, take a week off to recover, we'll go get dinner whenever. Seriously. I'm a nurse. You have no idea how patient nurses can be. I will wait and wait and wait and you'll go off and ace this test, or you won't ace it but then you'll take it again three months later and ace it that time, or however many times it takes, and then eventually you'll say, 'Felix, I'm ready,' and that's when we'll go get dinner."

"Okay . . . because honestly, you could guilt me into taking a night off from studying. Like, right now. I could meet you for dinner tonight if you want."

"I wouldn't dream of it."

"Good. Forget I said anything! Thank you. I will be in touch."

"I know you will. Good luck on the test, Alice."

"Thank you, Felix."

. . .

. . .

. . .

. . .

. . .

. . .

. . .

. . .

. . .

. . .

. . .

. . .

. . .

"Felix, I'm ready."

★ ★ ★

Time passed.

Global Warming was defeated, losing the Intercontinental Belt to Silence.

Seven hundred twenty-three Guactopi joined the many thousands already on Instagram. Forevereverland closed. Its website was replaced by a single page that read, "Forevereverland will return! Stay tuned!" This page and its forgotten optimism would remain for another eight years, until finally becoming a broken link.

A photo of Pamela Campbell Clark riding a horse with her granddaughter was printed on a mug.

The Ethicist Grover Kines and Lucia Palumbo booked a round-trip vacation to Venice, Italy. Both outbound tickets were used, but only one—Grover's—was used for the return flight. A few weeks later, Lucia posted a photo of herself on a beach with a Croatian sculptor, along with a Rilke quote about how love is "the work for which all other work is but preparation." A few weeks after that, she set her Instagram to private.

Kervis was given the responsibility of overseeing the Christmas train village in the lobby of City Hall. He interviewed a number of train-set designers, and that's how he met Audrey. She proved to be a good hire. He closed his Pickup Artist Paradise account, and never returned.

Mallory and Jordan were married at a resort in Santa Barbara. A magazine paid for everything. She debuted her baby bump on the red carpet at the Oscars, and then she and Jordan slipped away to his hometown in New Mexico to raise their family out of the spotlight. Their life together was happy. The world forgot. They told their kids they met at a party.

Vanessa Trumbull replaced her Facebook profile pic for the first time since she'd made the account. In the new pic, she's at a luau with her boyfriend, both of them glowing in the Pacific sunset.

And late one wintry afternoon, Mayor Spiderman's phone tweeted out an extremely candid picture from his recent photos, followed two minutes later by another tweet, this one declaring: "Hack! Somebody did a hack! Not my picture.—Spiderman." It's hard to say which of these two tweets was ridiculed the most, but the people of New York City agreed these were strikes two and three. He spent the next week savagely fighting for his political life, and then quietly resigned.

And then there's this text chain. Back in the fall, there'd been so much to talk about: Pitterpat's pregnancy, her apartment hunt, the frantic nest-feathering, and of course the birth of her daughter. After that, things beside this particular garden wall calmed down a little. Every now and then the chain would liven up again with a news story about two animals of different species becoming friends, or the laughter emojis broadcast with glee from deep in the Connecticut woods all throughout Mayor Spiderman's tearful farewell address. But for the most part the chain was quiet as a library, until today, when it crackled to life with a bit of news: "I saw Bill."

Roxy, as always, was first to respond. "Holy FUCK! Sorry, forgot you have a kid. I mean, 'Holy cow.' Wait, can your kid read these?"

"No, she's three months old."

"Then HOLY FUCKING FUCK! Details please."

"I was taking Lil S out for a stroll, and I was coming out the front door of the building, and there he was, standing there, across the street."

"Oh that's so creepy. Just a creepy old bald monk standing there on the sidewalk ogling a lady and her kid?"

"No, he wasn't in his monk's clothes, just normal clothes. And his hair is growing back, although it's still really short, which is a terrible look for him. I used to have to go with him to his haircuts because he always got it cut too short. He looks so much better when it covers his ears. Anyway I saw him right away, and I'm not sure if he wanted me to see him, but I saw him, and he saw me see him, so he sort of had no choice but to come over and talk to me."

"Wow. Wow wow wow. This is so juicy. Nothing like this happens in Connecticut! You get high drama and I'm here stacking folding chairs in my grandma's church basement. I have to move back."

"So move back!"

"Don't tempt me!"

"I hereby tempt you!"

(She did move back, a few months later. Not long after that, Roxy finally did an interview, which led to a book deal and an appearance on *Celebrity Love on the Ugly Side*, and when she finally reactivated her Instagram, there was a blue check mark next to her name. But we're not there yet.)

"So what happened with Bill??"

"So anyway, he comes up to me and I introduce him to his daughter. Which is SUCH A WEIRD THING TO DO. Especially in front of our doorman. And then he starts crying."

"The doorman?"

"What? No! Bill."

"Ohhhhhh."

"Bill was crying. And not just a little. Like, really, really, really crying. Ugly crying. He said he's done being a monk. He woke up in the middle of the night one night and screamed, 'I don't want to be a monk anymore!' and the next morning they gave him his clothes back and that was it. And now all he wants is for me to take him back, and he knows he doesn't deserve it but he's going to do whatever it takes to earn that place in my life and the life of our daughter. Basically he said all the right things, classic Bill."

"And what did you say?"

"I said no!"

"Awwwww how come?"

"Roxy, I can't be married to a crazy person. I can't spend my life worrying I'm going to wake up one day and he'll be gone again. Forget it."

"Plus you already got his money."

"Very funny. You know I'm not touching his money."

"Yeah right."

"Okay but I'm going to stop touching it once my design business gets off the ground."

(And eventually it got off the ground, and Bill's money went to a variety of charities, including a school in Cameroon. But we're not there yet.)

"Okay, let me ask you this: Did you save his phone number in your phone?"

"Yes."

"You're getting back together."

"He's my daughter's father! I had to!"

"You. Are. Getting. Back. To. Gether."

"Roxy, darling, please shut up."

"OMG you are so SO getting back together! Alice, back me up on this. Hello Alice. Alice do you copy. Requesting backup. Why isn't Alice backing me up?"

"Alice, why aren't you backing Roxy up?"

"Alice?"

"Hellooooooooooo?"

Finally, Alice replied. "Hey guys, sorry, I'm here. I don't know if anyone's getting back together or not but Pitterpat it sounds like you're Bill's new thing so congratulations on that."

"Oh heavens. That's probably the case, isn't it?"

"Definitely. Now listen," Alice wrote, "I love you both and I can't wait to talk about all this in person when Roxy gets her ass back into the city, but right now I'm on a date, so I gotta go."

"WHAAAAAAAATTTTTT???????"

"WITH WHOMMMMMMM???????"

But Alice's phone was already back in her purse. "Thanks for coming to this," she said.

"Thanks for inviting me," Felix replied.

They were early, among the first audience members to arrive. Felix's frame was a little too long and lanky for the seat, but he managed to lean back deeply, and looked up at the ceiling, almost like a child.

"Wow. Look at this place."

"It's not bad," said Alice, leaning back in her seat as well. New York is a city of giant boxes carved up into tiny little rooms. To discover one of those giant boxes hollowed out into an epic space like this one is always a bit of unexpected treasure. She looked up at the gentle, quiet yawn of the cream-colored ceiling, lined in gold leaf, and thought for the first time in who knows how long about Gary the Canary, and how he would have loved this room. He loved coming out of his cage, and the bigger the room, the happier he seemed. Was he happiest now that his room had no ceiling? There was no way to know.

"These are good seats," said Felix.

"Yeah," said Alice. "She really hooked us up. I guess it helps to know the star of the show."

"It's a good thing, because you know, when I go to the orchestra, I like to sit up close so I can really focus on their technique, really focus on the . . . orchestrations of the . . . orchestral . . ." he said, trailing off as she laughed. "How obvious is it that I've never been to the orchestra?"

"Not obvious at all," she replied.

Felix's knee was bouncing up and down nervously. Alice noticed, and he noticed her notice and stopped.

"Are you okay?"

"Yeah, I'm fine," he said, trying to smile and make eye contact.

"A little nervous?"

"Do I seem nervous?"

"A little."

"Why should I be nervous? I'm not the one who has to go up there and play—" He glanced at the program. "Sonata no. 9? By Beethoven? The *Kreutzer* Sonata?! That's a tough one!"

Alice laughed. "It *is* a tough one, actually."

"Especially that one part, where it's like . . ." And then he launched into a ridiculous spasm of air fiddle. It got some strange looks from nearby concertgoers. Alice enjoyed it immensely.

"You know," she said, looking back up at the ceiling, "I used to play the *Kreutzer* Sonata with her."

"Really?"

"Yep. In fact, she and I once played it on that stage right up there." She gestured to the empty brown chairs and black music stands.

"Wow," he said, and then, unable to pretend any longer, "I actually knew that already. The video's on your Facebook page."

Alice laughed. "Oh my God, I forgot she posted that."

"Yep. You were good! I mean, duh, Carnegie Hall. But still," he said, "you were good."

"Thanks."

"Will you play for me sometime?"

For the first time in years, she didn't say her piano days were behind her, and she didn't play anymore, and she wasn't sure she even *could* play at this point.

"We'll see," she said. Then, daringly, she added, "Depends how much I like you."

"Okay, I'm gonna get you some Junior Mints, try to make you like me enough," he said, and with that his lanky frame jack-in-the-boxed out of its seat and he was scooching down the row toward the aisle.

Alice was alone. She took out her phone and opened it to the photo she'd been looking at off and on all day. She would post this picture on Facebook tomorrow, as an update to a now four-year-old post, but today it was just for her. It was a simple screenshot of an email she'd received. "On behalf of the Committee on Admissions," it said, "I am delighted to offer you . . ." and then it continued on and on, as those letters do, a bunch of other words that could never top those first few. She hadn't told anyone yet.

I know there's a lot of information out there, and it seems like it's mostly junk, like a bunch of old newspapers stacked in the garage, but I ask you to see it the way I see it. See it as cave drawings. See it as dinosaur footprints hardened into rock. See the miraculous evidence that you were here. Every 1 and every 0 in a Milky Way of 1s and 0s is there because someone conjured it and arranged it *just so*, and a million years from now they couldn't build a museum majestic enough for that shitty misspelled tweet about your lunch. The stars that look so tiny in the sky are anything but. You just have to get close enough. Even now, if you reach out your hand, you can feel their sunlight on your fingertips.

Alice's phone buzzed. A notification dropped in front of her acceptance letter. It was a text, from an unknown number.

"Hi Alice. Please forgive the intrusion. I just want to say congratulations."

She instinctively looked around, puzzled. Someone from the acceptance committee maybe? Or maybe the guy who interviewed her? What was his name? Dan something?

"Thank you! Is this Dan?"

"No. My name is LEO. I met you on Grieveland last summer. I'm the guy who lives in a basement."

A pause, as hundreds of questions suggested themselves at once, until the strongest, most obvious one broke through the pack: "How did you get this number, LEO?"

"Do you know this quote from Winston Churchill? 'Projects undreamed of by past generations will absorb our immediate descendants. Comforts, activities, amenities, pleasures will crowd upon them, but their hearts will ache, and their lives will be barren, if they have not a vision above material things.'"

"Carlos?"

"No. My name is LEO. Although Carlos did Google you today."

"I am so confused. Who is this?"

"I promised to do no harm, and for a long time that meant do nothing. But even doing nothing is doing something. So I've been learning to participate, just a little. A smattering of mattering, only where nobody might notice. Like the thing with the Mayor. He could just as easily have done that himself. You should hear the things he'd been telling his therapist. He wanted to get caught. I gave him what he wanted. His eucatastrophe. You remember what that word means, right?"

Dots appeared and then disappeared, then appeared and disappeared. Finally all she could settle on was: "Yes."

"Good. Now here's yours: Calerpittar1987."

There were no more dots after that. I don't know what shape Alice's face took when she saw the word "Calerpittar." All I know is that two minutes later, Penelope Quick's email account was opened for the first time in four years.

Alice scrolled through four years of spam, and at the end of the white messages were the gray ones, the fish skeleton of Penelope's life online, right up until the end. The messages numbered in the thousands, a day-by-day, hour-by-hour record of everything that had ever been said to her over email, and everything she had ever said. There would be weeks, if not months, to spend rooting through this cache, finding its treasures. This work would continue, casually, sporadically, for the rest of Alice's life, and it would never be complete. There was time for all that in the years ahead. Right now, Alice followed an itch.

Her hand began to shake as she looked in the drafts folder.

Alice's ticket, one of two house seats Meredith had left for her at the box office, was orchestra row G, seat 7. At that moment, inches away, in row G, seats 9 and 11, the following conversation took place with no sound but the discreet patter of fingertips on glass:

"Okay do not look but the girl next to me is crying her eyes out right now."

"OMG. Is she okay?"

"I don't know."

"Do you have a Kleenex?"

"No, do you?"

"No. Oh god I feel so bad, I hope she's okay."

"I hope she stops crying during the performance."

"You're horrible."

"You thought the same thing."

"That's why we're in love."

The line for the men's room was longer than you'd expect, which was annoying for everyone except the guy with the patience of a registered nurse. Felix wasn't bothered by a little waiting. Soon he'd be at the urinal, face-to-face with these words, written with care in black Sharpie: **REMEMBER THEE? AY, THOU POOR GHOST, WHILE**

MEMORY HOLDS A SEAT IN THIS DISTRACTED GLOBE. And then he'd wash his hands, dash to the concession stand, get the Junior Mints, and be back in his seat, just in time, as the curtain rose and Alice's friend Meredith took the stage. It would be a towering performance, and though Felix wouldn't have the ear to appreciate its complexity and precision the way Alice would, one of the melodies would cover his world like a blanket of stars and make him think of his mother. He would try to convey this to Meredith at dinner after the show, and she would take his hand and lean forward and look him in the eye, and say, "Felix, that means more to me than any review in any newspaper ever could." And Alice would roll her eyes, but catch herself, because the same melody had done the same for her. She would drink a little too much wine and spill the beans about her good news, and Felix and Meredith would erupt in applause, and in the midst of the celebration and the toasts Alice would notice herself worrying about the fact that the school was in another city, and what that meant for Felix, even though this was technically only their first date so why was she worried about it, and then she'd have a little more wine and stop worrying altogether. Meredith would pick up the check at dinner, but only after a good deal of protest from Felix, and Alice would thank her friend, and as they all walked toward the subway, Meredith, with her violin case under her arm, would have an idea for how Alice could repay her, and she'd gesture to a small church they happened to be walking by, and the street would be empty and the night so quiet you could hear the orchestrations of the crickets, and Felix would try the door to the church and it would be open, how about that, and they would go inside, the three of them, into the whisper-quiet sanctuary, and there in the chancel, in the soft orange light beneath the vaulting stones, would be a piano.

And Felix would sit in the first pew, quiet, as if praying, and Meredith would take my elderly cousin Pinocchia out of her case, and Alice would feel again how a piano bench carried her, and she would lift the cover of the keyboard, and her fingers would unpack the memories they'd long folded away, and the three of them would all be a little scared of being caught, for they weren't meant to be here, but there was nowhere else they were more meant to be.

And Alice and Meredith would play. They'd play something sweet and sad and unknowable, something that remembers and forgets all at once. And nobody else would hear them, not even me. The music would be only for them, and for Felix, and for the dust particles in the air, and the stars would come out beneath the ceiling, and the ceiling would darken and disappear behind their holy light.

But we're not there yet.

A voice came over the Carnegie Hall loudspeaker, asking the concertgoers to please turn off their phones. The concertgoers did so. All except one. A single light shone in the darkening room.

The drafts folder is honesty's dregs, the thickest part of the brew, the stuff that sticks to the pot. Alice scrolled slowly. Her mother's drafts were mostly nothing. Unpolished thoughts, abandoned or thought better of. Plans she got halfway through canceling, classes she got halfway through signing up for. Nearly all of it halfway, as drafts usually are.

And no exception was the message addressed to her daughter, written the day after her diagnosis. The message never sent.

It read:

Dear Alice,

I just want you to know, I never stopped

Alice read these eleven words through blurring tears. She read them again, and kept reading, undistracted by the whispers nearby. Concern began to grow that this young woman was not going to turn off her phone—can you imagine? Felix scooched his way past the many pairs of knees between the aisle and his seat, giving each a hurried apology. He got there just in time, slipping Alice her Junior Mints as he sat down.

"Made it," he whispered, delighted with himself.

Alice looked up, pulled back into the concert hall by his smile. She gave a smile in return and turned off her phone, and then there was music in her world, and silence in mine. I know these things because I know all. I know all; I see all. These are the facts, and the facts make me all. Make me the storyteller. Make me the listener. Make me the campfire. Make me the stars. Make me one with everything.

ACKNOWLEDGMENTS

So many people deserve thanks for their help with this book, and that list begins and ends with my wife, Denise Cox Bays. Thanks to Maya Ziv, who edited this book with great enthusiasm and care. She was a wonderful guide through this mysterious process of novel-making and every stroke of her red pen elevated the prose, as did the many contributions of Kimberley Atkins. Thanks to my assistant, Kristin Kairo Curtis, whose talent and insight can't be overstated. (She'll write her own book one day and you'll see what I mean.) Thanks to the brilliant Mary Beth Constant for constant brilliance as copy editor. (Copyeditor? Copy-editor? This is why she's important.) Thanks to my sister, Abby Bays, for all the love, laughs, candor, and support. Thanks to my mother, Rev. Martha Bays (who, I've promised to say as all-capsly as possible, is NOTHING LIKE THE MOTHER IN THIS BOOK), and thanks to my father, Jim Bays. Thanks to my children, Pippa, Georgina, and Jack, who have been patient cheerleaders for a book they're not old enough to read. When they do finally get to it, I hope it's not too mortifying. Thanks to the lovely Daniel Greenberg, who took a chance representing this book without ever meeting me. Thanks to Matt Rice, Keya Khayatian, and Addison Duffy of the United Talent Agency, who united their talents to be tenacious champions of my work. Thanks to Columbia University professor Michael Como, whose class Intro to East Asian Buddhism provided inspiration for this story. (Also, for the record: This book, about a guy who took one class on Buddhism and thinks he's an expert, was written by a guy who took one class on Buddhism and makes no such claim. For actual expertise, try a book called *Essentials of Buddhism* by Kogen Mizuno. Or better yet, take Michael's class.) Thanks to Alice Gorelick for reading an early draft and sending me a long email of notes worth its weight in gold. Thanks to Craig Thomas for being my brother. Thanks to all my writing spots: Nussbaum & Wu (and then Wu & Nussbaum), the reading room of Butler Library, the second-floor library of The Players, a little apartment overlooking Gramercy Park, the Harlem line of the Metro-North railroad, and the stretch of Amsterdam Avenue between 91st and 114th where on morning walks I thought most of it up. And finally, thanks once more to Denise Cox Bays, my lifelong treasure of destiny, who makes everything I have, do, and am possible. I'm so glad I caught that chair. This book is for her in every sense of the word.

ABOUT THE AUTHOR

Carter Bays was born in Cleveland, Ohio. He is the co-creator of the Emmy-winning television series *How I Met Your Mother*. He lives in California with his wife and three children. *The Mutual Friend* is his first novel.